12

THE
RIPPLE
EFFECT

PAUL GARRISON

THE RIPPLE EFFECT

wm

William Morrow

An Imprint of HarperCollinsPublishers

This book is a work of fiction. The characters, incidents, and dialogue are drawn from the author's imagination and are not to be construed as real. Any resemblance to actual events or persons, living or dead, is entirely coincidental.

HarperCollins books may be purchased for educational, business, or sales promotional use. For information please write: Special Markets Department, HarperCollins Publishers Inc., 10 East 53rd Street, New York, NY 10022.

FIRST EDITION

Designed by Jeffrey Pennington

Printed on acid-free paper

Library of Congress Cataloging-in-Publication Data

Garrison, Paul, 1952–
    The ripple effect : a novel of suspense / Paul Garrison.—1st ed.
      p. cm.
    ISBN 0-06-008169-4
    1. Fathers and daughters—Fiction. 2. Brothers—Death—Fiction.
I. Title
  PS3557.A738R57 2004
  813'.54—dc22   2003059397

---

04 05 06 07 08 WBC/QW 10 9 8 7 6 5 4 3 2 1

For AE

*Every*thing goes!

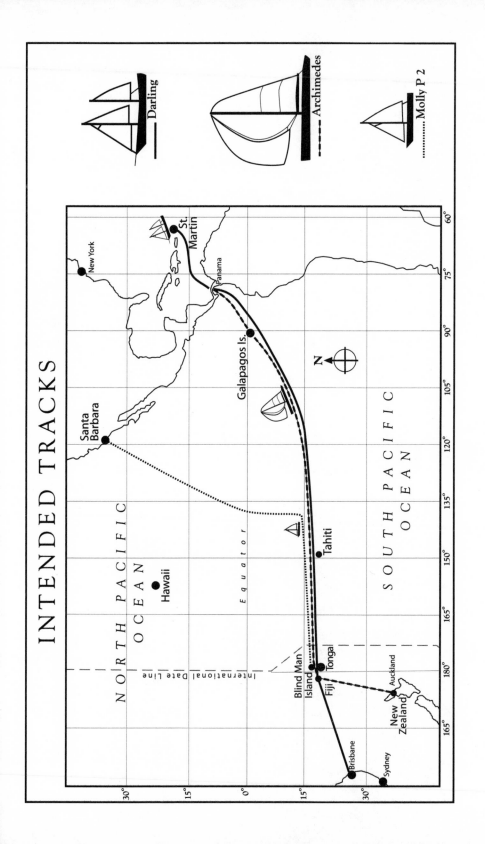

INTENDED TRACKS

Darling

Archimedes

Molly P 2

New York

St. Martin

Santa Barbara

Panama

NORTH PACIFIC OCEAN

Galapagos Is.

N

Hawaii

Equator

Tahiti

International Date Line

Blind Man Island

Fiji Tonga

Auckland

New Zealand

SOUTH PACIFIC OCEAN

Brisbane

Sydney

60°   75°   90°   105°   120°   135°   150°   165°   180°   165°

30°   15°   0°   15°   30°

BOOK ONE

THE
SWAN
POND

MARCH–APRIL 2002

T HE "SWAN POND" AT ANSE Marcel on the northwest coast of St. Martin, a popular Caribbean tourist island between Anguilla and St. Barts, was a lousy place to disappear if you'd ever devoted body and soul to getting rich in New York. Hidden up a narrow, twisty creek and ringed by dense vegetation, the natural cove might have sheltered pirates or escaped slaves in a simpler time. But in the month of March 2002, it was a marina for blue-water charter yachts. Tucked ashore among the bougainvillea, a five-star health club resort—the ritzy type the French called a *privilège spa*—offered a clear view of million-dollar hulls, flawless teak decks, lofty masts, and polished chrome. Sooner or later a Wall Street guy would run into somebody he knew at the Swan Pond.

So Aiden Page kept his head down while he scrubbed diesel soot off the transom of a Swan 44 he had just delivered from Martinique. When he did look up, it was to whisper Hail Marys that on off days, between last week's clients flying home and the next en route, the only people to recognize him—the boats' deckhands and cooks, and the shore-based mechanics, riggers, and varnishers—would know him as "Chuck," a taciturn charter captain from some landlocked place like Kansas or Iowa where Chuck must have learned to sail on lakes.

He appeared, at first glance, similar to the other paid crew cleaning the boats this brilliant winter morning in the high season—a seafaring man in cutoffs and a faded polo shirt, face tanned, hair and beard bleached yellow by the sun. Squint lines radiating from his eyes suggested he had left his twenties far behind; his perpetually bowed head hinted at disappointments or remorse; but a restless vitality and a handsome face offered the possibility that the best years stretched promisingly before him, if only he could get out of this current mess.

He had a sailor's broad hands, and arms hard with muscle. But his legs betrayed the camouflage of the working seaman: unlike most professional crew, whose lower limbs were spindly from years confined to small decks, Aiden Page's were still muscled from daily workouts at the Downtown Athletic Club. If anyone noticed, he hoped they would take him for a pumped-up race boat gorilla from the "Heine," the annual Heineken Regatta that the island had just hosted. Though at an athletic five-ten and one-seventy, Aiden Page was built more like a bowman than a winch grinder—and had the scars to prove it: an *O* branded on his left cheek by an errant jib's stainless-steel clew ring; and a pale crescent on his chin, which never took the sun, courtesy of a foredeck face plant in a club race back on the Sound.

Thank God the fierce tropical light made everybody wear sunglasses. If there was one aspect of his appearance that would give him away to anyone who had ever met him, it was a distinctive feature shared by several of that arm of the Page family that emigrated from Kiltimagh in County Mayo—one eye bright blue, the other bottle green. Blue for dreaming, green for money, his father used to laugh. And look where that had got them.

When the transom was clean, he got busy Windexing the ports.

A pretty crew girl in a bikini bottom and loose shirt, who had already made several attempts to get friendly, leaned down from the high-sided Halberg-Rassey ketch moored beside the Swan. "Newsprint works better than paper towels," she said. "The ink makes the glass shine." She handed him a section of the *New York Times,* which was stained with coffee cup circles and crinkled like parchment by salt spray.

Aiden shut his mind to a generous flash of braless brown breasts. He couldn't risk hooking up with anyone who would ask questions. So getting laid would have to wait until he worked himself a lot farther away than the Caribbean. He was dreading the arrival of Friday's charter clients; he didn't recognize their names on the manifest, but he couldn't breathe easy until he had scoped them out at binoculars' distance to make sure they had never met.

The newsprint worked as advertised, until the paper got wet. He reached to wad a fresh sheet. It was sprinkled with head-shot photos, and the sight of his own face knocked the breath out of him, like the boom had whipped across the coach roof and smashed him square in the chest.

"Hey." The pretty girl was back, peering down from her side deck, looking a little puzzled by the stricken expression on Aiden's face even as she said, "We're taking our van into town. Want to come for lunch?"

Aiden crumpled the paper and ran below.

The Swan's owner, who was in St. Martin on vacation, sat at the nav station, reading bills from the charter company. He looked up at Aiden stumbling down the companionway. "Chuck, can you explain—"

Aiden hurried past the nav station, around the saloon table, and locked himself in the forward head. Heart pounding, breath storming through his lungs, he spread the sheet and tried to focus on the print.

Headlined PORTRAITS OF GRIEF, the page was laid out like a high-school yearbook, with full-face photos and six-inch biographies. Aiden, who had deliberately not looked at a newspaper in six months, surmised that the *Times* had committed to posting an obituary for every single person who died in the September 11 terrorist attacks.

Smiling up at him was a picture he remembered well. He'd kept a copy on his desk, right next to Morgan's. The publicist's photographer had shot him and Charlie at a company party, arms over each other's shoulders. They were grinning happily at the camera, back in '99 when you could do no wrong and the money would flow forever.

CHARLES PAGE AND AIDEN PAGE
Brothers Inseparable in Life and Death

Charlie and Aiden. Aiden and Charlie. While in no way two peas in a pod, recalled friends and family, the "boys," as they were also known, were a team to be reckoned with. Charlie was older, steadier, and more worldly. Aiden flamboyant, the cutup. When they raced sailing dinghies as kids, Charlie was always helmsman, while daredevil Aiden leaned so far in the hiking strap he occasionally fell overboard.

On a memorable Christmas several years ago, Charlie chartered a jet to take employees of the HHH & Company investment bank and their families to the remote Tonga Islands in the South Pacific. Aiden organized sailing canoe races across the Polynesian lagoon and acted as bookmaker for the high-stakes betting. He and Charlie were the odds-on favorites, but lost to a long-shot dark horse: Aiden's teenage daughter Morgan. "It turned into a very expensive race," one banker recalled ruefully. "The mail-room clerk who bet on the kid went home a lot richer."

Charlie was HHH's CEO, Aiden his CFO. Aiden also served as HHH's fire warden, a job he appeared to take much more seriously than most things in life. When last seen, the brothers were shooing traders, bankers, accountants, lawyers, and secretaries into the stairwell that led out of the North Tower.

Aiden could not help but notice that "Brothers Inseparable in Life and Death" were bracketed by better people. A fireman, last seen going *up* the stairs, and a nurse who had stayed to tend to a burn victim in the lobby. Community volunteers. Churchgoers. Perfect parents.

He reached inside his polo shirt and touched trembling fingers to the simple gold crucifix that he had given his daughter for first Communion. Perfect parents. Who would forever be missed by their children. Which was the part that really destroyed him. Even worse than leaving Charlie to die.

MORGAN PAGE WAS AFRAID OF the subway.
She had loved the trains before 9/11. They had been her magic carpet. It was the first thing she learned when they made her move to the city. You ran down the steps and in five minutes you were a million miles from your mother's apartment. Summon the courage to change to the IND or the BMT and you got another million.

But now she rode her bike. You'd have to be too dumb to live to let yourself get trapped underground when the next attack came. Fortunately, all winter long it had hardly snowed, so she could ride everywhere she had to go. She rode to school, when they moved temporarily to Brooklyn after the attack. After school she would ride all the way up to Central Park. Outdoors, away from crowds. Sometimes it was easier to skip school and ride straight to the park.

She could bike to Chelsea Piers to swim, but didn't do it often. It was scary when you thought about a bomb exploding in a truck in the parking garage under the pool and getting sucked down a funnel of water to the jagged wreckage. She could bike to her piano lessons in her teacher's snug little brownstone studio, which seemed pretty safe because it was so small; except even there you could feel through the walls the thumping of a helicopter as if they were attacking again. And she could bike to her shrink, who had an office in "Shrink Land," a tree-lined section of the West Village where a lot of her friends went before 9/11. Her turn, now. Twice a week.

This was Tuesday. It had been a long weekend. Even weirder than usual.

"Osama came to my room last night."

She slumped in the chair, staring at the grease stains the bicycle chain left on her sneakers. The shrink, Dr. Melton, was even older than her grandfather. He had been headmaster of a private school—except it was a progressive school, so they called him principal, like they did at her special public school, Stuyvesant. When he retired from school, he kept the kids for patients, and their parents for couples therapy, trying to save their marriages. Which was how her mother knew him. Which made Morgan wonder why she was here: Dr. Melton hadn't done squat to save her parents, so what was he going to do for her? He was small, with round cheeks and little glasses that reflected the light, so you couldn't really see his eyes. Like, what was he thinking? Forget it. You'd never know.

"He's even taller than people say," said Morgan.

"Who is taller?"

"Osama . . . He's really, really tall."

Dr. Melton gave a little nod and his glasses flashed. "You say Osama. Are you referring to . . . ?"

He had this way of asking, without asking, that was really hard not to answer. Morgan said, "Yes. Osama bin Laden." Anger she had never known before seemed to be always bubbling under her skin. She could hear it in her voice, a mean sound like a box cutter slitting cardboard. "Who do you think I'm talking about?"

"And what did he do this time?"

"Like last time. And the time before. Like I told you already. He just stood there, looking down at me."

"Where were you?"

"In bed."

"Asleep?"

"Until he woke me."

"How did he wake you?"

"By standing there."

"Were you afraid?"

"What do you think?"

"I wasn't there, Morgan. I only know what you tell me."

She looked back at her sneakers. "Yes."

"Yes what?"

She touched the jade dragon she wore on a chain around her neck. She had bought it in Chinatown. Dragons meant good luck, the saleslady told her, and jade meant that goodness would protect the person who wore it. She had been holding it in her sleep, tight in her hand, when the terrorist came back to her room. Unbelievably tall. Thin as a rope.

"Yes what?"

"Yes! I was afraid."

"What did he do when you awakened?"

"He reached up and starting unwinding his turban. He just kept unwinding. Yards and yards of white cloth just 'un' and 'un' and 'un.' When he got down to his skin, it unwound, too, and he kept unwinding it, stripping it from his head and his face. I could see bones. His whole skull. All bones. But he kept unwinding and stripping the bones away, and inside . . . there was his brain. Like in a cup."

She looked up right into the glare of his glasses and asked in a small voice, "What is happening to me?"

"Let's talk about that, Morgan."

"I mean, before—until Christmas—it was just school blowing up and the tunnels caving in and water rushing . . . This is much worse. It won't stop. It's on my mind all the time. I can't stop obsessing."

"Did he touch you?"

"What do you mean?"

"In your dream, did Osama bin Laden come on to you sexually."

"Yeeuch. God, you're weird."

Dr. Melton watched her shrivel up in the chair, trying to disappear inside her own arms. She was a short, stocky little fifteen-year-old, solid as a fireplug. She had a turned-up nose that made her look younger than her years, and a firm jaw that made her look stronger than she was. A pretty face—though hardly the beauty her ice-queen mother was. Nor had she inherited the raffish elegance her tall, handsome father had possessed in such abundance—though she had also been gifted, if that was the proper term, with his strangely compelling blue and green eyes.

In ordinary times, before 9/11, she was the type of girl mothers hauled into his office seeking solace for not having dates and fitting in with the hot crowd at school. While guiding her to an understanding that her parents' divorce wasn't her fault, he would have searched for ways to assure Morgan that she might spend high school and college with fewer boyfriends than the hottest girls in her class, but would have many deep friendships, while concentrating on the things she was good at—her science projects, her music, her sailboat racing. He also knew, but couldn't say, that around the time she turned thirty, some smart, decent guy ten or fifteen years older would see her for the treasure she was. Happy days awaited. But it was a long wait until then. She would be waiting half her life. Still, it would have worked out. She was, at heart, an optimistic kid—or had been before 9/11. She had even had a boyfriend of sorts before 9/11. A boy pal.

"How's Toby?"

"I don't know."

"Don't you talk?"

"Naw. I feel so stupid, like I'm too scared to get on a train to visit my best friend? I really let him down. I used to take the train out all the time, after we moved."

"Can't Toby take the train into town?"

"His mother won't let him."

Melton sighed. Psychiatry careers would be made, country homes refurbished, and trust funds established with the profits from undoing the damage wreaked by obsessively protective suburban parents.

Before 9/11 he could have handled Morgan's problems by rote. At worst, she'd have grown up with awful taste in men. Now he didn't know. Though he did suspect that she was in deep trouble and he was feeling increasingly inadequate to help her. At least she was still talking, but wouldn't be much longer, he feared. With spring upon them and summer promised, most New York kids were getting over the attack. Left behind would be those too embarrassed to admit their fear, their isolation, and their misery. And he knew that when a kid went underground, a kid was lost.

"What about your friend in Tonga? What's his name?"

"Paea."

"Do you write?"

"No."

"Didn't you tell me he wrote you?"

"He's like ten thousand miles away."

Melton nodded. Person by person, friend by friend, she had stripped herself of connections.

"How's school?"

"Okay."

"Your mother called me."

He liked how she could not lie. A blue eye and a green eye focused hard on his and she said, "The school told her I skipped some classes."

"Where'd you go?"

"Riding my bike."

He waited. She wouldn't lie, but she could omit—a trait she shared with her father, who had been a world-class omitter of pertinent specifics. Finally, Dr. Melton asked, "Where?"

"Up to the park . . . Up the river . . ."

"What do you do there?"

"I look at the boats."

"Are there boats in the winter?"

"A couple . . . They're for sale . . . Sometimes I just want to get on a boat and check out."

"What does 'check out' mean?"

"Disappear."

"Where?"

"Thin air."

Melton smiled. "Your mother expressed another worry ... And I must admit I've never heard this one from any parent ever before."

"What?"

"She says you don't use your cell phone enough."

"I check in."

"She means that you're not running up minutes talking with friends like you used to."

"Oh."

"Is that true?"

"I don't have anything to say to them ... And they sure don't have anything to say to me— How can I be into flossing? They're all excited buying 'poodle skirts' at the Goodwill. Like nothing ever happened?"

"Is it lonely?"

"I don't know." Her father used to hold her hand on the street, when she was little, but as she got older he started throwing an arm over her shoulders like they were best friends. The night before the attack, they had lingered outside her mother's building, talking, kidding around. A woman passing stared at how handsome he was and Morgan had looked her right back in the face as if saying, *He's with me. He's mine.*

Dr. Melton asked about her grades, which were going down, and the science competition she had decided not to enter. "I just don't care anymore ... Mom's trying to make me go to Oxnard."

"What is Oxnard?"

"California? Like a retirement place? It's near L.A. She wants me to stay with Grandpa."

"Would you like the change?"

"He's so sad. I can't do it."

"Your grandfather lost both his sons ... Maybe he could use some help. Why not try it over spring break? Your mother could be right. The change might do you good. A different view out the window for a week."

"She just wants me out of the house so she can bring her boyfriend home." And with that, Morgan went back to inspecting her sneakers.

"Let's imagine," Dr. Melton asked her, "that you are looking back on your life two years from now—let's say from senior year. What would you regret then, about what you're doing now?"

She shook her head.

"Or not doing?" he coaxed.

"Not doing? I would regret that I didn't stay all night in my dad's office the night before it happened."

"Haven't we talked about that? It was a school night. You stayed past your bedtime, helping him."

"I could have slept on the couch."

Melton covered his mouth before he could voice the obvious: *And died with him?* But she saw it on his face and answered resolutely, "We would have escaped, together."

Again his face betrayed him.

She denied it in a rush of all her hopes. "We would have woken up early. I would have brought him home and made Mom cook breakfast. So we wouldn't even have been there."

Dr. Melton tried to shift to a more productive line. "Let me ask you this. If you had the power here and now, what would you most like to do?"

"Nuke Saudi Arabia?"

"Would you really drop atomic bombs?"

"*Neutron* bombs."

"What's the difference?"

"Radioactivity. Neutron bombs only kill people. They don't blow up buildings, so the wind wouldn't blow fallout onto India."

Dr. Melton smiled. "I'm sort of relieved to hear you joke."

Morgan Page said, "I'm not joking. Though, actually, since you ask . . ." And now she did look up. "I would prefer to be in an airplane flying over Saudi Arabia while a mega-tsunami washes it away."

"A *mega*-tsunami? I presume you mean a particularly enormous tidal wave."

Suddenly animated, she said, "It would start with a landslide in India. On the coast of the western Ghats? One of the mountains would fall into the sea. And the wave would race across the Arabian Sea. It would drown the desert and flood the Persian Gulf and the Red Sea all the way to the Suez Canal."

"That would be some wave," Dr. Melton said lightly.

"Half a kilometer high at least."

"I'm too old for metric," said Dr. Melton, looking for her reaction, hoping she would smile, or at least give a teenage sneer. "What is that in feet?"

"Sixteen hundred and forty, point four one." No smile. No sneer.

"Are you studying this in school?"

"We did tsunamis and volcanoes in Geology. I combined it with a 'What I did on Christmas Vacation' paper I did a couple of years ago for Physics. Wave phenomena and fluid dynamics?"

Melton ventured another smile. "Volcanoes, wave phenomena, fluid dynamics, and Christmas vacation? That sounds like the ultimate in multitasking."

"I saw volcanic vent holes in the South Pacific." Cold as ice.

"Still, isn't it hard to imagine an entire mountain falling into the Arabian Sea?"

She looked at him, eyes bright as emerald and sapphire. "God could do it."

"God . . . Yes . . ." Not an eminence in most of his patients' reveries. "Do you think God would do something so horrifying to all the innocent people in Saudi Arabia?"

"Why not? He did it to all the innocent people here."

Why not, indeed, although as revenge fantasies went, Morgan's were pure Godzilla. Which was an enormous relief. Too many of the children who came to him since 9/11 harbored fantasies far less grandiose and therefore more dangerous. Landslides and mega-tsunamis might reek of mass murder and genocide, but it was much easier for a child to get a gun. Angry as she was, this child wouldn't hurt anyone. She was more a danger to herself.

"Would you call this one of the things you're 'obsessing' on?"

"Yes—no! . . . Yeah, maybe . . ."

"Morgan, would it be fair to say you are bitter?"

"Would it be fair to say I'd be wack if I weren't?"

"Would it be *accurate* to say you feel bitter?"

Her eyes filled and she said nothing, even when he coaxed her with the thought that bitterness stemmed from anger and that anger was a necessary stage in the healing process. At last, mercifully, her fifty minutes ended. Although he hated finishing on such an empty note. What had he given the child to take with her?

"I'll see you Thursday. If you get that Osama dream again and it's too much, remember you can always call me. The service will find me in an emergency and I'll get right back to you."

Morgan slung her book pack over her shoulder and fished her bike-lock key from her jeans.

"Daddy telephoned last night."

Dr. Melton looked at his watch to hide his dismay. Adult patients pulled every stunt in the book to prolong a session, hustling extra time for their money. Teens, whose parents paid the bills, bolted out the door. That this child was standing stock-still, earnestly awaiting his reaction, cut to the heart of his fears. He was suddenly over-whelmed by a stark vision, his own hallucination. He'd been flashing on it often since 9/11. Chased by soldiers in some wartorn place like Kosovo, he was hiding in the bottom of a well. If he looked up at the bright circle of sky overhead, he knew that he would see Morgan Page holding a hand grenade.

What to say? An only child, unusually close to her father, had observed his financial and emotional distress and had tried to help—acing every admission test and interview to gain entrance to an elite tuition-free public school instead of an expensive private school. But unable to stave off the divorce, she blamed herself as even the healthiest children did. Nor could she accept why her father had been the one to die instead of her. Overwhelmed, she was counteracting survivor guilt with denial. And when that failed, Dr. Melton feared, her next attempt to right the wrong might well be self-destruction.

"Your father is dead, Morgan. He and your uncle were killed when the terrorists crashed hijacked airplanes into the World Trade Center."

"He telephoned."

"Where did he call from?"

"Some island."

"How do you know?"

Her expression shifted, as if she had changed her mind about confiding something very important. "I can't believe he could just vanish, like you blew out a candle."

"How do you know he telephoned from an island?" Melton repeated, but he saw that he was too late. Her face was closing up, layer upon layer, and when she finally answered him, her thoughts were hidden like a wall safe behind a painting.

"He and Uncle Charlie always kidded about running away to an island."

"Any island in particular?"

Morgan shrugged.

"To retire?"

Morgan shrugged, again. "I don't know."

"Did you dream about the telephone call after an Osama dream or before?"

Her chin came up and her strange eyes bored into his. "It wasn't a dream. I didn't dream it."

"What did he say?"

Morgan held his gaze for a frighteningly long moment. He was back in the well, waiting for her to release the grenade. Abruptly, she hung her head, the picture of dashed hopes and rejection. "Nothing. He hung up on me."

"How do you know it was him?"

"He was drunk."

"How do you know he was drunk if he hung up so quickly?"

"He called me Kitten."

"And . . . ?" Melton looked again at his watch. Now where was this going? "What does Kitten mean to you?"

"He only called me Kitten when he was drunk."

FOR AIDEN PAGE, THE TERRORIST attack on the World Trade Center had not been "like a movie."

People on the street, people watching TV, people watching from uptown and Brooklyn and across the river in Jersey, people stampeding from the dust cloud, all told the reporters that it was like a movie. But if, at a quarter to nine in the morning on the ninety-first floor, you were bent over your desk, holding your head in your hands in total despair, wondering whether you would go bankrupt or to prison first; if you knew you could never find another job to earn the kind of money you needed to support your family; if you had maxed out your credit cards to pay the home-equity loans you were tapping to pay your mortgages; and if you had spent the night fearfully combing your computer for e-mails the U.S. attorney for the Southern District of New York had ordered you to "preserve"; then the first plane smashing into the floor above you was not at all like a movie. It was like God drove His fist through the building and roared in your ear, *It's your lucky day!*

Smoke billowed from the air vents. In the time it took him to grab his whistle and flashlight and herd twenty-two employees into the stairwell, it was gushing through the ceiling tiles. Debris cascaded by the windows. Water poured in from the halls, ankle-deep. If the fire burned through the floor above, wouldn't it collapse the ceiling and obliterate every disk and paper file in HHH's office?

He swept through the cubicles and the trading floor again to make absolutely sure everyone was out. Here at last was an upside to the dot-com crash: six months ago, before they started firing people, they'd had a hundred more employees shoehorned into this space.

The thickening smoke drove him to his knees as he made a third pass, checking once more that there was no one left but him. He double-checked Charlie's office. Empty. Probably at a breakfast meeting. Thank God.

He crawled back to his own office, shut the door against the worst of the smoke, and took stock. Did he really want to try this? Did he have a choice? Job evaporating, divorce way past the point of no return, banks foreclosing on the house, the apartment, the country place, and suddenly a prosecutor breathing down his neck for reasons he couldn't fathom.

He had searched the files all night, and still didn't know if the prosecutor was only fishing. But the blame game was about to begin and everyone left standing on Wall Street in the fall of 2001 knew that such letters were a first step in a very dangerous dance, in which some would be invited to trade evidence for leniency, while those who protested their innocence faced a perp walk.

Either way—a protracted investigation or a swift and merciless trial—as the company's chief financial officer, he would take the heat. And the irony was that HHH's CFO, who was supposed to know everything going down in the company, but suspected he didn't, could no longer afford a lawyer.

Not a lot to stick around for. Nothing and nobody, except Morgan. And what the hell could he do for her anymore? Better to save her the shame of his failure. While his life insurance would take better care of her than he could.

Take this gift of fire, he thought. Stuff your briefcase with cash, disappear, and don't look back.

But he did look back—long enough to pull the CD of files that

Morgan had helped him back up the night before and stash it in his briefcase. Crawling to his door, he felt something under his hand. And when he saw what it was, he clutched it so hard that it bit into his palm. Morgan's crucifix. It must have caught in her sweater yesterday when she changed out of her school clothes for their weekly "Daddy dinner" upstairs at Windows on the World.

The smoke had turned black, too thick to see down the hall. He slithered under it, belly to the soaked carpet, and felt for the keypad that unlocked the chairman's private office. In that inner sanctum that Henry Ho Hong visited once a year was a wall safe hidden behind an oil painting of a nineteenth-century sailing vessel that sported the sharp bow of an opium clipper.

But deep in Henry Hong's office, where the smoke hadn't yet penetrated, Aiden was astonished to find his brother was there ahead of him. Charlie whipped around from the combination dial, eyes quick and dangerous. When he saw it was only Aiden, he flashed a tight smile. "You picked a hell of a morning to come to work on time."

"Slept on my floor."

He couldn't believe that Charlie had gotten the same message he had from the inferno roaring overhead. Charlie had had the balls to cash out his personal holdings at the first sign of trouble. Charlie was a star. Charlie got into an Ivy League college. Charlie spoke French and Chinese. Charlie had joined ROTC and, after the army, went straight to the top of Wall Street. Then he reached down and pulled Aiden up with him. Right into a cushy job at HHH, where Aiden— who regarded himself as little more than a glorified accountant— rode a kind and forgiving market until the NASDAQ collapse wiped him out. As long as Aiden could remember, Charlie was the "good" brother. Aiden was the "bad."

Yet Charlie the winner, Charlie the prince regent of an immensely wealthy investment house, had beat him to the safe. They called it "Dad's drawer" after their old man's desk drawer that always smelled of crisp, green fives, tens and twenties, folded in his money clip. HHH's held hundreds, a slush fund of C-notes to tip wine waiters and hookers to give the clients memorable service. Cash to close deals. Cash for down payments. Cash to tip security. Cash for antiques or a Harley, or a tax-free headsail. Cash for the unexpected.

Aiden watched Charlie calmly divide the banded stacks into two equal piles. At publicly held investment banking firms, even the rough-and-tumble traders had to take their clients to strip clubs on AmEx corporate cards; but private banks like HHH—founded by a Hong Kong refugee who kept all options open—played by their own rules. Twenty-seven grand each—hardly a new life, but enough cash to disappear without leaving a paper trail.

Aiden said, "What's going on? Why are you—"

He got back another tight smile and a wisecrack—the oldest cliché in the business. "No one stays on Wall Street a day longer than they have to."

Charlie flipped open his briefcase, dumped letters, files, business cards, and his BlackBerry onto the floor, and filled it with his share of the money, stuffing one stack in his jacket pocket. "All we're doing is ratcheting up the cycle."

"What about Mary?" Charlie's wife.

"Fuck her. She's running around on me anyhow."

"With whom?"

"Who cares?"

The room started shaking. They looked out and saw the trading-floor ceiling thunder down on the computers. Smoke and dust filled the space.

"Excellent," muttered Charlie.

Aiden darted into Henry Hong's marble bathroom to wet towels for their faces. The water had stopped running.

Charlie grabbed the towels out of his hand and dunked them in the toilet. "Let's go, pal. We're outta here."

"What about Dad?" Aiden asked.

"He'd do the same to us. Dad's a survivor. He'll get over it."

But what about Morgan? Aiden couldn't help her anymore. She was with her mother. He couldn't help anyone anymore.

There was more than cash in Dad's drawer. Down under the money, something equally valuable. Charlie ripped open a manila envelope full of passports, American and British, and handed him one. It had Charlie's picture, which looked very much like Aiden's, and the name of a stranger. "Remember, don't sign your own name."

"Where'd you get these?"

Charlie's reply was a puzzling, "You think you got the only letter from the U.S. attorney?"

"But—"

"Why are you breaking my shoes?"

Aiden bit his tongue. Don't ask stupid questions. Don't ask back when they were altar boys. Don't ask now. Shut up, do what Charlie says, and he'll look out for you. And plan ahead, too: folded inside the passport was a "six-pack" charter-boat captain's license in the same name.

Charlie hid all but one of the passports in his briefcase. Aiden shoved his into his pocket, and stuffed his share of the money in his briefcase. Charlie dropped his cell phone on the floor. The younger brother hesitated, reluctant to break the last tie.

"What are you going to do, call home? *Leave it!*"

Charlie grabbed Aiden's flashlight and led the way. But in the five minutes since Aiden had guided the employees out, fire had tumbled down the stairwell. They crawled through smoke and darkness looking for another.

"Whole building's going to hell," muttered Charlie.

It was an impossible thought: not just HHH's offices—not only the top floors of the building—but everything would be destroyed.

"Listen, buddy!" Charlie whirled around and kneeling face-to-face shined the light between them so they could make eye contact. "This is really bad. Anything happens, we get separated? Head for the island."

"We'll stick together. We're not getting separated."

"What did I say?" Charlie shouted.

"Head for the island."

"Okay. Let's go." At last they found the third stairwell. But it was dark with smoke and they heard people screaming, "Go up! Go up," and others yelling, "Down! Down!"

"Down!" said Charlie. "There aren't enough helicopters in the city to evacuate the roof."

One flight down they found the stairs blocked by a vertical maze of ragged slabs of Sheetrock. Aiden lifted a broken sheet, flung it aside, and picked up another. It was there, knee-deep in water—with voices from other floors still screaming, "Go up! Go up!" and "Down! Down!"—that they got separated.

The wet, broken Sheetrock was slippery as ice. Aiden's feet flew out from under him. He slid a full flight of stairs into darkness, banged against a wall, stood up, and slid into darkness again. When he stopped falling, he lay stunned, his head spinning. A minute? Two? He didn't know. Then somebody was lighting a Bic in his face and a flame-lit skinny little Spanish delivery guy was saying, "I got you, mister. Can you walk?"

"My brother—" Aiden looked up. Above the thick smoke loomed solid orange flame. It was roaring so loudly he could hardly hear the guy who was pulling his arm. The heat was sucking the air out of the well. He jerked free and started up the stairs. Halfway up he could smell his hair burning.

He stumbled back, shielding his face.

"No one left, mister. Just us—yo, he's probably gone down ahead of us."

Aiden clung to that hope and started down the stairs, leaping three at a time with the little guy scampering behind him. "Charlie!" he yelled at every landing. "Charlie!"

Thirty or forty flights down they found the steps blocked by an enormously fat woman exhausted and sobbing with fear. The Spanish guy took one huge arm and said, "Grab her, mister. We gotta get her down."

They carried and dragged her fifty flights past the cops and firemen who were slogging their way up to the fire. In the lobby, the Spanish guy said to Aiden, "Take her outside, I'll give the firemen a hand."

Head down, he walked out of the burning building and swiftly north through mobs of people staring at the skyline behind him.

IT WOULD NEVER seem like a movie—even six months later, waking before dawn, half-smashed, beside a sweet little college girl who was way too good a person for him to be with. If anything, the memory seemed like a dream that never happened, the kind you woke from not remembering more than bad feelings, and grateful it was over. That happened many mornings. But in seconds, it all came back and Aiden Page remembered far, far more about that September morning than he recalled of his gin-stoked wanderings last night.

Nausea rolled over him and it did not seem possible that within a few hours he would have to perform as Captain Kindly, settling the new charterers aboard and getting under way. He had really overdone it last night tanking himself up to a state where he could pretend that the little girl on the boat next door wouldn't ask questions.

The picture. Jesus H.! He had hidden the newspaper in the Swan 44's forepeak, under the berth he slept in when the owner or charter clients took over the aft stateroom. The paper was only three days old. Somebody must have brought it in a plane from New York. So it wasn't old news that the clients wouldn't remember. The clients probably read it before they left New York. Maybe it stuck in their heads—the brothers. Of course it stuck in their heads, how many obituaries did you read about brothers?

He slid out from under the firm, round leg she had hooked over his, stepped into his shorts, and sneaked out of her tiny cabin, past a deckhand sleeping on the pilot berth in the saloon and up to the ketch's cockpit, where he found his shirt and boat shoes damp with morning dew and spilled beer. Holding them in one hand, he climbed silently onto the side deck, where he swung across the safety lines onto the Swan.

The owner, thank God, had gone home and the cook hadn't slept aboard, so the boat was empty. He brewed coffee, showered, and felt the deep tremors that promised a savage hangover.

Quickly, he packed two seabags with what he had accumulated on the run. One held the tools of his trade—foul-weather gear and seaboots, bosun's knife, binoculars, a wool watch cap, a couple of GPSs, bearing compass, dividers, parallel rules, a handheld VHF radio, and a bought-for-cash cell phone with its now almost-maxed-out calling card. The other held a few polo shirts, some shorts and underwear, a bathing suit, and a pair of long pants that he hadn't worn since he sailed from Annapolis as last-minute replacement crew on a boat bound for Bermuda. Toilet kit and towel and a few paperbacks and that was it. He was out of here.

But where?

The boats were rafted stern to the finger dock. He managed to get off his and past hers without anybody calling to him and walked to the spa hoping he'd find a cab this early. There was no one in the lobby, no cabs out front, so he found a place in the shadows of the veranda where he could sit and wait for the staff to wake up but where early-rising guests wouldn't notice him.

The wind picked up a little as the sun cleared the horizon. Somebody's carelessly secured halyards began chattering against a mast. Crew stirred on the boats, yawning on deck over first coffees. He heard a vehicle on the road, but it was only a rusty van delivering cleaning crews from the town. Catch a ride with the van? He thought of the busy town with fear and the airport with growing terror. It was going to be very hard away from the water. On the water he was at home. He had kicked around for years, working the boats, until Charlie finally rescued him and made him finish up college and join him on Wall Street.

He wished he hadn't run away.

A ketch came up the twisty entrance creek. Aiden sat forward to watch closely, his troubles forgotten a moment, because the two-masted boat was coming in under sail—a fairly amazing feat considering the narrowness of the channel and the many bends. Tacking with neatly executed sail shifts, it emerged without running aground, dropped its main, its mizzen, and a working jib, and drifted a straight line across the postage-stamp harbor.

When it came to an exquisitely timed stop beside the main dock, Aiden stood up and started to clap, applauding the new arrivals' seamanship, before he remembered all the reasons to keep a low profile. He was not the only one who noticed.

The charter-company manager, a Frenchman representing new owners, ran onto the dock waving his arms. "*Bassin privé! Privé!* No mooring. No mooring. *Privé!*" Aiden had seen this happen before; the new manager did not welcome boat-bum cruising ketches with patched sails and laundry drying on the safety lines to the elegant Swan Pond. This one—an extreme example of the species, sprouting the hodgepodge of wind generators, self-steering vane, and solar electric panels common to the live-aboard cruising crowd—looked like an abandoned osprey nest.

There was an old woman at the helm. A second white head popped out of the hatch. Both had Australian accents.

"What's all the yelling, Sophie?"

"The Frog says we can't tie up."

"Tell him to get stuffed."

The helmsman called Sophie addressed the Frenchman. "We don't intend to spend the night. We want proper baths and a slap-up breakfast and we'll be on our way."

Aiden picked up his bags and hurried down to the dock, where the manager, who spoke perfectly good English, kept repeating, "*Privé.*"

"*Privé*, yourself," Sophie shot back. "What you are trying to say is that you don't want a battered old girl like this mucking up your posh harbor. Well, let me tell you, Monsieur Harbormaster or whatever you ruddy call yourself, when you've got the sea miles under you that she has, you'll not look so posh yourself."

"*Privé!*" said the Frenchman.

Aiden dropped his bags and called, "Heave a line."

"Thanks, mate. Gertie, get the bow." The old lady tossed a stern line that uncoiled neatly into Aiden's hand. He brushed past the Frenchman and flipped a clove hitch over the piling and hurried to the front of the boat to receive the bowline from the equally old Gertie, who flashed him a pretty, blue-eyed smile. "Bless you, mate."

The Frenchman was dogging his heels. Aiden said, "Could we give the ladies a break? Let them go ashore for their bath and breakfast. I'll watch their boat. In fact, I'll take it off the dock if they don't mind."

The manager protested that there would be many boats in this morning and no room. Aiden leaned close. "I have an awful hangover. Please shut up and do the right thing."

"Who do you think you're talking to? You're a fifty-dollar-a-day boat nigger. Get off my dock before I have you fired."

A severe expression crossed Aiden's face that people who had known them would have associated more with his brother Charlie. Sophie and Gert exchanged a quick glance, clambered off the ketch, and took his arms firmly from both sides. "No need for a dustup on our account, mate," said Gert. "Best we turn our other cheeks and sail away."

Sophie said, "We just thought it would be fun to luxuriate for a morning before we set sail."

Aiden calmed down, touched by their good-humored serenity. "Go ahead. I'll anchor her off for you until you're done."

"No, that won't be necessary." She turned to the Frenchman with a smile that would melt stainless steel. "Young man, would you be by any chance a Catholic?"

"But of course."

"I am Sister Sophie. This is Sister Gertrude. God has called us to spread His written word to those less fortunate by teaching their young to read."

"Yes, of course, Sister. Though I doubt you'll find many less fortunate here."

"Just as well: we're headed home. All we want is a last bath and good meal to sustain us on the voyage."

He looked at his watch. "Of course, of course. We can accommodate your yacht for the morning . . . and perhaps I could put a word in with the hotel manager."

"That would be so good of you." She turned to Aiden. "Young man, have you had your breakfast?"

"Shouldn't I watch your boat?"

"Monsieur will watch our boat. Won't you, dear?"

"But of course."

SOPHIE AND GERTIE tossed the health-spa menus aside and demanded "a good fry-up."

Aiden had contrived to sit with his back to the open-air breakfast room because the two old ladies drew a lot of attention as they charmed the waiter into producing the chef, who was in turn charmed into frying eggs, sausage, and bacon while apologizing that he could not produce kidneys or mince on short notice.

Aiden had already made a snap decision to drop the "Chuck" charade and use his own name. If he could persuade them to let him sail with them, they were supposed to hold his passport, as captains of their vessel. But that was yet another name and he would claim that Aiden was a nickname if it came up. He felt liberated to be Aiden again and almost lighthearted at the prospect of escaping discovery in the charter-boat world.

"Were you pulling the French guy's leg. Or are you really missionaries?"

"Only for the past forty years. Before that, I was a poet and Gertie danced."

"You've sailed that boat for *forty* years?"

"She's got a steel hull. One of her sisters carried Bernard Moitessier numerous times around the Southern Ocean."

Aiden wondered how the steel ketch sailed. Moitessier, a great circumnavigator, and as romantic a sailor as he was bold, had boasted about his in his books. But Aiden had never met a sailor who didn't love his boat. True, she had cut a trim figure tacking up the creek, though attributable largely to the skill of her operators, and those rugged masts could carry a lot of sail. But "fast" thirty years ago was pretty poky today, and at thirty-nine feet long and twelve in the beam, she could be a real dog. As if beggars had a choice.

"Not to worry. *Darling* will outlast us both."

"So long as we keep ahead of the rust," Gertie added.

"Where have you taken her?" Aiden asked.

"Indonesia. Africa. South America. We were last in Georgetown, Guiana. We usually go up the rivers and preach at the settlements. What brings us here is we were on our way to New York to show support. But we've given up on that. We had to admit we're getting a little old for this sort of thing."

"It's time to go home."

"Where's home?"

"Brisbane."

Aiden looked from one faded pair of eyes into the other and echoed in astonishment, "Brisbane? You're sailing all the way to Australia?"

"We can't afford to ship her."

"That's a long voyage."

"Only way home."

"By any chance would you like to take a deckhand?"

They traded quick glances. It was, Aiden thought, like watching fencers touch foils.

Sophie said, "Perhaps."

It was the kind of "perhaps" Aiden associated with the head-mistress at the private school he had sent Morgan to before he went broke. It promised nothing.

Gertie asked, "Are you sure you could stand being cooped up with two old ladies on such a long voyage?"

"I can relieve you of a lot of watch standing. And I'm pretty good at fixing stuff."

Breakfast arrived. The nuns held hands and reached for his and bowed their hands. "Thank you, Lord, for this bounty of your land. May it sustain your daughters at sea, if it pleases you. Amen."

"Amen," said Aiden. He hadn't said grace since his grand-mother died.

Gertie looked around the open-air breakfast room, which was fill-ing up with trim, carefully coiffed women in their thirties and for-ties. "I am so glad we stopped here ..." Her gaze fell on Aiden. "Perhaps we *could* use a deckhand. As Sophie said, we're getting a little old for this."

"Brisbane's on the east coast of Australia, right?"

"We're north of Sydney."

"What if I went with you partway?"

"Well, we thought we'd work our way down to Margarita, then do Bonaire, Curaçao, Aruba, before we hop over to the Panama Canal."

Every stop in the tourist islands off the coast of Venezuela increased the risk of bumping into somebody he knew. "But if you had a third person standing watch, you could skip the ABCs and cut straight across the Caribbean."

"Rough passage."

"But faster. You could make the canal in a week."

"Perhaps ..."

"April winds are easier," said Gertie.

"I suppose he could help us through the locks."

"Actually I could crew for you as far as——" He was getting used to covering his tracks and he hesitated only an instant before he said, "Fiji," instead of Tonga.

Again the glances. They had caught the hesitation and he could tell it made them cautious.

Sophie eyed him sharply. "We could even drop you in American Samoa, if you want?"

"No. No, Fiji would be fine . . . But you'd still have to sail another three thousand miles alone."

"Not to worry. She'll smell the barn after Fiji."

"Through the Panama Canal and across the better part of the Pacific?" Gertie mused.

"I'll pay for my food."

"Actually, that's a good point, Soph, we would have to reprovision. Young men eat like horses."

"Before we rush into this . . ." Sophie looked Aiden in the face. "Common sense says you should never hire a complete stranger to crew for a long voyage. Once we're at sea, there's nothing but good character to prevent you from slitting our throats and throwing our corpses overboard."

"Doesn't look the type," said Gertie.

"Perhaps."

"Can you tell us a little about yourself, Aiden? You look like a sailor. Are you?"

"Not in your class," said Aiden. "But I've crewed various boats since I was a kid. Quit college to bum around the Caribbean and the Med. I've raced, a bit. I've lived on boats. And I used to own a forty-two-foot sloop, which I sailed with my wife and my little girl."

"Where are they?"

"I'm divorced."

Sophie probed his face with eyes that seemed to see right through him. It was like reporting to a wise grandmother and he was glad he had formed a story close to the truth. No big lies in what he said, just gaps. She said, "I'm sorry. Divorce can be so hard. I've noticed people are well into it—and deeply relieved, at first—before they experience an overwhelming sense of failure."

Aiden hung his head and prayed that she wouldn't ask about Morgan.

She asked, "Do you see your ankle biter?"

"What?"

"Your daughter. The child."

"No."

"That's a shame . . . How old is she?"

"Fifteen."

"You don't look old enough."

"We married at twenty."

"Can you navigate?"

"Only with a GPS. I've never learned to use a sextant. But I've got two GPSs. And I'm good at piloting and dead reckoning. I can keep a log."

"In Fiji the immigration officer will demand a return airplane ticket before he lets you disembark."

"I have an open ticket. And some money."

"How often do you get off your face?"

"Beg pardon?"

"You smell like you really hit the turps last night."

"Hit the—?"

"Got drunk," said Sophie.

"Oh. No, that's not my regular thing. I mean, I like a drink, but I don't usually get drunk. Actually, I never want to drink much at sea."

"Have you ever spent more than a week at sea?" asked Gertie.

"My brother and I sailed a thirty-eight-foot sloop from Los Angeles to Honolulu and back. About two weeks each way."

"Did you enjoy it?"

"Very much. I liked being away from land."

They looked at each other. "What do you think?"

"Seems a decent bloke."

"Fit as a Malle bull."

"Right . . ."

"We can't pay you, Aiden."

"The ride to Fiji will be plenty," said Aiden.

"Well, if you come with us, we'll be at sea for months. What are we in—late March? Reckon we'll be shipmates into July before we reach Fiji. So there's one thing you need to know, Aiden."

"What?"

"Gert and I are a couple."

When she didn't say what they were a couple of, Aiden said, "I'm sorry, I'm not following you." His mind had raced off again. From Fiji he could catch some kind of a ride back to the Tonga Islands and, once there, work his way up to Blind Man. Henry Ho Hong would take him in. Find him some kind of work in his organization. He felt lost without Charlie. But Henry Hong would make a place for him to start a new life.

They were staring at him like he was an idiot and he said, "I'm sorry, I'm still not following you."

"We sleep in the same cabin."

"Well, I can sleep in a pilot berth or up the forepeak, if you prefer."

"Gay."

"Beg pardon."

"We are gay," said Sophie, taking Gertie's hand and raising her voice so it carried about the breakfast room. "A pair. Together. We are lesbians."

"But only for the past forty years," said Gert.

"Forty-one, actually."

"You say forty-one, I say forty. Shall we call the whole thing off?"

"No."

"Can you deal with this, Aiden? Sailing across the Pacific Ocean in a boat full of dykes."

"Well, sure. I mean it's none of my business."

"Just so you're comfortable."

"Are you allowed to do that?"

"*Allowed?*" Their eyes flashed like sabers.

Aiden backpedaled, rapidly, saying, "Being nuns and all, I mean. You know ..."

"We've been through our crisis of faith, so to speak. We concluded that we were not cut out to be celibates, much less silent, or even cloistered."

It was Aiden's turn to look at them sharply. Behind the smooth delivery of the facts of their lives lurked pain and confusion and a strong hint that even after forty years, matters of faith remained unresolved. He had had high-school friends who'd become priests, and from their experiences he knew that "marrying the Lord" demanded a lot more than a simple "I do." If he weren't angling for a free ride he might ask, if they didn't want to be celibate, silent, or cloistered, why answer the call?

Gertie looked away as if she had heard him speak the unspoken question and had no easy answer. "Obviously, we could not remain officially members of our order. But we still try to serve the Lord."

Sophie smiled, a little wistfully. "Having managed to remain contemplative—against all odds—we expect to be called to discuss dogma in the next world."

"Of course," Gertie chimed in, "with the priest scandal there will be a rather longish queue, wouldn't you think?"

"What priest scandal?" asked Aiden.

They looked at him. "The child molestation?"

"I've heard those rumors since I was an altar boy."

"Aiden!"

"What did I say?" Why did they make him feel twelve years old?

"It's in all the newspapers. Priests have molested small boys. And sometimes girls. Not to mention the occasional adult. The cardinals covered it up." They were staring harder, and he felt like he was falling down a black hole.

"I haven't read the papers since September eleventh."

"It's on the BBC. Don't you listen to the wireless?"

"Not since September eleventh." No papers. No radio. No surfing at the Internet cafés. When he saw a TV in a bar, he turned his face from it.

Sophie asked, "Did you know someone who died there?"

He nodded, saying, "Several," while thinking, the brother I abandoned and my poor father who thinks both his sons were killed, and my little girl, who I abandoned, too, and is now dead to me for-ever.

He heard her say, "I'm sorry, Aiden. We were insensitive to that. It never occurred to us. I suppose that we assumed that because you're from Los Angeles . . ."

"No, that was my father's boat we sailed to Hawaii. He moved out there after our mother died. We were raised in New York, so yes, I knew several people in the twin towers. But I still can't believe it happened."

A confused, uncomfortable silence spread across the table. Aiden began to worry. They thought that grief had made him a little weird. Crazed with grief could be a pretty good cover; who would press a weeping nutcase for the details? Except who would sail with a deckhand who was acting certifiable?

Sophie reached out and laid her wrinkled, sunbaked hand on Aiden's.

If she apologized again, he was prepared to say it was all right and that he was fine. If she said they had changed their mind about taking him with him, he would plead to be given a chance. But instead of apologizing or rescinding their offer, she fixed him with a knowing gaze.

"One great advantage to sailing with lesbian nuns, Aiden. You can talk about anything, anytime. Anything you want." It was no joke. She was looking right through him, through his soul and into the empty space beyond.

"And since you're already Catholic," Gertie added, "we won't have to waste words to convert you."

Sophie finished the thought with a smile half-humorous, but still probing, "Too far at sea to summon the priest, we can even make a case for being allowed to hear your confession."

ONLY FOOLS SWAM AT NIGHT when the big predators fed close to the islands.

But in the Polynesian South Pacific—eight time zones and ten thousand miles to the west of Aiden on St. Martin and Morgan in New York—on the boat deck of a motor yacht big enough to call a ship, Charlie Page steeled himself to jump overboard the instant he saw the twin pinnacles of Blind Man Island rise from the starlit sea.

The red glow of his handheld global positioning device told him they were on course to pass close to the island—an irregular heap of coral-rimmed volcanic rock three hundred miles north of Tongatapu. But when the motor yacht climbed to the crest of a tall tradewind roller, he still saw only a vast and empty Pacific, oily in the starlight. He shoved the GPS in his pocket and cupped both ears with his hands to listen for the telltale pounding of surf. All he could hear was the wind and the distant rumble of the engines.

The GPS didn't lie. It had to be there.

"Charlie, what are you doing out here?"

He jumped. The yacht's owner, a woman whom he had left sleeping off multiple orgasms and numerous Cape Codders, had come out on deck bundled in a terry robe. Her mane of silver hair glowed in the starlight and her fingers sparkled with jewels.

He had to get her back to her cabin right now. No one could know he had gone overboard right here. Might as well BlackBerry the feds: *Come get me.*

She took his arm, firmly. Widowed wealthily, she was used to getting what she wanted at the instant she wanted it. Her small fingers dug hard in the muscle. "It's cold out here. Come to bed."

"I can't sleep. I'll be in soon."

"The balls of youth. Where do you get your energy? I'll tell Cook to bring warm milk." With her other hand, she stroked his bare leg. The eight-carat rock on her ring finger flashed, only to wink out when she reached up his shorts. "Well, *someone*'s finally sleepy."

"I'll be right in."

"I'll wake him up. That'll bring you in."

"Not now."

"I owe you one." She shrugged out of her robe and arranged the folds to cushion her knees. "Several ones."

"Carol, not—"

She knelt. "When you get to know me better, you'll find I'm a girl who pays her debts."

He kept it light, teasing like she was. "Wasn't I paying my fare to Fiji?"

He had hooked up with her on the long flight from Paris to Tahiti. Rich, bored, and too horny to think straight, she had been up for anything, including an apparently aimless wander along the Coconut Milk Circuit, visiting islands here and there at Charlie's request while hewing a course designed to shave close to Blind Man Island. He reached down and stroked her hair. "Go to bed. I'll make the next installment in the morning."

"If you think I'll let this go at Fiji"—she paused to envelop him with her lips—"you've got another *thing* coming."

He actually liked her. She was totally up-front—never a mean drunk—and usually passed out before the night got too long. He had no desire to hurt her. But at that moment, hardening to her experienced touch, he saw the island's peculiar double peaks carve a familiar notch out of the stars.

It looked much farther off than he had hoped and it was falling rapidly astern as the big yacht plowed past at eighteen knots. A long swim getting longer every moment. God help him if the seas weren't running toward the beach.

He scooped her off the deck and into his arms.

"Hey, what are you doing? I'm just getting started."

Still as skinny as the first night she scored with her long-dead husband, she was light as a feather. Charlie timed the vessel's roll and jumped easily onto the bulwark.

She looked down at the water foaming far below and twisted in his arms like a worried cat. "Hey, what are you doing?" she asked, again. But Charlie could feel in how lightly she struggled that she had had life so easy for so long that she couldn't quite believe her instincts.

"Don't worry," he promised. "I won't drop you."

He waited, timing the big yacht's roll, again, to clear the hull.

She opened her mouth in an astonished shriek just as they splashed into the surprisingly cold water. When she thrashed to the surface, five feet away from him, she had swallowed too much water to scream. Not that the watch would hear in the distant, air-conditioned wheelhouse.

The yacht hissed through the dark beside them.

Quite suddenly it was past, exhaust ports thundering. Propeller wash billowed and buried them in seawater. Then just as suddenly, the thunder faded and the loom of the hull grew small. It would steam 160 sea miles before Carol's maid brought her late-morning breakfast.

Alone in the dark, coughing and struggling to stay afloat, she screamed in abject terror, "We'll die, we'll die."

Splashing would alert the sharks that a creature had surfaced, too weak to defend itself. Charlie Page kept his hands and feet entirely underwater and swam a strong sidestroke—smoothly, quietly, away.

5

IF THE SUBWAY WAS SCARY, then an airplane made you want to curl up and cry.

Morgan couldn't believe she was going until she was strapped in. What got her on the plane was that she was so pissed off that they had taken her favorite nail clippers that for a while she couldn't think about being afraid. Then she was in and the doors were closed and the stews were checking seat belts and they were rolling backward from the gate. She thought of standing up and screaming, but they would probably put her in jail and that would be even worse. Besides, what would happen to Roscoe?

He was yowling in his cat carrier, belted in on the seat beside her. He was part of the deal she had cut with her mother. If she went, Roscoe came with her, with a ticket for his own seat, so they couldn't make him ride in the hold. It wasn't like her mother couldn't afford it. Dead, Daddy was all of a sudden worth big bucks, again, worth a lot more than alive, with life insurance and all the charity funds.

They'd given her a whole lecture at check-in. Don't let "your kitty" out. Yeah, right, like I'm going to let my cat get lost on your stupid airplane. Like I would allow that to happen to my beautiful cat, who has been my friend since I was ten years old, which is like one third of my fucking life. Like I didn't learn to sew so I could line the inside of his carrier with velvet so he doesn't scratch his poor nose when he tries to get out? Like how stupid do you think I am? Stupid as my mother thinks?

Her mother had been panicking that she would back out at the last moment; the closer it got to the time to leave, the more she babbled.

"Grandpa says that boy you liked still lives next door." Her mother had dangled that news flash like she was a shark and it was raw meat—like she would get on a goddamned airplane to California for some stuck-up, pumped-up surfer who wouldn't give her the time of day if she was the last girl in America. The same mother who lasered a disappointed expression at her blue jeans and white sweatshirt and proclaimed, "You know if you would wear the same color top and bottom, it would make you look taller and slimmer."

The way to deal with her mother was to ignore her totally while pretending to listen. So she had said, "Thanks, Mom, I'll change at Grandpa's," while her mind was fixing tighter and tighter on the sturdy little fiberglass sloop her grandfather kept tied to the dock behind the condo. It was a simple boat—almost ugly, with no teak on the decks, only Nonskid Awlgrip. But Daddy and Uncle Charlie had sailed it all the way to Hawaii, once. So it might be ugly, but it was geared to go places.

"Grandpa will be so happy to see you," her mother kept babbling.

"I'll try to cheer him up." Like a sad old man whose only children had been killed really wanted a fifteen-year-old crazy girl hanging around his condo. *Cheer up, Grandpa. Everything's going to be fine as soon as I change colors.*

"This will be good for you."

"That's what Dr. Melton said."

Like sitting around a dark house watching a poor old man cry will really stop my nightmares and hallucinations. She knew what she was in for. Grandpa had moved in with them after the attack, alternating between hanging out at the family support center, crying in his whiskey at Moran's, and sitting alone with the lights out. Only after her mother had Daddy declared officially dead had Grandpa gone home. But not before he made them have a horrible funeral.

"I'll miss you," her mother had lied as she helped her into the cab.

Looking around at what she had a funny sensation would be her last sight ever of New York, Morgan had nodded when her mother said, "We'll talk on the phone." The truth was she would never know when it was safe to call. Her mother's boyfriend could be there at any time. Sure enough, her mother had actually said, "Keep your cell phone on." As in, *Don't call me, I'll call you.*

To that Morgan had offered no answer. But when the cab pulled into traffic, she had been horrified by a sudden vision of her mother consumed in fire. It looked so real. She could see her beautiful hair flaming, and her eyes widen with fear, and her chiseled lips twist in pain. Morgan had stabbed at the window switch. It didn't budge. "Open the window, open the window," she screamed at the driver.

"It don't work, lady."

Morgan had shoved the door open and yelled over the roar of the street, "I love you, Mommy!"

Her mother returned her usual two-finger waggle as she turned back under the same awning where Morgan had said good-bye to her father the night before the attack. She closed her eyes tightly and prayed to God that she hadn't dreamed his call.

The jet engines raced. The plane began to shudder. Roscoe freaked.

Morgan leaned close to his carrier and put her face to the velvet-wrapped bars and whispered, "Hey, cool it." But he got worse, howling like an ambulance stuck in traffic—an anguished *yowl-yowl-yowl* of helpless misery that broke her heart.

People were staring. The woman in the aisle seat said, "I hope this isn't going to go on the entire flight."

"He's scared."

"Can't you give him a pill?"

She was terrified that the other passengers would complain so the stews would take Roscoe. She closed her eyes and thought about waves to calm herself. If she were calm, Roscoe might take strength from her calmness. The neatest thing about waves was that molecules of water remained in place while the wave rolled past. A wave didn't *carry* water—even when it bashed you hard. A wave rolled *through* water and rolled on. I'm that molecule, she thought. I'm going to sit here, no matter what happens, no matter what tries to roll me. She opened her eyes and stared through the mesh at Roscoe. Sometimes you could talk to Roscoe with like brain waves. *Cool it, Roscoe. Just stay where you are and let it all roll by. We'll stay, you and me.*

Daddy once told her, "Don't be afraid to be silly."

Hey, Roscoe, remember the Happy Days?

Every summer, they had cruised the Maine coast. Her and Daddy and Mommy. And Roscoe, the Boat Cat. *Remember, Roscoe? Do you remember the* Molly P? *What a beautiful boat.* He probably didn't. It was too long ago. They hadn't sailed last summer. By last summer—the summer before the attack—Mommy and Daddy had sold *Molly P* and Morgan got shipped off to Grandpa's for vacation. Without Roscoe. She had sailed with Grandpa in his little sloop, but just for day sails. Grandpa was okay on land, but he was a lousy seaman—freaking out and yelling—and it wasn't anything you'd remember as Happy Days. And when she got home in August, there was no home because they had separated and her mother had taken her to Manhattan, saying, "No way I'm going to be single in the suburbs."

Roscoe howled louder. Her thoughts were making him crazy.

The woman stabbed at the overhead call button. The seat belt held her down, so she couldn't reach it. She started looking around for a flight attendant, going, "Stewardess! Stewardess!"

Morgan covered her ears and hunched over the cat carrier, whispering, "Please, please, please."

I'm losing it, she thought. I'm going to crack up right here. I'll start screaming. They'll kick me off the plane. I'll be arrested and they'll take Roscoe.

The rage boiled up. Like when you dumped pasta into boiling water, she thought, and all of a sudden before you could stop it, it bubbled out of the pot and all over the stove. She wanted to kill the woman.

What if she screamed for the flight attendants first?

What if she said that she thought she saw the woman had a gun in her bag?

Suddenly she could see it all happening, like on a monitor. The flight attendants would come running. They'd try to search the woman's bag. The woman would get mad and wrench it back from them and the other passengers would jump up and grab her and pull her out of her seat and hold her down on the dirty floor that two hundred people had just walked on while they searched her bag and then her clothes and frisked her like a criminal.

And when they found no gun, Morgan could say, *I'm sorry. I'm really, really sorry. It must have been that little black makeup bag. It looked like a gun. I was scared. My father was killed by the terrorists. I'm so sorry. I was scared she was a terrorist.*

And what could they do? Pick the woman up off the floor and give her a free drink?

She felt a funny smile jerk her mouth.

The woman was loosening her seat belt to reach the call button. Morgan leaned across the cat carrier, right in her face. "He paid for his ticket just like you did. So why don't you pretend he's a screaming baby and leave us alone?"

Just then the plane rolled to the head of the line and, without stopping, thundered down the runway. There was no way the woman was going to get the stews' attention, no way they could throw Roscoe off now.

In a weird way, Morgan realized, anger had made her strong.

To Roscoe she said as the plane began to lift, "I never made you ride on the bike, did I?" That shut him up, too.

"Thank you, Mr. Cat."

She sat back and closed her eyes, keeping both hands firmly on the carrier in case anyone tried to take him, and let her mind sail away on Grandpa's sloop.

6

W HERE'S THE BOAT?"
Grandpa's Oxnard town house backed onto a Channel
Islands canal. But the slip where the sturdy little sloop lived had
nothing in it except empty water. It must be in the yard, she thought,
getting something fixed.

Grandpa answered in the same grim monosyllables he had
greeted her at the airport. "Sold it."

"*What?*"

"Last week."

"Why?"

"Who's going to use it?"

"I would."

"You?"

"I brought my PFD." She kept blinking at the empty space.
Daddy had given her a combination safety harness and personal
flotation device the last Christmas before the Happy Days ended.
Down payment on a promise to one day sail *Molly P* in the Bermuda
Race. "We could handle it, together. Like we did last summer."

"You don't live here. You come out for a week. I can't afford to
keep a boat around for once a year."

"But, Grandpa . . ."

She couldn't believe it. The realization that there was no boat
knocked every hopeful thought out of her head.

She felt her mouth quiver. She looked helplessly up and down the
canal; there were more trees than she remembered, palm trees and
regular trees like at home, but everything seemed smaller than last
year. And the boats docked behind each town house were mostly
powerboats.

"What are you crying for?"

The tide was out. The concrete bulkheads loomed tall, like barricades. The floating docks looked flimsy. Before she knew what was happening, huge tears were spurting from her eyes.

"Jesus H. . . . Ah, you poor kid. You thought we'd go sailing and it would be like with your father . . . I'm a horse's ass. I never thought . . . Morgan, I'm sorry. I'm so stuck in my mind I can't . . ."

She could hear in his apology and see in his long face that the reminder that both his sons were dead was her cue to say it was okay, it didn't matter. But she couldn't bring herself to say it. It mattered so much she could taste it. Bitter, bitter taste of disappointment. Worse than disappointment that the boat was gone. Shock. Shock how important her fantasy about sailing after her father had been to her. Shocked it had actually been a plan. Sort of.

More than sort of. Who am I kidding? she thought. A lot more. She had packed her harness and foul-weather gear to go sailing, but hidden under them in her seabag were her father's binoculars, bearing compass, dividers, parallel rules, both his GPSs, and his triple-knit wool watch cap, along with several Pacific Ocean charts. The North Pacific sheets were his from the Hawaii crossing. Those for the South Pacific she had bought downtown on West Broadway.

She couldn't stop crying. It was like she was finally crying for the first time since the attack. Really crying. Like a tsunami of tears that she couldn't stop if she wanted to. Through their blur she saw Grandpa getting madder and sadder at the same time. Who cared? Screw him. She had her own problems.

The tears shook her chest and stung her eyes and even seemed to drown her breath. From a distance she heard her grandfather say, "Jesus H. Okay. Okay. Relax already. I'll call your mother, tell her to take you back."

"No!"

"Then stop crying."

"I can't."

She heard the familiar tough side of him suddenly come back. A side no one had seen or heard since the attack. He used the same tone on her that she used on Roscoe when the cat was really, really a pain. She had never heard her father talk that way—only Uncle Charlie, and then rarely. It was the Grandpa voice that cut nobody any slack.

"Hey! Make up your mind. It's either me—no tears, or you can bawl your eyes out with your mother. Your call . . ."

Morgan swallowed hard, thoroughly cowed by the brusque old man, even as part of her secretly rejoiced. Her father was gone and her mother was acting like a total jerk, but at least her grumpy old grandfather was finally behaving like somebody she could trust. He might be a pain in the butt, but at least he was like he used to be. But how could he sell the boat? The boat was the whole reason she came . . .

"Well?"

Her mother would kill her. Or make her come along to the boyfriend's East Hampton house, which would be worse. One thing for sure, she wouldn't let her stay alone in the city while school was out for spring break. "I'll stay."

"You sure?"

"Yes."

"Okay. Go in the house. Wash your face. I'll grab your bags, we'll get you settled. What the hell is all this stuff? Three bags for a week?"

"I brought my foul-weather gear. And my seaboots. And Daddy's binoculars."

"Jesus H—don't start bawling again."

"I'm not."

"Then what's wrong? You look like you're going to cry."

"I'm hungry."

"Didn't they feed you on the plane?"

"They stopped doing that."

"Jesus H. . . . Look, *Jeopardy!* is on in a minute. We'll grab a pizza after. And tell that animal to keep his claws off my furniture."

"He doesn't claw stuff." Except, sometimes, rugs.

• • •

GRANDPA HADN'T THOUGHT to buy any food for the house, but he had remembered kitty litter.

Morgan set up Roscoe's cat box and let him out of his carrier and fed him one of the cans of Sheba she had packed. Then she took a long, long shower until *Jeopardy!* was over. Grandpa complained the steam would ruin his wallpaper. But he took her to a pizza place, which he called "a hell of a lot better than some frozen chain pizza." It was actually pretty good because they had a veg pie covered with amazing greens. A stop for ice cream put the fear of God in her that she would gain thirty pounds before she escaped.

Back home, Grandpa popped a beer and said, "Let's watch the boats," which meant sitting on the deck that hung over the water beside his empty dock, with a view of the channel that turned and twisted through houses and palm trees. Everything looked soft in the mist that had clung all afternoon and was growing thicker. She couldn't see the Pacific Ocean beyond all the houses, but she could smell the salt.

People were heading in for the night. They were mostly in motorboats and everybody waved—"Hi, Charlie"—to Grandpa.

When he waved back—"Hey, I got the grandkid visiting"—the neighbors would wave to her, grinning like they were really relieved that he wasn't sitting inside in the dark.

"Remember the kid from next door. Chris?"

"Sure." The football player.

"Here he comes." Grandpa nodded in the direction she was look- ing, watching a mast slip between the condos as the invisible hull proceeded up the channel. "Parents bought a boat . . . Hey, maybe he'd take you sailing."

Yeah, right. Like this full-of-himself football surfer would take her anyplace. Still, when she saw the boat creep into view around the bend, she began to hope. She ran her eyes hungrily over its lines; she wanted to imagine it as a sleek and purposeful shark, but she had too sharp an eye to see it for more than it was: a boxy coastal cruiser whose headroom belowdecks was at the expense of wind-catching freeboard. Her father and Uncle Charlie used to bark at slow boats. Suddenly, wanting to feel close to them, she said, "Bowwow."

Grandpa made a face. "Not that one. The little guy behind him."

A little racing sloop with a deep blue hull rounded the bend behind the coastal cruiser and Morgan broke into a smile.

Not a shark, either, but a very sleek cat. Even putting along on an outboard motor with her sails furled sloppily and sheets all tangled, it looked fast and stable. "Cool. A J/27."

"Yeah. They don't make 'em anymore."

"Ooohh. That is hot." It was old-fashioned compared to a light-weight J/80; no retractable bowsprit for an asymmetrical spinnaker, a bigger cabin than a modern racer, but she knew just looking at it that it was still a neat little pocket rocket that begged to be pushed.

Her grandfather laughed. "It's older than you are. They bought it cheap."

"Are they racing it?"

"Ask 'em."

She had seen J/27-class races on the Long Island Sound. In the stiff winds of autumn it took five or six people to crew the boat. But for cruising, she was sure, the sea-kindly little sloop was small enough and simple enough to single-hand. Low freeboard and low center of gravity would let it sail closer to the wind than most. Downwind, its flattish bottom and fin keel would let it surf to fifteen knots. At sea in the trade winds it might make 150 miles a day.

They pulled into the slip beside Grandpa's.

"Hey, the kid wants to know are you racing?" he called down from his deck.

"Naw, we're selling it," Chris called back. "It's not big enough." He threw an affectionate arm around his father and grinned. "My cheapskate dad thought he was getting laid off, but he didn't, so we're going to buy a real boat."

"What kind?" Morgan asked.

Chris's dad puffed his chest. "Forty-foot Beneteau. Two state-rooms, two heads, room in the cockpit to party."

Bowwow, thought Morgan. She glanced at Chris, who was all tan and blond and even hotter looking than last summer. But as soon as they made eye contact, he looked away. Like, *Who is this short New York chick whose skin is pale as snow?* Although later, when she drifted down for a closer look at the J/27, he did speak to her, saying, "It's a hot boat . . . But racing's not their thing."

"I'll bet you'll miss it."

"Naw, they're right. It's way too little."

THE LONGER THE BOAT, THE faster the boat," said Grandpa. "The faster the boat, the faster the passage. Less time at sea."

"But little boats used to go to sea."

"The faster the boat, the better chance you have of sailing around bad weather."

"Tania Aebi sailed around the world in a twenty-six-footer." A foot shorter than the J/27.

"So did Robin Knox. And I'll bet you dollars to doughnuts they took bigger boats next time."

"A really good little boat can sometimes point higher and go faster than a bigger boat."

"Not in heavy weather."

"Daddy told me Mr. Hong said a Windsurfer won the Hong Kong Round the Island Race."

Grandpa gave her a funny look. "Mr. Hong? I wouldn't believe a word out of that chink-boy clip artist."

"Daddy liked Mr. Hong."

"Yeah, well, your father liked to like."

"What do you mean?" she asked, wondering if her father had told him about his scary letter from the U.S. attorney. But he didn't answer. Just flipped on the TV. As if to say, *Case closed.*

GRANDPA HAD A gazillion sailing books on wooden shelves in the back of his rec room. She brought another to his lounger chair, where he was watching TV.

"Look at these old people. They sailed all the way around the Pacific in a thirty-two-footer."

"What do you think made them old?"

"Ha ha. And then they took it around Cape Horn."

"Finish the book. They ran aground on Chile."

"Ellen MacArthur won the single-handed transatlantic in a twenty-one-foot Classe Mini."

"Wasn't her next boat sixty feet?"

"How big was your boat? It was a lot smaller than Daddy's."

"Thirty-eight feet."

"I thought it was smaller." She went up to the guest room, where she had plugged her laptop into Grandpa's Internet cable. She came back with a triumphant, "I just checked it out. I found sixteen boats under thirty feet that circumnavigated the world."

Grandpa turned up the volume on Jay Leno. "Why are we arguing about boat size?"

"Mom says you like to fight."

"Yeah, well, your mother's an uptight WASP who never got the difference between arguing and fighting. We're not fighting. Are we?"

"No."

"We're having a discussion."

"Right."

"Do you have a bedtime?"

"Only when tomorrow's a school day."

He was smiling, a little. He was joking about bedtime. A commercial came on and he got up and went to the bookshelf and came back with *The Long Way* by Bernard Moitessier. "This guy raced in the first single-handed Round the World—little boats, but all longer than thirty."

"Thirty is little."

"Nine started the race, one finished." He handed her the book. "Keep it. It's yours."

She suddenly felt close to him and safe. They sat awhile, Grandpa watching TV, Morgan flipping through the pages, discovering that Moitessier had stripped his thirty-nine-foot steel boat of a ton of excess weight. "Grandpa. He dumped his engine. No generator. No radio."

"Yeah, he had a slingshot to shoot messages to passing ships— guy was a complete lunatic."

Jay Leno made a joke about Al Qaeda terrorists. Grandpa flipped to Letterman.

"Grandpa?"

"What?"

"If I were to tell you something, would you promise to not tell Mommy? Or anybody. Ever."

"What?"

"Promise?"

"Yeah, yeah, I promise. What?"

"Daddy telephoned me."

The old man sat up straight in the chair. His face darkened. His eyes got slitty and mean. "That is not *fucking* funny."

Morgan was prepared for that and she said, firmly, "I'm not joking."

His eyes, so mean a second earlier, got wet. "Please don't do this to me."

Morgan fell silent and stared at the rug. When she finally gathered the courage to steal a glance at him, she saw tears running down his wrinkles. She had really thought for a moment that he would listen to her. Listen. And understand. And maybe even help her with her plan. Instead, she had made the old man cry.

He hoisted himself slowly out of his chair and shuffled to the door. It was like he was twenty years older than when they were talking about sailing. Suddenly he whirled around and asked, "He didn't really call? You had another dream, right? You dreamed it."

"I don't know, Grandpa." She inspected him with sidelong glances and decided that he would be no help. He would never understand. Worse, he would just get in her way.

"But you said it like you meant it."

"I really don't know. Sometimes I think he called, sometimes maybe it was a dream. Sometimes I don't know what's real anymore."

She watched anger drive hope from her grandfather's face. But wasn't what she had just admitted true? Sometimes, she didn't know. Then she hated herself for doubting. To doubt was to kill her father. Or, worse, abandon him. But what if she *had* dreamed it? Even the part about him calling her Kitten. If I had dreamed his telephone call, wouldn't I dream it was real by dreaming he called me Kitten?

"COULD I LOOK at your boat, Mrs. Lloyd?"

Chris's mother, a smiley, blond California lady, said, "Sure." She pulled a key off a peg inside her kitchen door. "There's a lock on the hatch."

The decks were dirty. They hadn't even hosed off the salt when they tied up last night. She stood in the cockpit, automatically coiling the sheets they'd left in heaps, while she traced the running rigging with her eye and inspected the mast and the boom. At least they'd stretched a blue canvas boot over the boom to protect the mainsail from the sun. She peeked under the canvas and was relieved to find the Dacron hadn't yellowed. In fact the sail looked almost new. The winches turned freely. The jib lead cars had some corrosion; the deck tracks they rode were caked with old salt. It looked like they never bothered to shift the cars but just took the wind as it came instead of working to shape the sails. Which, on a racer like this, was a crime.

She moved the tiller. The rudder swung freely and took such a big bite of water that it shifted the boat sideways in the slip. You could scull her along with the tiller if you had to. She had not seen many keelboats with a tiller. People preferred to cram a big wheel into the cockpit, no matter how small the boat, because they thought it looked cool. But she had learned to sail on dinghies and steering by tiller was second nature to her. She liked the direct control. Besides, she had heard her father say that tillers were a lot better than wheels because they had fewer parts to break.

I'm in love, she thought. I love this little boat.

The hatch lock was a padlock, like a school-locker lock without the combination. She opened it, pocketed the key, and slid the hatch open.

"Yuuccch."

A stale bilge smell ballooned up like a hundred old gym towels. Fanning the air in front of her face, she stepped below and crouched in the low space, which was about a foot shorter than she was. Despite the low ceiling, the boat had a head, a pretty little bronze kerosene cookstove, and a mini–ice chest. No shower, no refrigerator, no freezer, no microwave. No generator to run all that. No inboard engine to charge the single twelve-volt battery.

"I'm still in love," she said aloud, though it was really, totally basic. Like in no radar, no weather fax. She wondered how long the battery could power the lights. On her father's *Molly P* they had had four humongous batteries, each twice as long as this one.

No nav station. No radios except for a short-range VHF handheld, and a little receive-only shortwave. No way to radio more than fifty miles. No charts. But if you already had charts—like California coastal charts and Pacific Ocean charts and Tonga Islands charts that you had bought downtown at New York Nautical and hidden from your mother in black plastic bags under your foul-weather gear—you could spread them on the pilot berth, and read them kneeling on the cabin sole. And if you had ironed wax into the paper before you left home, you could fold them to the section you were sailing and take them up to the cockpit and not worry about them getting wet.

The cabin ceiling and sides were off-white trimmed with teak.

Molly P had been all teak and mahogany below and had glowed like candlelight. But the white was kind of clean looking and plenty of light came in from long, narrow ports on either side of the cabin, so even if you had to stay inside in heavy weather, it wouldn't be like being locked in a closet. So what if there wasn't enough headroom to stand? Minimal freeboard and a deep-down center of gravity were worth it. The wind wouldn't push the sleek hull and coach roof like a kite, so you could sail close-hauled right into its teeth. In fact, the cabin was kind of cozy. Besides, you'd spend most of your inside time sleeping and it wasn't like she was as tall as Mommy or Daddy. A person could cook sitting or kneeling on a sail bag, or, in good weather, stand up and stick her head out the hatch.

Ducking, she stepped forward, through the oval opening in the bulkhead that separated the main cabin from the forward V-berth and head. She undogged the foredeck hatch, admitting the breeze to air the stink out of the cabin. The V-berth was jam-packed with sail bags.

"Cool."

Whoever had owned this boat before Chris's clueless family had bought it must have raced it in all kinds of wind conditions because it had five different-size jibs—the triangular headsails in front of the mast—ranging from an enormous wind catcher of a genoa jib for a regular breeze down to a stiff little storm jib, which, as her father used to say, you'd sell your mother for in a gale.

There was even a brand-new spinnaker—a big balloon of a headsail—that had never been out of the bag, and a whole bunch of extra line. The anchor was a crappy little lunch hook, which puzzled her because the sails and the running gear were first-rate. She guessed that maybe the previous owner had really dug this boat and, when he traded up, took his favorite anchor with him like a memory.

"Hey!"

The boat rolled as Chris clomped aboard. He stepped down from the cockpit and saw her passing through the opening from the forward cabin. "What are you doing?"

"Your mom said I could look around."

"Want to buy it?"

"I wish . . ." She had in fact considered that and actually went on line to see what they cost, which turned out to be four or five times the max on the Visa her mother gave her to travel. Besides, even if she had the money, they would make a parent sign papers. "Does the outboard motor charge the battery?"

"Yeah, it's got like an alternator? Puts a charge in it for the running lights and the cabin lights."

But only until the outboard motor ran out of gas. And on a long passage you'd want to keep your gas for emergencies and motoring in and out of port.

"How much gas do you carry for the outboard?"

"Couple of quarts in the motor and a three-gallon tank."

You'd definitely need a second auxiliary tank. Except where would you stow it? You couldn't keep gas belowdecks. The fumes could blow up. Have to lash it down in the cockpit, where you'd stub toes every time you forgot it was there. And how long would it last?

"What's she like under the kite?"

"Spinnaker? I don't know. We never put it up."

"You're kidding."

"I told you. They just bought it and now they're getting a new one. Racing wasn't their thing . . . I mean they didn't even get around to putting a name on it."

"Yeah, I wondered about that. A no-name boat . . ." She realized that he was staring at her, kind of shifting from foot to foot, like he was nervous or something.

The weirdest thought came to her. Way weird. But he was acting like he wanted to be here with her and didn't know what to say. Like he liked her, or something. For a second she imagined a whole new life. Stay at Grandpa's. Go to school out here. Date a football player. Just go back to being a kid. Except, what about her father?

Besides, there was no way this incredibly hot-looking guy liked her. So why was he staring at her? Probably because she was from New York, Morgan decided. Like she was from this exotic place that wasn't boring California. Or was it something else—something heavier than just liking her? Like maybe Chris sensed that she had a secret. A plan. And without really knowing why, Chris wanted to hang around somebody who knew something that nobody else did. Somebody who knew she had to act.

It struck her hard, all of sudden, that she didn't really care if he liked her. But she could use it. She asked, "You want to go sailing?"

"Us? Just us? I don't know if I can handle it alone."

"I'll help you. I can sail. Can you ask your mom?"

Chris's mother gave permission. But they couldn't leave the harbor.

While Chris piloted them down the canal on the little outboard, which was mounted on a lifting bracket beside the rudder, Morgan chose the smaller genoa jib for their headsail, hanked it on, and led the jib sheets back to their winches in the cockpit. Chris motored under the bridge into the main harbor. Morgan raised the jib and the mainsail and the little boat came so alive it gave her goose bumps.

She hadn't sailed in a year and she felt clumsy. But the boat was forgiving. It really was a pocket rocket—so quick off the line and fast in the turns and amazingly responsive to the tiller, even underpowered with a jib too small for the light harbor breeze.

She doused that headsail and ran up the bigger genoa in its place. Just then the wind picked up, but the boat felt so steady—so big-boat-like—that Morgan knew she must have a ton of lead ballast low in her keel. The winches were quality, Barients, which was good because while she was a strong girl, she was small. Powerful winches would make up for that.

Chris said, "The guy we bought her from said don't reef the main before you reduce the jib."

"I see that."

"He said you could leave the main full in thirty knots."

"Wow." She depowered by tightening the backstay, which flattened the jib and the main. The boat straightened up, willing to adapt to too big a headsail.

"What are you doing?" Chris asked.

"You never used this? It's the backstay adjuster. Hauling on this block and tackle tightens the backstay and bends the mast to flatten the sails and spill the wind—this is such a cool boat."

That Chris was having fun, too, became obvious when he asked, "You want to try the spinnaker?"

She did, very much. But with the plan that was ricocheting inside her mind, she didn't want anyone to know how fast she really could sail, so she said, "No way."

She steered toward the last outcropping of palm trees and town houses that marked the mouth of the harbor. A fat fishing boat with a high bow and tall cranes was plowing between the stone jetties that cut through the beach. Beyond an offshore breakwater the Santa Barbara Channel was speckled with whitecaps.

"Would your mom mind a lot if we went out a little ways?"

Chris grinned large, checked out nearby boats to make sure none contained people who knew his parents, and said, "I won't tell her if you won't."

They sailed between the stone jetties—a tight squeeze as half the channel was taken up by a bunch of dredging pipes and tank floats—butted into a strong chop, and continued around the breakwater into the channel swells. The little boat maintained headway—slicing through the smaller waves. The bigger ones tossed her around, but she still sailed closer to the wind than the much larger *Molly P* could have done. All in all, Morgan thought, she was a very nice, very stiff little boat built to race near shore and weekend cruise if you didn't mind roughing it.

Miles across the water the Channel Islands reared out of the mist. Santa Cruz and Santa Rosa, she remembered from her charts. Closer in, oil rigs poked up like mushrooms. Closer still, a car carrier that looked as big as an island steamed swiftly up the channel. The rigs, the hilly islands, and the huge ship made the Pacific Ocean beyond seem much smaller than it was. Sort of the way, she supposed, that the J/27's lead keel, low freeboard, sleek hull, and bold sail plan made the boat feel bigger.

Morgan told herself it wouldn't really be stealing. It wasn't like Chris and his parents loved their J-boat. It wasn't a special friend, like *Molly P* had been to her and Mommy and Daddy. Chris had made that clear; it was just an object they were getting rid of to trade up to a Beneteau—which was like trading a racehorse for a cow. So it wasn't like stealing something precious from a person, really, but more like giving an abused pet a new home.

She started a mental list of stuff she had to buy.

When they got back to the dock and she had to show Chris how to rig the spring line, she realized that he hadn't a clue how to close up the boat. All he knew was that the mainsail was supposed to be covered from the sun and the jib taken off the head stay and stowed below. He didn't question her leaving the jib sheets in place. Or the jib halyard shackled to the pulpit, close at hand. While his mother smiled—"No problem"—when Morgan returned the key she had "forgotten" long enough to make a copy of.

I T W A S T W E L V E H U N D R E D M I L E S across the Caribbean Sea to Panama sailing a shallow dogleg to skirt the dangerous coast of Colombia. The winds would be lighter close to shore, but Aiden's captains, he was relieved to see, preferred to wrestle the weather than the drug smugglers and pirates who were known to prey upon lightly crewed small boats.

The women claimed that they had been boarded often in their meanderings to serve the poor, but had always managed to buy the raiders off with offerings from their stock of steel fishhooks, sewing needles, and reading glasses. As smugglers intending to steal a boat for a onetime delivery worth millions were not likely to be impressed by fishhooks, they plotted a westerly course that would take them to 13 North 76 West before cutting southwest for Panama. And Aiden kept a sharp watch for high-speed Cigarette boats, particularly as they neared Punta Gallinas that thrust far into the sea.

It was a rough passage even without pirates. Sophie and Gert had hoped for somewhat easier conditions, supposing early April to fall within the usual transitional period between the Caribbean's windy seasons. But strong, relentless easterlies kept blowing, building steep following seas that chased the ketch, and broke around her in white foam.

"Like rabid mastiffs." Sophie laughed, repeatedly adjusting the self-steering to ride them at the safest angle.

The women were superb and unflappable seamen, as good as any he had sailed with, and intimately familiar with the old ketch, whose tapered canoe stern split overtaking seas that would have pooped a boat with an ordinary square behind.

"So tell me, Aiden," Sophie said, looking across the cockpit where Aiden was keeping a weather eye for rogue waves. "What sort of work did you do before your divorce?"

He had managed to keep his story thus far to a simple dropped-out-and-ran-away-to-sea. But as they sat face-to-face in the cockpit early in a ten-day passage, there was really no way to avoid what was a typical shipmate's polite question. He had to either answer with an out and out lie, which he didn't want to have to later defend, or stick close to the truth.

"I was an accountant."

"Like a chartered accountant? What do you call them in America, CPA?"

"Certified public accountant."

"And what did you count?"

"Beg pardon?"

"Which business did you serve counting their money?"

"Oh, banking."

A low roar caught their attention. A crest was breaking close behind the boat. Sophie seized the helm. *Darling* picked her face up and skittered ahead. Free of the breaking wave, she slowed in the next trough. Sophie reengaged the self-steering.

"Banking? Were you rich?"

"No."

"But rich enough to own a forty-two-footer. What sort of boat was it?"

"Hinckley."

Sophie's brows rose. "Rich indeed."

"I meant not as rich as most people on Wall Street. A lot of people I knew were ordering their boats custom-built."

"Wall Street? . . . What sort of banking?"

"I worked for a private bank. We managed wealthy clients' portfolios."

"Wall Street," she mused, smiling, teasing a little. "It must be a rather inactive existence counting other people's money. A bit passive?"

"It was," he admitted. "I mean when you stop and think about it, what kind of a life is getting rich by earning tiny percentages of tiny percentages of tiny percentages?"

"When did you stop and think about it?"

"What do you mean?"

"You said 'when you stop and think about it.' After the bust? Or after the attack?"

Aiden got uncomfortable. "We always thought about those things on the Street. Nobody wanted to stay on the job longer than they had to . . ." His face fell as he recalled where last he had heard that. Then, oddly, the memory of Charlie brought a sudden smile. And a brighter memory, though steeped in mystery. "Now and then I got a chance to do something a little more 'real.' Last year my boss asked me to run a buyout of a tugboat company out on the West Coast." Henry Hong's super-secret deal. *Tell no one. Not even Charlie.* What a mind blower that had been. "It was interesting. If I ever went back I'd look for a more nuts-and-bolts job. I could become an art dealer."

"Art? Seems quite a step up for an accountant."

"I bought a lot for the boss."

"What sort of art?"

Aiden grinned. "Paintings. They told me I had an eye for 'wall power.' "

"Investment art."

Aiden didn't answer; he felt a little stung that Sophie looked down on his achievement.

"Were you a 'dot-comer'?" she asked with a smile.

He gave the theatrical moan she expected, and the rueful, "Unfortunately." Since he'd already let her nudge him into spilling Wall Street and banking, it seemed almost inevitable that he would admit to going broke, too.

"Did going bust contribute to your divorce?"

Anyone else he would have told to mind her own business. But the old women were absolutely uninhibited when it came to personal questions. They already knew Morgan's name, his ex-wife's name, the year of his mother's death, and how his father had fled to California. All he had managed to keep for himself, so far, was Charlie's death.

Maybe it was because they had seen it all; maybe they had *done* it all. But they projected a serenity that seemed to reduce life's problems to minor events, and crises to vague annoyances. Even now, as she waited for Aiden's answer, and noticed a wave twice as tall as the others suddenly race up behind them on a course that would drop five tons of seawater on the cockpit, all Sophie did was detach the wind vane with a casual flick of her wrist, nudge the tiller, and mutter a quiet, "Move your arse, *Darling.*"

Darling obliged and the tall sea exploded next to the boat instead of on it. Aiden ducked the spray that rattled harmlessly on the mizzen sail, and looked up to find himself back under Sophie's bright-eyed scrutiny.

"Did going bust contribute to your divorce?"

"I guess so."

Sophie raised an eyebrow.

Aiden said, "Of course it did. Partly because we never had to think about money. Which was strange, actually, because we didn't start off rich. Our first six years we bummed around on an old boat. We even had the baby on the boat. Then we had some low-rent years when I was getting my degree. But by the time I went bust, we had gotten used to either making huge amounts of money or being able to borrow it. All of a sudden we had to deal with paying back. I mean until then we didn't even talk about it and all of a sudden we were yelling."

"Money is a vicious mistress. Particularly when you've got a child to care for."

"I had to take her out of private school." He turned his face from her and eased a sheet to make an unnecessary adjustment to the headsail.

Sophie reached past him and cranked it back where it belonged with two clicks of the winch. "Was that so terrible?"

"I thought so."

"What did your daughter think?"

"I don't know," he said brusquely.

Up came the eyebrow, again. And an apparent change of subject. "I've always been in awe of people who have children. What an inescapable responsibility."

"It was partly that . . ." Again he brightened. "Morgan tried to help. She insisted on switching to public school. She's a great kid." His face fell. "But her helping made it even harder to deny that I was a complete failure."

"For losing your money? How could a man with a child like that be a complete failure?"

"You don't understand. That's easy to say out here." He nodded at the puffy white clouds in a pretty sky and the ketch slipping through the breaking seas like a dolphin. "This is a kind of paradise with no responsibility except to keep from drowning and not run into any-thing. But back home, I got used to being successful. I got used to people admiring me. It was hard to lose that. You know, hard to admit I couldn't hack it. I wasn't a player anymore."

"Surely a stock-market collapse implies considerable company. You were hardly the only bloke to lose his shirt."

"Yeah, but not everybody lost. You have to question who you are. How did I screw up? Then you wake up one night and ask yourself, 'Was it all too easy? Couldn't any idiot have raked in the dough?'"

"Well, you must have proved yourself to get the job in the first place."

"My brother got me the job."

Out of nowhere Sophie asked, "I wonder about the greedy cheats. Is there a pattern that leads step-by-step to the destruction of morals? Or is it perhaps the willingness to turn a blind eye to the moral questions?"

"In my experience, people were too busy to bother with questions."

"Is a successful businessman ultimately a human who beats out his fellowman?"

"Most people I knew earned their success with long hours."

Sophie skewered him with a probing eye. "Were they too busy to rock the boat? Or too comfortable?"

Aiden looked away. *He* certainly hadn't rocked the boat. Had he, he might know why the U.S. attorney had come after him.

9

DADDY AND UNCLE CHARLIE HAD outfitted Grandpa's boat for their Hawaii trip. Last summer when Morgan had sailed on the sloop, it had been as totally geared for blue-water cruising as the *Molly P.* With radar, radios, EPIRB, weather fax, Sea Talk integrated navigation system, tools and tons of spare parts, it had been equipped to communicate, observe, predict, and survive.

Whereas the pretty little J/27 had nothing but a short-range VHF, an outboard motor with an anemic electrical alternator, and running lights. Period. Her rigging was old. And the anchor sucked. But at least she had some good sails.

Not that Morgan had time for second thoughts—much less to look for another boat. She had already blown a day and a half of her trip. Her ticket home was for Sunday. If she wasn't aboard that J/27 and out of here in five days, she'd be back on the plane to New York, mother, and school. And Osama crowding into her bedroom at night.

It was hard to tell herself she wasn't crazy, though she tried to put that from her mind while she went on the Internet to surf the marine supply stores. She was checking out the latest small long-range radios—and trying to figure out how to install it and power it. As far as she could tell, the outboard motor alternator produced six amps of electricity and the radio required thirty amps to transmit. So maybe she didn't need to transmit. All she wanted to hear was the weather. Her head was spinning when an instant message popped up—her lost friend Toby from the burbs.

RU still at special science school?

Stuyvesant, she typed back.

Toby went right into a homework question, like he wasn't mad that she hadn't written him even once since the night before the attack. *U know how U were always going on about how a single molecule of water stays in place while waves roll past it?*

It does.

Why doesn't it move?

A wave carries energy from one location to another. It's a disturbance that travels.

Like Eminem on tour?

Morgan saw her face reflected in the window and was amazed by her huge smile. She was so happy to hear from him. If you could have a boy as a best friend, it would be Toby. She fired back, *The audience is not the show.*

?

The wave medium is not the wave.

Kewl. So how do I set up an experiment to prove it?

Morgan typed, *You don't experiment to prove. You experiment to observe.*

Thanx, teach. How do I set it up? I gotta do it for Science.

Define the problem, dude.

OK ... Is a molecule of the wave medium temporarily displaced from its rest position or does it travel with the wave?

Hypothesis?

I believe it is only temporarily displaced, because this geek girl told me so.

Design experiment to test the hypothesis—keep it simple. Morgan waited a moment, then typed, *Hello?*

Toby typed, *I'm gonna be a lawyer. I don't want to do this shit. Helllllp!*

Since he was ten, Toby had acted like the ultimate gonna-be-a-lawyer guy. Morgan took a deep breath and typed, *Hey, Mr Lawyer. Can I ask?*

?

She typed her question straight, no abbreviations.

How serious is a letter from a United States attorney ordering someone to preserve computer files?

She had been thinking about the letter, ever since the phone call. It was one thing she had definitely not mentioned to Dr. Melton when she told him about helping her father that last night in the office. Or anyone else in the world.

From civil division or criminal?

Morgan could still see the letter like it was laser-printed on her brain. It had said, BY HAND, and was dated that day, the last day she saw him.

?

Civil sues you. Criminal prosecutes you. Civil is expensive serious. Criminal is jail-time serious.

No way her father committed a crime.

U doing a paper?

4 Ethics.

Serious enough to pretend to be dead? True, he had seemed really pissed that she saw the letter when he left her alone in the office to change her clothes. But he said it was just a business thing. Civil. Expensive. But wouldn't that be Mr. Hong's money? Except she had noticed his hands shaking. Coffee, he had claimed. He was going to be up all night searching for those files. It wasn't something he could let a secretary do, which was too bad because he was pretty dumb about getting help from computers. So Morgan had offered to open up a folder for him and break it down into subfolders and files. When he admitted he was afraid he would accidentally erase everything, she organized it so he could burn a backup on a CD.

I'm still waiting for helllllllllllllllllllllllpppppppp!

Get a long tray. Fill it one third with water. Add some sand at one end to make a beach. Like a smooth slope? Measure where the water meets the sand. Okay?

Then what?

Make waves.

How?

Blow the water with a hair dryer from the other end of the tray to make waves. Measure where the water meets the sand.

A guy in class said to do it with high-intensity sound waves.

Just borrow your mom's dryer. Keep it simple and keep your data in a notebook. Include all observations, even those that don't seem important. They might be useful later.

Then what?

Conclusion: If the water is higher, then the waves carried the water to the beach; if the water is the same, then the waves only passed through the water.

KEWL.

U really should do a bunch of trays to increase your sample size.

Give me a break.

OK, but you need a control. One other tray with water and beach but no fan. And get started like right now. You need time in case something goes wrong.

What else did they teach you in superschool?

Don't drop the hair dryer in the water or you'll electrocute yourself. LOLBMHATC.

Morgan smiled. Toby was the first person she knew to combine Laughing Out Loud with Banging My Head Against The Computer.

BTW my parents are driving me into the city tomorrow. You want to hook up for coffee?

Can't. I'm in California.

SUP?

Nothing she could tell him or anybody else, so she typed, *NMU? NM.*

Hey, have you ever sailed on a boat with a wind generator?

My uncle had one. He said it almost chopped his arm off. So he got solar panels instead. Why U want 2 NO?

GG. Really gotta go. Like right now.

L8er.

Morgan typed *CU* with a cold feeling that she probably never would.

Yell if need help Ethics.

"I don't," she said to herself. "I've got bigger problems."

None of that mattered anymore. Except the weird thing was, if her father had done something terrible—which she could not believe—and was about to get caught, it might at least explain why he would run away. And be even more proof that he was alive. But it couldn't be criminal anyway, had to be civil. Like a white-collar thing, which might be sort of criminal, but not really terrible.

When he got mad because she saw the letter, he had claimed he didn't want her to worry. But he hadn't hidden it; it was sitting on his desk. Almost like he secretly wanted her to see it? Like he was *asking* her to help him. And after she saw it, didn't he let her format the file for his research? And set up folders and files? It wasn't like he had to hide it from her. So it couldn't have been that serious. She shoved from her mind any more thoughts of what he might have been caught for. She had to focus on stuff she needed for the boat.

If she couldn't have a powerful long-range radio transmitter, she absolutely had to have a weather fax—a combination receiver and printer to print out weather maps. She started obsessing on it. She absolutely, *definitely* had to have a weather fax. The little boat wasn't fast enough to sail around bad weather without a ton of advance warning.

She could buy a little handheld weather station that would measure barometric pressure, humidity, wind speed, and windchill. But that was not the same as regular printouts of approaching weather systems that she could use to predict what would happen in the next five days.

Then all of a sudden she completely lost her nerve. It was like talking to Toby reminded her that she was only a fifteen-year-old girl. There was no way she could sail alone across the Pacific Ocean and cross the equator down into the South Pacific all the way to Blind Man Island. It was crazy.

There were huge ships in the Santa Barbara Channel passing up and down the coast between L.A. and San Francisco. Just one mile down the coast was busy Port of Hueneme—car carriers, fruit ships, and tankers. The other day she had seen them passing the Channel Island Harbor mouth—long rectangular hulks of red or green or black plowing through the water like buildings on their sides. They would make dodging tugboats in the Long Island Sound look like bumper cars.

From the guest-room window she could see the little boat. And boy, was it little. At that moment—while she was staring at it with one hand over her mouth and the other stroking Roscoe so hard that he tried to get away—a Cal 46 came up the channel, a big boat like the *Molly P.* That was a boat to cross the Pacific. If you were big and strong enough to change sails without a crew.

But Tania Aebi, a New York girl and bike rider like her, had circumnavigated in a boat one foot shorter than the J/27. While Ellen MacArthur, who won her class single-handing the Atlantic when she was twenty, was only five-two. As small as racing rock-star bow "man" Martha McKechnie—who worked Daddy's old position on the foredeck. Hadn't Martha McKechnie proved that a girl with brains, guts, and agility could work spinnaker pole, sheets, and sails as well as any boy, without the muscle? And wasn't Morgan Page a full half inch taller than either of them?

Define the problem.

I want to find my father. I *have* to find my father.

Hypothesis.

I believe that he is alive on Blind Man Island.

Why?

Because he telephoned. Because he was losing his job and lost all his money. Because I saw a letter that made it sound like he got into trouble and maybe he thought that his only hope was to run away.

Why Blind Man Island?

Because ever since the Christmas party, Daddy and Uncle Charlie had always joked that they'd retire young to Blind Man Island. But not really a joke. Often, late at night, she had heard them talking in *Molly P*'s cockpit, or down in the den, or at the ski lodge, drinking whiskey in front of the fire, saying that Mr. Hong, who was like king of the island, really meant it when he told them there was room for them in paradise. Joked—not joked—that Mr. Hong would give them huge plots of land instead of a pension, where they could build houses and sit on porches with views of the Pacific and anchor their sailboats in the lagoon.

Hypothesis. Her father knew he would be safe on Blind Man Island. Safe from bankruptcy. Safe from failure. Safe from the United States attorney.

Design experiment to test the hypothesis. Keep it simple. Go to Blind Man Island. I can't fly there. I'm a kid. Last time Uncle Charlie took us on a private jet to Tongatapu, and then on a little plane to another island, then a boat to Blind Man Island. No way a fifteen-year-old can fly there alone without her mother finding out and stopping her. She remembered Daddy had gotten them visas. How would she get one? Or maybe it was just a passport. She had hers with her. Too young for a driver's license, she had brought it for picture ID at the airport. And even if I did somehow fly to Tonga, how do I get to Blind Man Island, which is like three hundred miles away in the middle of nowhere?

Keep it simple. Sail to Blind Man Island.

Sample size: Only one of me, one boat. One cat.

Time: Allow enough time for experiment to be repeated. And enough time for screwups. Keep a detailed notebook. Log. Include all observations—especially weather. Even those that don't seem important.

Formulate a conclusion: Explain what actually happened; don't have to prove hypothesis. The goal of an experiment is to observe what actually happened. This is crazy. Start over.

Define problem.

Am I nuts?

Hypothesis.

Yes. Only a nutcase would try to sail across the Pacific Ocean in a stolen sailboat. But—big but—how could a nutcase successfully sail across the Pacific Ocean in a stolen sailboat if she wasn't sane enough to sail and navigate and survive storms? If I did that, maybe I wouldn't be nuts anymore.

Design simple experiment: Equip the boat. Sample size, only one of me, one boat, one cat. What if they catch me? I can't let them catch me. Because they'll stop me from helping him. Conclusion: I am even crazier than I think. Wondering about my father is making me crazy. I have to know. I have to find him. I have to help him.

Roscoe pulled free and hid under the bed. Morgan hugged herself as hard as she could.

Control.

Find another girl who thinks her father wasn't killed in the

World Trade Center. Make it a girl who didn't know why she lived when everyone died. And make that girl sit at home and do nothing.

EVERYTHING SHE BOUGHT for the voyage had to fit into her L.L. Bean book pack so she could smuggle it past her grandfather. She rented a bike and helmet, undid her ponytail, braided her hair into pigtails, and pedaled three miles from Grandpa's condo to a chandlery she had located on the Internet. She walked the bike through a door with a sign that read SUPPLY AND HARDWARE; BOAT-YARD OFFICE OPEN SEVEN DAYS.

She wanted to browse the stuff she'd seen on their Web site, but was stopped by a man in a pink shirt and blue cap with gold letters that said PRODUCT ADVISER.

"Is that your bike?"

He said she had to leave her bike outside.

Morgan pleaded that it was rented and she was afraid it might get stolen. The pigtails did the trick. They made her look younger— as young as twelve—and he relented. But then he wanted to know what she wanted.

"I need a weather fax." She named the brand and model she had seen on the Web site.

He looked down at her. "Do you mind if I ask how you're going to pay for this, little girl."

"Visa."

"Okay," he said slowly. "Could I ask where you intend to use it?"

"It's not for me. It's for my father. For Father's Day."

"Oh! Okay. I get it . . . Except Father's Day isn't till June."

"He's away. If I get it today, I can hide it at home and surprise him."

"Good idea."

"And I need a solar panel."

"What is Dad going to use it for?"

"Charging handheld batteries and the main twelve-volt for the weather fax."

"Doesn't he have a generator?"

"He keeps saying he wants a solar panel to do a trickle charge. Do you know what that is?"

"Sure. Good idea. So he doesn't have to run his generator all the time. Does he sail offshore?"

"Sometimes."

"How big a boat are we talking about?"

"Not very big. He wants the smallest panel."

"How big is not very big?"

"Twenty-seven feet."

"So he's doesn't go very far offshore. Why doesn't he just top up the battery when he gets home at night?"

"He's a blue-water sailor. He already sailed to Hawaii."

"Well, *excuuuse* me."

The man showed her what she was asking for. Measuring two feet by three feet, the grid of blue glass and aluminum and its mounting brackets were way too big to hide in her pack. "Can you wrap the box like in brown paper or something in case he sees it?"

"I'll wrap it in an old chart."

"No. If he sees the chart, he'll guess."

"I'll wrap it inside out. Blank side out."

"Okay." She had to figure out what to tell Grandpa was in the box.

The man said, "Okay, just so we understand each other; this weather fax is not the kind he'll interface with his own radio. It has its own receiver."

"I know. And can I get a handheld weather station?"

"Are you sure you want to give him so many presents on Father's Day? I mean when he gets the bill he's going to be maybe a little upset."

"It's for my uncle, too. He doesn't have any kids, so he gets his presents from me."

The weather fax—a combination receiver and printer—barely fit in her backpack. She stuffed the weather station, cushioned in its box, into the front pocket, along with spare rechargeable batteries and two battery chargers, one for Daddy, one for her uncle. She bought some shock cords to strap the flat solar-panel box on the back of the pack.

Then came the hard part, waiting for the Visa approval.

What's a fifteen-year-old girl doing buying all this stuff with a credit card? She knew a kid at school who bought cameras on his card to trade for drugs, until they caught him. Would Visa call her mother? All she could do was pray that her mother was partying in the Hamptons. Except it was March. A private party. Just her and the boyfriend. She closed her eyes and prayed. Dear God, make them be having sex so they don't answer their cell phones.

The verification machine went *chunk, chunk, chunk.* A strip of paper slowly emerged. The man tore it off, read it, and handed it to her to sign.

"Wait. I want that South Pacific sailing guide. He wants to go there sometime."

The man started a new bill. "Anything else?"

"Oh my God. I almost forgot. He wants a first-aid kit."

"Good idea."

"And a sextant."

The man in the pink shirt said, "Why not come in for that tomorrow? You've bought a lot of nice presents. Maybe you should think about the sextant."

"Okay—do you sell them?"

"Not many anymore."

"Do you sell the books that go with it?"

"You can get the tables in a little calculator now. Or I can sell you a MyStars program your dad can run on his laptop and a top-of-the-line plastic Davis Mark 25 sextant for about three-fifty. But why not a wait a day to think about it?"

She was running out of room, anyhow. But then her eye fell on a canvas-bound log with leather piping. The canvas was green, the piping gold. "I want that log. And a fancy pen to go with it."

He said, "It's on the house," and gave her the log and a gold-colored pen, and she pedaled off, swaying under the backpack. She had to buy a ton of vitamins and a huge sack of brown rice and a lot of bottled water.

But no. Heavy stuff like months and months of food and water would have to wait until she had sailed so far up the coast that no one would suspect she had stolen her boat. Pedaling home, she suddenly squeezed the brakes a couple of blocks from Grandpa's. An old boat guy in a sailing cap had his garage door open and boat stuff all over the driveway. Younger adults were watching from their front door, like they were his kids and worried he needed watching.

"Are you selling this stuff?"

"Anything you want. They got rid of my boat."

"What's this?"

She picked up a foot-long torpedo-shaped tube with fins. It was black and scored with long scratches that exposed the metal.

"That's a taffrail log. Measures how fast your boat's going after you drop your fancy GPS overboard."

"I thought so." She weighed it in her hand. Everything else on the boat was stripped-down basic, why not this?

"Genuine antique. See, here's the line and the indicator dial in the box. Cost you a thousand bucks on eBay."

"How much from you?"

"Ten bucks."

"What are all these scratches?"

"Fish teeth biting it."

"Five bucks?"

"What do you want it for?"

"I'm going to give it to my dad. We're going to sail in the Bermuda Race."

"If you can afford the Bermuda Race, you can afford ten bucks."

She gave him the ten. "Do you have a sextant?"

"Do I have a sextant? I have a sextant that hasn't been out of the box since it was last serviced. And none of your plastic crap either. Solid brass. Genuine Weems and Plath. Cost you a thousand bucks on eBay."

"Where is it?"

"They have it. It's in the house. They won't let me take it out."

"Could I buy it, tomorrow?"

"Eighty dollars."

"Do you have the book that goes with it?"

"What, do you think I'm senile? Of course I have the almanac— 2002 edition. Cost you a thousand bucks on eBay."

CHARLIE-BOY, YOU COULDN'T MAKE THIS up. Palm trees blowing in the trade wind. Snow-white beaches. Turquoise lagoon. Willing maidens. Does it get any better than Blind Man Island?"

Not if you own it, thought Charlie Page.

The Pacific Ocean surrounded Henry Ho Hong's paradise, empty as far as the eye could see, in shades of a blue so rich it almost seemed unnecessary to think about tomorrow, much less order your thoughts today.

"Does it?"

Henry Ho Hong was a broad-shouldered Cantonese. He wore a dusty rose pastel summer suit with a fine necktie—one of the few Charlie had seen in the South Pacific outside a church. London tailoring and the exquisitely soft hand of Dupioni silk managed to conceal whether he was powerfully built or merely fat. A smooth, apparently guileless face proclaimed his youth; a perpetually satisfied expression, his power. If he had any doubts, they resided behind small, opaque eyes.

Charlie made him ask one more time before he answered, "No, Henry. It couldn't get better than this."

"Which is why I will explain the ground rules and emphasize I enforce them strictly."

Midafternoon, Charlie Page sat in a hospital bed cranked upright so he could look out the window at a scene as beautiful as any in Polynesia. The hot rainy season had ended and the palace gardens descended in full flower to the lagoon, whose diamond-clear waters reached through the surrounding reefs and white surf to the dark and boundless deep. Beautiful it was—paradisiacal beyond doubt—but the border between land and sea was a violent one and swimming ashore had stretched even his legendary luck.

The cracked ribs still hurt, as did the flesh-and-bone bruises. The concussion spawned headaches and he was plagued by vicious flareups of the coral infections that the doctor flown up from New Zealand claimed to have subdued.

He remembered little of that night in the dark and cold water. What memories he did have were chiefly aural: the fading rumble of the yacht. Carol's fainter and fainter screams ending in a shriek. The near silence of crests collapsing on the waves. Then the ominous rumble of the surf, when the current took him until he felt sure he was not so much swimming as strapped to a cruise missile aimed at the beach. He could still hear the crunching sound explode in his skull when the wave that cartwheeled him across the razor-sharp coral threw him headfirst on the sand.

"Number one rule, no arms on the island."

Charlie Page climbed out of bed and limped to the powerful Bausch & Lomb 60×80mm spotting scope that was mounted on a tripod in the window. He focused on one of the Tongan soldiers patrolling the gardens between the palace and the dock. "None?"

True, they weren't brandishing weapons, but there was a tough defense-force tradition in these islands that went back to fighting the Japanese in World War II. The men in the garden packed powerful little Berettas under their knee-length *vala* skirts and he had discovered that their Gurkha sergeants carried keys to an arsenal for a ninety-man light reaction company.

"My 'palace guard' are armed, of course," Henry admitted with a theatrically indulgent smile for Charlie, as if to say, *You know this shit, Charlie. I'm not telling you anything you don't already know.* Smile receding, he said, "They are very happy. The Tongans have their wives, their children, and irrigated vegetable plots in the hills. My Gurkhas rotate regularly home to Hong Kong and Nepal. Everybody is happy and secure."

Head spinning with fever, Charlie climbed back in bed. "Especially you with your own private army."

"I meant, as I should think you understood, arms for sale. We have no weapons warehouse on the island, no trace of the business is allowed here. For the same reason there are no 'abused natives' on Blind Man Island, and no abuse of the environment: *nothing* to draw attention."

"What about that resort project you're building on the windward side?" Eight miles across dense jungle and steep hills, as the pelican flew; fifteen by boat—the only practical way to get there.

"Greenpeace certified," Henry shot back. "Environmentally friendly construction practices and materials."

Charlie shrugged: typically slippery Henry Hong to invent "certification"; it was highly unlikely that Greenpeace had even heard of the island, much less "certified" blasting a man-made harbor out of the living coral that clung to the volcanic rock. Besides, HHH's resort consortium hadn't amounted to more than the sort of half-baked, unfinished projects the South Pacific was famous for. All he had glimpsed of the construction site on the steep northeastern shore when Henry treated him to a motor-yacht ride around the island was a half-finished harbor with an abandoned pier that led to a hole in the ground. "I get the impression construction kind of ground to a halt."

Henry waved him off impatiently. "I don't do details."

"You used to."

"Jin-shil is project manager."

Charlie eyed him closely. How the hell rich *was* Henry? Make-work projects bankrolled by moguls desiring to keep their wives out of their hair were common, though not on the scale of building a resort complex with its own harbor. On the other hand, the beautiful Jin-shil was no ordinary wife.

"What's it costing you, pal?"

But Henry returned a pleased smile. "Zip. Jin-shil's father and his *chaebol* buddies are paying for the harbor."

"Does the king of Tonga know you're letting a gang of South Korean monopolists call the shots?"

"No, no, no. No shots. The South Koreans are silent, nonvoting investors. I made that very clear to Jin-shil. When we're ready to build the actual hotel, they've been told they can join the consortium." He grinned. "I believe that Texas oilmen refer to such partners as 'mullets.' "

Charlie said, "I don't think of *chaebol* as mullets. Killer whales are more like it."

"It's a tax dodge for them. All they want is their names kept out of it."

"Who will control the consortium? Jin-shil?"

Henry's grin got bigger. "I'm in love, Charlie-boy. I'm not stupid."

"You're a pisser, Henry. I'll give you that."

Henry sobered, immediately. "My business arrangements make me 'king' of this island. But never forget that we are 'guests' of the real king. And of our 'honorable noble nephew.' "

There were thirty-three hereditary nobles in the kingdom of Tonga, each addressed as "Honorable." Henry and Charlie had made their particular honorable—a favorite nephew of the king, whom they had dubbed, privately, "Noble Nephew"—the wealthiest in the monarchy. "We will never embarrass him or the real king by drawing any attention to Blind Man Island."

Most of the Tonga monarchy's 176 islands—which were scattered like stars in heaven over forty thousand square miles of ocean—were as uninhabited as Henry's had been before he constructed the enormous water distillation plant that turned seawater into something you could drink. The generator that powered the distillery, the storage tanks, and the multiple satellite dishes for encrypted phone service and high-speed Internet were concealed in a dense grove of coconut palms planted for the purpose, while the deep-water wharf for the monthly LPG fuel deliveries appeared from any distance to be that most common of South Pacific sights, a rusty, coral-encrusted shipwreck.

Very HHH, thought Charlie. Henry Ho Hong was the ultimate Hong Kong man adept at papering over unpleasant reality with an averted gaze, a smile, a timely disappearance, or discreetly armed guards at the door.

"I am fully aware," said Charlie, "that we are the king of Tonga's 'servants,' through his nephew, whose ass we have bailed out, repeatedly."

Theirs was, in fact, a benign relationship compared to many foisted on gullible South Pacific islanders; last year Charlie had had to intervene when a Christian sect persuaded their noble to invest in a secret process to make natural gas out of seawater. Only this month Henry had discovered that Tongan officials had been conned into issuing flags of convenience to a shipping line whose vessels almost surely served the same murderous Al Qaeda that had bombed the World Trade Center and Henry's own offices.

"The less the king knows of us, the better. Better for us. Better for our noble. Fortunately Tongatapu is far away."

"We stay under the radar," said Charlie. "We don't want to be like Al Qaeda bringing down fire on the Taliban."

"Cleverly put, but still not accurate. The Polynesian monarch is in no way, shape, or form like the Taliban were. And the kingdom of Tonga is no Afghanistan and never will be."

"But we could be Al Qaeda?"

"We can and will be many things," said Henry Hong. "But in the kingdom of Tonga we will be well-behaved *guests*. That way, no matter how hot it gets anywhere else, here we are safe. A safe harbor in a world of giants is no small thing. Why did *you* come here? You came because I told you if you ever had to run, run here. Here you are safe. As long as you're careful."

"Any more rules I should know about, Henry?"

"Don't fuck the servants."

Charlie grinned. "I had a feeling there was a security camera in the ceiling."

"And particularly don't fuck the soldiers' wives. Do you want to get killed?"

"I thought you said I was safe here."

"I can protect you from nations, not vengeful husbands."

"Husbands add to the excitement." Not to mention how much soldiers' wives could tell you about Henry's security arrangements. Particularly when they were as bold and observant and self-confident as Salote, whose husband was away in Canada, looking for work in Vancouver's Tongan expatriate community.

"Excitement is what the Hong Kong girls are for. Plus, they're better looking."

"That depends on your tastes, my friend. Give me a Tongan woman any day. They're strong, they're smart, and they know who they are."

"With the Hong Kong girls you're guaranteed variety. I don't allow them to stay more than two weeks."

"Why not?"

"They get bored." He shook his head, in mock astonishment at human idiosyncrasy. "They're so excited at first—come play in paradise. Meet rich men—but this is, after all, an island and they are young, so I cycle in a fresh quartet every two weeks."

Is your wife bored? Charlie wondered. Is that beautiful Korean engineer with the teacup breasts and the thighs to ride to the moon bored, Henry? What does Mrs. Jin-shil Hong do for kicks in Paradise? Because to tell the truth, a strange light shines from those beautiful eyes like she's got some essential screws loose.

"I repeat my rules because you are a man who takes what he wants," said Hong. "Much of what you might want here is yours for the taking. But certain things are not, and knowing the difference will make your new life more comfortable."

Most Chinese Charlie had done business with resisted eye contact at the exact key moments when a New Yorker would get in your face. Henry was no exception. As he uttered his last, unmistakable warning, he looked out the unglazed window. His gaze lighted briefly and significantly on his Tongan guards, then drifted to the headland that reared above the white sand.

A two-masted *wa a' kau lua*—a double-hull voyaging canoe—rounded the headland.

"Speaking of the devil we know, our honorable made good time."

In came its sails, the inverted triangles folding to its masts like origami. Thirty oarsmen scrambled down to the splash rails and began paddling. The helmsman manned the starboard sweep and steered toward the narrow cut through the fringing reefs.

"Knock-knock?" inquired a musical voice, and Jin-shil poked her head in the door. She was dressed in ceremonial Tonga costume with a red plume on her head, ankle-length *vala*, and a blue and white blouse that bared her shapely arms and was cinched at her hourglass waist by an intricately patterned *kiekie*.

"Our 'honorable nephew,' " she announced, "has come."

Henry rose smiling from his chair beside Charlie's bed. "Thank you, dear. You look lovely."

"I look local." She had studied at Columbia University, Henry had explained when Charlie commented on her fluent English.

"I'll be right down."

"How are you doing, Charlie? Feeling better?"

"Much better, Jin-shil. And you?"

Jin-shil smiled—"I'm always better"—and disappeared down the veranda that connected the rooms in this wing of the rambling house they called a palace.

Charlie said to Henry, "I'm looking forward to seeing him again."

"I'm afraid that won't be possible, just yet," said Henry Hong.

Which was, of course, where this whole rules charade had been headed.

Charlie decided to keep spinning it out. "I trust our honorable," he said, innocently. "He won't blow my cover." This was neither wishful thinking—or braggadocio. The Tongan economy had been wiped out in the stock market crashes, thanks mostly to the king-dom's elite acting on awful advice about the Internet. But their hon-orable had prospered, thanks to HHH & Company, which had steered him early into initial public offerings and out before reality caught up with price. Plus, Charlie had sufficient knowledge of his private investments in the kingdom to keep him loyal. What he had no control of—yet—was Henry Ho Hong.

Who shook his head, no. "It wouldn't fit my plan for you. For the moment I am going to keep you under wraps."

"What plan?"

"Your 'resurrection' presents wonderful possibilities."

"Meaning?"

"I promise you we won't waste them . . ." He turned back at the door. "By the way, what's your latest thinking about your brother?"

"What do you mean?" The pain flared inside, a burning in his belly that rushed like fire up his spine, seared his brain, and nearly burst his chest. Henry was still in the doorway, watching.

Charlie Page had always known he was different—that he cared about nothing that made other people tick. At least until he had lost Aiden. It was now seven months and they had not heard a peep out of him. Couldn't he have searched the flaming dark longer? The answer was a guiltless no. But a guiltless no could not lighten the overwhelming loss, or mitigate the crushing finality, or even relieve the alien sting of regret.

"What do I mean?" Henry echoed "I mean what I meant last time we discussed your brother. Could Aiden have somehow survived the attack? Is it possible that he, too, escaped from the building and ran away like you did?"

"Two miracles in one family? I doubt it."

"If he did, what would he do?"

Why was Henry asking this? Charlie wanted to shout, *Why don't you let Aiden rest in peace?* But he felt too weary to struggle. The antibiotics were still gnawing at his edge, leaving him terribly slow on the uptake. "I told you. We agreed to hook up here."

"Which was sensible. Meaning he'll come here, too."

"Yeah, well, I wouldn't lay out the welcome mat just yet. Like I said, two miracles would be a bit much to hope for."

"But if he did, you're still quite sure he would come here?"

"Henry, not to put too fine a point on it, you're our only friend in the world."

Henry got very Chinese for a second, bowing his head and murmuring, "You honor me." Then he got paranoid. "Charlie, you just used the phrase '*our* only friend,' as if you *know* Aiden is alive. I truly hope that if you actually know he's alive, you would tell me. I could help him get here. He's not as resourceful as you. He could be stuck somewhere hiding from his shadow, just waiting to get caught."

Charlie Page sat up in bed. All of a sudden his head was very clear. He swung his feet to the polished teak floor and walked toward Henry. He stood nearly a head taller than the broad Chinese and Henry backed up a step.

"What is it, Charlie?"

"I just remembered my last thought that morning—just before those fucking Arabs blew up the building." He stared down at Henry.

"What?"

"It wasn't so much a thought as a question. You see, just before the plane hit, I was standing at my desk asking myself, Who tipped the U.S. attorney that HHH and Company was not a hundred percent, shall we say, kosher? Who handed them my head and my brother's head on a silver platter?"

"Well, you've had seven months to think about that. Any ideas?"

"Oh, I think I know who ratted us out, my friend. I just don't know why."

Henry Hong looked him full in the face and said, "Me?"

"Why, Henry? Why'd you do it?"

"Without a 'why,' you don't know who did it. Because no one would betray you without a very good reason."

"I gave you no reason to rat me out."

"Then clearly I didn't do it."

CHARLIE WATCHED THE honorable's landing from his bed.

The Tongan was about his and Henry's age—a tall 250-pound guy in his late thirties, as hip to the modern world as could be expected of anyone born in a remote archipelago where the biggest claims to fame were proximity to the international date line ("where time begins") and exotic postage stamps celebrating a simple world of bamboo and thatch *fales,* subsistence farms, canoe and sailboat fishing, and moonlight shining on the palm trees.

But paradise was sinking. Obsessed by rapidly rising sea levels that threatened to submerge Polynesia's lower-lying islands, their honorable blamed the modern world's contribution to global warming. Henry Hong and Charlie Page had played upon his fears like a violin duo.

Money was the power to change the world, their line went; banks attracted money; offshore banks, loosely regulated, attracted the most money. Of every offshore bank Henry Ho Hong now controlled across Polynesia, their earnest Tongan sat on the board of directors.

The wind was picking up, rattling the palm trees outside his window, and swooping down to the lagoon to pluck at the ankle-length skirts worn by the women who had come to greet the noble. "Henry, you *are* a pisser," Charlie muttered to himself.

He climbed off the bed and limped to the spotting scope. The instrument's magnification and the ultracrisp resolution made it seem he was standing on the dock with them. Standing beside Henry's beautiful wife.

Charlie watched carefully as the noble nephew disembarked from his huge canoe. Was this a social visit? A chance to cavort with Henry's Hong Kong girls far from the eye of his straitlaced Christian uncle. The spotting scope showed a face alive with nervous anticipation. But did he look like a guy about to cheat on his wife? Or like a dutiful nephew who had finally mustered the courage to strike out on his own?

Charlie scrutinized the other faces. Obedient soldiers of the honor guard. Expressionless Gurkha sergeant—half the size of the big Tongans and twice as tough. Smiling Chinese—wait, I know that guy. The smiling Chinese gripping Henry Hong's hand in both of his was one of the investors from Henry's tugboat hustle and had been an early investor in HHH & Company. Lately, he had shepherded Beijing's efforts to revive industry in North Korea. But when Charlie had last met him, at the UN, he had had the strong impression that Mr. Ping-li was reluctant to leave the diplomatic sanctuary. It was interesting that Henry wanted Ping-li, as well as Noble Nephew, to believe that Charlie was still dead.

The greeting party moved inland and out of his line of sight. Charlie got back in bed, his head swimming again. "You will always be safe here," Henry had promised. It had worked. Charlie in trouble had fled here—put himself in Henry's hands. Safe on ice. Like protective custody, with emphasis on the custody.

W HAT'S IN THE BOX?" GRANDPA asked.

"Jigsaw puzzle."

"Jigsaw puzzle?"

"I found it at a tag sale."

"How you going to get it on the plane?"

"I'll take it apart and put it together when I get home."

"You should have done that instead of riding around with it like a sail on your back. You're lucky the wind didn't pick you up and toss you in the drink."

Out of nowhere she heard herself answer, "They lost the original box. I wanted to study the picture."

She recalled that her mother once said, "If I didn't know better I'd sometimes think you were Uncle Charlie's kid instead of Daddy's."

"Why?" she had gasped, utterly taken aback.

"You've got a calculating side to you—I don't mean it in a bad way—but you see the big picture." Morgan could not recall what she had done, only that her mother had gone on to explain, "Those are Uncle Charlie traits. Poor Daddy hasn't a clue— What's wrong?"

Morgan could still remember staring with her mouth open like a cave. "Are you telling me something about Uncle—"

"What? No! Oh, for goodness' sake. Don't worry, Daddy is really your daddy."

"Are you sure?"

"Of course, I'm sure, for goodness' sake. I was just thinking out loud." She had taken Morgan's hands and looked her straight in the eye. "I can tell by the look on your face that you're wondering. So I'll ask you, would I have said such a thing if it was true? Your daddy is your daddy. I guarantee it. I should know." She laughed. "Remember, I was there."

Morgan believed her absolutely. "Then where did I get my calculating side?"

"Probably direct from Grandpa," her mother had replied, adding with a big smile, "Or maybe from me."

"Maybe from both of you."

"God help us."

"What did I get from Daddy?"

This was back in the Happy Days, and her mother had kissed her forehead and hugged her close. "A warm heart. And beautiful eyes."

"Uncle Charlie's eyes are like mine, too."

"Oh no they are not," she said, shaking her hard for emphasis. "Yours and Daddy's are like sunshine. Uncle Charlie's are cold as the moon."

Morgan didn't remember him as cold. In fact, she had liked Uncle Charlie. He said cool stuff. Usually cooler than Daddy. Uncle Charlie taught her to race to win. He often took her aside for really serious talks about how to win. Forget your mistakes during the race. Think about them later. Write them down and plan how you'll do it next time. Don't overload your brain with details. Stick to basics.

Daddy would say, Feel the wind. Feel the wind. Feel the wind.

But it was Uncle Charlie who taught her, Don't be afraid of the other boats. Get in their face and make them blink. Stay in their face until they blink. She found it really hard to get close. So he taught her a trick: watch the wind-direction indicator on the competition's boat—so as not to be distracted looking up at her own mast for apparent wind angle when she should be watching ahead. You had to get close to do that.

"Watch where you're going!" her father coached in the kids-and-parents Optimist race at sailing camp. The Opti was a seven-and-a-half-foot kids' racing pram. Uncle Charlie and Daddy were folded into theirs with their knees jammed over their chins. "Get your head out of the boat."

But Uncle Charlie barged between hers and Daddy's. Gunnel to gunnel, he whispered, "Keep your head *in* the boat. Go fast. Make the other guys get out of your way——"

The memory of that Parents' Day was so strong it made her smile like she was back on the Long Island Sound. Back in the Happy Days until Grandpa interrupted, "Hear me? The neighbors asked us to come sailing Saturday."

"Saturday?"

"I told them yes. You're not leaving till Sunday morning— Hey, why the face? I thought you'd like it. Chris is coming. In fact, his mom told me it was his idea to invite you."

"Oh, yeah. It's great." It meant she had to make her move Friday night. It was so soon.

"But don't get your heart set on it. They've got somebody coming to look at the boat tomorrow. If he buys it, obviously we can't go sailing."

"*Tomorrow?* When tomorrow?"

"I don't know. What does it matter?"

SHE WENT ON-LINE and downloaded all the weather reports she could find. An infrared satellite image of the Eastern Pacific showed thin clumps of white cloud floating above an almost infinite blue sphere. On the right side spiderweb lines marked the West Coast. The rest was empty clouds and blue. The spots she thought were dirt on her monitor turned out to be islands, minuscule specks of land, nameless and far, far away. I am surely nuts, she thought. And not only that, but when I'm out there, I will have no way to get these weather pictures.

But she had no time to worry.

She pedaled as fast as she could to an ATM and took out the two-hundred-dollar max her card allowed and raced back to the tag sale. The old guy in the sailor cap was arguing with his kids, who were telling him he had to come inside, now. "Hey, stop it," he yelled at them. "I got a customer."

"The sextant? Do you still have it?"

She snuck it past Grandpa and raced out again, pedaling the long busy roads to a strip mall, where a kid with headlight eyes was leaning on a No Skateboarding sign whispering, "E? E? E?"

She wheeled the bike into a health-food store and used her credit card again to buy three huge bottles of multivitamins and a box of herb tea, some bottled water, and a bag of brown rice. Outside, she approached the kid hustling E. He was pretty dorky looking and in New York would have lasted about four seconds, but he probably didn't have much competition in the retirement community.

"Got any uppers?"

After concluding her transaction, she raced back to the condo and retreated to the guest room and tried to figure out how to get her grandfather out of the way while she sneaked out with a bulging backpack, the flat solar panel, her seabag full of foul-weather gear and charts, her travel bags, her laptop, and her first few days of food and water.

HE WATCHED CBS *News at Eleven* and then switched over to Jay Leno, surfing back to Letterman. Then he watched the late shows, flipping between Conan and Craig, and then Daly with last call and all of a sudden it was one-thirty in the morning. "Why are you staying up so late?" he asked.

"I'm getting tired. I think I'll go to sleep. Are you?"

"Yeah, in a minute."

"Good night, Grandpa."

"Good night, honey." They were starting to repeat the eleven o'clock news when she heard him still surfing. She turned out her light and stared out the window. The J/27 was almost near enough to jump to. Almost. But not carrying bags and a cat.

After a while she lay down on the bed with her hands tucked behind her head and listened to the TV droning up from below. The noise drifted around the dark room. Suddenly she saw a tall, thin shadow move through the shaft of light that spilled in the window from the dock light. It was a man so thin he was almost two-dimensional, and even before he turned to let the light slash across his face she knew who he was. Her throat filled; she couldn't scream, she couldn't call for her grandfather. But she spoke anyway, saying, "You can't be here. I'm in California." Osama reached up and began unwinding his turban. "I'm everywhere you sleep, little girl."

"I'm not sleeping— Oh my God!" She sat up with a start.

Oh my God. I fell asleep. What time is it? She looked at her watch in terrible despair, fearing the daylight. Two forty-five. Downstairs the TV was still going. But she couldn't wait a second longer. She ran downstairs to complain to Grandpa that the noise was keeping her up, that he should go to bed, too, that they should both be sleeping. But he was already fast sleep, sprawled on the lounger, mouth open, snoring softly. She started to turn the TV off, but decided that the racket would mask her noise.

In her room, she captured Roscoe and shoved him, struggling, into the carrier. Then she put on her backpack, grabbed the carrier in one hand and her seabag in the other, and headed down the stairs. She got through the kitchen and out the back door, where she put down the bags and whispered, "I'll be right back. Please be quiet."

Through the kitchen, past the living room, up the stairs, she picked up the big, flat box that held the solar panel and the bag that contained her clothes, food, water, and laptop. She crept down the stairs and got out the door.

"Morgan?"

She put everything down and stepped back into the room. Her heart was pounding so hard it was shaking her chest. Her face felt cold, like it had turned white as snow. She couldn't look at him.

"Did I ever tell you I was first in the family to get to Wall Street?"

Something told her not to answer.

"Got my broker's license when I was twenty-two. Thought I was hot shit." She stole a look. His eyes were half-closed, like he was caught in a dream. He mumbled something she couldn't hear. Then his voice got louder and Morgan stood there praying he wouldn't wake himself up.

"Didn't know that the Jews I was working for got banned by the SEC, so they made the dumb Mick front for them." He laughed. "You think I cared? I didn't give a damn how I got there. I was in like Flynn . . ."

She waited, holding her breath. His head nodded onto his chest and he started snoring.

She tiptoed out the door, put on her pack, grabbed Roscoe, and crossed the dark square of lawn to the neighbors' slip. She dumped the bags at the edge of the light that shone down on the floating dock, which was higher. The incoming tide would make it harder to drive the boat under sail alone. But she could not risk making noise with the motor.

She ran back for the rest of her stuff and carried it to the pile in the shadows.

This was it. She had to enter the light, load everything on the dock, and board the boat, at which point she would have no excuses, no plausible story if someone happened to see her.

Now, she told herself. *Do it now.* She looked back at the row of condos. Not a one had lighted windows. Maybe they were all asleep. Or maybe someone was standing in the dark, looking out.

She felt the wind on her face. A gentle land breeze, puffing toward the sea as the ground cooled faster than the water. Just enough to sail her off the dock into the canal. If she could raise the sails without too much noise.

Now.

Roscoe should be last; if she left him alone on the boat, he'd howl. She put on her pack, picked up the panel and the food and clothes bag, and stepped into the light. It was like crossing a pond on thin ice. Onto the dock and into the cockpit. She opened the hatch with the key she had copied, swung the food and clothes bag, her pack, and the panel into the cabin.

Then she grabbed Roscoe and her seabag. The cat was shifting uneasily. She left his carrier on the cockpit sole, knowing he would freak in the dark, smelly cabin.

Her heart was pounding and she could hardly breathe for the fear. The town houses loomed from all sides—a hundred gaping windows, any one of which could hold some insomniac staring out at the silent boats.

She loosed the stern and spring lines and threw her weight against the bowline to walk the boat out of the slip. The fair, slim hull started moving with a rush. She got tangled around a piling, and had to let go. For a horrible moment she saw the boat getting away from her. She jumped for the bow and shoved off with her foot. The rubber fender squealed like a car alarm.

Caught between the tide and the soft breeze, the boat drifted aimlessly in and out of the light pools that dotted the water. She found the jib that she had folded so carefully after sailing with Chris and dragged it to the bow. The tack came out of the bag first. She shackled it to the foot of the forestay, snapped the hanks to the forestay, and bent on the sheets and the halyard. The sail rose with a loud crackle of fluttering Dacron.

A shadow loomed. The drifting boat was inches from banging into the high bow of a power boat that stuck out from the dock on the other side of the canal. Morgan pushed away, and ran to the tiller. The wind was breathing over her right shoulder. She yanked the starboard jib sheet. The sail gave an anemic flutter and the little J-boat started slowly toward the harbor.

She glanced back. A man was standing on a second-floor deck, smoking a cigarette. She could see a big-screen TV flickering in the room behind him. He was staring right at her. She waved. He turned and went inside. To watch TV? Or call the cops? She wouldn't know until she heard the sirens, but right now she had her hands full trying to steer and see around the sail that blocked a sizable portion of her view.

The maze of canals and slips looked completely different at night. The shore was marked by the town houses—most with a boat in the backyard—all shining backdoor lights, dock lights, and security floods mirrored and smeared by the water. At each intersection she had to try to decide whether to continue straight or turn. It was like driving around a suburb of cul-de-sacs where all the houses looked the same. It was too dark to read the street names on the bulkheads, but she would not know them anyhow.

She was hesitating at an intersection of two narrow canals when she finally saw the water widen ahead and, suspended over it, the lights of the bridge. There was the main harbor lined with the marinas, which were brightly lighted and dense with sailboat masts. She saw other boats moving in the distance, though none under sail. Fishing boats, she thought. Who else would head out in the middle of the night?

She looked back. Grandpa's town house was back there, somewhere, but she doubted that if she turned around now she could find it without daylight. Safe at last to start the outboard. She tugged the pull cord ten times with both hands before it finally bubbled alive with a high-pitched growl. She engaged the propeller and tried to figure out where exactly the mouth was. It was like looking for a friend at a carnival.

She locked the tiller with a loop of shock cord and pawed through her seabag for her father's binoculars. Much better. She swept the dark for flashing channel buoys indicated on the chart.

Closely set red and green sidelights indicated a boat coming her way on a collision course. She edged over, closer to the stems of the docked boats lining the canal, to give it plenty of room to pass. But when she ducked her head to watch under the jib, she saw the boat shift course and continue right at her.

Police, she thought. The smoker called the cops.

She heard them shouting. She couldn't hear over the motor. They came closer.

"Lights! Turn on your running lights."

Duh! The harbor patrol would stop her in a second.

She jumped below again. Unlike *Molly P*'s electrical panel—which looked, with its rows and rows of switches and circuit breakers, like you could control an entire advanced-placement Physics lab with it—the J/27's consisted of four toggle switches under white on black name tags. She felt for them on the bulkhead beside the companionway and hit the wrong one. The cabin light flared on, blinding her. The next switch over was marked POWER LIGHT. And the next RUNNING LIGHTS. There. Now the J/27 showed red and green sidelights on its bow, a white on its stern, and—halfway up the mast—a white masthead light indicated the sailboat was under power.

She scrambled back to the tiller, blinking frantically to clear her vision. The boat the man had yelled from was about to pass close. Morgan wanted to call thanks. Better some stranger than the harbor patrol, but she didn't want them to hear a girl's voice. A voice in the dark solved the dilemma for her. "Asshole!"

She speeded up the motor, and mouthed a silent "Up yours."

Now the harbor got wider and the shore fell aside like opening arms. She swept the distance again with the binoculars, searching for the way out. She couldn't find the flashers marking the mouth, but she did notice several more fishing boats all on the same course, and scoping ahead of the lead boat, she finally saw the flashers marking the entrance and the whole picture fell into place.

Just when she knew where she was, the blue flashing lights of police or harbor patrol or coast guard came straight at her. She clamped the tiller between her knees to raise the binoculars. They were shaking so hard the lights all blurred. The flashing blue light was speeding across the harbor on a course that would cut her off. They had a searchlight, too, pointing like an angry finger. A siren whooped. A man yelled in a bullhorn.

Suddenly, right in front of her, she heard a high-pitched engine and a startled girl shriek, "Whoa!"

A Jet Ski flew out of the dark and cut across her bow. She caught a glimpse of two figures in string bikinis—thighs clamping the jet ski like a pair of Valley Girl Godivas. They were gone in a flash, racing toward the town-house canals, followed closely by the blue-flashing boat whooping its siren.

The J/27 bounced on their wake and Morgan felt a giddy grin tug at her face. She wasn't the only criminal on the water tonight. Ahead, she saw more fishing boats, a parade of them heading for the mouth. She took a deep breath, speeded up the motor, and got in line.

She steered to the right side of the channel between the long stone jetties that cut through the beach, keeping a lookout for the dredge pipes. As she rounded the breakwater, the first big wave lifted the bow like wind gusting under a newspaper. With a headline screaming YOU ARE LEAVING THIS HARBOR AND CAN NEVER COME BACK.

Even beyond the lee of the breakwater, the seas were relatively moderate, the broad Santa Barbara Channel being protected from the Pacific by the offshore islands. But under motor power, the boat was nowhere near as steady as the last time under sail and she bounced and pitched and rolled like an empty bottle.

She raised her mainsail. It luffed, flapping hard. A wave slapped the bow. The little sloop lurched into a trough with a stomach-tossing thud. Down in the cabin, Roscoe began to howl.

Morgan felt her way back to the cockpit, steered off the wind, and sheeted in. The boat heeled, and skimmed ahead. Morgan felt she needed the bigger jib. But no sail changes in the dark, thank you very much. She shut off the outboard. In the sudden quiet she could hear the bow cutting the water and the muted thunder of the fishing-boat engines.

A boat that had come out of the Channel Islands Harbor behind her began to overtake her. Its bow loomed high and sharp and she started to get afraid that they wouldn't see her lights. She should have brought a big flashlight to shine on the sails. But they steered clear, passing her boat at a safe distance. As she was between them and the lights of Oxnard, she saw fishermen lining the rails, drinking beer and talking and gazing back at the harbor, and down at her little sloop. Now that she saw they weren't going to run her down, she was afraid they would see her in the cockpit. Then all of a sudden the thought hit her: Out here, I'm just another boat. No one knows I'm me.

AIDEN AND THE TWO OLD nuns were standing watches four on, eight off. Gert came up from her hammock with mugs of tea for all. Sophie stayed until Gert got settled, then took hers below to enter course, speed, wind, and barometer in the log.

Aiden stayed in the cockpit. He should catch a couple of hours' sleep before his next watch, but it was a bit cramped inside the rolling hull and he preferred the fresh air. Besides, with the steeply following seas tumbling after them in the starlight, it didn't hurt to have a second spotter just to be on the safe side. So while Gert stood by the helm, ready to override the self-steering, and Sophie napped below before taking her turn to cook breakfast in the cool of early morning, he supplied a second set of eyes and ears and cranked an occasional adjustment to the sails. Relieved of the minute-by-minute responsibility of captaining the boat, however, he could let his mind wander down some strange paths where Sophie and Gert's questions had begun to point him—paths that led him further back than the attack. Back to that fucking letter.

In the year and a half after the dot-com crash wiped him out, he had scrambled around like a coal miner in a crumbling tunnel, madly propping and bracing so it wouldn't collapse. The prosecutor's letter had dropped the entire mountain on top of him.

But how was this for irony? Thanks to that letter, he had wonderful memories of his last visit from Morgan. After they got past his upset over her accidentally reading it—and he had come around to blaming himself for leaving it out—Morgan had asked if they could order in instead of taking the elevator up to Windows on the World.

"Pizza. Sushi. I don't care."

"But you look so nice. Come on, don't you want to go have a real dinner?"

"Da-ad. Windows on the World is like *really* expensive."

"Don't worry about it, we're still on Mr. Hong's tab. Come on, I want to walk into a fancy restaurant with a pretty girl on my arm."

"Yeah, right. Listen, Dad, you're going to be all freaked about this letter."

"I'm not freaked."

"I know you're not. Let me just help you set up the computer." She started typing. "They want a ton of files, so we'll get organized."

Aiden said, "I know how to use my computer."

"I know, but you seem to have a problem with files. Files and folders? Look at this, you're dropping single files directly onto your C-drive— So let's eat in and get started and you can whip through this and not have to stay all night."

There was no arguing, he recalled with a smile. It was exactly like her approach to homework. Do it now. Get it done. Play later. By the time a waiter came down with menus, Morgan had scanned the U.S. attorney's letter into the computer and was typing notes as they read it aloud, together. Long before the busboys wheeled dinner in on a cart, she lifted her earnest face from the monitor and said, "See? Your main folder is named 'U.S. Attorney Request.' Inside are subfolders, which we can name now. You were saying, proposals . . . negotiations . . . contracts . . ."

He said, "Then give each of these people I was dealing with a separate file."

"Good!"

She was opening files from names he read from the letter when something caught Aiden's eye.

"What did you say?" Morgan asked.

Unaware he had spoken aloud, he said, "Nothing . . . It's just that they want all these e-mails about buying stocks and trades and offerings and all."

"Well, yeah, I mean isn't that why we're doing this?"

"But here's a whole separate line of inquiry about privately held companies. This towing outfit. This construction company . . . Deals I did for Mr. Hong."

"What's the difference?"

"Real stuff instead of paper."

"Paper deals don't count?"

"They count. They're where the money is. But they're just numbers, pieces of pieces. These deals—these 'real deals,' are stuff you can grab on to. Bulldozers, drills, trucks, tugboats, whatever."

He had watched Morgan type in a blur of small fingers.

"Okay, I named a new subfolder 'Real Deals.' And I opened files inside it called 'Tugboats, Bulldozers, Trucks, Drills, and Whatever.' " She flashed him a happy smile he would remember for the rest of his life, and asked, "What else?"

Before he took her home, she set it up so he could back up the entire U.S. attorney folder onto a CD. In the car he had told her, "You're a lifesaver. I hope I'm not screwing you up with all this grown-up garbage."

"Do I look screwed up?"

"Not more than usual—but, seriously, that idiot marriage mediator told your mother and me that parents of only children make them grow adult too soon."

"I'm too short to be adult."

He had returned to the office much calmer. By morning, however, reality had firmly reasserted itself. The prosecutor was only one of his problems. And there was no way that "organized" could keep his whole life from going to hell.

The CD was in the bottom of his seabag, still in its stiff plastic protector. Though at the moment, he couldn't read the disk if he wanted to. There was no computer on Sophie and Gertie's boat, wind and solar generators for their shortwave receiver and running lights being the limits of their advanced technology. He could hit an Internet café in Panama, if he felt he could stand it. He'd gone into one once in Martinique. It had made him crazy, jam-packed with boat people and backpackers e-mailing home, checking their messages, sending pictures. Which was fine for people who existed. He did not exist. He had no home and no past.

Frankly—and frank thinking was getting to be a habit under the influence of Gert and Sophie—he didn't want to read it. It was just a record of some business dealings that had become, the instant he had escaped the World Trade Center, as remote to his life as Roman history.

Even if the U.S. attorney dropped his investigation, it wasn't as if he had a life waiting with debts canceled, homes restored, and a terrific new job lined up. As guilty as he felt for abandoning Morgan, running away had saved him the agony of floundering through the final days of a hopeless endgame. And her the humiliation of watching it.

NIGHT HAD ALWAYS BEEN MORGAN'S favorite time sailing with her parents. She would sit with her father all through his turn at *Molly P*'s helm, proud to have him all to herself. It was not often they risked piloting in the dark, preferring to spend the nights in harbors. But she had longed for night passages. She loved the enormous stars, the empty blackness, and the fact that at sea, at night her parents didn't drink. Of course, when she got tired she could curl up on the cockpit cushions and sleep with her head on his lap, which she couldn't do here with fishing boats roaring around and oil wells and drilling platforms and workboats and tankers and the lights of huge ships plowing along the murky horizon.

She was tired and cold. She put on her foul-weather jacket and zipped it to the neck. Then she drank a Coke in hopes the sugar and the caffeine would keep her awake.

This was a night of many firsts. First time she ever stole anything. Anything at all. First time sailing alone in the dark. First time ever she was the only one in charge of a real boat all by herself. This might not be big, but it was a real boat. In fact, she had never been so alone in her entire life as she was at this very moment, a mile offshore in the night. Not ever biking around New York, where there were always faces. This was completely alone. Except for Roscoe howling.

"No way I'm letting you out until daylight," she called down the open hatch. "Sorry."

It was no wonder the poor cat was pissed. Down in the cabin, the waves rattled loudly against the thin hull. But she couldn't catch a cat in the dark if he started running around and falling overboard.

At least his howls would keep her awake. She felt more exhausted than simply sleepy, totally physically exhausted, a kind of hit-the-bottom crash after the sky-high high of the exhilarating scramble out of the harbor.

Listening for fishing boats and tracking ship lights and worrying about oil rigs, and monitoring her handheld GPS so she didn't accidentally steer into the surf, she finally saw a bright Holiday Inn sign rise from the lights on the shore. According to the *Coast Pilot* pages she had printed off the Internet, she was passing Ventura Harbor, only five miles west of Oxnard. That meant she had still had twenty-five miles to go before she passed Santa Barbara. More than six hours at the four knots she was poking along.

She intended to sail straight through to Santa Cruz before she stopped to provision, 130 miles up the coast from Oxnard inside Monterey Bay. The cruising guide called it the last bastion of sixties hippiedom. That would make everybody there pretty old, but maybe less likely to ask a girl a lot of questions. And as the first big harbor after Santa Barbara, they'd have plenty of boat gear and grocery stores.

But it would take her at least a full day and night past Santa Barbara. And fighting a lot rougher sea after she rounded Point Conception and Point Arguello—and met the full Pacific outside the lee of the Channel Islands. A full night and day of dealing with this coastal stuff. Uncle Charlie always said any idiot can sail at sea, coasting is what will test you. Well, thank you, Uncle Charlie, she was more than tested. And thank you, Mr. Cat, for keeping me awake.

Could she even stay awake that long? Would it be better to provision immediately and head straight to sea? Santa Barbara had a yacht harbor where she could buy all kinds of offshore freeze-dried cruising food—enough for months—long-life ultrapasteurized juice and milk and a powerful flashlight and gas and oil for the outboard and whatever million other things she thought she might need on this last chance to load up.

The problem was that the long thirty miles by sea between Oxnard and Santa Barbara was a very short distance by freeway. Soon Chris and his parents would wake up and report their boat stolen. Then Grandpa would find her room empty and her stuff gone and everyone would put two and two together. The cops or the coast guard or harbor patrol or whoever traced stolen boats would draw a circle around Oxnard equal to the miles the J/27 could sail overnight. With luck, the cops would look at the weather and the northwest wind and figure she ran downwind to L.A. or San Diego. But all she needed to get caught would be one Coastie to know the J/27's sailing qualities and think, Naw, what if she sailed close-hauled north? That would put her into Santa Barbara sometime this afternoon. Look for the boat-thief girl in Santa Barbara.

She was too tired to think.

But only out of the coastal shipping lanes could she put her head down.

There would be thousands of sailboats in Santa Barbara. It wasn't like she would stand out the moment she sailed in. Besides, they wouldn't even start looking until afternoon. Maybe she could get there sooner than expected.

"What do you think, little cat? Worth a try? . . . Yeah! But fast. Like a lot faster than this!" Which meant going up on the bow to change headsails in the dark.

She jumped below to get her light-breeze wind catcher—the big genoa jib. Dragging the headsail into the cockpit and up to the bow, she could almost hear Daddy yelling what he yelled every time she went on deck: "Safety harness! Hank on! Hank on!" Dad was right. It wasn't like Roscoe could stop the boat if she fell overboard.

It took forever feeling around the dark to lower the small jib and raise the huge triangle of genoa and she got soaked by a couple of waves splashing over the bow. But it was worth it. The genny filled like she had netted a tiger. The J/27 came alive in her hands, and by the time the first hint of dawn reddened the hilltops, she had no doubts that she had stolen the right boat.

BARKING WOKE HER up, confused by the cold mist dripping from her hair, until a pelican gliding past told her that she had dozed off at the tiller and that the barking was not dogs, but seals. She jumped up and looked around. The boat was okay; no ships bearing down on her. They were sailing quietly in a low cotton-white fog that clung to the water. Above the fog she could see a big hill a half mile ahead, and a mile or so beyond it—just where the *Coast Pilot* promised—the white pillar of Santa Barbara Light.

The sun was lighting the red tile roofs on the city's hillside houses. Her watch said nine-thirty.

"Whoa, little cat, we did better than this afternoon, didn't we? Yeah, yeah, I know what you're thinking. No way we could do all our shopping and get out before afternoon."

She started the outboard. "Now all we have to do is find the sea buoy. Look for a green, Mr. Cat. Green on our right."

Roscoe, who had been pacing the wet decks since she let him out at first light, gave her an angry look and a telegraphic message that if he was bigger he would kill her.

"Screw you." She yawned, taking him off guard to grab him suddenly and lock him safely in his carrier.

"Just while we're shopping," she promised, spreading the chart on her lap and raising her father's binoculars to probe the fog for the sea buoy. By now she should be able to see that outermost channel marker. Maybe she'd passed it in the fog.

"Inland from the sea buoy we're looking for a red 'number four' on our right, Mr. Cat. Red, right, return. Then a green 'three' on our left. Remember how to remember? 'Even red nuns have odd green cans'?"

She was so sleepy she couldn't think straight. "Red four, red four, where are you?"

The sun and a light breeze scattered the fog and suddenly, dead ahead, she saw a cluster of sailboat masts. The harbor. It looked like a painting she'd seen of Sioux Indians heading home across the plains, guided by smoke and their tepee poles, and she steered toward the welcoming sight. But she should have seen the red buoy by now.

There was a green can, rising on the swell. But it was far off on her right, and slipping behind her. She was heading straight for the masts. But the can told her that she was way west of the channel.

"*Wait!*"

Did she overshoot the sea buoy in her sleep? Now she remembered a warning in the *Coast Pilot*. Something about the masts. She throttled back on the motor. A dark shape reared ahead of the boat. Huge, square stones. The seawall.

"Oh, shit."

In front of the seawall, dangerously close, the waves were crashing on a sandbar. She felt a breaker shove under the hull—felt the water snatch command from the wind and the motor—felt it lift the boat to throw it on the sand.

She shoved the tiller hard over and gunned the outboard. The motor wasn't worth much. But the big rudder bit and swung her from the beach. She felt the keel nick bottom. Instantly, she threw her weight to leeward to heel the boat further—which would angle the keel slightly upward—and held her breath. Instead of striking bottom, the J/27 struggled out of the breakers.

Morgan let out her breath and raised the binoculars with shaking hands. There was the green three, and there was the harbor entrance, and now everything was suddenly clear. An immensely long wharf stood on pilings that leaned every which way like heaps of bones. Smaller red and green buoys marked the fairway.

She steered past the long wharf into the harbor.

Inside, it was the kind of beautiful spring day when everyone went sailing, and the place was jumping. She motored in circles, dodging sailboats, whale watchers, sport fishermen, and tour boats, while trying to scope out the docks and read the Santa Barbara printout of the *Coast Pilot*. She finally oriented herself by the fuel dock on the end of a long pier that thrust into the basin between two crowded marinas.

It looked like at least a thousand sailboat docks. In the slips beside the fuel dock was a floating dry dock—a square, blue barge with SANTA BARBARA BOAT LIFTS painted on its side—houseboats, workboats, fishing boats, and sailboats, older, smaller boats locally built that she didn't recognize, less big-bucks flash than Newport or Marblehead. More like a cute little harbor in Maine.

Clustered around the basin were a bunch of stores and restaurants and tourist stuff. Hoists lined the fuel-dock pier like a row of preying mantises. Fishermen were using one to haul boxes up to a truck. But what riveted her attention was a coast-guard cutter moored to the fuel-dock pier and an orange harbor-patrol launch. Everyone on the cutter seemed to be asleep, but the patrol launch was nosing around the channels like a curious shark.

•   •   •

"TRANSIENTS," SHE READ in the *Coast Pilot*, "should report to the harbormaster for guest-slip assignments."

Oh shit. Should have read this earlier. *Hi, Mr. Harbormaster. Where should I park my stolen sailboat?* Should have thought ahead. Now what? Stupid. Stupid. Stupid.

Her brain felt like Jell-O. All she wanted to do was sleep. Should have read this earlier.

"I don't know about this," she called down to Roscoe. "What do you think? . . . Oh boy."

You couldn't just drop anchor in the busy harbor. And you couldn't keep on sailing circles very long before the harbor patrol got suspicious. You could go to the fuel dock, but you couldn't leave your boat for three hours of shopping while buying six gallons of gas. There were a thousand slips. A few must be empty. But you couldn't just pull into an empty one because before you tied your first line, someone would yell, "Hey, what are you doing in Joe's slip?" If it was at all like back home, people waited years for slips and paid a fortune and were kind of real mean about them. Should have planned ahead. Now what? Turn around, drive out, and sail a hundred miles to Santa Cruz? "What do you think, cat? Santa Cruz?"

She drove into the gas dock. She needed gas anyway and it would give her time to think. They were really busy, with yachts and huge fishing boats arrowing in from all over the basin, and the guy pumping gas didn't look that thrilled to top up a measly six-gallon tank while fifty- and sixty-footers lined up.

"Can you sell me another tank?" They didn't have a tank, but they had a plastic five-gallon can that was almost as good. She bought two of them, and oil to mix in the gas, and had them both filled. "Don't stow them belowdeck," the man warned, "or you'll blow yourself to kingdom come."

Wondering if she looked that stupid or that young, Morgan paid in cash, then got real nervous when the guy had to run for change. Too young to have her own boat?

Had word traveled up the coast?

The gas dock was too low down to see anything. She raced up the steep ramp to the main pier to see if any cops were coming. All she saw were boat people on their boats and tourists walking the pier and the seawalls. Now what? Now what? She had to find a place to leave the boat. There was another whale watcher with people leaning on the rails. Across the harbor was a launch ramp; SUVs were backing trailers down into the water and people were winching boats as big as hers off them. Could she pretend she was waiting for a trailer? No. There was no place to leave the boat unattended.

Looking toward the shore that the fuel dock thrust from, she studied the floating dry dock again. The marina stretched almost to the shore that was formed by the stone seawall. In the last row of slips were fishing boats. There was a row of restaurants and shops and behind them, inland a few hundred feet, a boatyard with cranes rising above the low buildings that housed the shops. Past the fishing boats, tied to the marina's innermost pier, was a splintery old wooden barge that looked way out of place. Most of the harbor was as bright and clean as homeroom on the first day of school. But the barge, listing slightly, appeared to be a sinking ruin. Except for a brand-new shiny sign. She raised her father's binoculars to confirm that it read in round script with a flourish of curlicues:

Wayne's
Boat Lettering
Service Dock

"Hey!" The gas guy was calling up the ramp. "Here's your change."

"Can I leave my boat a sec? I have to talk to the lettering guy."

"Make it quick."

She ran full speed up the long wharf to the land and careened left through a bunch of people drinking take-out coffee and along the seawall—slipping and sliding on mats of yellow seaweed—past a yacht club on the beach, down the marina ramp, and onto the wooden barge. "Hey! Anybody here? Hello!"

It was a little barge, no bigger than a suburban deck, and in the middle stood a hut that looked like a wilderness-camp outhouse. She banged on the door. She looked behind the hut. Nothing but a rusty bike with bald tires. She knocked again. Finally, a sleepy, bearded face opened up. "What?"

She recoiled from ancient beer breath. "Can you do a boat name?"

"Sure. Come back tonight."

"Now."

"Now?" He stepped out, squinting at the sunlight. The harsh glare revealed a raw scab on his cheekbone and deep wrinkles forming around his mouth. His beard was long, streaked with gray. Stringy hair grazed his shoulders. It was not as gray as his beard, but his skin looked like he had been left in the sun a very long time. "Now?" he repeated, backing through his door like a turtle in danger.

"Please. It's a surprise for my dad. It's his birthday. It will be the coolest present if I can get the name on his boat before he gets back."

"When's he getting back?"

"Noon."

"What time is it?"

"Ten-thirty."

"Shit . . ." He stared blankly, then bloodshot eyes finally focused on her face and he mumbled, "Excuse the language, kid. Didn't realize you were a kid."

"Should I bring the boat? It's on the gas dock."

"Okay. Bring the boat. Oh God, and then get me some fucking coffee. Excuse me, kid. Lots of coffee."

"Thank you. I'll be right back."

"Are you old enough to pay me?"

"How much?"

"A C-note. And I don't take Visa."

She must have gaped. He said, "A C-note is a hundred dollars. Cash. For both sides. It's my one-time-only prebreakfast special. And I'm hoping it's a short name."

A hundred dollars? She would have paid her last *two hundred* for the dock space. She raced back to the fuel dock, apologized profusely to angry adults, shoved off, motored the boat past the floating dry dock and through the clear waters behind the fishing boats, and moored alongside the splintery barge. The way the letterer looked at the J/27 she could tell right away that he was a boat guy who knew enough to like it.

"What's that noise?"

"Roscoe—my cat. I'm going to lock the hatch. He hasn't had his rabies shot." That should keep Wayne from poking around. "I'll see you later."

"Kid. We made a deal."

"What do you mean?"

"The deal was coffee. Lots of coffee. Light, two sugars."

She ran to the coffee shack at the foot of the fuel-dock pier, bought him three and herself one and a bag of muffins when she realized she was starving.

"I have to buy a ton of groceries. Can you recommend a store?"

"Yeah, there's a Vons on State. You can borrow my jalopy if you want. Go up Chapala."

"I don't know how to drive."

"What?"

"I mean I don't have a license."

He stared. "Oh, I guess you don't. You got a cell? Okay, punch in my number . . . Okay, take my bike. Call me when you're done. I'll pick you up in the truck."

"Thanks. Later."

"Kid!"

"What?"

"The name?"

She stared blankly. He held two of the coffees to his temples and said very slowly, "What name do you want me to paint on your father's boat?"

"Oh. Molly P. No wait, Molly P the second. *Two*. Is that too long?"

"Roman numeral two?"

"Right."

"Molly with a *Y*?"

"Right."

"What color?"

All she could think about was getting to the grocery store. "I don't know. Gold?"

"I won't paint gold on that boat. It's too cool. I mean the boat, not the gold. What color does your dad like?"

"Blue and green."

The boat letterer studied her over his coffee. "Like your freaky eyes. No offense, kid, but they are weird."

She didn't know if that was an insult or what and she was too tired to care. Besides, time was flying. She said what Uncle Charlie used to say. "I only see them in the mirror."

Now he was really staring at her. "I used to do portraits. Man, I would give anything to paint you."

"My dad's getting back at noon."

"Okay. Okay, tell you what I'll do. Blue *M*. Green *O*. Blue *L*. Green *L*. Blue *Y*. Green *P*. Blue number two. Forget the roman."

"Okay."

"Should I reverse them on the port side?"

"Sure."

"Hey, you better get going if you're going to finish shopping before I'm done."

• • •

THREE MONTHS OF food? What if she were becalmed? Or the boat damaged? Or forced off course by bad winds. Four months to be safe. She and Daddy used to talk about what they'd bring on the Bermuda Race. But that was only four or five days. Four months. Sixteen weeks. One hundred and twelve days.

She rolled a cart down the aisles, throwing in cans of tuna fish and jars of mayonnaise and bread-and-butter pickles. She piled in a dozen loaves of bread and lots of crackers. Saltines if she got seasick. Pasta. Tons of pasta. Spaghetti, linguine, orecchiette, lots of orecchiette. She loved orecchiette. Forget butter. It would spoil too fast. Olive oil. Bottles of olive oil—no, tins were lighter and wouldn't break. Gallons of olive oil. You could live on olive oil a long, long time. She had a fleeting thought of getting very tired of olive oil and immediately pulled twelve huge plastic jars of peanut butter into the cart. Canned chicken caught her eye. She had never tried it, but she liked chicken, so she threw in a bunch. They had canned ham, too. But she hated ham. Canned cheese? Another new experience. She stumbled upon a camping section: fifty freeze-dried meals in a bag. Add boiling water. Kerosene for the stove? There was a hardware store down the street they told her. Coffee. Tea. Coke.

Thank God they had square boxes of ultrapasteurized juice. She bought every kind of juice she liked. Two quarts a week of long-life milk. Forty-eight quarts of long-life milk. It didn't seem possible. Besides, Roscoe never drank the stuff. She bought twenty-four. A quart a day of water? Half a quart. She had already filled the boat's water tank at the gas dock and she had read about sailors catching rainwater in their sails. She got another huge cart and piled it completely full with liter bottles of water. Cat food. She took all their Sheba cat food, only enough for two months. Bags of dry food. They didn't have the special crunchy dental nuggets for his teeth.

What did she absolutely need? Kitty litter. Soap, tampons, sunblock—she was terrified of skin cancer—shampoo, she recalled, lathered better in salt water than soap.

"That's a lot of food," the checkout guy said when she wheeled up three carts.

"It's for my parents' boat."

"How many people?"

She thought fast. Four months was sixteen weeks for one person equaled eight weeks for two. "Eight of us. We're going out for two weeks."

"Where to?"

"Catalina and Mexico."

"That's cool." He started ringing up stuff.

Morgan relaxed, past the first hurdle. Santa Barbara was a boat town, after all. People bought a lot of food in boat towns. Though the checkout guy still made a joke about all the cat food. And another joke about kitty litter when she claimed that her parents had three cats. What else? she thought. What else?

"Whoa," said the guy when he came to all the tampons. "Lotta ladies on board."

Morgan thought her face would go red, but her mind leaped instead to the gym-towel smell and she ran back for baking soda and vinegar and a stiff brush. He asked, "You need a can opener?"

"Ohmigod. Thank you, thank you." While she searched out the can opener, she spotted a rack of books and grabbed a dozen paperbacks.

Everything seemed fine until the checkout guy read the Visa printout. "You got another card?"

"What's wrong?"

"They rejected your card."

She froze inside. They'd canceled her cards already? It didn't seem possible. Wouldn't they have to go through her mother? Could they have already called her in New York and found her at home or on her cell and got her to agree to shut Morgan down? Now what?

Exhausted, and absolutely stunned by this sudden reversal, she felt the anger rising in her blood. This damned store clerk was wrecking her whole plan.

"You want to try another card?"

She heard her voice cut sharply. "What?"

"They did me at the gas pump. Up by 101? They go, like, your card sucks. Give us the money. Man, I was pissed. My other card had like maybe twenty bucks left on it? I gave it to him and I thought, If he eighty-sixes this, I'm going to lay rubber out of here . . . You got another card?"

The guy was standing there with this goofy California grin like he was saying he didn't care if it took all day. He wasn't like the gas-dock guy. She felt suddenly bad she'd gotten mad at him. She calmed down and remembered her backup American Express. But that had been on her father's card, so it was shut down, too.

"Do you have an ATM?" He pointed to the back of the store. "I'll box your stuff."

"You better wait till I get the cash."

"It'll work. I got a good feeling."

She had her own savings account that had been opened when she was little for the Christmas and birthday checks from older relatives who didn't know what to buy a kid. Until this trip she wasn't allowed near it. It was always called "for college," but when she agreed to visit Grandpa, she had asked her mother to let her have a bank card to draw on it in case she had a problem while traveling and her mother was so glad to see her go to California that she took her to the bank and set it up. Best of all, the savings account had a huge five-hundred-dollar limit.

Maybe her mother didn't think to shut it down, too. Maybe she couldn't.

But as she slid the bank card in and out, she wondered, Can they track me to this store? How much time do I have to get out of here? The machine was way in the back of the store. She was trapped if cops suddenly came charging in to arrest her. Wait. Wait. She was getting crazy. This was as bad as Osama, imagining this huge bank computer going *beep, beep* to the California Highway Patrol computer. *Beep, beep, beep.* "Morgan Page, boat thief age fifteen, of New York City is trying to get money in the back of a Vons in Santa Barbara." The ATM went *thunk, thunk, thunk, thunk, thunk* and spit out five hundred dollars.

"Whoa," said Wayne when he pulled into the parking lot in a filthy Toyota pickup. "Looks like you bought out a Costco."

"The whole family's coming on this cruise."

They filled his truck and drove back to the harbor, borrowed wheelbarrows from the boatyard, and wheeled the boxes to the barge. When Morgan unlocked *Molly*'s hatch and pulled Roscoe's carrier out so he would get some fresh air and be out of the way, Wayne looked down into the little cabin and echoed, "The whole family."

Morgan wondered what to say. Wayne kept staring down the hatch, rubbing his face. But when he finally spoke again, he said, "So what do you think?"

"What do you mean?"

He stepped back and pointed at his handiwork.

Molly P 2

Lettered just aft of midships in alternating light green and light blue, it looked fabulous. In fact, it looked so fabulous that for a second she could believe that she was really about to surprise her father for his birthday.

"I chose a face called Benguiat. I think it goes with the boat. The contrast? She's got classic lines and Benguiat's kind of modern, in an old-fashioned way—you know, modern like fifty years ago. Like Broadway or the Bernhards?"

"I'll be out of your way soon. Soon as I load up." She paid him his C-note and said, "Thank you."

"You want a hand stowing all that?"

He didn't wait for an answer, but just started walking boxes across the barge and down into the cockpit. "Man, where are you going to put all this?"

It seemed impossible. There was some room under the berths in the main cabin. And behind the port berth was a low stowage space under the cockpit seat. But the starboard berth, which was placed farther aft to make room for the galley, used that space for its occupant's legs and feet. While the V-berth in the bow had to be shared with sailbags.

"First thing we do is get rid of a ton of packaging."

"Right. Right." She recalled doing that when cruising the Maine coast with her parents.

Wayne stuffed a big garbage bag with excess cardboard and plastic. Morgan chose the spaces low down in the center of the boat for stowing the heavy cans and juice boxes and water bottles. Lighter things went forward, under the sails, lines, and anchors, which she had to leave accessible, and aft under the low space beneath the cockpit. Slowly the mound of stuff in the cockpit grew smaller. It finally came down to six cartons of pasta and freeze-dried meals with no place to go except one of the berths in the main cabin.

"Port or starboard?" Wayne asked.

Her head felt like it had already imploded.

"You want to sleep on the down side, right? So you don't roll out of the berth. So you sleep to leeward and the food goes to windward."

"Right," said Morgan, understanding that when the boat heeled, she was less likely to get thrown out of the leeward berth because gravity would press her sleeping body against the side of the hull.

Wayne stuck his head out the hatch and looked at the sky. "The winds'll be mostly east in the channel tonight, but if by any chance you're heading offshore, you'll find them mostly north and west. So figure out what tack you'll sail on and we'll lash this stuff on the windward bunk."

Morgan hesitated. The tack she would sail would tell him a lot about where she was going.

Wayne covered his eyes and rubbed his whiskered face. "Kid, I got one question."

"What?'

"Where are you *not* going?"

"What do you mean?"

"I mean just let's suppose somebody asks me where you went. What do I tell them?"

"I—I don't know what you mean?"

"Yes, you do. You've stowed food for a family. But there isn't enough *room* left in here for a family of gerbils."

"So?"

"So tell me where you're *not* going. That's where I'll send anybody who asks."

"Mexico."

"Olé, kid."

Morgan shifted the boxes to the starboard berth and tied them with bungee cord Wayne gave her, raised the lee cloth just to be on the safe side, and lashed it to the handholds in the ceiling. They went out on the barge and checked the sloop's trim. She was down at the head, her bow tipping too low. They went back aboard and moved some stuff around and checked again. *Molly P 2* sat level, but much lower in the water than when Morgan had sailed in empty.

"She's not going to be a speed demon anymore. At least not until you eat and drink a bunch. Okay, I got another question."

"What?" Enough talk. She wanted out of here, now.

Wayne nodded at Roscoe, who was glaring from the padded grille of his cat carrier. "The cat know how to steer?"

"What? What are talking about?"

"If it's only the two of you, and you can't trust Roscoe with the helm, who steers the boat when you sleep?"

"I'll balance the sails. She tracks really well. She'll hold a course."

"That's cool on a broad reach, maybe. But what do you do when the wind shifts, or short seas start slapping her about? Don't you want a wind vane?"

"Sure. But I don't have one."

"I got an old Monitor in the yard."

"Really? Could I buy it?"

"Naw. It's my dad's business."

"Your dad?"

"You're gaping at me like, 'How could anybody that old have a dad?'"

"No, I didn't—"

"Well, my dad is *really* old. So old, he's got shitloads of junk he won't miss. Why don't you take it? You can hook it up when you got time. Pretty simple. You ever use one?"

"My parents had one—have one."

"I'll get it for you. How you fixed for tools?"

"Okay, I guess."

He opened the wooden chest that served as the bottom step of the two-step companionway and poked through the contents: a coil of rigging wire, some crimps, a small bolt cutter, and three sizes of wooden cones for plugging holes in the hull, a vise grips and a multi-blade screwdriver. He nodded, grunted to himself, and climbed out of the boat.

He returned with the wind vane and water paddle and tubing and various connecting parts of a Monitor wrapped up in a spiderweb of bungee cord. "Here's the manual. Stash this, I'll be right back."

He brought her a heavy plastic box. "There's a bunch of tools in here. Nothing matches, but it's mostly quality. There's a drill you'll need to install the Monitor. You can charge the battery with your solar panel." He peered over the stern. "You know, you might be able to rig it off that outboard motor rack . . . Maybe not—where would you stash the motor? Anyhow, here you go. You'll work it out."

"Why are you doing this?"

"Doing what?"

"Being so nice to me."

Wayne rubbed his face. "I don't know. Except sometimes by helping out, you get to sort of ride along?" A frightened expression crossed her face. "No, no, no. I don't mean ride along with you, I mean ride along, you know, in your head. Man, you're skittish . . . Or maybe I'm remembering how I screwed up a stunt like this when I was your age . . . Got caught. Turned out I wasn't that good at planning ahead."

"I know how to plan ahead. I do science in school. I know——"

"You got a sewing kit? To repair your sails."

"Uh, no."

"Needle? Thread? Palm iron? Fid for splicing."

Morgan said, "I have my dad's sailor's knife with a fid."

Wayne said, "Okay, okay. Stay here, I'll be right back."

He shambled off toward the boatyard, returned with a canvas bag, and showed her sewing gear, thread and light cord, and several rolls of chafing tape. "No offense, kid, but you're proving my point: when you're a kid, the future is kind of a murky concept—which is cool, because if you knew about it, you'd never get out of bed in the morning. Problem is, going to sea is all about the future—like always asking what's going to happen, then, and how can I prepare for it, now?"

"Thank you for all this."

"Some people might say 'thanks for nothing.' What kind of 'nice' is it aiding and abetting a fourteen-year-old putting to sea in a twenty-seven-foot boat without even a single-sideband radio?"

"Fifteen."

"Well, that's an entirely different proposition, isn't it?" he asked with a smile that made her smile.

"I have a VHF for talking to ships that get too close."

"Excellent. You can hail ships for weather reports, too, you know."

"Really?"

"They're usually glad to help if they speak English."

"I speak French. Sort of. I mean from school."

"*Excellentissime!* Kid, where are your parents?"

The blood rushed from Morgan's face. "Oh, please don't——"

Wayne stared at her long and hard. Then he said, "Open your eyes. You're looking at a fifty-six-year-old part-time painter, full-time drinker. I'm living on a stinking barge in the back of my old man's boatyard. I'm not a cop or a teacher or a mommy or a daddy who's going to tell a kid what she can't do. But I might worry a little less about you if I knew where you stood with them . . . Are you a runaway? You don't look like a runaway."

Morgan pulled a sealed sandwich bag from her wallet, unfolded her cutting from "Portraits of Grief," and handed it silently to Wayne. He read it, stared awhile, read it again, and folded the page reverently. "Well, Morgan, sounds like he died a hero."

"He didn't die."

Wayne looked at her. Then, to Morgan's enormous relief, he said, "Okay," and handed back the page. They locked eyes for a long time and Morgan felt tears well because at last someone accepted that what she had hoped with all her heart might actually be true. Wayne pulled a square of stained paper towel from his pocket and gave it to her to dry her eyes.

"Listen, why don't I drill a few holes for you and rig the Monitor?"

"How long would it take?" She was tempted. It would be incredibly helpful to have self-steering before she set out. But time was flying. There could be harbor patrol and cops all over here in any second.

"Couple or three hours. You could catch some sleep—which would not be a bad concept at all. You look beat."

Morgan shook her head. "No, I better get going."

"Kid—I'm not going to rat you out at this point, am I? I mean, where's the profit, right? Go below, sack out, I'll install the Monitor."

"I don't have much money left."

"Don't worry about it."

"But you can't just give me all this stuff."

"It's not mine. I borrowed it." He looked around. While not in plain view of the main harbor, Morgan's boat was certainly not hidden. Tourists were marching by, though they tended to gaze on more attractive sights than Wayne's barge. "You know, I'm going to run a workboat alongside yours—give me a platform."

Morgan waited nervously, still half-afraid he would return with a policeman now that she had gone and spilled her guts. But he came as promised, alone, steering a flat-sided, stripped-down, sun-blasted fiberglass boat with a shuddering diesel and a stink that smelled like Wayne had a day job hauling garbage. When he got done tying it alongside, it shielded *Molly P 2*'s hull from the harbor, the fuel dock, and the nearby berths.

"Let me just show you what I'm going to do. So when it breaks—and it will, everything does—you'll know what to fix. See, I'm going to mount her here on the stern. And I'll lead the pendulum lines through these blocks I'll attach to the stern rail. I'll bend these chains from the lines to these jaws I'll mount on your tiller." He demonstrated how the chain fit the jaws and how easy it was to shift the links to fine-tune the boat's course without messing with knots.

"Do you have to make holes in my tiller?"

Wayne groaned. "No good deed goes unpunished. Okay, I'll find some stainless straps. Don't worry, I'm not the kind of guy to drill holes in your tiller. Get some shut-eye."

She went below thinking she was too scared to sleep, started to stretch out on the port berth, and the next thing she knew a gnarly old guy with beer and coffee breath was shaking her shoulder and whispering what her mother said every morning of her life: "It's wake-up time."

She was so groggy she couldn't figure out where she was. Slowly it came back: the hull deeply laden with food and water; the new name in blue and green; the wind-vane self-steering; the snaggle-tooth old guy with gray hair and gray beard and beer breath.

Wayne handed her a container of coffee. She sipped it slowly as an overwhelming list of details churned in her head.

"Still going sailing?" he asked.

It took her a long moment to say, "Yes."

"Let me pass you some local knowledge . . . Let's say I were *not* sailing to Mexico, I would head straight west out the Santa Barbara

Channel and past San Miguel Island and hold my course west for at least a full day and night. Further out you go—the further off-shore—the less ships to run into, the weaker the California current, and the better the wind."

"I know," said Morgan. "That's my plan."

"Yeah, well, plan on fog, too, while you're at it. Until you're at sea. I found an old radar reflector, so I ran that up on your flag halyard." He pointed up at the top starboard spreader, where an aluminum ball consisting of three circular reflector plates hung like a Chinese puzzle. "It will paint a bigger target on the ships' radars."

"We had one on my parents' boat."

"I imagine they had radar, too."

"They had everything."

"Yeah, well, like they say, 'Heads up in the shipping lanes.' "

"I know . . ."

Wayne stuck out his paint-spattered hand. "It's been a privilege to meet you, Morgan."

She said, "I can't thank you enough. If it weren't for you—"

"Hey. You got the boat. You sailed it here. You got your food and water. All I did was a couple of details. And, if I were you, I'd bon voyage my ass out of here while the going is good."

She motored quickly out of the maze of floating docks. Wayne was right. Time was flying. The sunlight had grown richer as it sank west, and she saw a fishing boat coming home under a cloud of seagulls.

She passed the coast-guard cutter, still tied to the fuel-dock pier.

Then she saw the orange harbor-patrol boat sitting smack in the middle of the channel. Two officers with binoculars were scanning the boats heading in and out.

Oh, Daddy. Help me.

I T WAS ALREADY NIGHT IN the Caribbean. Aiden Page was alone at *Darling*'s helm, steering by Alpha Centauri and Beta Centauri, the hooves of the Centaur, which were about to sink into the southwest sea. That he could see the lowest stars in the constellation promised new skies after they transited the Panama Canal and angled closer to the equator. Soon he could set his course by the fabled Southern Cross.

He was also tracking red and green sidelights and white masthead lights to keep a safe distance from the merchant ships converging on the Canal, while his ears were tuned for the revealing *thrumm* of a poorly trimmed sail and the threatening *shlussh* of a dangerous crest he might miss in the star glow.

He managed this on his own internal automatic pilot, which allowed some of his attention to drift toward memories of his helter-skelter years at HHH & Company. The "girls'" questions had got him thinking. As he had told Sophie, his brother had nailed him the job, just as Charlie had talked him into coming home and finishing school and gotten him hired at the investment house that Merrill Lynch had gobbled up. He blamed all her questions—thanked them, actually—for dynamiting his head loose from the insanity of September 11 and the lunacy that followed. Would he run again, if he had the choice? Jesus H., he thought, I don't know. But what did you do *before* the war, Daddy? What did you really do at HHH?

Had a ball, he thought, before it went to hell. A blindman's ball. Jesus, he and Charlie. Everything they touched turned to gold. Early in March of 2000 he had calculated his personal worth at cracking $10 million. And Charlie's was probably five times that. On paper. He remembered joking with his wife that if they sold everything right that minute, they could pay off the mansion, the Manhattan pied-à-terre, the ski house, the vehicles, and the boat, stuff Morgan's college and trust funds, and still have money in the bank. Not enough to retire on, of course—not after taxes, but, Jesus H., what a heap of money. Hard to believe that was only two years ago.

The day the NASDAQ topped 5000 he had promised himself that he would bail at $20 million. What was that? Two days before it sagged? Halfway through the collapse, they still could have sold everything and kept only the boat and gone back to the way they lived before Charlie dragged him to Wall Street. Living on a boat, like they did when Morgan was born. Debt-free. A hell of a lot better boat. Time on their hands. Happy days.

Aiden rapped his fist gently on the old wooden helm. The funny thing was, as he looked back at the 1990s, it was hard to remember how they spent their days. Months of meetings and phones would blur by—phone calls day and night; phone calls from the car and the boat on weekends. Unlike Charlie, he took long weekends, trusting in the cell phone to keep him abreast of the action. Charlie didn't seem to mind. Most of the week, Monday through Thursday at least, they were still a team—walking the walk in boardrooms and trading floors. *Here come Charlie and Aiden.*

We got something you might be interested in here, Charlie.

Talk to Aiden.

Aiden, how you doing, buddy? Looking good. We got something Charlie thought you might like.

Or, from the surviving white-shoe firms: *Good afternoon, Aiden. Your brother suggested . . .*

Let me clear it with Charlie, I'll get back to you.

Or. If it was really hot: *We got something here might interest you, Charlie.*

I got twenty minutes—Aiden, I'll catch you back at the office.

Later, back at the office, Aiden more than once said, "You know this so-called sale is really a loan. We're *lending* them money, but they're booking it as *income*."

Big smile from Charlie: "These guys are doing gangbusters. Stock's tripled. They've got a brief interruption of cash flow."

"Their stock price has nothing to do with it. They can't meet their obligations without our loan."

"It's only a loan if we call it a loan. Maybe you could work the language. What is this, Thursday? *Molly P* still out at Block? Hell, tell Penny to book a seaplane—you can get this done by tonight."

"No skin off my nose." Which became his standard face-saving way of admitting that if you were going to whore, you should at least demand top dollar. And top dollar he got—a very cushy life with a solid future; all he had to do was pretend to be blind.

DADDY! GET ME OUT OF this.

But it was Uncle Charlie who, like magic, whispered in Morgan's ear, *Get close! Get in their face. Make them move.*

Quickly, she hoisted her sails. She had a new name painted in big bright letters on her hull. And the Monitor self-steering vane sticking up straight as an orca fin changed their silhouette considerably. Praying that the Santa Barbara harbor-patrol officers were not racing sailors and didn't know a J/27 from a Beneteau, she stuffed her hair under her cap and headed straight at them.

It felt like the start line, jockeying to cross in the best position when the cannon fired. Boats cluttered the channel—big sloops and ketches heading out to clear the land before dark, day sailors racing in, fat motorboats churning waves. The water was crisscrossed by wakes, like it was boiling.

A sport fisherman cut across her bow, and forced her off the wind onto a course that would T-bone the patrol boat. She came about as fast as she could, sails crackling like gunfire. The patrol guys whirled fearfully toward the sound.

"Sorry," she yelled over her shoulder, as if she had just missed clipping the race-committee boat. "He cut me off."

Dodging and weaving, she put a hundred yards between her and the patrol boat and came about on a course that took her past the wharf that formed the harbor mouth and into open water. She glanced back. They were looking the other way.

"Yes, cat!" she yelled down the hatch. "We are outta here!"

Buoyed by a hull full of everything she could think of, a solid nap, and a million cups of coffee, she jibed about and ran west. *Molly*—in that instant Morgan decided that *Molly P 2* was too big a mouthful for this little beauty and from now on she was plain *Molly*—settled into a miles-eating broad reach.

The Santa Barbara Channel grew wide as the continent and the island chain veered apart. To her left and ahead, Morgan could see lights begin to glow on the oil rigs. To her right, evening cloaked the California hills.

The wind shifted, gusting from east through south to southwest. The seas began to build. She debated reducing sail while she could still see to work on deck. But the wind, instead of getting stronger, died. Then the lights on the land and the offshore structures disappeared as fog rolled in from the Pacific.

THE COPS TREATED Wayne's father with the respect due a prominent businessman. The old man had served in the navy and at seventy-eight still wore a crisp blue shirt to his boatyard every day. The razor creases in his trousers were as sharp at night as when he had started work early in the morning and he stood so straight that he looked—Wayne was known to grumble into his sixth or seventh beer—like he had swallowed a mast. His shipshape office—frugally ensconced in a houseboat he'd seized for nonpayment—was lined with fifty years' worth of Rotary and Lions plaques, framed good-citizen citations from the City of Santa Barbara, faded autographed pictures of famous old movie-star yachtsmen Sterling Hayden and George C. Scott, a framed letter of thanks from the Santa Barbara Fishing Association, even a proclamation from the state legislature up in Sacramento hailing his contributions to the public good. A small portion of the cops' deferential courtesy encompassed Wayne, too, until he blurted, "If I had health insurance and life insurance and a pension and a gun, I'd be a cop. But I don't, so don't ask me to do your job."

"Since when do you have to worry about paying for your health insurance?" his father demanded.

"I don't, thanks to you, Dad. Not the police."

The cop doing the talking said, "Come on, Wayne. Cut the counterculture bullshit. This isn't 1969 and we're not picketing oil rigs. All we're trying to do is ensure the little girl's safety. What's the big deal asking your help with that?"

"Safety at sea?" Wayne asked. "Is that what's troubling you? Let me put your mind at rest. She struck me as a better seaman than most of the turkeys I see steering mega-yachts to Mexico."

"Mexico?"

"You didn't hear it from me."

They looked at their notes. "And what was the name you lettered on the stolen boat?"

"On the boat I didn't know was stolen?" Wayne waited for their reluctant nods. "On the boat I didn't know was stolen I lettered 'Roscoe.' R-O-S-C-O-E."

"*Roscoe?* Funny name for a boat."

Wayne shrugged. "I don't name 'em, I just paint 'em."

"Did she say why she named it *Roscoe?*"

"No," he said, playing up his obstreperous hippie rep so the cops wouldn't hear the lie.

"Do you have an idea?"

"It's the name of her cat."

They added to their notes. Wayne stole a look at his father, whose stone face looked like someone had chiseled on it in Poster Bodoni Bold: **AT AGE FIFTY-SIX WAYNE SHOULD STRAIGHTEN UP, GROW UP, AND TAKE AN INTEREST IN THE BUSINESS.** It was not a new thought.

"And what color did you paint the name?"

"I don't remember."

"*Wayne!*"

"Gold."

BECALMED IN THE fog, Morgan drifted in circles, straining to hear invisible ships. Afraid to start the motor, afraid she couldn't hear, she clutched her VHF radio to warn any that came too close, constantly comparing her GPS position to her chart. As terrifying as being run down by a ship was drifting aground to be smashed in the surf.

The *Coast Pilot* said the fog was worst from August to November, so she kept expecting it to clear. But the cold, wet murk lingered all night—as she alternately dozed in the cockpit and started awake— her gear slick with condensation.

She heard the muffled groan of foghorns, some seemingly nearby, others in the immeasurable distance. The glow of a searchlight blossomed in the dark, a ship bearing down on her. She looked up at the mast spreader where Wayne had hung the radar reflector. Of all the stuff he had given her, the radar reflector felt like the most valuable. Did the ship's radar see it? She keyed her VHF to radio a warning. But she was afraid. What if it was a patrol boat? Suddenly the light went out and in the blackness she heard machinery, then silence.

Sometime later she sensed light again, but with it came a foul smell. Gas, she guessed, the light the white-orange flare on an oil rig. Then another light, this behind her, the herald of a weak dawn, the sun poking futilely at the fog. When it was bright enough to see the top of her mast, she heard a hollow rumble. It grew metallic, like softly beaten steel drums that got louder and louder until it became a rhythmic pounding—deeper and deeper, but still hollow. The fog was full of tricks: she couldn't see her own bow, but now the sound seemed to come from overhead, as if it were a big helicopter. But what helicopter would fly in this fog?

She kept turning her head, seeking to get a fix on where the noise was coming from. She looked over at Roscoe, barely visible until he retreated into the cockpit to sit beside her. Out of his cage since dawn, prowling the decks with his old surefooted "boat-cat" ease, he was suddenly anxious.

"What is it, Boat Cat?" she whispered. The sound was all around them. It was like the boat was inside a drum.

Roscoe stared at the bow. His long body went rigid, head up, yellow eyes turning dark as wary alertness turned to fear.

"Oh shit!"

She threw herself over the stern and yanked the outboard start cord. Once. Twice. Three times. Scalp prickling, she looked over her shoulder ahead of the bow where Roscoe was staring. A black shape that loomed as tall as a "Shrink Land" town house parted the fog.

She yanked the cord again. The engine started with a high-pitched whine. The little propeller churned. The boat moved slowly. When the two vessels were close enough for Morgan to see the ship's anchor, its bow wave lifted the sloop and shoved her on its side as it rumbled past.

She had stupidly left the hatch open. The wave spilled into the cockpit, filled it in an instant, and cascaded below. It soaked her berth and her open seabag of clothes and Roscoe's litter box. But the boat straightened up and the fog began to lift as if the ship that had nearly blasted her to smithereens had dragged it away.

The wind hardened in the east and filled her sails. The sky cleared, the horizons spread. She saw oil rigs, in close formation, cranes rising like masts on a fleet of Spanish galleons. They fell astern, and when she found San Miguel Island—the westernmost of the Channel chain—on her port beam and Point Conception on her starboard, she stopped worrying about drying out the cabin and got busy sailing.

She had the main and the big genoa both pulling downwind and the boat was screaming along at hull speed and starting to surf a little when they quite suddenly left the Santa Barbara Channel and entered the Pacific Ocean. It was like turning a corner from a quiet city block onto a broad, windswept avenue.

The waves were big. The temperature dropped twenty degrees. The wind whipped around the compass then settled in the northwest and blew hard. The seas grew orderly, as if they had traveled a long way, unimpeded. Even the light changed, like walking out of a cramped house into the sun.

In an hour the mainland had totally disappeared and San Miguel looked far behind her. As that last island continued to sink below the horizon, Morgan again fixed on the fact she had admitted earlier, but was suddenly branding her consciousness. She had never single-handed a boat before. As the kid, she had always been number three aboard *Molly P,* under Captain Daddy and First Mate Mommy, barely ahead of Roscoe. Now every decision was up to her, every problem hers to solve before it became a crisis.

Such as right now, the strong wind was making the boat heel too sharply. She had to replace the genoa with a smaller jib. But the decks were wet from spray, slippery, and steeply angled. So before she reduced sail, she set about rigging jack lines—short, strong lengths of rope to which she could clip her safety harness when she climbed out of the cockpit.

As she worked, she kept looking back at San Miguel's jagged, rocky coastline. Here and there gleamed a white sand beach. The beaches were the first to disappear. She noticed that her wake was riled by the drag of the outboard motor. It would be a long time before she used it again, so she figured out how to operate the lifting bracket and raised the shaft and propeller up out of the water. The boat felt like it had shrugged off a restraining hand. And San Miguel sank in her wake as *Molly* descended the curve of the earth.

A FUNNY THING HAPPENED TO Wayne. Only it wasn't so funny and it left him fearing that he'd screwed up the kid's chances. Early the next morning another cop woke him up, banging on his door. Plainclothes. Not a local, at least no one Wayne remembered. He caught Wayne a little off balance—tired and hung—handed him a container of coffee marked SWEET AND LIGHT, and asked, "The little girl in the sailboat? . . . You think she'll come back here?"

"Nope." Wayne fumbled with the lid.

"You think she'll drown?"

"Drown? Hell, no." Same thing they were trying to pin on him yesterday, like they thought Morgan Page was running away from home and that it was his fault.

Sure enough, the cop got all righteous and said, "No thanks to you."

Another man might have tossed the coffee in the guy's face for a remark like that. Wayne got the lid off and took a grateful sip.

The cop said, "Look, we're talking about a fifteen-year-old girl. Maybe has some problems. Maybe needs some help."

"I told you yesterday. As far as I'm concerned, she was helping herself."

"What if I told you she bought dope the day she ran away."

Wayne was surprised. "Dope? What are you talking about? The kid's not a doper."

"Amphetamines, from some mall rat in Oxnard."

"Go pills?"

"You heard me."

"Oh. Well, what do you expect?"

The cop looked puzzled, but shifted quickly back to moral out-rage. "What do you mean, what do I expect? I'm telling you the kid has problems and now you've sent her off sailing around stoned."

"Not stoned. She's single-handed. If she bought speed, it was because she knew that some squally night she might need go pills to stay awake at the helm."

The cop looked around. He was tanned like everybody else in Santa Barbara Harbor. But there was something about him that said he wasn't quite local. Busy East Coast eyes. "Look," he said. "I'll level with you. Her grandfather told me that the girl's father was killed in the World Trade Center."

"She told me she was getting the name lettered to surprise him."

"That's the point, isn't it? He's dead. She's pretending he isn't. The girl needs help . . . And I've got a funny feeling you can help me find her."

"When cops say they'll level with me, I say it's time for a lawyer. Thanks for the coffee. I'm going back to bed."

A meaty hand blocked the door. "Who said I was a cop?"

"Who the hell are you?" asked Wayne, a little afraid now.

"A friend of the family."

" 'Friend of the family'? Is that code for 'private detective'?"

"It's code for 'I don't have to read you your rights.' "

Wayne backed up.

The guy pushed into the messy little cabin. "It's also code for 'there's nothing to stop me slapping you around to get some simple information out of you.' "

Wayne reached for his cell phone. The guy knocked it out of his hand.

"I'm asking you nice as I'm going to, buddy. Please help me undo the damage you did."

"Hey! I didn't do any damage. She knew what she was doing. She had everything she needed to stay at sea for months."

"Months?"

"I told you she's no dummy. And let me tell you something else: If she's got problems—and I didn't see any—they won't get in her way when she's sailing."

"Months?"

"You heard me."

"I'm from back east. I wasn't aware it took months to sail to Mexico . . ."

Well, screw you, too, "friend of the family," thought Wayne. And happy hunting. It's a goddamned bigger ocean out there than you could ever dream . . . Still, it stayed in his head all day and all night, that he had told the private detective more than he should have.

BOOK TWO

VOYAGE
TO
PARADISE

APRIL–MAY 2002

O N BLIND MAN ISLAND, CHARLIE Page slept round the clock for days. He awakened clearheaded, with a powerful conviction that his body had finally thrown off the coral infections and that he was on the mend. His thoughts, too, firmed up in the course of a shower and shave and coffee.

He knew now that he had wasted years finishing second best to Henry Hong before he learned a costly lesson: Henry Hong was never what he appeared to be and never had been. The "rules of paradise" that the boss had laid down were only smoke to hide the truth that this island was not a safe haven, but part of a larger plan.

They had started off as equals, way back in Charlie's Wall Street apprentice days. Same age. Same step, relatively, on the career ladder. Same ambition to own it all.

The white-shoe investment house that had hired Charlie on the basis of his special operations service in Soviet-held Afghanistan had assigned him to investigate the prospects of an old New York family–owned tugboat firm that wanted to go public. He had met with Henry, the tug firm's Hong Kong partner, who had brought in

enough modernization money to get himself appointed chief financial officer.

It had been a make-or-break moment for each of them. Charlie
knew he'd gotten the assignment because the Connecticut WASPs
who owned the investment house thought it expedient to send an
Irishman to the rough-and-tumble waterfront. And it was soon
apparent to Charlie that Henry was overextended, having underestimated the shrewdness of the tugboat scion.

Charlie's job perks had included access to a venerable midtown
club and one of the more worldly of the senior partners had
informed him that Hong Kong Chinese were suckers for private
clubs. More than dinner out or barhopping or strip joints, Chinese
businessmen wanted to dine and drink brandy in a private club. So it
was over brandy that Charlie revealed that he had learned that
Henry was hanging on by his financial toenails. Then he had wondered aloud if Henry would not be wise to take his marbles and go
home and let Charlie's firm take the tug outfit public without him in
exchange for a modest finder's fee.

Henry looked sad. He explained that he had always been a refugee.
"I am a child of poverty," he said. "You cannot begin to imagine
the desolation in the aftermath of the Great Cultural Revolution.
People ate grass." Charlie recalled stories his grandmother told of
Irish farmers dying with their lips stained green. He had a strong
suspicion that Henry, who was broadly educated, knew those stories, too.

"When I was ten years old, I saw Hong Kong gleaming across the
bay, so I decided to 'sprit.'"

Even then Henry was adept with accents, sounding Chinese
when he wanted to, British when he wanted to, and lately, New York.
So "sprit" for "split" was by choice.

"Wasn't the border closed in those days?"

"I swam Tai Peng Bay. I swam with the sharks. They didn't
bother me."

"Professional courtesy?" Charlie had asked.

Henry grinned back. "I gave you that one."

"Thanks, buddy."

"Ten years old, I start a business filling out forms for refugees trying to get papers to stay."

"When did you learn how to read and write English?"

Henry had skated across a blank page of his résumé with a casual, "Picked it up here and there."

"In China or Hong Kong?"

"A bit of both. Before you know it, I've got a few businesses and some investors. Many businesses, and then I'm having some troubles. So I figure it's maybe time to 'sprit' again."

"Is that when you came to New York?"

"Cambridge and London." Henry Ho drained his snifter, stood up, and said, "What do you say we take a walk, old chap?"

He steered Charlie up Fifth Avenue to Fifty-third Street.

"You see that building?"

It was a former town house next door to a Doubleday Bookstore shoehorned into several floors of a similar five-story building. Its Beaux Arts facade had been neglected and Charlie wondered why they both hadn't been knocked down and replaced with one of the fifty-story office towers taking over the avenue.

"Nice little building. What about it?"

"Aren't you surprised to see it there?"

"Yeah. There's not too many of them left. I doubt it will be there next year."

"It will be there in ten years. If not twenty. Or thirty. Or a hundred. Do you know why?"

"No, but you are going to tell me."

"That building—devoid of renters and paying enormous city taxes—is hostage to the estate of a Hong Kong gentleman who died five years ago. His children and his mistress and *her* children are feuding over his will. If they agreed to share, they could sell that single building for more money than the old gentleman ever dreamed of, thanks to New York's current construction boom. It would be very wise to share. But we have a great Hong Kong tradition of pissing our money away in endless and extremely expensive court battles from which only the lawyers emerge intact. In other words, Charlie-boy, how do you propose to buy me out?"

Neither the white shoes nor the gnarly tugboat captain had loved him for it, but they had taken Charlie's advice and settled generously with Henry, who promptly "sprit" back to Hong Kong, so suddenly that when Henry called to say good-bye, Charlie asked if his plan from the get-go had been to stage a public offering for the express purpose of holding it hostage to double his share of the take. To which Henry Ho Hong had replied, "Everyone's got to make a living somehow."

Suddenly, just as the stock market began to soar, Henry Ho Hong came back to New York. It was in the midnineties—'94 or '95. (In Charlie's mind, the Clinton years had already blended into a blur of money and sex, a time of great expectations with few disappointments and politics a comic sideshow.) Henry had looked enormously prosperous, though by then Charlie was no longer impressed by six-thousand-dollar suits and thirty-thousand-dollar watches or even bodyguards and chauffeured Bentleys. But he was chafing for a move up, himself, so he had cleared his calender for a last-minute lunch and after a meal lavish by even M&A-on-the-client standards, he took Henry back to the white shoes' club and over brandy asked, "What's up?"

"Always to the point. I like that about you, Charlie."

"We've been talking bullshit for three hours. What are you up to these days?"

"Many interests, Charlie. Many interests."

"If this is a con, I'm not rich enough, yet, to make it worth your while. Come back in ten years."

"You're too modest, Charlie. They've made you a partner."

"I'm a glorified wage slave and you fucking know it."

"You've achieved the Wall Street dream. You'll retire at fifty with millions."

Charlie let his anger show, partly to signal Henry not to fuck with him and partly because he was angry at having gotten trapped on a velvet treadmill. "The days of 'millions' being a big deal are over and you know it. People who earn 'millions' are servants for people with billions. If you are half as successful as you're pretending to be, you know that's a fact."

"Point taken, Charlie-boy."

"I'll make you an offer. If you stop calling me Charlie-boy, I won't punch you in the face."

"Right here in your club?"

"Right here in my club."

"Do you really think I'm here to con you?"

"I don't know why you're here."

"Then why did you agree to meet on short notice? It couldn't have been convenient. You're a busy man. You've got clients. Decisions to make. Meetings."

Charlie Page gave that some thought before he answered. "I agreed because I like you, Henry. I don't know what makes you tick, but I do know that you are no fucking wage slave and I like you for that. You have a sense of humor. And when you put on an act, at least you don't forget it's an act, unlike the assholes I have to work with on a daily basis. What's up?"

"May I ask one more question, first?"

"Shoot."

"Have you ever been bent?"

"Bent?"

"Crooked, illegal."

"Oh, you mean like you were when you organized that rhino-horn smuggling scheme?"

Henry Ho Hong hadn't bothered to hide his surprise. In fact, he had laughed. "Very good, you've done your homework."

"I wondered why you had to 'sprit' from Hong Kong."

"I was invited back. All was forgiven. But you haven't answered my question. By 'bent,' I meant behavior like the sort that got you asked to leave Princeton."

"I was asked back, too," Charlie replied, struggling to hide his surprise, only to be surprised again when Henry said, "I believe you had a kindly cardinal in your corner who had influence with the police as well as the college?"

Charlie had conceded that Henry's research was at least as good as his. Almost on impulse, yet with a strong suspicion that Henry's detectives, or whoever he paid for information, had ferreted out other things, he added, "Yeah, I've been bent. Not only then, but when I was a kid. And a bit in the service."

"What did you do in the service?"

"People usually wanted to buy something I could find it for them."

"And as a kid?"

Charlie shrugged. "Same as Princeton. Dealing drugs."

"For the money?"

"I liked the edge it gave me. And I knew that the crazies I got to deal with could teach me a lot."

"Excellent. Ever kill anybody?"

"I honor the nondisclosure oath I gave the army. What's up, Henry?"

"I have partners interested in taking another shot in New York."

"I thought they already had."

"What do you mean?"

"Aren't they the guys with Donald Trump's balls in a rattrap?"

"Your blowhard builder put his own balls in a rattrap. My friends merely changed the cheese. But I'm referring to others. Of course you would remember some names from our tugboat days—but these are basically investors looking for diversification in a safer atmosphere than China."

Charlie still recalled sitting up straighter. Communist China was "modernizing" itself into a market economy. Henry would act as a conduit for high-up Chinese officials skimming money from the dying system. A lot of money.

"Well, this is very generous of you, Henry. *My* 'partners' will be impressed. Might even elect me to the compensation committee."

"I want nothing to do with your partners or their firm."

"Then why are you talking to me?"

"I'm starting an investment firm. I want you to lead it."

To this day on Blind Man Island, Charlie still recalled the powerful jolt to his heart and lungs. He could hardly breathe, much less conceal his astonished delight. Henry's offer had promised a life changer on the level of the white shoes giving him his first job. It was the kind of opportunity that would make him, overnight, a wealthy man. And in a very few years, powerful, too. The stock market was gathering steam. It looked like the bulls would run for years, making it a wonderful time to wield large funds on the ground floor.

But it would also change forever his relationship with Henry Ho Hong. For as powerful as it would make Charlie Page on Wall Street, Henry would control the spigot from which the money flowed.

"Why me?"

"I know you."

"We haven't spoken in four years."

"I've seen you operate. You damned near blew me out of the water, and when I threatened to reverse it on you by tying the deal up in court, you made it work for both of us. Win-win for all parties. I know few men who can both win and lose to advantage and you're the only one I know on Wall Street."

"Why would I give up a partnership to become your employee?"

"A bank! Charlie, I'm offering you your own private bank. Brim full of funds for you to invest as you see fit. It's a license to print money."

"Who's the boss?"

"I will hold the title managing partner, Hong Kong. You will be senior partner, New York, and the chief executive officer and anything else you want to be. It will be up to you to employ a financial officer, traders and bankers and analysts; you can make any of them junior partners if you choose. But you will not need salesmen to beat the bushes for investors because I will supply the money."

"What exactly does a 'managing' partner do?"

"Keep his distance."

"Are you going to stay in Hong Kong?"

"Not necessarily, but I promise I will be in New York only rarely. And when I do come, I won't stay long."

Charlie shook his head. "How do I run a bank when everyone sees you parachuting in whenever you feel like second-guessing me? Where's my credibility? I'll get people saying, 'Let me talk to your boss.' "

"No, no, no. I will be a *silent* managing partner. Silent as the grave."

Charlie had still looked skeptical.

Henry said, "I promise you, that the last thing I want is a high profile. *You* will be the high profile. I will be invisible . . . What do you say, Charlie-boy?"

He hadn't punched him in the face and now—seven years later—and seven months after the Al Qaeda attack—he was Henry's guest. Or prisoner—if you wanted to look at the situation worst case—because he sure as hell wasn't getting off this island without Henry's help. Best case, Henry had a plan for something big with a big part in it for him. But even best case, he was a man without a country. A man who would like to have an island like this. Or even this island . . . The fact was, he had always gotten on well with their tame Tongan noble.

"Knock-knock?"

Jin-shil walked into his room. "Hello, Charlie." She was wearing a Tongan costume similar to the one she had donned to greet their noble, so it looked like the king's nephew was still on the island. No surprise; Polynesian sea voyagers did not drop in for an afternoon. She closed the door behind her, stretched her arms high, removed the red feather from her hair, looked at it the way a woman who shopped at Tiffany might look at a product from Kmart, and let it float to the floor.

"Henry's busy with our guests. He asked me to see how you were getting on here all alone."

"Tell Henry I'm sorry I missed all the parties."

"Little to miss," she assured him. "The honorable is worried about terrorism. It's all he'll talk about. Thank God we're all in bed by ten."

"I thought he was worried about the Pacific Ocean drowning his atolls."

"He wonders if the two phenomena are connected."

"Someone should tell him that terrorists don't drive enough SUVs to contribute to global warming."

Jin-shil smiled. "I had some success convincing him that terrorists can't afford to work so slowly."

"How'd you manage that?"

"I made a pretty speech. 'Dear Honorable,' I said, 'speed is their strength. Terrorists can only hold power in the ephemeral—the mind, the idea—things that can't be bombed by the United States Air Force. The instant that an idea takes shape, it is vulnerable. Therefore the terrorists must execute an idea swiftly as a shooting star.' "

Charlie looked at her, suddenly interested in a new way. They had spent little time together and none alone. The strong sea light showed that she wasn't all that young, he realized. She held herself like a girl in her twenties, but she had the voice and sense of self of a woman nearer his own age. And there was a depth to her quite beautiful face that hinted that she was perpetually reflecting upon new ideas she found interesting.

"Where," he asked, "did you meet Henry?"

"Shipwreck."

"Beg pardon?"

"There are volcanic islands in these waters that rise so suddenly they're not on any chart. My ship struck one. Only I survived . . ."

Charlie knew that her ship would not have been the first to come to grief on an uncharted "mountaintop" in the volcanically lively Tongan archipelago. Even the high, reef-rimmed Blind Man Island—a hodgepodge of peaks and cliffs on the northeast, and coral reefs to the south, had not existed before an eruption in the seventeenth century. But something in her strange eyes told Charlie she was putting him on.

"Henry rescued you?"

"In a manner of speaking."

Although it was only late morning on Henry's paradise island in the middle of nowhere, he felt as if he were bantering with a woman newly met in a hotel bar—a far-from-home, free-form ballet of bright advance and flirtatious retreat. *Whose ship?* he wanted to ask. And where was it steaming out here at the end of the planet? And—most of all—where did her loyalties lie?

He said, "I'm curious. Henry claims that he doesn't warehouse arms on the island. So why do you need a light reaction company? It looks to me like you've got a full ninety-man complement."

"You have a good eye, Charlie."

"I was a soldier once. What are they protecting if you keep no weapons on the island?"

"That's not entirely accurate," she replied without hesitation. "Because the light reaction company *itself* is a weapon. Henry can lease it out for surgically precise operations like hostage release, or hijack termination, or as a potent antiterrorism force. Terrorism's strength, in addition to speed, is flexibility. The light reaction force is fast and flexible, too. We can load it on a plane or helicopters and zoom it anywhere at a moment's notice. Henry believes he has created an extremely commercial tool. He can lease the unit to stop a terrorist attack."

He had asked Henry once how he had gotten into the arms trade and Henry had answered that it seemed like a good idea at the time.

"Or spearhead a political coup?" he asked Jin-shil.

"No!"

"Why not?"

"Coups are high-risk operations. If one went the wrong way, how would he get his light reaction company back? That would be very bad business—enough questions, Charlie. Unless you really want to talk business."

She moved closer, until she was standing beside his bed, pressing the mattress.

"Talking business still beats being stuck in bed while everyone else is at the party."

"Poor Charlie. You come so far and no one gives you a party."

He could see her thighs swelling against her skirt. She wore a musky perfume. And when she inclined her head, her glossy hair veiled her cheeks. Charlie was wondering if he was reading her signals right, or was she just cock-teasing him, when she began casually unbuttoning her blouse.

"There's a camera in the ceiling," he whispered.

The next button revealed her necklace, an exquisitely worked gold heron poised on the swell of her breasts as if about to spear its dinner. Two more buttons. She parted the cloth and raised her head. Her hair fell back and he saw an immensely strong light fill her eyes. "I unplugged the camera."

Charlie had a fleeting thought that the security system would record the time the camera went off-line and the duration of the breech. Who cared? He would deal with that later. He deserved this. Deserved Henry's wife. And his whole fucking island. Henry-boy, you're definitely right. It doesn't get better than this. A beautiful, bored wife right here in paradise.

Jin-shil watched him study her body. "I'm afraid that my breasts are smaller than you prefer."

"No," he said. They were not small, though it was clear to his practiced eye that no plastic surgeon or silicone artist had ever been near them. Still, he would have said anything to make this lovely woman his ally, for he was getting some wonderful ideas that went well beyond taking her to bed. Though that was certainly where they would start. But no lie was necessary and he added, in one of the most honest statements of his life, "Your breasts are perfect."

"But much smaller than that Tongan girl you had the other night."

He covered his surprise with a lazy smile. "*Who?*"

"The soldier's wife?"

"Did Henry tell you that?"

She shook her head. Her smile was serene. "I watched the security video."

Oh wonderful, he thought. A sensuous, elegant, intelligent pervert. His famous luck was back with a vengeance.

"You put on quite a performance for that simple girl. Must have ruined her for her husband...I wonder if you're ready for an upgrade?" She leaned closer to his mouth. Charlie raised his head and took the nipple she grazed against his lips.

He teased and kissed while she pressed harder and harder against the mattress. She was trembling before he reached between her legs to lift her onto the bed. She straddled him light as air. "Close your eyes," she whispered, trailing her fingers over his face. His whole body shuddered when she reached down to draw him inside her. The man without a country was coming home, he thought. Every feeling in his body spiraled into their connection.

"Wait for me?" she asked, rising and falling with slow deliberation.

"Impossible if you keep doing that."

"You opened your eyes. Please shut them."

"I want to look at your face. I want to watch you get close."

"Shut them, please?"

"Why?"

"It's easier for me."

He saw the strange light again and did as she asked. Good old Charlie, anything to please. Besides, she was absolutely right. The explosions they were heading toward were going to be tidal—why not ride toward them forever? This was the ultimate no-rush woman. Were Koreans into Zen? Who knew? The way she felt moving on him, they probably invented it.

"What kind of engineer are you, Jin-shil? Erection?"

"Shhhh."

"Demolition?"

"Geological."

"Earthquakes?"

"Volcanoes." She arched her back and leaned forward and touched a breast to his lips again. Her breathing grew quick, then harsh. Suddenly, out of the blue, she whispered, "Henry says you're a man who takes what he wants."

Charlie Page released her nipple to whisper back, "Yeah, well, it takes one to know one."

"And Henry knows you so well."

He opened his eyes, alerted by her tone. "What is that supposed to mean?"

"Close your eyes."

"How well?" he asked.

"Very well." Grinding softly against him, breath quickening until she whispered, "But not as well as me."

He opened his eyes again, and discovered that she had removed her necklace and unhinged the gold heron's legs and beak to form a slender needle-sharp blade that was plunging toward his eye at the speed of light.

TO HEAR AND see and know too late to act was the curse of a vengeful god. Thought flew ahead of motion, his brain a thousand beats quicker than his body. It was, he supposed, a punishment he deserved. But not the deeper curse, which was worse than death:

"Henry knows you so well" told him that Henry Ho Hong had beaten him again.

A hundred last thoughts, a thousand questions—his brain avalanching at supernatural speed even as his body stalled: a new angle on the blue sea, the green lagoon, the camouflaged power plant. What else was camouflaged? What was a weapon? Nothing Henry claimed was ever entirely true. No weapons on the island? *What was a weapon?* An airplane was a bomb; a necklace a stiletto. Were weapons hidden behind the machinery that was in turn screened by the dense grove of palm trees? For a nanosecond he thought he heard the palm leaves rattling in the trade wind. But that beach was too far away and what he heard, he knew, was his agonized explosion of breath as Jin-shil's blade pierced his bottle-green money eye.

Flayed nerves jolted muscles that swiveled his body away before her weapon slid into his brain. He screamed in agony. But driven by anger deeper than pain and hotter than loss, he reached for her wrist instead of his bloody eye.

THE CARIBBEAN HAD SETTLED DOWN the last couple of days. There was no need for wave spotters and the women were sleeping, leaving Aiden alone on night watch with his memories.

Once in a blue moon would come a private visit from Henry Ho Hong. A touch-baser, Henry called them. A hearty hello for Aiden. Maybe a catered lunch in the dining room—never in public. Then Henry and Charlie would disappear. Later, how's Henry doing?

Already left.

Until one time, just after everything started going to hell, when Charlie was in San Jose, trying to persuade Silicon Valley venture capitalists they had showered with money to give him a break. From that doomed enterprise, Charlie was scheduled to fly transpolar to London for a meeting Henry Hong had arranged with a German whose huge fortune seemed to be weathering the storm. Out of the blue, Henry himself suddenly appeared at the World Trade Center. Materialized, like a smiling Chinese ghost.

Aiden, I want you to do something for me.

It was a little out of his normal duties as the company's financial officer—more an M&A thing. Henry Hong was making a play for a privately held West Coast tug-and-barge company in trouble. Top secret, Henry told him. Tell no one. We have to move fast and quiet before anyone else finds out.

Halborson Towing of Portland, Oregon, was a third-generation family firm with aging boats, a fair-size truck fleet, valuable docks, and an even more valuable recently purchased parking space for a container depot. Borrowing heavily to build their container depot, the family had gotten overextended when the EPA ruled that the land was contaminated, Henry explained. Whoever bought up their bank loans could seize Halborson Towing for twenty cents on the dollar.

Henry ordered Aiden to create a corporate entity. As the numbers were relatively small, it wasn't a big deal, something he could pretty much set up in a week without interfering with his regular work. Then it got weird.

Henry said, "I remind you, this deal stays quiet."

"Sure, Henry."

"Discuss it with no one. Use outside lawyers."

"Don't worry, I'll tell no one but Charlie."

"No one. Not Charlie."

"Not Charlie?"

"Not Charlie. Not even Mary."

"Mary?"

"Mary Page . . . your brother's wife."

He could still feel the chill in his heart. "Excuse me, Henry. Why would I discuss anything with Mary Page?"

"I think you can answer that better than I."

It had felt a lot like a taxicab jumping the curb and throwing you through the window of Saks Fifth Avenue. There was Henry with his Chinese smile. And there was me, thought Aiden, mouth open wide as a garage door, eyes darting like two cornered rats.

"Understood?" asked Henry.

"How did you find out?" It was all he could think to ask.

He had been having an affair with his brother's gorgeous wife, right under Charlie's busy nose, and who finds out: a guy in Hong Kong? Go figure. But oh my God, it was the worst crime he had ever committed, betraying his brother. Not just his brother, but the man who paved his way into a beautiful life. He felt no guilt toward his own wife. Whatever he and Penny had, had died with the money and she was dumping him like the failure he was. But to betray Charlie . . . He still didn't know why he'd done it. Mary kept telling him it was just sex. Enjoy it. But if that were all, then there had to be some other sexy woman in New York City other than his brother's wife.

"It doesn't matter how I know," said Henry. "And he'll never hear it from me—as long as you honor our bargain."

"Swear you won't tell him!" He would have to kill himself if Charlie ever found out. Or if Morgan found out. Anyone else he could face. But neither of them.

"No need to swear," replied Henry. "We each hold a secret. No one must ever link my name with Halborson Towing. And your brother must never link your name with anyone who is—what's that Yiddish word?—shtupping—his wife." The way Henry said it, Aiden recalled, made it sound like he wasn't the only one. He almost smiled at the memory of a pang of jealousy. Almost, because that hurt, too.

But tonight, as he drove the ancient steel ketch through the Caribbean Sea under a million stars, another question he had wondered about started reverberating again. Why was Henry so bent on keeping the deal secret? It hadn't involved anything illegal or even unethical. Nothing that would provoke prosecutors, like bribing stock analysts to tout crappy offerings or trading on insider information. People bought up loans all the time.

Henry Hong had almost made a go of it with Halborson, and would have if it hadn't been for some awfully bad luck. Instead of looting the company, he had installed capable managers. The site was cleaned up, the container-transfer operation flourished, providing plenty of cargo for the truck fleet. They had begun expanding into trans-Pacific barge tows—until an accident nearly destroyed the entire enterprise, when a dynamite barge exploded, sending a brand-new oceangoing tugboat to the bottom and blowing the superstructure off a Japanese coast-guard cutter that had stopped the tow for a routine inspection.

So why the big secret?

That would be his second question when he finally got to Blind Man Island.

First question: Why did I get a letter from the U.S. attorney? And why did Charlie get one, too? Were we simply convenient targets in the busted-bubble blame game? Or were we more? Was the prosecutor's next step a plea-bargain threat? *The line to turn state's evidence forms here, Mr. Page. You want to be first on line. There is no second. A deal for testimony?*

Or to put it bluntly: What the hell was really going on at HHH & Company?

A question, Aiden Page was forced to admit, he might have asked years ago if he hadn't been having such a good time.

IT TOOK A LOT LONGER to get offshore than Wayne had predicted, and Morgan Page was three and a half days getting slapped around by wind shifts before she finally connected with the northeast trades. South and west she flew on a port reach—the wind blowing over the left side, the boat leaning to the right—with the full main pulling and the big genoa round and fat as a balloon.

Her weather handheld showed a steady barometer, lower than it had been during fitful winds, but not so low that it threatened storms. The grueling days of constant sail and course changes were over for a while and *Molly* sailed in such perfect balance that Morgan could have disengaged the self-steering and handed the tiller to Roscoe.

Now that the port reach caused the boat to heel to starboard, she shifted the extra boxes to the berth on the left side of the cabin—the new high side—and made her bed on the right. Roscoe resisted the change, until he discovered the pleasure of the cavelike back end of the starboard quarter berth, where the foot and leg space extended under the cockpit.

Morgan wondered where she had gotten the idea that the Pacific was a warm ocean. Running downwind wasn't as cold as it had been beating into it, but crossing 29 North—a line of latitude that paralleled the desert stretches of Mexico's Baja Peninsula—she was still wearing a thick fleece under a heavy foul-weather jacket and her father's triple-knit watch cap.

She knew she should take advantage of the easier sailing to install the solar electric panel to power the weather fax. Her Internet printout was five days old; the weather it displayed had moved onshore and halfway to New York by now, while her barometer and the state of the sky predicted only a day or two ahead. But she was nervous about screwing up the solar panel. She caught some sleep instead. Still putting it off, she pulled up the floorboards to clean the awful-smelling bilge. But when she went to mix up baking soda and vinegar, she discovered she had no bucket.

Of all the stupid—how could she even bail if the bilge pump broke? You had to have a bucket; it was a coast-guard rule. Grandpa's stupid neighbors had probably planted petunias in it.

The boat had had a single medium-size cook pot in which she had boiled pasta, and as she started to lean over the side to fill it, it occurred to her that the rushing water might rip it out of her hands.

She bent a safety line through one of the handles, but they didn't look very strong, so she held on with both hands when she bent over the wooden rim of the cockpit to dip the pot. It filled instantly, and the weight of the water and the force of the boat's momentum jerked her hard against the cockpit and sent shooting pain through her ribs.

She almost dropped it, but hung on for dear life, wondering how she would cook pasta without it. When she got it aboard, she hunched over, saying, "Ow, ow, ow," until the sharpest pain ceased. She could not afford to lose that pot, ever. Nor, she realized with a chill, could she afford to get hurt. Ever.

She had discovered a ripped sail in the forepeak, which the original owner must have kept for patches. She pulled it up to the cockpit with scissors and sewing kit, cut a circle and a rectangle, and sewed them together forming a cloth bucket. Hemming the top over a ring of stiff rope for strength, she fastened another piece of rope for a handle, bent a line around it, and tossed it over the side. It filled and she pulled it aboard, feeling proud. Even though the soft top collapsed, it held several quarts. She carried it below and dumped it into the bilge, sloshed in some vinegar, and scrubbed at the slime. When she pumped out the wash water and did several rinses, the boat smelled good, though a little like a pickle. The electric bilge pump began groaning as it ran down the battery, a stern reminder that she had to tackle the solar panel.

Once she got it laid out in the cockpit, mounting it turned out to be simpler than she had feared. Hinged plastic mounts clamped around the stern rail, making it easy to swivel to the best angle toward the sun, or remove it completely to stow belowdecks in heavy weather. The tricky part was not dropping the blue glass panel overboard while attaching it to the brackets; she wrapped it in a line, which she tied to the backstay just to be on the safe side.

The hardest part was running its cable down to the battery in the cabin. She absolutely refused to drill any holes in her deck, so she led the wire along the cockpit coaming and through the main hatch, duct-taping it all the way so she wouldn't trip on it. Connecting to the electronics panel was a piece of cake compared to her last electrical experience: wiring up a resistance-sensitive superconductor in physics class with copper leads and silver electrical paint; here, some wire nuts and tape did the job.

Then all of a sudden she was back in the twenty-first century, or at least on the edge of it. The shortwave receiver began whistling static. Tuning it could wait; she turned eagerly to the weather fax.

The first page rolling out of the machine freaked Roscoe, who got double-freaked when, in her excitement, she squeezed him too hard. She pored over the printed weather chart, absolutely delighted. Now she had a week-wide window on the weather coming her way. A depression would pass well to the north. Another, drifting across her intended path, could be avoided by altering course a little farther west, where, the chart showed, the trade wind might even blow harder.

"Boat Cat, we are rocking!"

There was something super-liberating about being able to study the one single area of the vast ocean that applied specifically to her. More charts unreeled: sea states, water and air temperatures, barometric pressure, and winds. Studying them, while boning up on the weather section in her Pacific cruising guide, she realized she had to hurry out of this sector of the eastern North Pacific and get to 140 West and 10 North before the hurricane season cycled up in May. May and June brought hurricanes powerful enough to sink ships, not to mention twenty-seven-foot boats.

ENRY HO HONG RETURNED FROM a tour of the hill farms that his water treatment plant irrigated to find his wife huddled in a silk robe in their airy bedroom suite. The windows were open to the soft wind and champagne was chilling in a gold bucket, but he could not help but notice that she looked less content than distracted.

"Where," she asked, "is our honorable guest?"

"In the arms of many Hong Kong girls. Did you enjoy yourself this morning?"

"Very much."

"How would you like to celebrate?"

"Could we watch the video?"

Henry laughed. "Happy is the voyeur whose beautiful wife is an exhibitionist. Particularly if he's not the jealous type."

"I lied to him. I told him I unplugged the camera."

"I think that falls in the category of a little white lie," said Henry Ho Hong. Jin-shil had led him to believe that she had been raised by strict Christian nannies, which he assumed explained why she took the strangest things seriously.

"I should be punished."

"Whenever you want, dear. Just say the word. But wouldn't you rather watch the video first?"

"Video first," she said, to his relief. Perhaps he loved her too much, but he was not the ideal husband for an erotic masochist.

She touched the switch that caused an enormous high-def screen to rise from a marble plinth, and patted the bed beside her. The ceiling camera had recorded sound as well as image. Henry Hong laughed out loud when he heard her tell poor Charlie Page that she had arrived by shipwreck.

"You neglected to tell him that it was you who wrecked the ship."

"Shhh. It's coming." She pressed her fingers to his lips.

All hands had drowned, including her husband, a brilliant seismologist with a vicious streak who—Henry Hong imagined—had failed to perceive the subtleties underlying her tastes in abuse.

Suddenly Henry Hong leaped to his feet. He gaped at the screen in horrified disbelief. "You killed him!"

"Look."

Hong couldn't believe what he saw on the screen. Blood was gushing from Charlie's eye. Yet he seized Jin-shil's wrist, twisting the knife from her, sprang to his knees, and backhanded her with a blow that sent her flying out of camera range. Then, breathing hoarsely, he staggered out of sight, leaving the camera's dead eye to linger on the bloody bed.

"Where is he?"

Jin-shil flashed on Charlie's eye. Green light. Red light. "He ran."

Hong snatched up a phone. "He can't have gone far in that condition. He must be on the grounds."

"I already have the Gurkhas looking. I told them he attacked me."

"But why? Why did you do it?"

"For you."

"For *me*?"

"I heard him threaten you. He thinks you betrayed him."

"I didn't betray him. I don't know who betrayed him."

"He could destroy our life together."

"I didn't—did you plan this? I mean, I thought you wanted to amuse yourself screwing him." He stared at her, stunned. Charlie Page was hardly the first houseguest whom Jin-shil seduced into performing unwittingly for the hidden camera. But it was a game. Not violence. Not murder. "But—"

"I'm sure the Gurkhas will catch him."

Henry Hong sobered rapidly as he calculated the threat. "They damned well better. He's one dangerous son of a bitch." He radioed the captain of his guard and stepped out on the veranda to receive his report.

The Gurkhas hadn't found Charlie yet. By now they knew he was not on the palace grounds or in any of the buildings. The captain feared he had either fled into the nearly impenetrable interior of the island or made his way off on a boat. Discreet as he was loyal, the captain had already made the wise decision to keep it in the family and leave the Tongans out of it.

"How the devil did he get off the grounds? He's bleeding to death."

"He might have had help."

"Who?"

"The Tongan woman's gone, too."

"Bloody, bloody hell."

The Gurkha, who had served the British in Hong Kong as a young soldier, knew the difference between an officer swearing at him and one who was swearing at a situation. "Quite, sir."

Henry Hong went back inside. He still could hardly believe what he had seen with his own eyes.

Jin-shil was sprawled where he had left her, like a cat digesting. "I would like something to drink," she said.

He busied himself opening the Bollinger that was chilling in the gold bucket. They had moved into new territory and he was glad to have a simple task to concentrate on. He removed foil and muzzle and popped the cork in the quiet way he had been taught by an English butler he had hired years ago to teach him better manners than those of ordinary men. Even slick Charlie didn't know how to open champagne properly. Still trembling, he carried the glasses to his wife. But when she thanked him warmly, and pressed against him, his hard round face brightened. Of all his riches and all his good fortune, nothing equaled her.

He raised his glass. He wanted to say something that would demonstrate that what happened with Charlie would never stand between them. He wanted to assure her that he, too, had always flourished in a corrupt world that crushed the good and rewarded evil. And that if there was any difference at all between them, it was merely that he had had to learn detachment, while to her it seemed to come naturally.

He directed her attention to the twin hills that topped Blind Man Island, their lower slopes crisp and green in the clear air of an April autumn, their pinnacles bare as polished steel. "Like two mountains," he started to say, when he felt her pager vibrate through the taut flesh of her hip.

"I am so sorry, dear," she said. "I've been expecting this call. I must take it. I'll be quick."

She selected one of several satellite phones from a drawer in her night table, took it to her chaise longue, and beckoned him to sit where he could stroke her foot.

Her caller spoke Korean, which Henry did not understand beyond the sex phrases she had taught him. She nodded reassuringly at him and pressed her foot harder into his hand.

To her caller she said, "Go ahead."

"Sorry to bother you, Comrade."

The Workers' Party Operations Department's senior agent in New York owned a Garment District *kal bi* restaurant, Sam's, which provided "Sam" with an American-sounding nickname along with deep cover in the city's prosperous and respectably Christian Korean business community. The ranks of the private investigative firm he kept on retainer had been vastly strengthened since 9/11 by early retirements of elite NYPD detectives and there was little they could not learn quickly.

Jin-shil had trusted the man with an emergency number known to few. She did not, however, reveal more information than was necessary. Standard operating procedure, even before the Arabs goaded the West to tighten security. And this particular agent had been too long in New York City to remain ideologically untainted. Thus, when Charlie Page had washed ashore last month, she had ordered him to investigate *both* the Page brothers, even though she had Charlie right here in her sights. Nonetheless, they had in common years of living in the American city—Sam was raising a family in an upscale New Jersey suburb—and thus they conversed in a colloquialism-laced expatriate New Yor-korean that would have drawn blank stares back home in P'yŏngyang.

"What's up?" she asked, arching her foot against Henry's soft hand.

"Nothing new on Brother Number One. Dead for sure. But it is just possible that Number Two Brother got out before the buildings fell down."

Jin-shil's face closed flat as a block of ice. But she couldn't fool Henry. His hand stiffened on her foot and he looked at her with concern. She formed a smile and shook her head. When he still looked worried, she reached down and placed his hand higher up her leg.

"What do you know?"

"His daughter stole a boat."

"So what?"

"My detective and I both wondered why a fifteen-year-old honor student from a comfortable family with no history of drugs—or any of the ways kids go wrong here—would steal a sailboat in California. Right out of her grandfather's backyard."

Jin-shil interrupted coldly: "May I continue to assume that their top detective handles this entire affair himself?"

"What are you hocking me for? I told you he would."

"Go on."

"Apparently the kid equipped the boat for a long voyage. This was no prank. My guy called me with a very strange thought. Why does a New York kid steal a boat in California?"

"And?"

"What if she's looking for Daddy?" Sam asked.

"That's quite a leap of thought."

"Until her grandfather leveled with him. It turns out she told Grandpa that her dead daddy telephoned."

"*When?*"

"That's all the old man knew. Grandpa figured she was dreaming.

The kid's had problems since the attack. They sent her to a shrink—a psychiatrist."

"I know what a shrink is. I was four years at Columbia, for Christ sake." Three, to be strictly accurate: freshman, huddled in a dorm room as frightening as any orphanage administered by Christians in Seoul or the Operations Department in P'yŏngyang; sophomore, spiraling into psychosis while learning to smile when smiles were expected; junior year, abroad, alternating between Switzerland's Institut für Geologie and private hospitals, where science and drugs honed a knife edge onto her memory of a childhood gang rape by American occupation soldiers; senior year, back at Columbia, honors, the destruction of several tenured marriages, and a voracious mastery of a downtown nightlife no one ever found in *Time Out* or *Zagat.*

"Sorry, Comrade," he replied, sounding not at all sorry. "It's been a while since we've had any face time," he added, so dryly—"Comrade" so ringing of irony—that Jin-shil was tempted to recommend to Operations that Sam suffer a fatal car-jacking the next time he cruised the transvestites at the Lincoln Tunnel. But with a coup by the faithful against the excesses of Chairman Kim brewing in the Democratic People's Republic of Korea—and progress under way in the reabsorption of South Korea into the North—Jin-shil chose not to destabilize the DPRK's New York cells.

"Go on."

"I told my guy to brace the shrink. He tried every trick in the book. But the doctor wouldn't talk. So I called a buddy of mine who can get into telephone records on the q.t. It turns out the phone at the kid's mother's apartment registered a three-second international cell-phone call from the French side of St. Martin. That's an island in the Caribbean. I flew down there—myself—spread some green around, and triangulated the call to a marina. I heard about a guy who might have been Page working as a charter captain. Which fits his background—all this sailboat stuff."

"Where is he?"

"Before I got there, a man who might have been him sailed

away with a couple of old ladies who might be headed for Australia."

"You are linking a long chain of mights."

"Understood," replied the intelligence officer, with no apology.

"What else?"

"If it is Aiden Page and if they are sailing to Australia, I'm told they'll probably go through the Panama Canal. Sometime next week . . . They tell me it's easier than sailing around South America. Is it possible that the guy is heading your way?"

"I have no idea," Jin-shil lied.

"I'm wondering if the little girl might think he was headed your way? From California, she could sail in your direction."

"My husband and I inhabit a speck of land six thousand miles from California in the middle of the biggest ocean in the world." All true, if somewhat disingenuous. One in a million people could locate the Tongan archipelago on a map. One in a hundred million Blind Man Island. And of those millions, how many would notice that almost nothing blocked those six thousand miles of ocean between his island and California? In theory the little girl could sail here almost directly without ever touching land.

She said, "Thank you, Comrade," and switched off the phone.

A curious child. The Tongans still talked about her from when she had come with the company party. The pale, small *pälangi* girl who won the canoe race. The other whites had never sailed the island canoes until the day of the race. But Morgan Page had made friends with the soldiers' children and had sailed on the lagoon every day.

"What is going on?" Henry asked.

Jin-shil related a bare minimum of what she had learned.

The most obvious and valuable spy craft they had taught her in P'yŏngyang—and vivid proof that the thirty-eighth parallel was a temporary border imposed by the West—was that no outsider could distinguish between a beautiful woman from South Korea or North Korea. Henry had no reason to question that her source of information was a supposed childhood friend who was now a top agent of the

South Korean Intelligence Service. Nor reason to doubt that she herself was the daughter of a wealthy, reclusive South Korean industrialist, instead of an orphan.

Henry even accepted her claim that her father's fellow magnates were willing to be silent, nonvoting investors in her resort project in exchange for total secrecy to protect them from the tax man. Why shouldn't he believe her? The peoples of North and South Korea were divided by a political border, not by ethnicity. And the money was real, only the source was bogus: Workers' Party Operations Department instead of South Korean *chaebol* hiding skimmed profits. But he did protest when she said, "I'm going to Panama."

"I'd rather keep you here."

"Don't be silly," she said sharply.

"You think he's heading here, anyway. Why don't we just wait for him?"

"We can't risk waiting. If Aiden Page is still alive, he is dangerous. If he's stopped at a border. If he's caught up in a security sweep. If he's ever arrested, he will talk."

"He can talk till he's blue in the face. I am nearly divested of HHH and Company. I will soon be home free."

You may think you're safe, she thought, racking her brain for the means to convince him that Aiden could wreck everything. But how, without revealing the true nature of her "resort project" on Blind Man Island's windward coast?

"You were as relieved as I when we thought that Al Qaeda had got rid of them," she reminded Henry, trying to steer him back toward the U.S. attorney threat.

"A stroke of luck."

But the luck had been all Charlie and Aiden's, thought Jin-shil, who had gambled and lost.

The risk had seemed small, when she first tipped off the United States attorney about the brothers Page. Betraying the Pages had required no approval from her handlers in P'yŏngyang. Whereas ordering the New York cell to murder them would have.

She had sent the prosecutor tantalizing hints of bribed stock analysts and rigged initial public offerings that she had gleaned from Henry's laptop. Nothing that could hurt Henry. He was safe in Hong Kong and Blind Man Island and had started divesting anyhow. All she had intended was to frighten the brothers into fleeing to Blind Man Island, where Henry had always promised safe refuge, and where she could neutralize them until her project was complete.

Then everything that could go wrong went wrong, thanks to the fucking Arabs. Now, of course, she wished she *had* killed them. It had always been an option if "plan A" didn't work. Instead, the Arabs did the job for her. An unexpected, unwitting gift from the jihad. Or so it had seemed until Charlie Page swam ashore.

"You were as appalled as I when Charlie Page showed up alive," she reminded her husband.

Henry displayed a rare expression of temper. "Not as appalled as I am now that he's lurching around out there like a wounded tiger."

"Now who's worrying too much? We live on an island. How long can he hide on an island?"

"Japanese soldiers hid on islands like this for the entire length of World War Two and ten years after. Bloody hell, Charlie's been a soldier."

"Our Gurkhas are *still* soldiers," Jin-shil said calmly. "The problem is *Aiden*. If he babbles to a prosecutor, who knows what they'll turn up? What if the U.S. government gets the idea that you sold arms to terrorists? That's the sort of thing they're concentrating on now. It's a different world since 9/11, darling, and we could lose everything."

To her relief, Henry finally looked troubled. "Who knows every end user I sold to? I certainly don't."

"That's my fear. You are vulnerable even if they only want to make headlines. Aiden would let them put words in his mouth. Wouldn't it be ironic—and so sad—that just as my resort makes it possible for you to retire from the arms trade, Aiden should betray you to the prosecutors?"

Henry shook his head. "Why, every time I find a home, does something attack?"

"Let me go to Panama."

"No. I have clients at the Panama Canal. Customers and suppliers. They will be happy to serve. And I will be happy to keep you here."

Jin-shil thought furiously. It was not usually difficult to keep her husband in the dark. Henry Hong was no fool, but he was deeply preoccupied with his strategic shift out of Wall Street and, eventually, the arms trade into the offshore banks that were expanding his influence across Polynesia.

What Jin-shil had led him to believe was the initial stage of a typically slow-moving South Pacific resort project on the other side of Blind Man Island was actually almost finished. And barely in time. Events were accelerating in P'yŏngyang and Washington eight months after the Arab attack, five months after the United States routed the Taliban, and four months after the Americans declared Iraq and North Korea their enemies. Among the faithful—the core of true believers in a united Korea—it was agreed that America would attack Iraq first. Simply because Iraq was the easier target. For the time being, North Korea could try to protect herself with ten thousand artillery pieces dug in at the border.

These cannon were aimed and primed to fire in seconds at Seoul and the thirty thousand American troops still occupying South Korea. But it would be a brief respite. As soon as the Americans overwhelmed Iraq, they would turn their might on the PRNK.

At which point, Jin-shil was sure, they would move their troops out of artillery range and leave the citizens of Seoul to their fate.

North Korea's only hope was nuclear weapons. But to develop enough weapons to defend herself, the PRNK needed time to process enough fissionable material. Time that could be bought only by some new way of deterring the United States. Gaining that time and that deterrent shield was Jin-shil's goal—her gift to her country for all the gifts it had given her. Before the Americans maneuvered their soldiers out of range of North Korean cannon, she would arm her country with a bigger "cannon." Aimed at densely populated port cities that even God could not move out of range

Charlie Page could no longer stop her. But Aiden Page, whether he knew it yet or not, had the power to destroy.

"I will not rest easy until they mail us his head."

Henry smiled. "I was thinking more along the lines of having him brought here, alive."

Jin-shil smiled back and pressed her heel into his hand. "Grant me one favor."

"Anything," he said. "So long as you stay with me."

"I will. But may I please use my contacts in Panama?"

He eyed her curiously. "I wasn't aware you had contacts in Panama."

"Friends of friends," she answered casually.

"Professionals?"

"Professional enough to help me track down a handsome arms dealer to share my life."

Henry opened his face in an expression of mock astonishment. "Was that how your ship happened to sink off my island?"

"Surely you're not surprised."

"At this point, nothing you would do could surprise me," Henry replied. He still spoke with affection, but he qualified it with a cold reminder that he was not to be trifled with. She could build her harbor and her resort without interference. She could dupe her lovers and flaunt her videos. He would even oblige when she demanded her punishments, though his heart was not in them. All that was a game. But in matters that Henry Ho Hong deemed within his own sphere—the business of arms and the manipulation of Tonga's elite to establish a secure home for the first time in his life—he was boss. "Therefore, let me make it perfectly clear: if they find Aiden, I want him brought here, alive."

"They will find Aiden," was all she would promise. "He cannot hide."

THE OCEAN SEEMED BIGGER AND wider and emptier with every mile in *Molly*'s wake. The sky grew immense, infinitely blue on clear days, white with stars on clear nights, deathly black when there were clouds. Sometimes when Morgan Page thought that it wasn't possible for a boat to be so small or space so large, she retreated into the tiny, jam-packed cabin, which felt as snug as the backseat of her parents' car used to feel when they drove to Vermont.

The seas were growing bigger, too, and a little scary. Clear of the land, they rolled with forceful symmetry. The troughs between the crests got wider and wider, the evenly spaced, round crests taller, until *Molly P 2* seemed more a mountain goat than a twenty-seven-foot sailboat climbing long slopes and descending into deep valleys. Sometimes the waves were spaced so far apart that for long minutes in the troughs all Morgan could see were the tops of the seas ahead and behind.

Then, up out of this watery prison *Molly* would take her, lifted by an overtaking sea, thrust into the sky, and held for a panorama of horizons so far that she thought she could see to Hawaii. Except Hawaii was not ahead of *Molly*. Hawaii was 1,500 miles to her right, west, off the starboard beam. While she and *Molly* and Roscoe were angling southwest on a 6,000-mile diagonal toward Tonga.

Morgan settled into a routine of watching for ships, preventing lines and sails from chafing, cooking one serious meal a day and snacking in between, and tending the sails. It left too much time to think. And a person could really feel stupid thinking about some of the stuff she was thinking about.

Where was I, she wondered, what was I doing while my parents were getting angry enough to divorce each other? Where was I? The first fight she overheard had shocked her. They had never shouted—like some of her friends' parents did—and all of a sudden they were yelling at the top of their lungs. It suddenly dawned on her that on the trip to Blind Man Island they hadn't started yelling yet, but that even then she knew something was wrong. That's why I went sailing with the Tongan kids. I had to get away. Nobody even noticed when her friend Paea took her offshore all day, sailing halfway around the island in a canoe.

I'm getting depressed, she thought. The boat was a mess, clothes and gear and food everywhere. All her bread was covered with blue mold. Her mother always said every boat was an autobiography.

Why am I thinking about her, of all people? She tried to tap memories of her father instead. She opened the *Times* "Portrait" and studied his picture. But with Uncle Charlie hogging the camera, the photo didn't show how handsome he looked dashing along on his long legs.

Depressed, and lonely. She would not see another face until Blind Man Island. Six thousand miles. Twice the distance of New York to Europe. On a direct course that would traverse nothing but salt water, crossing the equator at 140 West—hoping to shorten the distance through the doldrums' dead calms and thunder squalls—then angling southwest to 17 South, where she would make her westing, downwind, to Blind Man Island. No one along the way to ask questions. No customs officials demanding boat registration and quarantine cards and passport and port clearances.

She went below to warm up, after taking a careful look around while the boat perched on a crest. "Hey, cat, how you doing?"

Roscoe was not at all depressed. In fact, he seemed so happy that she guessed he had forgotten land. In high-cuteness mode, he stretched, raised his head to be patted. "Hello, little lion." He watched intently as she knelt on the cabin sole beside her rumpled mattress. She had forgotten blankets. She had found one musty beach blanket in the boat, but she slept in her clothes and, when it got really cold, in her foul-weather gear, too.

She smoothed the berth and spread out the western North Pacific chart she had inherited from her father, and the crisp new South Pacific sheets she had bought at New York Nautical, and penciled in her latest GPS fix. On the small scale chart it looked like nothing had changed. She was still very close to California, high above the equator, and far, far away from the South Pacific and the ink dots that represented Tonga.

If she turned around this very minute, she could be home in New York in less than two weeks. It was easy to imagine the sequence that would follow. The neighbors' boat returned safe and sound; no damage done, even improved with a beautifully lettered new name and a self-steering Monitor. Chris's parents probably wouldn't even press charges. If they did, her mother would hire one of Daddy's lawyers. They would coach her to act like the little-girl-orphaned-by-terrorists and send her back to the shrink. At worst— after everyone got done screaming and crying—the school would put her on probation.

But what if her father really, truly was out there, somewhere? So lonely, so confused, that when he telephoned her he couldn't talk. He would have been injured when the buildings fell. He could have some kind of amnesia. And forgotten everything, except her. He had remembered her. Why did he hang up? What if he were a lot more confused than she was? Maybe the sound of her voice had frightened him. If she wouldn't help him, who would?

For courage, she focused on the girl sailors whom she had always tracked on the Web: Tracy Edwards, who led *Maiden* in the Whitbread Round the World Race with the first-ever female crew; Tania Aebi; Linda Greenlaw, the fisherwoman bossing a crew of men; Allison Jolly, Olympic sailing gold medalist; Emma Richards, Isabelle Autissier; and her two faves, Ellen and Martha, who were both five feet two inches tall, a half inch shorter than she was. "Can't say 'Chill out' when you're tired," Ellen MacArthur wrote in her Web site.

None of them would turn around. If I ever met them, she thought, I couldn't look them in the eye—or would they give me a look? Like, *What are you, wack? You're not a rock-star sailor. Give your mom a break. Go home, finish school. Let your poor father rest in peace.*

Would Ellen really say, *Full on! Go for it!*

Wouldn't Martha McKechnie say *Be smart . . . ?*

Morgan looked around the cabin. It was really a pigsty. "My boat looked after me well and I've looked after her," Ellen wrote in another Web mail. "I haven't been lonely at all."

Yeah, well, maybe that's what's bugging me. Maybe I should treat *Molly* better.

She put junk away, rearranged food and water, threw the blue bread overboard, and scrubbed the sink, the head, and the cabin floor. While straightening up tools, she discovered a length of Velcro, which gave her a bright idea. She measured off a piece, glued the prickly side to her "hockey puck" bearing compass and the fuzzy side to the ceiling over her berth. Now she could find it in a flash when she needed to take a bearing. On what? A million miles from nowhere . . .

At least, whenever she awakened, she could see instantly whether *Molly* was on course. She lay on her berth, listening to the water clatter past the hull, watching the compass needle drift. A few degrees port, a few degrees starboard, as the self-steering negotiated the constantly shifting wind and waves. And what would Tania Aebi say? *Practice navigating with your sextant,* is what she would say. *Don't count on electronics.* But she had sailed a long time ago. Tania didn't even have GPS. Just an old-fashioned sat-nav. Which reminded her. She had already connected her battery chargers to the electric panel to keep her GPSs and laptop alive. Now she added the handheld VHF radio charger, just in case by some miracle she ever saw a ship or another boat out here in the middle of nowhere.

She wished she had a long-range radio. A powerful single-sideband transmitter. And while I'm dreaming, a generator to power the transmitter. Whom would she radio? she asked herself. Daddy, of course. He might be on a boat, like me, still on his way to Blind Man

Island. What would I say to him? Funny thought, Daddy. The first thing that popped in my head.

Remember the letter? Of course you remember the letter. Mr. Organized Accountant was so freaked he couldn't get organized and I had to do it for you. You said it wasn't important. You said they were just playing the blame game. So many investors lost their money, so somebody had to get blamed. Your hands were shaking.

But we ended up having fun that night, didn't we? Eating a Windows on the World dinner at your desk like it was room service in a fancy hotel. She hadn't expected fun when he got so upset that she saw the letter, but he got over that, and they had a good time working together on his files.

In the Town Car when he took her home, he even said, "Hey, this was good practice for the Bermuda Race. We'll be a great crew under pressure . . . One way or another, honey, we'll sail that race. I promise."

Six hundred miles from Newport to Bermuda in four or five days didn't seem like that big a deal now. But that night she had clung to his promise and let herself hope that everything would work out and he could buy the *Molly P* back. Even though she had said to him, "Don't worry about it. We'll have other fun." Then a funny thought had struck her and she had asked, "Dad, why would the U.S. attorney think you did something bad if you're broke?"

"What do you mean?"

"I mean, if you did something bad, where is your stolen money?"

Dad had laughed and laughed. "I'm going to call up and ask them that in the morning."

She knew of course that it couldn't be that simple, but it did seem kind of odd, and she thought maybe he thought so, too. Why investigate some poor man who had lost everything? Why not investigate somebody who had come out of the stock-market crash rich? Like Mr. Hong?

Do you have a radio, Dad?

If I had a radio, could I just broadcast, *Calling Dad, calling Dad?* Somewhere in the South Pacific. Could you answer? Would you answer?

BOOK THREE

PANAMA

MAY 2002

"A IDEN, ARE YOU BY ANY chance gay?"

"No, Gert."

"Well, don't look now, but there's a fellow at the bar can't take his eyes off you."

They had made it to Colón, a poverty-stricken port city on the eastern terminus of the Panama Canal. The boat was anchored on the flats. Oppressive heat and the frequent rain showers that forced them to shut the hatches made it like trying to sleep in a sauna. So like most boat people waiting to transit the Canal, they spent the nights holed up in a loud, smoky, slightly-less-hot marina bar.

Tonight they were celebrating the victorious end to a full week of wrangling with Canal Authority bureaucrats. Tomorrow they were on their way. Paperwork in order, *Darling*'s tonnage measured, her transit fees paid, ship ID number issued, and pilot booked. They even had their crucial line handlers ready to help them work the boat through the locks in the morning—three husky Panamanian deacons lent by a priest Gert and Sophie knew from their days of dodging paramilitary death squads in Colombia.

"Maybe he's after one of you. Or both."

"No, it's you he fancies, dear. He's too young and fit for us—my Lord, he is fit—and quite handsome, too."

"Yeah, well, he's in for a disappointment," Aiden said casually, though he wasn't feeling casual at all. They were teasing him about a gay pickup, but he was worried that somebody he knew was staring through the smoke thinking, Should I get up, walk to their table, and ask, *Aiden Page? Didn't you die in the World Trade Center?*

"Go on, Aiden, take a squizz."

He swigged beer from the bottle to mask a "squizz" at the bar.

The guy wasn't exactly staring, although a second glance revealed that he was watching their table. But Aiden didn't know him. Nor had the old girls called it correctly.

"You two have warped sex on the brain. He's not gay. He's with a good-looking girl."

"The Sheila just arrived," said Sophie, who was facing the door. "Before she walked in, he was eyeing you like a chocolate."

"I wish *she'd* eye me like chocolate." He looked again, wondering if she had the face to go with the killer body. She turned his way and his heart nearly stopped.

"You've gone white as a sheet," said Sophie. "What's wrong?"

She looked exactly like Charlie's wife—his lover, Mary. She made eye contact and smiled. It wasn't Mary. She just looked like her. He still had Mary on the brain. He returned her smile and told Soph and Gert, "That is one terrific-looking woman."

"Don't let us stop you. Just get back by morning."

And Gert said, "Soph's right, Aiden. It's going to be a long, lonely haul across the Pacific. You might as well grab something while you can."

"It's okay, girls. I'm doing fine. Besides, she's with a guy."

Gert shook her head firmly. "Trust me, Aiden. They are not a couple."

Sophie said, "Why don't I go get another round and invite them over?"

"No."

She was already on her feet, ignoring his protest. "Same for everyone," she asked, and toddled toward the bar.

"I don't believe she's doing this," Aiden said to Gert.

"Sophie's fond of you, Aiden. She wants you to set sail with happy memories."

"You two are impossible."

"It's good to see you smile, Aiden. You came aboard an unhappy man. By the time we drop you in Fiji, we'll have you laughing out loud—oh, here she comes. That was quick. I guess the young lady didn't need much encouragement."

"I hope she didn't encourage the guy, too."

Gert reached out and patted his hand. "Not to worry, Aiden. Sophie knows which team you play for."

Unlike the boat folk killing time in the joint, the couple was wearing clean, stylish clothing—tailored jeans and a silk cowboy shirt for the guy; tight, leather hip huggers and a silk midriff-baring handkerchief-size top for the woman. Based on their outfits and expensive jewelry, and the fact that both appeared to have showered recently, Aiden pegged them for upscale types transiting in a luxurious motor trawler or a crewed sailing yacht. They were obviously American and Gert's guess that they weren't a couple panned out when the woman, Jerry, shook hands with Aiden and introduced the man as her brother Joe.

Jerry still reminded Aiden a lot of Charlie's wife—similarly coiffed blond hair, long and swept back from her brow, ice-blue eyes, legs to the moon—which made him very glad that Joe was a brother instead of a husband. Maybe she didn't look that much like Mary, but both were of a type that turned him on. He wondered where to take her when he got her out of here. That she would come with him appeared a foregone conclusion. She was sending broadband signals with her eyes, her smile, and the occasional light touch with her red fingernails.

They talked about the awful weather and how the city of Colón was so dangerous that the duty-free stores had guards with machine guns. Jerry and her brother were cruising to the Galápagos. From one ear Aiden heard Gert and Sophie engage Joe in a lively debate about the advantages of a ketch rig over a sloop. Joe, who owned a Baltic 70, was a loyal sloop man, but conceded that a single big sail took a lot of muscle.

"What do you call her?" asked Gert.

Jerry leaned across, pressing against Aiden. *"Baltic Nights."*

"Oh, I like that," said Gert, and Sophie asked, "What does it mean?"

"I don't know, I love the sound. Joe kind of liked it, too."

"Easy to remember," said Joe. "Same as the builder."

"The C?" asked Aiden, expecting that Joe and Jerry would have sprung for the comforts of the "Classic" luxury-version Baltic 70.

"No," said Joe. "We've got the racing machine."

"How many crew?"

"Eight Malaysians."

"Wonderful sailors," cried Sophie.

Joe smiled. "I get the impression they had plenty of practice as pirates."

Aiden felt Jerry's knee touch his under the table. She leaned close to his ear and mock-whispered, "Your place or mine?" Shades of high school, when he had found it easier to find girls than somewhere to take them.

"I don't have a place."

"You'll like mine . . . Joe?" She touched her brother's arm. "Aiden and I are starving. We're going to get a bite. Anybody hungry?"

"No," said Gert. "We are not."

Joe hesitated. He looked at his watch. "Naw, I'll have the cook make me something later. See you back at the boat. Nice to meet you, buddy—Aiden."

Outside in the loud, dirty street lit by the glare of neon signs, Aiden said, "I haven't been aboard a Baltic in years. Beautiful boat."

"You can see it if you insist. But I'm staying at the casino."

"I don't feel like gambling."

"Don't you like taking chances?"

"Not on my last night ashore."

They took a cab through the ramshackle city to a parklike section that was near the water and planted with tall palm trees. The casino was past a big church, down a long driveway in a three-story hotel. Rows of arches on the ground floor and tall windows above gave the impression of a combination Moorish castle, federal courthouse, and unusually stylish yacht club. Guests were drinking at tables in an outdoor café in the front entry yard—an open-air lobby protected from the rain showers by a striped awning.

Inside, the main lobby was packed with middle-aged gamblers wearing tropical shirts and gold jewelry. Most were accompanied by attractive younger women and many were trailed by bodyguards. Jerry led him up a marble staircase to a fair-sized suite on the second floor.

"Nice place."

The living room had a grand piano. French windows, closed to preserve the air-conditioning, led to a balcony.

She gave him another welcoming slow grin. "Sure you don't want to go downstairs and gamble?"

"Positive."

"Said like a man looking for a sure thing."

Aiden stepped close. She even smelled like Mary. "I'm looking for a memorable good-bye."

"How memorable?"

"Something that will last on a slow boat across the Pacific."

Jerry nodded thoughtfully. "That's the way I'd like to be remembered." She kissed his mouth and trailed fingers down his spine. "Stay here. Let me change." She stepped into the bedroom and closed the door.

Not only did she smell like Mary, she even kissed like Mary . . .

But why, he wondered, was he suddenly anxious? The kiss. It was Mary's good-bye kiss, when one of them had to get home and there wasn't time for another round.

Aiden stood there a moment, wondering. Jerry was a nice little dream interlude come true. Except . . . maybe I'm paranoid, but I've seen this movie. Girl brings drunk to hotel room, where her friends roll him for his wallet and watch. But where was the profit in robbing a scruffy boat guy? The hotel room cost more than he was carrying.

He walked quickly to the French windows and flung them open. No muggers on the balcony. He leaned on the balustrade and looked down. Laughter rose from the outdoor café. Shadows played on its awning. Maybe he just got lucky.

He went back into the suite. On the polished sill under the front door, a reflection moved. A hotel guest? Room service trundling by? Behind him, Jerry stepped out of the bedroom. Aiden was not entirely surprised to see her still fully clothed, and leading two heavy young guys in muscle shirts.

Serves me right, he thought. A horny teenager would have seen it coming sooner than I did. "What is this?"

"It's a kidnapping, asshole. What does it look like?"

Kidnapping? That came from so far out of left field that he stopped backing away. He was dead. Who would kidnap a dead man? "I hope you don't think the nuns can afford ransom."

"Not my problem."

Of all the boat people waiting to transit the canal, why did they choose him? "Who sent you?"

"Can't tell you that."

"Can't or won't?"

Jerry flipped open a compact and laid a line of coke on the mirror. "When you're the best, you freelance." She inhaled and added, "If it's any consolation, you got popped by the best." Then, as if to emphasize that the best had all the time in the world to savor their victories, she laid another line. "In fact, if they sent Joe and me after

Osama"—up her nostril went the line—"it would be bye-bye, Al Qaeda . . . Bye-bye, Aiden."

The "best" were expensive. He had not looked any more prosperous than anyone else in the bar.

Jerry walked around him, out the front door, and called over her shoulder, "Be a good boy or they'll hurt you."

That much he could figure out on his own. He felt his left leg starting to shake. He was scared and confused and he wished he was a tougher fighter. He'd won his share of fistfights way back when he was a kid—an affluent Catholic high school being one of the few civilized institutions left in America where you could get punched hard in the teeth by a fellow A student. While the Old Man—quick with his fists and quick to take offense—had taught his sons to box as a matter of course.

"Someone hits you, you hit him back. Counterpunch!" Out in the backyard wearing light gloves. "Counterpunch." *Bam*, in the face. "Get your fucking left up!"

Aiden had never taken to it like Charlie had. That was their upbringing in a nutshell. The Old Man liked to fight. Aiden would just as soon walk away. Charlie wanted to win.

Charlie learned better ways to end a fight. "Change their expectations. Make them deal with your game. Never play theirs."

Whatever the hell that meant, he had about one second to figure out how to change this situation before it got worse. The muscle men were starting into the room, fanning to take him from both sides, arms in motion, a confident swagger in their walk. They were so coked their eyes looked like nails. "The lady make good advise, señor."

His leg was shaking harder. But through his fear, he heard an element of bluff. *Kidnap* was the key word. They weren't supposed to hurt him and sure as hell not kill him. *Kidnap* meant keep alive. At least till they got around to mailing fingers. But whom would they mail the fingers to? He was dead. *Who would kidnap a dead man?*

When one flicked eyes at the door behind him, he was certain they had a partner covering the hall. Aiden picked up an armchair. They rushed him from both sides so that he could only hit one of them with the chair. But he was already moving toward his real target.

No one worked the bow who was afraid of heights. He faked a throw, charged between them, rammed the chair through the French windows, crossed the terrace in two long steps, and leaped over the balustrade.

The striped awning ripped like wet paper. Instead of sliding down it onto the hedges that surrounded the café, he tore through it like a spear and landed, wildly off balance on a table full of drinks. It flew out from under him, but the people he tumbled into absorbed the impact of his fall, so that when he finally hit the pavement, he felt sharp pain in his shoulder and hip, but didn't break anything.

Women screamed. Men shouted and drew weapons.

Aiden scrambled to his feet, shoved past someone trying to stop him, jumped a low hedge, and ran up the long driveway, racing for the distant road. Feet pounded behind him, someone yelled, and a car squealed. Over his shoulder he saw three guys running after him, and a car turning a one-eighty, sweeping headlights over the casino gardens, a pool, a statue. It screeched up the driveway; high beams hurled his shadow ahead of him.

He dodged a taxi and a limousine and an SUV full of singing drunks. Its driver had to slam the brakes to miss hitting him and his passengers yelled as they were tossed about the vehicle. A beer bottle soared, blazed in the lights, and bounced off Aiden's shoulder. He kept running. Behind him, the fastest of his pursuers had drawn far ahead of his partners and was catching up. Aiden veered off the driveway, along some outbuildings behind a wall, and ducked into an alley between them. He rounded a corner, stopped, planted his feet, and waited for the footsteps.

Why me?

The footsteps neared, the quick, light patter of an athlete.

He landed a perfectly timed left as the guy turned the corner full tilt. But although the man went down, like a boom had swatted him off the coach roof, stopping to throw a punch had taken longer than Aiden had thought and his friends were right behind him.

He sprinted for the dark at the end of the alley and turned another corner, skidded on wet grass, and wove through a stand of palms. If only he could keep moving, the attack was his to control. God bless the Old Man for teaching him how to make a proper fist, or he would have broken his hand on the guy's face.

He heard waves splashing a breakwater and could see in that direction the lights of ships at anchor. And here came their car again, down a service road that wandered through the compound. Headlights probed the trees. He couldn't stay here. They would trap him against the water. He had to get off the casino grounds, back to the center of town. Darting shadow to shadow, circling through the trees, he skirted a dark swimming pool and crossed some tennis courts. He navigated by the loom of a square church tower, while his mind revved furiously. This was no ordinary grab-the-nearest-yanqui. But if, of all the people in the bar, they had come for him, that would mean that someone knew that Aiden Page was not dead.

A hammer blow slammed against his ear and knocked him to the ground, his head ringing. He heard shots and bullets tearing through the trees and he realized one had grazed his head. A thirty-secondth of an inch closer would have exploded his skull. Were the kidnappers stoned out of their minds? Or been ordered to shoot to kill if he escaped? He scrambled to his feet. The rules had changed, catastrophically.

He ran, crouched low to the ground, and headed for the dark church. With it between him and the gunman, the shooting stopped. A desperate desire to burrow into the building or hide in its graveyard overwhelmed his spirit. His gut told him to keep running while he had breath in his lungs.

BLANG . . . *BLANG* . . . *BLANG* . . . *BLANG*.
Morgan awoke in her berth with Roscoe in her arms. Something was wrong.

She had reduced sail before she lay down an hour ago and *Molly* was standing tall and rising and falling in tune with the seas. She shined her penlight at the compass she had Velcroed to the ceiling. On course. What woke her?

She listened to the hull rushing through the water, heard the familiar creak of the genoa sheet straining its winch, heard the regular slap of wavelets striking the bow. Heard the tempo increase as the boat surfed a willing sea.

Blang . . . blang . . . blang . . . blang.

Something was striking the mast. The impact reverberated down the hollow aluminum spar into the cabin a foot from her head. Ringing like a slow, sad bell.

Frightened, she snapped on her harness, ran out on deck. It was cold and dark. Thick clouds hid the stars. The wind felt like fifteen knots and the seas were big. She shined her flashlight up the mast. She saw nothing hitting it. But she could still hear the ringing, the mournful *blang . . . blang . . . blang.*

The sound echoed memories of the double funeral with empty coffins.

When the city delivered urns of ashes from the death site, it had been Grandpa's idea to bury them in full-size coffins even though by then everyone knew that the pieces recovered were small enough to inhale and most would never be found. Her mother gave up trying to talk him out of it. She had wanted a simple ceremony. But Grandpa had argued—yelled, pounded the table, screamed, and spit, "This is for your daughter!"

Morgan hadn't wanted it either. Then cousins and uncles and aunts chimed in until it turned into a huge family drama. Instead of simple, they ended up celebrating mass at the gigantic stone church on Ninth Avenue, which had been Grandpa's parish growing up in the neighborhood the older Pages called Hell's Kitchen.

The organ had played "Amazing Grace," and when the thunder finally faded and the stones stopped shaking, Morgan herself had been expected to sing "Danny Boy." Like it was one of the family picnics that usually ended with cousins in fistfights. "Danny Boy" was not exactly the Catholic Church's favorite music for a funeral mass, but the older Pages were mega-Irish and Uncle Charlie had contributed heavily to the rebuilding fund. When they went to arrange the details, Grandpa was already upset because the old priest he would have preferred to say the mass had the flu. The young replacement priest had asked if maybe Morgan would sing something more sacred with the choir and Grandpa started shouting. "Two sons! Jesus H., will it wound God's ears to hear the song of an orphan?"

The priest had to go along. Just as she had to go along. Standing in front of two hundred people while she tried to fill a space the size of an airplane hangar with a voice that sounded to her as thin as a pennywhistle. She would have died or run from the church, or burst out crying, if it hadn't been for the kindness of the organist, an incredibly handsome guy who had asked what part of the song scared her most.

The high G, of course.

Why don't we take the entire piece down a step? he suggested. Knowing she only had to lift "there" to an F was a huge relief. And the day of the funeral, when he saw the tears in her eyes, he told her, "I know how you feel. I've been playing 'Amazing Grace' six times a day for a month. When it seems like we'll all grieve forever, I try to remind myself why we have to do this."

"Why?" She recalled the box-cutter sound in her voice.

He pretended not to notice. "Music braids grief with memories. So I try to leave my tears at the door. You can pick them up on the way out."

When it was time for her to sing, he moved from the organ to the piano and made her sound better than she was by filling in her empty spaces with "colors" she would have chosen if she could.

The relatives loved it. At least it had given them something to say to her beyond "Sorry Daddy is dead." Grandpa went home happier than he had come and even her mother admitted later that it was probably good for all concerned to have closure. The day had ended with Morgan storming out of the apartment screaming that she didn't want closure. Which got her sent to Dr. Melton.

The noise stopped. But now her heart was pounding; two hundred people crying at a funeral had made it seem like he was really dead. Like maybe he was. She started to cry, but bit her lips and pressed her face to the salty wet hatch to stop the tears. The wind was cold. She ducked below to make some tea and had just removed her PFD harness when the noise started up again, *blang, blang, blang.*

Peering up from the open hatch, she traced the rise of the mast with her flashlight. No halyards tapping. Nothing on the first spreader, which crossed the mast about twelve feet off the deck. Higher. Her heart pulsed and her stomach dropped. The radar reflector was banging against the top starboard spreader.

"Oh shit."

Her hand flew to her throat and for a long moment she clasped the good-luck dragon she had bought in Chinatown. Like the jade talisman, the radar reflector had taken on magical importance and she truly believed that Wayne's kind gift protected her while she slept. If the ball of aluminum circles fell in the water, she would lose her best protection against ships running her down in the dark. Juggling flashlight in one hand and binoculars in the other, she focused on the tip of the spreader. The reflector's bridle was tearing loose from the flag halyard that Wayne had used to haul it up.

With fear came rage and she heard the voice in her head condemning the crazy old drunk who'd probably stopped for beer while he was attaching it. I don't mean that, she thought. I'm sorry.

She harnessed up again, clipped onto the jack line she had rigged up the center of the coach roof, went to the mast, and tugged gingerly at the flag halyard to lower the reflector. But, as she feared, the torn bridle had tangled and the halyard was jammed. How long before the rest of the bridle parted? A day? Or a minute? Who knew? Not her, until she climbed the mast.

The mast stood nearly forty feet above the water. The upper spreader, twenty feet above the cabin roof. How was she going to climb up there? There were no mast steps. She had no bosun's chair. Okay, she could fake a bosun's chair together with rope. But who would crank the winch?

She didn't have the upper-body strength to climb the mast like a monkey, much less pull herself hand over hand up a shroud the way she had seen really strong boys do. Still, she tried, stepping onto the boom and attempting to shinny up the aluminum spar. She slid right down.

Back to a bosun's chair. Back to who would crank the winch. She had seen her father haul himself to the masthead using only a block and tackle. But he was a real bowman, and they were expected to be monkeys. Besides, where would she get block and tackle? *Molly 1* had had miles of rope and a bosun's locker full of extra blocks. *Molly 2*'s were all in use in her rigging. She shined the light around the boat. The darting beam swept the black swells, and landed on the backstay adjuster, a strong block and tackle.

If she could lengthen the halyard to reach it . . .

Her mother had taught her basic knots and she could tie the important ones in the dark. Except a rolling hitch, which she never could learn. But no knot would fit through the blocks. That meant splicing extra line onto the halyard. She hadn't spliced in ages, and had never done it well, probably because when she was ten years old, some snot-nose boy had snickered that splicing was a girl thing, like sewing.

Her head was spinning faster than a CD. This was insane. Nor did it seem fair.

She yelled into the dark, "All I want to do is not get hit by a freakin' ship," and tugged the flag halyard again, hoping it would miraculously unjam. It didn't. The hell with it, she thought. If it falls, it falls. Then she thought about trying to sleep knowing that big ships couldn't see her.

No choice. Keep it simple. She found a short length of heavy line and tied two bowlines in it. The first knot formed a loop big enough to fit around her hips as a rough-and-ready bosun's chair. The second knot formed a smaller loop, an "eye," to which she shackled the spinnaker halyard. Pulling the halyard raised the big loop, which she did until it was as high above the boom as she could sit in it. She led the end of halyard down the hatch, where she could see to splice by the cabin light.

The halyard was made of braided line and braided line was very hard to splice. She cut open the soft outer cover, revealing the strong core within—three-strand, thank God. She unlaid those strands, unraveling twelve inches of the halyard. She unlaid twelve inches of the line she intended to add on and started splicing by interlacing the strands. It took her an hour and four tries to get a splice thin enough to fit through the blocks and strong enough, hopefully, to bear her weight.

Next she went to the stern, tied a strong rope through the backstay's eye, tightened the backstay adjuster, secured the backstay with the strong rope, and tentatively slackened the adjuster. The stopper line she had created with the rope took the strain, creaking and groaning, which allowed her to detach the adjuster blocks.

She led the lengthened halyard through a block at the foot of the mast, back to the stern, through the backstay tackle, and forward again to the mast. She climbed onto the boom, stepped into the bosun's-chair loop, and started pulling the halyard. Straining against the resistance of one quarter of her own weight, she pulled four feet of line to raise herself one foot. An inch for every four, three inches for every foot.

It was still heavy going. She rose slowly, swinging like a yo-yo, banging into the mast, bouncing off, and crashing into the shrouds. Her arms got tired and she couldn't stop to rest because she had nothing to cleat the halyard to. They were burning by the time she reached the first spreader on which she could stand and catch her breath.

Twelve feet above the cabin, feeling the hard push of the northeast trade wind, she had the strangest realization that the boat was happy. It didn't give a damn if it had a radar reflector or not. It was loving being here, loving the steady wind and the orderly seas that the wind piled in regular rows. It surfed down a swell, flew across the trough, and slowed only to climb the next swell.

"You're just like that cat," she whispered. "I'm the only one around here who worries . . . Which means you're both in trouble, since I'm getting so weird I'm talking to you like a person." She looked around. Ahead, the sea was dark. Dark, behind. She looked to left, the east, and there, too, loomed the darkness of deep night.

It struck her that she could not see to work in the dark. She had to wait for dawn. But the sail blocked her view to the west. For all she knew, a giant tanker was about to run her over. Was she supposed to just wait while some ship blasted out of the dark and sank her without warning? She had to stand watch. On the bow, ahead of the jib, so she could see. She lowered herself back down to the roof and went forward, where she held on to the head stay with the water rushing past her feet, watching and waiting for ships. Exhausted, she fell asleep and lost her grip. She woke up falling. Only her harness prevented her from slipping into the dark water.

To stay awake she pretended they were in the Bermuda Race. Pretended they were racing flat out for five days. Pretended her father needed her on watch so he could repair something or catch some sleep.

Drifting off, she slapped her face and pinched her cheeks. Pretend you're back in his office, running searches to fill that CD. Pretend Dad didn't take you home but that you both worked all night searching files.

"I don't even know what they're looking for," he kept saying. Over and over: "I don't know what they're looking for."

Pretend you had stayed with him all night.

Suddenly she was wide-awake, heart pounding.

If she had stayed with him all night, would she have seen something in the "real deal" subfolder that made her ask a strange question now?

You know what, Dad? I just got a really neat idea. What if the prosecutor started playing the blame game, but while investigating HHH happened to discover something different? Something about those "real deals." What if a "real deal" that Mr. Hong ordered made them suspicious? What if it was really bad? But you didn't know it was bad. You were just doing your job.

EVERYONE IN THE BOAT BAR and the Canal Authority waiting rooms had warned of pickpockets, armed robbery, and people's fingers cut off for their rings. Aiden made it unscathed across most of Colón. Then, within sight of the railroad tracks that served as a kind of DMZ between the poverty-blasted third-world city and the safety of the marina, when he thought he was home free, two guys spotted him from one of the many abandoned buildings.

Aiden hurried toward a group playing dominoes under a streetlight. No one looked up as the two rushed him. The leader had a knife, his backup a length of two-by-four. The guy with the knife looked like he knew how to use it, but when he lunged, he lost his balance and fell on his face. Only then did Aiden realize that they were muggers, not kidnappers, and both were so drunk they could hardly walk. After what he'd been through, it was a bad joke, and he stopped the other one with a severe look. The fallen drunk crawled away. The guy with the board dropped it and ran.

Aiden himself stood rooted in the street, stunned by a revelation. Only Morgan could possibly know he was still alive. Only his daughter—thanks to that brief, unforgivable telephone call. But if there was one sure thing in his scrambled world, he knew that his child had not hired kidnappers.

Was there anyone else in the world who could even *guess* he was alive? Only Charlie. Had Charlie escaped from the twin towers, too?

Aiden's heart filled with a joy that obliterated fear and panic and confusion. Thank God, if he had. Thank God, thank God. Imagining seeing his brother alive, he could almost feel the guilt for abandoning him evaporate like a splash on hot stone.

But Charlie could never betray him, much less hire kidnappers who shot to kill.

It wasn't Morgan. And it wasn't Charlie.

He crossed the railroad tracks and hurried toward the marina, his brain racing so crazily that he had to concentrate on putting one foot in front of the other as the sky grew red in the east. He had been spared when the burning buildings collapsed. Better people died. And spared again tonight. Dead but not dead, was this his opportunity to make up for a wasted life?

At the marina he found a fisherman glad to row him out to *Darling* for a dollar. The instant he swung over the safety lines into the cockpit, voices from below chorused, "Look what the cat dragged in."

Up popped Sophie. "Did she send you off with a cuppa?"

"I'd love one."

"Coming right up."

On deck, in the strengthening light, which brought with it intense heat, they got their first clear look at him. "You've been in a fight," said Sophie.

"And lost," said Gert.

"I survived," said Aiden.

"What happened? You've blood down your ear. Here, we better clean you up."

They found additional cuts on his arm and back. From the fall through the awning, Aiden supposed, gradually becoming aware of new aches and pains as he sat for their Band-Aids and hydrogen peroxide.

"What happened?"

"I got rolled."

"By the Sheila?"

"No, afterward, on the way back."

"We assumed she'd keep you for the night, or we'd have told you not to cross the city by yourself."

Aiden gazed about the flats, inspecting the thirty or forty boats waiting at anchor. None was a Baltic 70; hardly a surprise. "Where's Joe's boat?"

"Weighed anchor in the night. Joe said something about moving her down the coast to Isla Grande."

Sophie shook her head. "That's what he said, but he's the sort to grease a palm to jump the transit queue."

There were four piers at the marina. The rising sun glinted off someone standing on the third. Binoculars, sweeping the anchorage. Even if Joe and Jerry weren't personally looking for him, their trigger-happy assistants would be, and it would be a piece of cake to inspect each of the boats on its slow passage through canal locks. This was no good. He'd bring it all down on Sophie and Gert and they were innocents.

When they finished patching him, he took their hands.

"Girls, I can't sail with you."

"Why not?"

"I'm sorry. I had every intention of going all the way. But something's come up and I gotta get off here."

"Are you in some sort of trouble, Aiden?"

"Yes."

"Can't we help?"

"No. And the trouble I'm in will make trouble for you . . . Can the priest find you another line handler?"

They exchanged a look. "Not to worry."

"If you see Joe or Jerry, start screaming. If anybody asks about me, just tell them I jumped ship."

They looked at each other, again, and he knew that all he had to say was, *Help me,* and they would do anything for him. "Aiden, are you sure?"

But even if they managed to transit the Canal and escape the port at Balboa, their boat was slow and the steel hull a prominent radar target, easily hunted down alone at sea. "Positive . . . I feel terrible about this. Can you two make it home okay?"

"We were already headed home alone when we met you in St. Martin and we're heading home alone now, so stop your worrying. We'll be apples."

"Thank you for understanding."

He got his money and his seabags. Sophie handed him his passport and a bacon sandwich. "God bless, Aiden."

WHEN FIRST LIGHT silvered the eastern horizon, Morgan climbed her mast again to repair her radar reflector. But just as she reached the upper spreader, the bosun's-chair line slipped and suddenly she was falling, the rope burning through her gloves.

She heard a scream—a startled, high-pitched shriek that had to be her own. *Bang,* one foot hit the bottom spreader. The impact broke her fall, for an instant. She got a grip on the halyard again and saved herself.

"What am I doing?" she asked herself in a sudden fright flare of lucidity. It's only a radar reflector. I probably don't need it anyway.

It was like singing at her father's funeral—if she stopped to think about what she had to do, she would never make it up the mast. She started up again, hand over hand, inch by inch, until she could sit on the spreader. Gasping for breath, muscles on fire, she took several safety turns with the line. Then she edged out on the spreader and reached for the reflector.

Just as she got a glove on the aluminum, *Molly* headed up.

Either the wind had suddenly dropped in a sort of reverse gust or a loopy sea had staggered her. But instead of skimming the water like a surfboard, the sloop suddenly slowed and stood straighter. Morgan, who for many days had been leaning to port to balance against the boat's heel, fell sideways and forward and, in trying to save herself, caught the flag halyard, which tore the reflector's last binding.

"Shit!"

With a dull flash, the reflector fell. She heard it bounce on the cabin roof and roll against the mast. Frantically, she unwrapped the turns she had taken around the spreader and let the line slide as she plummeted down, burning her hands again, and crashed onto the cabin roof just as the reflector rolled overboard.

Morgan sank in despair to the cockpit bench. But an instant later she jumped up, terrified that a ship was steaming her way on a collision course. Heart in her throat, she waited while *Molly* climbed atop the sea, revealing an ocean as utterly empty and devoid of ships as it had been for days. Why, she wondered, was she so paranoid? Dr. Melton would have an answer. But the simple fact was that she could see only twelve miles from the deck of the low-lying Molly, and in a half hour, a twenty-five-knot ship she couldn't see now could be on top of her.

She sat by the tiller with her head in her hands. What could she do? Leave her VHF on all the time in case a ship radioed? But the ship that didn't see her on its radar wouldn't radio. Stand watch on deck whenever rain, fog, or dark reduced visibility? Impossible; she would die of exposure or sleep deprivation. There was only one answer. She had to replace her radar reflector. You could walk into any marine supply store and find them in twenty shapes and sizes—circles, cylinders, squares, and triangles—some to be mounted on the masthead or a shroud or a stay from a halyard like Wayne's, only attached more securely. It occurred to her that this was the first time in her life that she couldn't just walk into a store. Even from a boat. When she sailed with Mommy and Daddy, they usually moored each night within a dinghy ride or short walk to a store. Even Blind Man Island had had a store—sort of. The Tongans called it the commissary and they could buy canned food and cereal and Coke on credit.

She looked ahead at the mast. Her bosun's chair was still swinging with the roll of the boat. Had she overdone it with the complicated cat's cradle of spliced halyard, block and tackle, and rope chair? Wouldn't it have been simpler just to tie a series of bowlines every six inches in a thick rope as footholds, haul it up the mast with the halyard, and climb it like a ladder?

She felt like a complete idiot for not thinking of that before. But the concept of keep it simple finally gave her an idea for a radar reflector. And again she felt like an idiot for not thinking of it sooner. It was like she had been staring through binoculars too long to see what was going on outside their field of focus, and she vowed that she would remember to "lower the binoculars" next time she was faced with a problem she couldn't solve.

"Hey, Boat Cat? Want some tuna fish?"

Roscoe rose from a dead sleep, hurried over, and rubbed her leg.

Morgan opened a can and emptied it into the plastic soup bowl Roscoe was using for his dish. Then, while the cat inhaled his favorite human food, Morgan rinsed the can with salt water, dried it, and opened her toolbox. She drilled a hole in the center of the bottom of the can and another in the lid and strung them both onto a length of wire, tying a knot between them to keep can and lid three inches apart.

"Want seconds?"

Roscoe attached himself to her leg again.

She opened a second can, gave the contents to the cat, drilled the holes, and added can and lid to the wire. She held it up. The cans were considerably smaller than the twelve-inch spheres that had formed her lost reflector.

"Thirds?"

The cat looked at her.

She opened a third can. Roscoe inspected his bowl, then settled down, chewing thoughtfully. Morgan added the third can to the string and used pliers to twist an eye into either end of the wire. She tied small stuff—light, strong cord—to the eyes and took the concoction out on deck, where she knotted the small stuff around the flag halyard with a buntline half hitch. Even though a buntline hitch would never loosen, she used sail thread to whip the working ends to be doubly sure. Then she raised her handiwork up to the second spreader. It looked like the cans that wedding guests tie to a bride and groom's bumper. It might not return as strong a radar echo as the "official" reflector, but she was betting her life that it was better than nothing.

TWO KINDS OF BUSES CROSSED the isthmus to Panama City on the Pacific side. Aiden took a sweltering rattletrap instead of the air-conditioned express favored by all but the stone-brokest yachties and sat near the front with his razor-sharp bosun's knife concealed under the bag on his lap. The ride gave him three hours to speculate. Who else might know—or guess—that he was still alive?

Henry Hong would know if Charlie had made it to Blind Man Island. Charlie would have told Henry about their plan to meet up there. But why would Henry Hong want to kidnap him? Why not just wait for him to arrive? It wasn't like he had anyplace else to go. Maybe Henry had some reason to be impatient, some reason not to wait. But how in hell would Henry know he was in Panama?

Maybe Morgan told someone about his stupid phone call. Who? Not her mother. None of her girlfriends. She had always been a private child. She held things closely, almost secretively. Possibly her pal Toby. But with HHH & Company blown out of business on September 11, would a child's whisper reach Henry Hong ten thousand miles away on Blind Man Island?

When the bus pulled into Panama City, he ran from the terminal to lose himself on the crowded sidewalks. He churned through the crowds, checking behind, gawking around like the other gringo tourists to make sure he wasn't being followed. Why? Why? Why? Why would Henry Hong—why would *anyone*—want to kidnap him?

Kidnappers kidnapped for ransom. Which made him a lousy candidate. Why else kidnap somebody? Hold him prisoner? Get him off the street? Lock him up? Like the U.S. attorney's implied threat to lock him up?

Criminals get kidnapped to keep them off the witness stand.

I am not a criminal, he thought. I may have kept my mouth shut when I should have protested. I may have looked the other way when Henry and Charlie played fast and loose with the language. But I never stole or cheated, no matter what the prosecutor might have been thinking when he ordered my files preserved.

But if I'm a witness, I don't know what I witnessed.

Was he a witness?

He went looking for an Internet café.

Events that the prosecutor thought he had "witnessed" were recorded on the CD that he had steadfastly ignored. But now, jostled and gawking on a hot Panama street, he realized that the CD might possibly contain what he knew, but didn't know he knew.

He hurried past the cafés nearest the bus terminal, fear driving him to find one where an American was less likely to go. When he finally did alight near a college campus, he bought coffee and an hour of computer time, and loaded in the disk.

His old e-mails made surreal reading seven months away from Wall Street. Essentials now seemed Mickey Mouse. Details, chicken feed, in negotiations that had engaged a man he no longer knew. He could still put faces to names, and smiles to joke lines, but he couldn't form a big picture, or distinguish any pattern pertaining to the requested material. Perhaps the prosecutor had been fishing, casting a wide net. When the situation was seen from this perspective, though, it appeared to Aiden that the government had not yet decided whether to investigate HHH as a criminal enterprise. Which made sense. He wasn't a criminal. *Was* he a witness? *What do I know that I don't know I know?*

His hour was up in a flash. He bought another. And another. Finally, he looked out at the busy sidewalk, debating whether he should stay longer. What have I learned? Nothing that told him what to do.

He did notice, as he had the night Morgan helped him put the files together, that some of the deals for which the prosecutors ordered records preserved were so-called real deals, involving direct ownership of actual, working companies. But he still didn't know what the hell that meant, if anything. Maybe at some point the prosecutor got more interested in the real deals. Such about-faces were common in any kind of investigation, whether by lawyers, prosecutors, or even accountants inspecting a company's books to determine its financial health. Red flags popped up in previously unnoticed areas.

Stay or run? Panama City looked big and bright and modern compared to the misery of Colón. More the kind of city he was used to. But there was no place here for him. He didn't know the language, had no friends and only a short-term canal transit visa.

A sudden loud noise snapped heads up around the café. Aiden was halfway to his feet, heart racing, when he saw that it was only a crate that had fallen off a truck, scattering pedestrians and sending several dogs running madly into traffic. The dogs settled it for him. If you don't know *what* was chasing you, you still had to run.

He hurried into the street. A taxi was stopped at a light. Should he take his chances at the airport? The passport Charlie had given him was now seven months old. Still good? And without credit cards, what kind of profile did you fit when you bought a ticket for cash in a city known for drugs and money laundering? He looked around, saw no one watching him, and hopped into the cab just as the light changed.

"Balboa Yacht Club."

THOUSANDS OF TONS of water swirled out the Miraflores Lock, lowering a 106-foot-wide "Panamax" freighter, a Canal Authority tugboat, a motor yacht, and Joe and Jerry's Baltic 70 down another step to the Pacific Ocean.

Jerry was getting bored. They had already come up 102 feet from the Atlantic, motored across Lake Gatun and through the Gaillard Cut, and down the Pedro Miguel Lock. Lakes and mountains were beautiful and all, and the locks were majestic, but enough already. One more lock to descend to the Pacific before drinks at the marina, where they supposedly had a decent clubhouse.

Except Joe hadn't waited and was already half in the bag. She might have to prowl the yachties for entertainment tonight, which meant cutting one loose from a wife or girlfriend. If she could find one who looked worth the trouble. Better to see what was cooking in Panama City's hotels. She was feeling antsy and regretted not having a little fun with Aiden Page before she handed him off. It would have violated her strict standards of security, but, hell, live a little.

The distinctive *ding-ding-ding* of the incoming-only sat phone was a welcome interruption. And not unexpected. Make it another job, she thought. Make it in Europe. Anywhere less hot, with more class. She went below, closing the hatch to preserve the air-conditioning, and stretched out on a white leather banquette in the saloon.

They couldn't call out on it. Only answer when the client's intermediary called.

"Joe and Jerry."

"You fucked up." Not the intermediary. But an angry woman she had never heard before. Most likely "the boss." Traces in her voice of a New York accent. Manhattan. Traces of something foreign. Asian. Korean, if she had to guess.

"No, we didn't. We delivered him to your Panamanians."

"Not according to my people."

Jerry took her feet off the banquette and sat up straight to say loud and clear, "They're lying. We delivered. Your people screwed up and they're blaming us."

"So you do know he escaped?"

"I heard shooting. I figured it was either a revolution or your people blowing holes in him. Either way, it was not my problem."

She waited for empty threats. Instead, the woman said, "We want him back."

Jerry said, "I *want* a red Lamborghini. But I also know that if I *really* want one, I have to buy it."

"One hundred thousand U.S.," the woman said.

They could do a lot better than that for pulling their fat out of the fire. "Each," said Jerry. "There's two of us." Double the first fee. Where, she asked herself, do I get my nerve?

"Done."

"Plus expenses."

"Done."

"Up front."

"Fifty thousand is already in your account. One quarter of two hundred thousand. You get the rest when you deliver."

Jerry said, "No. That's not how we work. We get full payment up front, just like last time."

"This is not negotiable."

"Let me quote my partner, Joe, on this subject. Anyone can snatch. Anyone can terminate. *Finding* takes special skills."

"This is not negotiable."

Jerry said, "Try to get your head around this picture: I tell Joe I've accepted your terms. Joe gets mad and slugs me. I pull a knife, and before you know it, there's blood all over. *And your guy's still running around loose.*"

Figuring she was going to win this argument, Jerry had already turned her mind to the tracking problem. With any luck at all, they could get lucky in Balboa and put Aiden Page in handcuffs by the end of the day. But if Aiden escaped, he would run on a boat. Thorough in the extreme, Jerry had researched Aiden Page, as she did every quarry, until she knew him like—forgive her—a mother. Aiden Page would always run on a boat. So she and Joe would start scanning the Pacific mariners' ham-radio and SSB airwaves. Order some software from their computer guy to pick up on key words. Let the program do the hard work and ring bells when key words came up. Like the name of whatever boat he skipped on. The names of the crew on that boat. Aiden's own name. His "Chuck" alias. His runaway daughter's name. And the name of the boat she stole.

The woman on the phone said, "Look up at your lead line handler."

"What?"

"*Look up at the side of the lock.* Your line handler is falling."

"What?" Jerry ran up the companionway into the thick heat. She heard a scream. One of *Baltic Night*'s crewmen tumbled thirty feet to the water. He landed with a huge splash. Joe put down his glass and dove off the boat with the speed that made him so wonderful in a fight. Two of the crew jumped after him and they pulled the line handler out, wet, scared, bleeding where he had scraped the wall of the lock.

Jerry looked at the sat phone. Of course they had planted a GPS locator in it. And of course it told them exactly where she and Joe were. And of course she couldn't throw it overboard if she wanted the job.

"You'll be relieved to learn he survived," she spoke into the phone.

"Next time it will be your 'brother,' and he won't," the woman said.

Jerry's father had been a baseball player and a successful major league manager, and he had taught her, "Sometimes the other batters hit them where your fielders ain't." In other words, *Don't get mad. Don't waste energy getting even. Win next time.*

"Message received."

"Here's another. You're not the only ones hunting. You just happen to be closest at the moment, though not by much . . ."

THE MARINA ON THE PACIFIC side was a lot more comfortable than the one at Colón, but the clientele was basically the same friendly crowd, either waiting to transit east or, having transited west, gearing up for the Pacific.

Aiden spent the afternoon in the bar, drinking beer and shooting the breeze about integrated radar, paneled laminate sails, high-capacity water makers, air-conditioning and teak oil with cruisers who had money, and nonskid deck repair and bargain bottom paint with those who didn't. He kept a close watch on the door, not only for Joe and Jerry's friends, but, as always, in dread of being spotted by someone who knew him from New York.

He was hoping for a berth on a fast boat headed for Fiji or Samoa, or one stopping there on the way to Australia or New Zealand. But he soon discovered that it was not a great place to meet people in a rush. Most cruisers were heading down to the Galápagos, four hundred miles off Ecuador as a first leg and most already had crew.

He met many Australians, who were headed home, including a wild bunch on a Maxi yacht who were going to make great time, but were already fully crewed, and several single-handers, each of whom told him that if he wanted crew he would prefer "a bit of crumpet." He also struck out with a couple on a fast catamaran, a dive-boat captain and filmmaker who had only recently met and were in no mood to share their love nest. Nor was he the only stranded sailor in the jumping-off place and the competition included deckhands younger and stronger than he was. One of them had a stainless-steel artificial arm—having lost the original, he explained to Aiden, in an electric winch whose salt-corroded switches had caused the machinery to start without warning. His "mate" had crewed on Maxis in the Southern Ocean. Dismayed to find themselves stuck in Balboa, they told their tale in a Ping-Pong blur.

"We had a boat."

"Archimedes."

"Hell of a boat, too."

"One-off Finnish design."

"She would have been a rocket."

"Flat as a pancake. Pull the floorboards up and there's the bottom in your face."

"Like she's so flat the bilge is like four inches deep?"

"Captain was an asshole."

"So are a lot of owners," Aiden interrupted. "Is he still here?"

"Who would sail with the bastard?"

Aiden signaled the bartender and ordered three more Red Stripes.

"Thanks, mate."

"Why'd you jump ship?"

"Found out who the asshole really was. Tom Slade."

"Who's that?"

"You're kidding? Capetown to Rio? Didn't stop to help *Orion?*"

Aiden said, "Vaguely . . . What was that, three, four years ago?"

"Claimed he never saw *Orion.*"

"Except his crew did."

Aiden recalled the scandal, if not the details. The first rule of the sea—some said the only rule—was stop to render aid. Battling for the lead in the race from South Africa to Rio de Janeiro, when the fleet was mauled by a Force-10 gale, Tom Slade had sailed past a sinking rival. Two men had drowned, and when the six who drifted for a month in a life raft were finally rescued, they gave angry testimony that Slade had refused to help. In the tight-knit world of ocean racing, Tom Slade had fallen from rock star to public enemy number one.

"Why'd you sign on with him?"

"We didn't make the connection until we got here. I was in high school when he did it."

"He posted for crew on boatingoz.com and we had to get to New Zealand."

"What's his boat called?"

"*Archimedes*—hey, where you going, mate? It's our round."

Aiden hurried down to the dock and found a club launch to drive him out to *Archimedes'* mooring. He easily spotted the racer on the outer edge of the crowded anchorage. She was a downwind sled as slick as a submarine. Her hull was bright yellow.

Archimedes looked like an extreme version of an already-extreme-design "Open 50," the workhorse of the around-the-world racing circuit. Fifty feet long, immensely broad in the beam from midships to her squared-off stern, she had a deck so flat you could have landed small planes on it if it hadn't been for the unusually tall mast. The small, shallow cockpit led directly back to a wide-open transom—necessary to drain the green water sure to sweep over her bow at speed. If there was any faster way to Fiji, it didn't float.

Aiden rapped on the hull—made of some exotic composite, which resonated like marbles dropped on steel. He knocked again. A head shot from the companionway hatch. An angry, tight-lipped face, barely softened by the puffiness of sleep, swiveled toward Aiden, who was standing in the launch, peering over *Archimedes'* safety lines.

"What the fuck do you want?"

"Ah, jeez, Cap, I hope I didn't wake you. I'm looking for a berth."

"I'm single-handing."

"You're going to *single-hand* this thing?"

"Soon as I finish the half-hour sleep you interrupted."

Aiden looked around the deck. Coffee-grinder winches to be manned by double gorillas. Water ballast controls. Spiderwebs of multiple running backstays. Open 50s were remote-ocean downwind racers, pure—though hardly simple—and while they could be single-handed by maniacal Around Alone types, they were usually crewed by eight or ten professionals inured to pain.

"If you are really single-handing, I'm a pretty good rigger. Why don't I give you a hand refitting her?" Show his skills, demonstrate he would be decent company on a passage, use the time to talk him into it. This monster machine was too good to lose.

Slade said, "Rack off."

"Guy back at Colón was selling a Harken furler we could adapt. He's practically giving it away. A lot easier than changing headsails all the time."

"Let's do this by the numbers, mate. Number one: This is not a lard-ass cruiser. Number two: Headsail furlers only jam when you're already in trouble. Number three: I've had it with crew: I'd rather sail alone."

Across the water a long, white Baltic 70 motored to a mooring. Aiden counted eight in its crew. Its sloped afterdeck held a satellite dome and the stern rail bristled with antennae. Too far off to read whether her name was *Baltic Nights*. The tall guy at the helm could be Jerry's brother Joe, or just a tall guy with an expensive boat. The blonde at his side could be Jerry, or just an expensive blonde. If they had bribed their way to an early start, as Sophie had suggested, they could have transited the Canal by now.

"I will crew for free, if you will drop me in Fiji."

"I'm not going to Fiji."

"It's on the way to New Zealand."

"If you know I'm going to New Zealand, you've been drinking with those self-righteous pussies who jumped ship. Bloody right they told you who I am."

"All I want is a berth to Fiji."

"But you know who I am."

"I know who you are."

"I'm sailing alone. I do my own rigging. Get off my boat."

The launch driver revved his motor. Tom Slade disappeared down the companionway. Aiden held the stanchion he was gripping. The driver's radio crackled.

"*Si?*"

Aiden did not need to speak Spanish to recognize "Baltic 70," nor to guess that the yacht club had radioed its launch to pick up a customer from the new arrival. The Panamanian started to flip his line off *Archimedes'* cleat. Aiden covered it with one hand and dug in his pocket with the other.

"Wait—*un momento*. Wait." Twenty bucks was real money down here, but the driver still raised two fingers for "make it snappy."

He sprang to the racer's deck, over the safety lines, into the cockpit, and stepped down the companionway. She was a stripped-out hellhole below, a long, low, tunnel-like workspace shoehorned between the water ballast tanks, heaped with sailbags and dirty laundry. Grocery boxes were not yet stowed, and the workbench was piled with enough tools and service manuals to maintain the boat around the world nonstop. A welding rig confirmed Aiden's guess that the owner had dumped the contents of his support van into the boat—saving shipping fees while turning the racer into a veritable seagoing boat shed—when he hired Tom Slade to deliver it to New Zealand.

Slade had already climbed back onto his bed—a sailbag—and pulled a dirty sheet over his shoulder. "What part of 'Get the fuck off my boat' do you not comprehend?"

"I know who you are. I know you sailed past a sinking yacht. And I also know that I've done worse."

"You've done worse? What did you do? Cook children? Feed them to their parents?"

"None of your fucking business."

Slade laughed bitterly. "In other words, nobody saw you do it. Well, congratulations, mate, next time I screw up, I'll do it in private, too."

"You'll find out it doesn't make any difference."

"Is that so? If no one knew what I did, I'd be leading America Cup challenges instead of begging for delivery jobs." He gestured around the hold; comforts consisted of pipe berths that folded down from the side, a two-burner kerosene stove, a pressure cooker, and a bucket that served as a latrine. "There wasn't much competition for this one. The owner had to hire me or sail it himself."

"If I tried to get my life back, everyone would know what I did, too."

Tom Slade lay back and shut his eyes and said, "You see, I have a problem despite my reputation—or perhaps because of it. I'm compelled to help people, even when helping them goes against my interests. Why did I hire those pussies? They were clearly not cut out for shipmates on a long passage—lazy slobs, spoiled mama's boys with too high an opinion of themselves to learn anything new, and not to be trusted on watch. But my warped need to help every sorry sod overruled my better judgment. I won't make that mistake again. So will you please get off my boat before I pick up"—he glanced at the tool bench for a serviceable weapon—"*light up* that gas torch and run you off my boat."

Aiden said, "I didn't mean that I don't *want* my life back." Although, thanks to Sophie and Gert hammering away at him, he wondered, Which life? The greedy life or an empty life? Erase Morgan from his past and what was left of value?

Slade jumped up, quick as a rooster. Aiden was surprised how small he was. He stood only five-six and was built somewhere between slim and compact, yet was so intense that he filled space like a bull. But halfway to the workbench, he stopped. Something in Aiden's words or the off-key way he spoke them had struck a chord with the disgraced captain. He rubbed his face. Then he steadied himself with a hand pressed against the low ceiling and looked Aiden up and down, shrewdly. "It looks like it's been a few years since you worked the bow."

"I can still fly the kite."

"With confidence?"

"With confidence."

"And you'll crew for free?"

"I'll pay for my food, too."

"There's plenty on board for the pussies—you drink?"

"Not much at sea."

"Yeah, well, I do."

"Maybe we should rig her for single-handing, then."

Tom Slade returned a thin, mirthless smile. "Get your shit."

Aiden held up his seabags.

"Okay, let's hoist some sail."

Her sails turned out to be as yellow as her hull. Hardly a stealth getaway boat, thought Aiden. But at least the Pacific was the biggest ocean in the world.

M ORGAN WAS ADJUSTING THE SLACK out of her self-steering when she heard a soft tapping sound aloft. She looked up, frightened that her new tuna-can radar reflector had somehow worked loose and was blowing against the spreader. But it was right where she had installed it, and the tapping came from a tan bird that was clinging to the halyard and pecking at the cans. It was a land bird, with no webs on its feet, and it actually looked like a mourning dove.

"Where did you come from?"

Surprised to see it a million miles from nowhere, she took a closer look through the binoculars. Definitely a mourning dove, but it looked awful, not as plump as she remembered them under the backyard feeder. In fact, it looked like it was going to fall over dead. She had read that lost birds that landed on boats usually died.

"Poor bird. You got picked up by a storm and blown away and you thought you saw the Santa Barbara Channel, didn't you? So you just flew and flew but you never found L.A. . . . You want something to eat?"

She watched, mesmerized by the desperate creature pecking at the cans. It descended wearily, spiraling down to the leeward safety line like a falling leaf.

"Look out for the cat!"

Roscoe crouched as still as the winch he was hiding behind.

"No, Roscoe!"

The bird hopped to the deck. Roscoe was on him in a flash.

Morgan forced herself to watch with a cool eye.

He ate everything including the feet. They had an agreement: once he caught something, he could eat it. Uncle Charlie had taught her that when she first got him, explaining that if she tried to stop the animal doing what came naturally, she would confuse him into becoming a clumsy hunter who would maim his prey, leaving her to put wounded victims out of their misery.

Now, out here, just the two of them, was no time to change the rules. Although in a lonely place where she measured her days with pencil specks on an empty chart, she would have loved to tame the bird and have another friend.

"JESUS H.," AIDEN greeted the dawn as he climbed into *Archimedes'* cockpit. "It sounds like an anvil factory down there." His ears were ringing. Whatever magical composites the Finns had used to shape the hull amplified every bang and clang that the fifty-footer made hurtling over wave tops and slamming into troughs.

His brain was ringing louder than his ears. Instead of sleeping when he was off watch, he had once again loaded his e-mail–file CD into the nav station computer and cycled through it. Again and again and again, as he had done every chance he got since they sailed from

Panama. He wasn't a criminal. Was he a witness? What, he kept ask-ing, do I know that I don't know I know?

Separated as he was from the events by time and distance, read-ing his e-mails gave a new perspective, like gazing down from the top of the mast and seeing the shape of the hull as the architect had first imagined it. But even in the clarity of dawn and tasting the salt spray on his lips, he still couldn't see the pattern. Although he was increasingly convinced that the prosecutor had started out fishing *before* he got interested in the "real" business deals, Aiden suspected that if the terrorists had not attacked, a subpoena demanding records involving direct ownership of actual working companies might well have been next.

He had isolated those deals by now. An international construction company. A chemical plant. A shipping line. And Halborson Towing, the trans-Pac barge outfit. But he had no idea of their significance. Or any guarantee that any of this really told him who had attacked him in Panama, or why.

"Now that you're up," said Tom Slade, who'd been steering like he was welded to *Archimedes'* helm, "you want to shake the reef out of the main?"

Aiden went to do battle with the yellow monster, although left to his own devices, he would have kept the reef in. The sloop was already pounding and the south wind was blowing harder than it had all night. But by now—after three frustrating days beating their heads against headwinds, or sitting becalmed, and still only two hun-dred miles out of Panama—he knew that this race captain would rather risk a knockdown than sail slowly.

Tom Slade took the adverse weather as a personal affront, out-raged by the simple fact that they would not get a boost from the southeast trades until well after they had rounded the Galápagos. Hoping for a break, he pored over the weather fax printouts, sat glued to the voice broadcasts, and eavesdropped every evening on the volunteer ham-radio weather networks, where boats throughout the Pacific reported the weather conditions at their positions.

Aiden could only hope that Tom would not report their own position. By now Joe and Jerry would have discovered that he had escaped from Panama on *Archimedes,* and the volunteers always announced their boat name when they joined the network. "Do you ever check in?" he asked.

"Not as a rule. I'm a hermit. Of course I'd report a dangerously low barometer or unusual swells . . ."

In his ceaseless quest for speed, Tom refused to use the autopilot on the grounds that he could drive the boat half a knot faster than it could. Two nights ago he had punched straight down the throat of a squall that most seamen would have sold their girlfriends to sail around. And last night he had steered right through Aiden's watch because the clutch of navigation computers he hung from his neck calculated that he could beat Aiden by a quarter knot in cross seas.

Aiden was impressed, if not humbled. It wasn't as if Slade had sailed the boat for years. He had just picked it up at Balboa. But already he seemed to know how to take advantage of each of her many quirks, including her inclination to go airborne for long intervals before pancaking into a trough. Whether they would arrive in Fiji in one piece was a question still to be answered.

"Want me to drive?"

"Naw, I'm okay."

"Want some breakfast?"

"Sure."

Aiden went back down into the thundering cavern. He had managed to get the hold straightened up: tools stowed before they started flying around like hand grenades; sailbags organized so he could find what he had to quickly; galley scrubbed; flashlights, fire extinguishers, hull plugs, and bolt cutters clamped within easy reach of the companionway. Most of the mess, he learned, was courtesy of the previous crew, who had bailed after transiting the Canal. Slade himself was not a slob, and once Aiden had straightened things out, they would stay that way.

The man could not cook worth a damn, however, and he couldn't care less what he ate, so Aiden took over the cooking as a means of self-preservation. He fried up eggs and bacon on one kerosene burner and created a facsimile of toast on the other.

Slade let him steer while he wolfed it down, then ran below to wash the dishes, which was the kind of seagoing manners Aiden appreciated. "You want coffee?" Slade yelled up the companionway.

"That's okay, I'll make it."

"Good." Slade galloped up the companionway and back to the wheel. "Never could get the hang of coffee."

"I noticed."

After they'd drained a couple of mugs, Aiden said, "Let me take over, I'm getting rusty."

"Okay, take a crack at it." He sprawled on a cockpit seat, but didn't close his eyes. "Break-dancing with the helm like you're doing will stir up a shit storm of turbulence around the rudder."

It took some effort for Aiden not to remind the racing skipper that he had been steering boats since he was eight years old, but he restrained himself in the interest of peace on a long passage. At least Slade preferred his steering to the autopilot. Finally, Slade took a long, hard look around the uncooperative sea, then closed his eyes— less out of belief in Aiden's skills, Aiden guessed, than from sheer exhaustion. In seconds, he was snoring.

Aiden shook his head, mostly in admiration. The man could sail. Thank God; the faster he got to Blind Man Island the better.

In fact, he sort of liked Tom. Liked his cutting humor when he occasionally opened up. He felt a certain kinship, he supposed. They were fellow outcasts, though for vastly different reasons. Tom Slade was running from his past. While he, who had escaped his past, suddenly found himself fleeing for his life in a bewildering new present.

"Aiden?"

Aiden looked from the water ahead, to the sails, to the compass, before he shot a quick glance down through the spokes of the wheel. This was a boat that demanded total concentration at the helm or it would suddenly end up sailing backward.

"What?"

"What kind of work you do, Aiden? When you're not crewing."

"Glorified CPA."

"Yeah? What glorified you."

"My title was chief financial officer."

"You don't seem like a bean counter."

"I didn't work very hard at it."

"How'd you get away with that?"

"In a bull market, everybody's a genius."

"Like downwind sailors," Tom Slade growled, and fell back to sleep, leaving Aiden to recall how every now and then he had actually tried to apply himself to the job. Which usually ended up in a fight with Charlie.

"Why does Henry want to buy a bankrupt site prep construction company that's been destroyed by second-generation inheritors? Why do *you* want to buy it?"

"The price is right."

"The price is debt. They've lost every asset they owned, all their machines, and they're in debt."

"We'll negotiate with their creditors."

"Why bother?"

"Because they'll be so grateful they'll give us a break."

"Look, I found another outfit in Portland—their competitors. They've been doing the exact same type of work and they've been doing it successfully. They did everything right that your yahoos did wrong."

"Why are they selling?"

"It's for sale because the founder looked at what happened to his competitor and decided *his* kids would do less damage getting nice jobs with charitable foundations."

Charlie laughed. "Smart fellow. Anyway, we're buying this one."

"Makes no sense—Charlie, I've run the numbers. There's nothing left. Why buy a gutted shell that's in debt?"

"Because Henry wants it."

"Henry? Why?"

For a moment, Charlie had looked perplexed, a rare sight. "Beats me. Henry says he wants it and that's that."

"Would you at least pitch my ideas to him? Show him the numbers."

"Sure. I'll get back to you."

A week later, Aiden had buttonholed Charlie in his office before the market opened. "What did Henry say about the contractor?"

"I just got off the phone with him. The answer is no."

"Goddammit, that makes no sense."

Charlie got angry, surging to his feet, eyes ablaze, voice rising. "It makes all the sense in the world. It's his bank. His fucking money. He's the boss."

Aiden started to protest.

Charlie sank wearily—another rare sight—to his desk. "What are you getting involved in this shit for?" he asked. "Here." He handed him a phone. "Take the ski lodge. Call Penny. Tell her to grab the kid and pack the car."

"I want to get this settled, first."

"It's settled. It's out of my hands. Go skiing."

"Are you going up this weekend?"

"No, I'm up to my eyeballs here. The caretaker just called. It's snowing like hell. You'll have a blast."

Except, Aiden recalled, that Morgan hated the cold and had reached the age when she'd rather spend the weekend with her friends, and Penny had volunteered to chaperon her school dance. So at the last minute he had gotten in the car and driven up himself. And who was at the lodge but Mary Page, who looked as surprised as she was pleased to see him and said, "Come on in, Aiden. Plenty of room."

28

T HE HEAT AND SUN WERE making her crazy. She knew
why. It wasn't just that the sun was ferocious, rising burning
like a white coal, getting hotter and whiter and bigger until finally,
at last, the mainsail shaded the deck in the late afternoon. It was that
sailing as fast as she could, she was still moving very slowly across
the biggest ocean in the world. Slow as a snail, which meant it would
be forever before she could find her father. Which meant she
obsessed on everything around her that she couldn't control. Like the
fact that, six hundred miles from the equator, it was so hot that she
sweated off her sunblock as fast as she rubbed it on. When the wind
died in the doldrums, it would feel like the subway in August.

She rigged an awning by stretching a line between the mast and
the backstay and draping the old sail across it. It was a precarious
arrangement: the boom and the mainsheets would swing through it
like a scythe if the wind suddenly shifted. It hadn't budged for
days—blowing a smooth, steady twelve and thirteen knots dead of
the northeast—but the possibility worried her, until she remembered her father tying a "preventer" to the boom to head off an accident jibe. She led a springy length of anchor line between the boom
and a solidly anchored cleat.

"See, cat. No surprises."

Roscoe was acting like he'd been born on the boat. Scampering
around the deck, jumping into the fold of sail where the foot met the
boom, and creeping behind winches, as if to spring out and catch
another bird, even though birds had vanished completely. She
watched him anxiously from her patch of shade under the awning.
He climbed into the fold of sail and curled up and went to sleep, baking in the sun.

"You'll get skin cancer, you silly cat."

But it was she who would get skin cancer, with her paper-white Irish skin. In sailing camp she used to wish she was Indian, or African-American, or even Italian. She'd go red as cranberries without sunblock, and if she missed a spot, that spot would blaze like a stoplight. Her lotions would never last the voyage; she had already gone through two tubes. Before she was halfway to Tonga, she'd be baked black, with eruptions on her face and arms. So she wore long-sleeved shirts, which made her sweat like a football player.

She wore a baseball cap and her biggest, darkest sunglasses, but the fierce light was everywhere, reflecting off the blue sea like ricocheting bullets. Approaching latitudes lower than the Sahara desert, she remembered a news video of soldiers there. She cut up another piece of old sail and sewed it to her cap so it shaded the back of her neck.

Her jeans were way too hot to wear, but she had to cover her legs. She sewed an ankle-length, wraparound skirt out of a piece of the ripped spinnaker. It shaded her skin completely, except that the tightly woven sailcloth didn't breathe and she was drenched in sweat. She sulked in her underwear for a while, obsessing on cancer. Then she took her scissors and carefully cut a hundred vertical slashes from the bottom to the waist, until it clung in shreds, shading her legs while letting the breeze cool her like a grass skirt.

"Aloha, cat."

Roscoe was fast asleep. What if the wind shifted and backed the big mainsail, and it slammed around and the boom broke the preventer? Roscoe would go flying. First thing the poor cat would know, he'd be in the ocean, meowing in terror as the boat sailed past. She stepped out from under the awning into the full heat of the sun, up onto the cabin roof, snatched him out of the sail, and dragged him to the cockpit.

"I'm obsessing about you falling overboard. I'll kill you if anything ever happens to you. Will you try the harness again, please?"

She had fashioned it yesterday out of light nylon line she had made by unraveling a short length of anchor line. Two loops under his chest and tummy and one to be safe just around his neck, all joined in a loop on his back, to which she bent a six-foot line she could tie to the lifelines, or the handholds on the roof, or the stern pulpit, or the companionway in the cabin.

"Hold still!"

She got him into it and tied him onto the lifeline. "Just relax . . . Shit!"

He'd set a new world record of eight seconds to get out of it. "Okay. Okay. Look at this." He was watching from a distance now, atop the coach room, determined not to get caught again. She went below, burrowed into the jammed forepeak, and fished out one of the long spring lines used for docking. Back in the cockpit, she held it in front of him. "See this. If you fall over, you grab on to this. I'm not kidding. If you fall over and I don't see you that second, you are gone. So if you do, grab on to this and yell your stupid head off."

She heard herself talking to him and it might have been funny, except for some reason she couldn't entirely understand, she was crying. Her eyes were all wet and a heavy lump got heavier and heavier in her throat. Well, it didn't take a genius or even a Dr. Melton to know why. "Don't you understand, you damned cat. I am so scared of losing you—Watch me!"

She tied the line to the aftermost lifeline stanchion and led it back under the stern pulpit and tossed the end into the wake. It streamed behind the boat for twenty feet. If he could get his claws into it . . . Maybe he'd have a chance.

"I'm going wack."

She was thirsty. She hadn't been drinking enough water. Maybe she was getting dehydrated. She forced herself to drink a whole bottle of warm water in long slugs, wishing, praying, thinking if she could have anything in the world right now, it would be to walk into a deli and buy a bag of ice.

She checked her GPS again and entered the new fixes on her chart. More than two-thirds of the way to her equatorial crossing; but less than half to Blind Man Island. She drank some more water and noted with satisfaction that the boat was sailing like a dream. Puzzlingly, however, the GPS showed her slowing down. Not only slowing down, but drifting east of the course she had laid out on the chart.

Morgan calculated the drift by measuring her distance from the position where she expected to be and dividing that by the time since the last fix. Then she got out her books.

"Duh!"

She had entered the east-flowing Equatorial Countercurrent. Probably before she crossed 10 North. *Molly* would be fighting it until they got within two or three degrees of the equator and joined the westward-flowing South Equatorial Current. As if things weren't slow enough already.

She stuck her head out the hatch and studied the water. Some sharp-eyed sailor might be able to see the current in the water, but not her. Although, when she studied the regular seas that the northeast trade wind was driving to the southwest, maybe she did see a disturbance, a jagged ripple of resistance, suggesting that the waves and current were moving in opposition.

She felt something cool on her cheek. The sun was sinking west, but it was too early to expect any nighttime relief from the heat. A puff of wind, not so cool, but definitely holding less heat. She ducked down to see under the sails. Ahead of the boat was a dark haze on the horizon, and when she looked closely, she saw ribbons of rain hanging from the sky.

First squalls of the doldrums?

She looked again and was suddenly galvanized into action. They were closer than she thought. She quickly released the preventer and hauled down the big genoa and took two reefs in the main. Hand-steering because the boat was unbalanced under main alone, she eyed the squall. If it was only rain, it would be beautiful to sail right into it and stand under it like a warm shower. If it was wind, she was ready, but thank God she had felt the temperature change. She could have blundered right into it. It was a scary reminder to pay attention. Squalls could be deadly. And there would be more of them as they neared the doldrums.

Feel the wind.

She registered another cool puff on her cheek, grabbed her binoculars, and studied the squall line. It was advancing behind a fierce white line of tall waves, like snowplows blasting through a blizzard. Thank you, Daddy. She altered course to sail behind it.

If only I could return the favor.

At least you're safe on dry land . . . Or are you? She shivered. She felt a deep chill that had not ridden on the wind, but attacked from within her. Daddy, when you ran away to Blind Man Island, did you run into a lion's den?

What if the U.S. attorney was really investigating Mr. Hong? What if he was just getting at him through you? What if Mr. Hong did something really criminal and the prosecutor thought you knew?

Was it the shipping company? You said they were crooks. She remembered him muttering angrily when she opened the shipping-company subfolder. "I warned him about this. I told him they'd get investigated for padding government contracts. I told Henry Hong it was a time bomb."

"Why didn't he listen?" she had asked.

"He said he was going to flip them. Sell them again, right away, so it wouldn't matter. He said he had Indian buyers lined up."

Daddy, even if you didn't know what he had done, what if Mr. Hong thought you did?

And she wished again she had a radio. Though how could she radio someone who didn't exist?

29

J IN-SHIL, ACCOMPANIED BY A GURKHA bodyguard and
two heavily armed boat boys, drove Henry's gas-turbine motor
launch around Blind Man Island to the construction site on the
windward side. Weaving through coral heads and battling the
bigger-than-usual swell, the twelve-mile journey took the custom-
built Rivolta 38 Jet Coupe over an hour even though the boat's
Kevlar-reinforced hull and the minuscule draft of the jet drive
allowed her to cross depths that would tear the bottom out of most
craft.

A skeleton crew of Korean laborers manned the pier, the rusting
crane that towered over it, and the shaft collar—a reinforced concrete seawall, six feet high, twenty feet in diameter—where drilling
continued day and night. Their prefab sleeping huts and cook shed
clung to the sides of the cliff above the sea line and only a very dis-
cerning observer could calculate that the huts would house far more
than the men seen on the surface. Particularly if they were bunking
in tiers as tightly packed as a submarine.

When Jin-shil jumped ashore, she could feel the distant drilling
vibrating up through the volcanic rock. The engineers waiting
beside the shaft bowed. The senior man extended her a hard hat,
respectfully, in both hands. But she lingered to examine the newly
installed storm lid. Set on rails beside the collar, the massive circle of
steel could slide over the shaft to seal it from cyclone seas. She gestured. Machinery ground and the lid trundled partway across the
collar, stopping short of the drill structure, which would have to be
disassembled to shut the shaft entirely in the event of a storm surge
flooding the lagoon.

Still she lingered, signaling her structural engineer—a servant wise in her ways, who sprang forward with blueprints and the latest seismic velocity profiles. The hydrothermally altered volcanic rock had caught them by surprise, being even less stable than early profiles had indicated and they had had a close call—which had shut them down for a year—when the lip of the shaft crumbled under the weight of the collar and a seismic wave set off by vibrations from the drill.

She had run out of legitimate ways to stall.

She braced herself to enter the shaft. Confined spaces terrified her, one reason she loved the open, sprawling house Henry had built for her. They conjured overwhelming memories of punishment closets in the orphanages; the cellar where she had hidden for a half a winter; and the abandoned freezer where the soldiers had left her to suffocate.

Locked in the dark, bleeding—torn body and soul—she had still looked to God, then, and He had sent a liberator—the vigilant Operations Department recruiting agent who smuggled her to a new life in the North. Now she looked up at the sun-splashed cliffs, to take courage from their heights, and let grow in her mind a silent mantra. *We are a small nation with many enemies. We have only our spirit and our wits.*

"HELLO, GORGEOUS," CHARLIE Page whispered as Jin-shil stepped into his crosshairs. She was wearing a red hard hat. The wind that rattled the leaves around his blind swooped down the slope and tugged at her blouse. He slowed his breathing to steady the shot.

He lay absolutely still, with only the tip of the muzzle extending from the rocks. Salote, the Tongan soldier's wife who had hidden him, stroked his back. His ruined eye was covered by a patch of bark cloth she had made for him. Her brothers had stolen the antibiotics that suppressed infection, and the rifle to avenge himself, and had made it clear that they didn't care much for Henry Hong's Gurkha officers. Nor did they miss Salote's husband, who had found work in Vancouver.

It was a two-for-one shot: obliterate Jin-shil for blinding his eye and rob Henry Hong of the woman he adored to repay him for siccing her on him.

"More guards," warned Salote. She provided as solid a backup as any he had known in the army: alert, observant, and even cooler under fire than he'd have predicted from her knowing smile.

Charlie pulled back from the scope. The three on the boat were joined by three Koreans. They were toting rifles, which made him pause to reassess his field of fire. He had no desire to die, no intention of taking foolish chances. But looking down on the cramped little harbor, he calculated good odds that he could kill her and get away. The cliffs were all the advantage he needed. The sheer rock walls would echo the report all over the place; the confusion would buy time to escape.

He found Jin-shil's face in the scope, again, just as she stepped into the crane bucket beside the engineer waiting for her. An imperious nod, and the crane operator swung the bucket over the shaft, where they had to wait while workmen lined the bucket up with the vertical rail that would steady it on its long ride down.

Aiming a superb weapon from the heights, Charlie was enough of a marksman to take her in midnod with a snapshot. Even with one eye. But he was suddenly more interested in where she was going than in immediately avenging the loss of his eye, and he let her go. He could just as easily get her when they brought her back to the surface.

This just did not look like what it was supposed to be. Add up all the construction—the crane, shaft, the concrete pier, the rusting rebar sprouting from the footings—and what was he looking at? Mainly a pier for a three-hundred-foot ship, beside a deep hole. He didn't know what it was, but it sure as hell was not a tropical resort-hotel site. He shifted the scope to watch the crane, which kept paying out cable until its massive drum was almost empty, down to the last row. A winch drum that big on a tugboat would hold nearly a mile of tow wire. Very deep indeed. Where was she going and what would she find when she got there?

Strange projects stood half-finished all over the Tongan Islands. All over the South Pacific, for that matter. Although the kingdom of Tonga drew its full share of crackpot schemes: down in the southern Tongatapu group seagulls nested on a launchpad built by Californians for tourist space-rocket rides; Internet relay stations, squash and seaweed farms to supply Japan, vanilla-bean ventures; and of course, the scam foisted by the religious cult that claimed to have a secret formula to turn seawater into natural gas.

Charlie allowed himself a grim smile. Maybe Henry Hong and Jin-shil were planning to launch space tourists out of that shaft—the steel lid on rails could easily pass for a missile-silo door—but whatever they were up to, it sure didn't look like a hotel.

The drum started turning again, wrapping up the cable.

When Jin-shil came up, he took another bead on her head.

Too much was going on here that he didn't understand.

He closed his eye on Jin-shil. His mind cycled back to the day in New York when Henry Ho Hong had offered him the bank; the day in the midnineties when he had failed to punch Henry in the face for calling him Charlie-boy. Instead of maintaining the line between them, he had caved for the money, saying only, "I feel like I won the lottery."

After that admission, Henry could afford to be gracious. "Luck has nothing to do with it, Charlie. You're the best man for the job."

And indeed I was, thought Charlie. He had not known precisely why at the time, though he had his suspicions. Suspicions he did not voice because he wanted the job too much, and whatever answer Henry would have conjured up, he would have accepted it. When he finally did ask, it was too late to get out.

Henry did not identify his investors. But with China hurling itself into a schizoid mix of foreign cash, crony capitalism, free-marketeering, and Communist Party quality control, it didn't take a genius to guess that Henry Ho Hong was serving an ever-increasing cadre of Mainland Chinese officials smuggling bribes out of the country. And Red Army generals stashing money they'd skimmed. Not to mention Hong Kong interests hedging bets in case the impending 1997 takeover blew the whole system to smithereens. By comparison, Wall Street looked like a safe haven and the U.S. secure. What better place to multiply illegal gains and in the process make them appear legal? Perfectly logical, if ethically dicey, though not quite illegal—which was exactly what Henry had wanted him to guess, he discovered later.

HHH & Company was a winner, as it could not help but be, pumping its steady cash flow into a rising market. Charlie Page built a reputation for deep pockets and a willingness to take risks—an uncommon combination on the Street. With great pride he moved up to lavish offices on the ninety-first floor of the World Trade Center and every day he would take time to just stop and stare out the window. The building really was like an airplane; people looked like ants, cars like slow-moving roaches. HHH's offices, which reflected Charlie Page's white-shoe apprenticeship and a burning desire to outdo his old bosses, had an old-fashioned feel, with walnut paneling ransacked from one of the Vanderbilt mansions and the nineteenth-century ship paintings beloved of Hong Kong Scottish taipans—Henry's contribution. But attitudes were strictly nineties modern; entrepreneurs seeking capital and hustlers launching public offerings found a willingness to invest in almost anything as long as HHH could climb aboard ahead of the general public.

The firm survived shortsighted investments in Atari game machines instead of software and Sony, courtesy of Charlie's brother; bungled hedging by a math-genius rocket scientist who should have stayed at NASA; excessive hope in the short-term future of Russian capitalism; as well as gangs of "new paradigm" boosters threatening, "If you're not with us, you just don't get it."

As long as Henry kept funneling money from Hong Kong, HHH & Company lumbered through the Greenspan "irrational exuberance" crisis of '96, the Asian collapse of '97, the Russian meltdown and Long Term Capital debacle of '98. Charlie Page reveled in the prince-of-the-city status accorded a Wall Street *macher*. He loved the money, the media coverage, the star treatment in the best restaurants, the countless invitations. But in his heart, it became impossible to deny that the man at the helm of HHH was like the captain of an oil tanker that fueled its engines with its own cargo.

It meant that he was probably in charge of a criminal enterprise. Worse, Henry could cut him off at the knees on a whim. Two reasons he should be paid more.

He had Concorded to London and boarded Cathay to Hong Kong.

Henry had not been pleased by the surprise visit. Midafternoon, he offered no brandy. Not even a cup of coffee. "I'm touched by your generosity," he said coolly. "You've traveled ten thousand miles to tell me 'things will get better.' " (It was '97 or '98, the Russians or Long Term Capital the crisis of the hour.)

"Things *will* get better," said Charlie. "It's all taking off again—this Internet stuff is amazing."

"Really? With AOL's network crashing daily, I understand that people are going back to the telephone."

"The country practically stops dead when their system goes down. That tells me they've got the subscriber base to own the world."

"You're still buying AOL?"

"With both hands."

Henry stared his flattest Chinese face stare.

Charlie said, "That's not why I came. I'd like a cup of coffee. Do you want to order it or shall I?"

Henry snatched up a telephone. "Coffee."

It arrived quickly in silver and china. Henry dismissed the servant. During the short wait, neither man had spoken. Now neither touched his cup. Finally, when Henry looked like he might break the silence, Charlie beat him to the punch.

"You don't mind losses, do you, Henry?"

"Would that our investors were so trusting."

"Our 'investors' don't exist. 'They' don't care about losses. In fact, sometimes 'they' like losses."

Henry nodded with a small smile. Jackpot. Again, Charlie spoke first.

"The bank is a front. We're money launderers, not bankers."

Henry's smile got bigger.

"The bank is a front," Charlie repeated. "We're laundering money, aren't we? That's what fuels this outfit."

"Whatever money comes into our firm leaves clean."

"But it's coming in dirty."

"You sound outrageously outraged. I must admit I'm surprised."

"Money laundering is a crime. We could be in deep shit."

"Only if we're caught and that's not likely."

"My cousins who are cops love criminals who think they won't get caught. They're more fun to catch. Is it drug money?"

"Do you care?"

"Yes. I told you I know drugs. People kill for drugs. On all levels of the business, no matter how high or low you go, murder is a tactic."

"Not one penny is drug money."

"That kind of money? Bullshit it's not drugs. If you want me to stay in, you have to level with me."

"Are you sure you want to know? You don't need to. We can keep on going as before."

"I hire people who don't need to know. But I need to know. Where's the money coming from? It's not skimmed Chinese money. They don't have to launder. They just want it out of China."

"It's mine."

"What do you mean?"

"I still funnel some Red Chinese money to keep friends happy. But by now ninety percent of the funds I send you represent my own personal profits."

Charlie was shocked. "Where did you get that much money?"

"Brokering sales."

"Of what? How could you make so much—Jesus H. Are you selling weapons?"

"Do you have a problem with the arms trade?"

"Not as much as drugs."

"Even though people kill for arms, too?"

"No, they kill *with* arms. But they keep the business clean, works better for everybody."

"So weapons don't trouble you?"

"Weapons are an excellent business, until you happen to supply terrorist customers who see Wall Street firms like HHH and Company as their enemy. Not to mention governments like mine and yours—what are you, now? Brit? Hong Kong?"

"I am a subject of the king of Tonga."

"Tonga?"

"An island group in the far western South Pacific. It used to be called the Friendly Islands." Henry smiled, pleased with himself. "I have many friends among the rulers. The weather is gorgeous. It is quite beautiful, extremely remote, and, best of all, sovereign."

"Sounds like a prosecutor's nightmare." Charlie laughed. "How the hell did you get into arms?"

"It seemed like a good idea at the time."

Charlie stood up and looked out at the thousand ships carpeting Hong Kong Harbor. He raised his eyes to the hills of China and tried to calculate how to make this work for him best. First time he'd come to Hong Kong, the Chinese hills had been blue in the distance. Now they were rendered pink by air pollution. He spoke to Henry's faint reflection in the glass. "Level with me. How did you go from raiding tugboat companies to selling weapons?"

"My first deal I did as a favor for a general who had stolen a shipload of AK-47s without a clue how to get paid for them. That's when I discovered the marvelous thing about the arms business. The buyer often needs the weapons ASAP because his enemies are shooting at him. So even though he's paying you the money, he thinks you did him a favor and saved his life."

"Doesn't it dawn on the sucker that you sold bullets to the guy shooting at him?"

"After the battle, sure, but by then he's liberated his people, so he suddenly needs a heap of police equipment—helicopters, surveillance instruments, prison supplies—to keep the liberated in line."

"But you see the problem. The rocket you sell to an embargoed state gets sold or passed on to a terrorist cell and one day it's crashing through our window."

Henry Ho Hong smiled. "So could a bolt of lightning."

"Especially if you're standing in the window waving a copper sword—"

"Is it a problem for you?" Henry pressed.

"No problem: because the way the market is heading, I'll make you so much money we'll both retire by 2002."

"Cheers." They picked up their cups at last.

"Will you tell your brother?"

"Jesus H., no!"

"I thought you were close."

"I love Aiden and I'll do anything to protect him. Anything. He's a sweet guy, but unfortunately, something of a fool. Which makes him a perfect chief financial officer."

Henry Ho Hong said, "I love you, Charlie. You must be at least one-third Chinese."

"Yeah, I love you, too, Henry. What kind of arms are we talking, here?"

"Whatever sells. Small arms to the Africans—assault rifles, grenade launchers, land mines—that's all they can afford. APCs and tanks in the Gulf. Missiles, diesel submarines, ballistic missiles and radar, et cetera to governments under UN embargo. Shoulder-launched surface-to-air missiles to their rebels."

"Which means that you're smuggling, too."

"I believe in free trade."

Charlie gave him the laugh Henry expected.

Henry said, "Thank God for the arms embargoes. My biggest competitors in the open market are the U.S., Britain, Russia, and China. Without the embargoes and the UN terrorists sanctions list, I'd be out of business."

"You sell to terrorists?"

"Who can take sides? One man's terrorist is another man's freedom fighter. Just as—look . . ." He hesitated, as if not sure he should say more. "Just as one man's weapon is another man's tool. Weapons are not always guns or explosives. Have I answered your question?"

"All but one."

"Shoot."

"What makes you think I'll continue our arrangement, now that I know what's going on?"

Henry gave him a tight smile. "Would doubling your take seem more fair?"

"Tripling would help make up for not being up-front with me."

Henry caved and Charlie flew home congratulating himself on how deftly he had handled his boss. But he soon learned, with a bitterness so sharp he could still taste it boiling in his throat, that his old rival had even more secrets, which he wouldn't tell. Worse, Henry Hong had once again left him in the dust.

Right after that meeting at which Charlie had accepted that he was the CEO of a criminal enterprise, Henry had acquired his private safe haven on Blind Man Island. While Charlie had moved up to a floor-through Park Avenue co-op, commissioned a Finnish shipbuilder to start construction of a hundred-foot ketch, and married an expensive wife, Henry Ho Hong had built his power station, his water distillation plant, and his palace, and started construction of his resort harbor on the far side of his island. The bone he had thrown Charlie had been to leave for a week of skiing in Switzerland so Charlie Page could impress family, friends, and employees by chartering Henry's own 747-400—a stretch-limo version of the four-engine Boeing wide-body—to fly everyone to paradise for Christmas.

With the dot-com collapse in 2000, the losses turned real—slow at first, then as sudden as they were devastating. The Henry spigot dried up. "When hundred-dollar stocks become penny stocks," he told Charlie, "I send my laundry elsewhere."

But where he sent his laundry was a mystery.

There was no way that Henry could have moved the sort of cash he funneled through HHH without Charlie getting wind of the lucky new recipient. The Street was too small a club. Competitors would have been smirking at him and bragging behind his back about their hot new accounts. But he heard not a hint of the new recipient. Only rumors here and there of Henry purchasing a construction outfit or a shipping firm, but nothing he could pin down, particularly when he was so busy scrambling to stay afloat.

For a full year after the crash, Charlie couldn't believe that the ride was over. But money melted. Debts soared. He had protected his personal fortune for a while, but the business kept evaporating. Then, suddenly, from a direction he least expected, federal investigators pursuing one of HHH's minor clients got interested in certain transactions. It had been even money whether bankruptcy or the prosecutors would get him first, when out of the blue—like the lightning bolt he had warned Henry about—Al Qaeda's murderers saved his life.

"*Shoot!*" said Salote.

He opened his remaining eye.

Jin-shil's face was still in his scope, the sight intersecting on her cheekbone.

"Kill her."

He shook his head. "Not yet."

"She killed your beautiful eye—*shoot!*"

"Too many guards," he lied.

It would be stupid to pull the trigger. Clearly, Henry and Jinshil's hole in the ground was no hotel. If he could figure out what the project meant to them, he could take double revenge. On her. On Henry. And come out of this owning it all.

EVERY NOON, MORGAN PENCILED HER GPS fix onto her chart. She measured the distance that wind and current had caused her to drift from her rhumb line and calculated small course changes to get back on track. In her log she entered her position, along with wind speed, sea conditions, weather. When talking to Roscoe wasn't enough to keep from going crazy, she also wrote news of the day.

This hot, horrible windless noon—becalmed on heaving swells—her neat block print was splintered like crackhead graffiti by the violent motion of the boat.

> I AM REALLY FUCKING TIRED OF BEING ROLLED AROUND LIKE A BOWLING BALL BY THE SWELL BECAUSE THERE IS NO FUCKING WIND IN THESE FUCKING DOLDRUMS. AND SO IS ROSCOE. THE DECK IS NEVER STILL FOR EVEN ONE SECOND. DROOPY SAILS ARE SWINGING WITH EVERY ROLL. AND THE BOOM KEEPS JERKING THE SHEETS. IT'S LIKE GOD GOES, "LET'S TORTURE THE GIRL AND THE CAT." IT'S MAKING ME SO CRAZY I FORGET TO READ THE TAFFRAIL LOG AND CHECK THE BAROMETER. SHIT!

Clinging to handholds, cursing the swell, she struggled up into the cockpit and out of the shadow of the awning into the skin-frying sun to read the dial of the tag-sale taffrail log, which was supposed to be trailing behind the boat, but today was hanging straight down like an anchor. The GPS had already told her boat speed—dead zero in the calm—and speed over ground—a knot from the North Equatorial Current. She worried what she would do if her GPS broke or the batteries died or Roscoe knocked it overboard. Use the backup.

But in case Roscoe trashed the backup, too, she was sailing with two records of her progress: the electronic one that tracked her to within a few feet of her position in the Pacific, and a deduced "ded"-reckoned position that she calculated from her speed, course, the current, and the time and distance sailed. She corrected her ded-reckoned position each day by the GPS fix and occasionally found it satisfyingly close.

Similarly, she backed up her weather fax with regular measurements of wind speed, temperature, and barometer. Her Skymaster weather station hinged open like a jackknife, to expose the screen and the little impeller that she held to the wind. What wind?

This morning, when she turned it on, it shrilled, *Beeeeee-eeeeeeeeeeeeeeeeeeeep!*

The high-pitched tone startled her and she nearly dropped it.

"Whoa! . . . What—ohmigod."

She had bought this model specifically for the severe-weather warning feature. The alarm tripped if barometric pressure dropped six millibars in six hours, which would indicate a vicious low was bearing down on her at high speed. The faster and deeper the drop, the worse the storm. The screen showed an eight-millibar drop in the past six hours.

She scrambled below to check the weather fax. "Oh shit!" There was the latest sheet, right in front of her, which she had been too narcked out by the heat and the relentless rolling to bother to read. A deep low forming to the west looked as big as Kansas. She stuck her head out the hatch.

While the sun still blazed through the thin veil overhead, the sky had turned fuzzy gray in the west. And the horizon had developed an edge she had not noticed before. Where the meeting of sea and sky had been indistinct earlier, it was marked now by a strong, low jumble that looked like a stone wall. Ten miles away? She tried to scope it out through the binoculars. More like six or eight. And moving toward her.

She immediately lowered the big genoa, stuffed it into the forepeak, and brought up the storm jib, blessing the original owner who had stowed it in an easily spotted red bag. She hanked on the tiny triangle of stiff, heavyweight Dacron, then she took both reefs in the main and lashed the excess cloth tightly to the boom.

She caught Roscoe, who was sprawled in the cockpit, put him below. It was hard to believe she would need foul-weather gear in the brutal heat, but she brought her jacket and her PFD harness up on deck. She slid the washboard into its slot and checked that she could slide the hatch easily closed when the storm hit. Then she sat down in the cockpit and wondered what else to do while the horizon grew taller and darker.

She took the solar panel below, out of harm's way.

Food. She should drink water and eat while she could. Too late to cook and her stomach was too unsettled by the constant rolling. Tuna without mayonnaise. Tuna straight from the can. She gobbled a few bites, couldn't stand any more, and gave the rest to Roscoe. She grabbed a freshwater bottle and fled the hot cabin.

The awning. She untied and stowed it.

It was hard to believe that anything would ever happen. The boat was still rocking and rolling. The sun, though obscured by cloud, still burned. And the air was almost too heavy to breathe. It was like waiting for a test to be passed out, wondering what you had forgotten to study and why the school hadn't fixed the air-conditioning.

"I can't stand waiting."

She took a deep breath of the thick air and climbed below to bag the genoa, which was all over the forepeak. By the time she got it in the bag, she thought she was going to throw up and sweat was pouring out of her skin. But crawling through the cabin, she paused to toss the empty tuna can before it flew around spilling oil. Back in the cockpit, she clipped her tether to a cleat. A cool puff of air felt like heaven on her wet body.

Ripples darkened the greasy-looking water and her spirits rose. Storm or no storm, any change beat the present. Another puff, even cooler. Heaven again. This one shivered the sails. Morgan nudged the tiller. *Molly* leaned a little and pushed her bow against the water.

"Yes, cat! We are out of here."

From the cabin came a terrified howl. Morgan shivered. The animal knew better.

In the distance the water turned dark gray, then black. Wind was building. Whitecaps suddenly sparkled. Her eyes shot to the mainsail, reefed as low as it would go. Should have doused it entirely. Too late now. The first ripples were arriving, behind them low waves, and behind them, closing faster now, whitecaps, stacked deep as snow.

The first gust punched the sails like a fist. *Molly* sliced into it, close-hauled, spilling excess wind and cutting a smooth track through the sudden chop. The whitecaps were racing toward her now. Leading the whitecaps came the second gust.

It shoved hard at the boat, and pushed her on her side. Morgan tried to head up into the wind again, but the boat leaned farther and she was caught off balance. Suddenly she was looking down at the water. She fell across the cockpit. Still trying to steer, she reached for the lifeline to keep from falling overboard. To her disbelief, the boat kept heeling, so far onto the side that the stainless-steel wire disappeared underwater. She missed the wire and fell hard against one of its stanchions.

The solid upright saved her from falling overboard, but at the cost of pain in her shoulder that seared her to the bone and ripped a scream from her throat. A wave broke over the bow and raced along the side deck and exploded into the cockpit. Warm water broke over her head. A second wave grabbed her with the force of a heavy animal and started dragging her out of the boat. She reached desperately for the tiller, but water and gravity pinned her to the stanchion. The boat whipped upright, throwing her onto the cockpit floor. She found the tiller and looked ahead.

She wished she hadn't. She had never seen such waves in her life. The whitecaps had tripled in number and tripled again into a hissing mass of foam and broken seas. Stacked closely, colliding, they raced in every direction like angry rioters fleeing tear gas. They slammed against *Molly*'s hull. She was cold, for the first time in ten days. The wind blew harder, lifting spray from the waves and blowing it like hail in her face. Her boat had never seemed so small, and it was fear, she knew, that felt so cold.

Then something raced across the waves, scattering them, like a giant kicking leaves. A huge gust hit the sails again and down *Molly* went. Morgan lurched across the cockpit, desperately scrambling to get her feet in front of her, stopped her momentum on the opposite seat back, and struggled back to the starboard side. She tried to steer into the wind. But the rudder was angled too far out of the water and the boat heeled so steeply that she saw the lower mast spreader touch the waves.

Another gust flattened the whitecaps. Morgan gripped the tiller and braced her feet. The gust doubled and over *Molly* went again. But this time Morgan kept her seat and steered up into the gust, headed her up, building speed, even as she spilled the worst of the wind. She watched the boiling sea for warning of the next gust.

Eerie darkness spread from the depths of the squall, obscuring all, and she could not see the next crazy blast until it struck. Spray stung her face. The boat staggered. It seemed the wind would push it backward. And in that moment when her forward motion ceased, a wall of water, taller than any of the waves, washed over the bow, pummeled the cabin roof, and crashed into the cockpit.

Shoulder-deep in the pounding rush, clinging to the tiller and the nearest stanchion, Morgan felt the stern sink under the weight of the water. The bow pitched up like a frail finger pointing at the sky.

If the next sea scooped under it, it would flip the boat backward. But her heavy keel held her down even as the water washed out of the cockpit and spilled from the scuppers. *Molly* rose, regained her precarious perch between water and air, and caught the wind. She forged ahead, and shrugged through the next sea, then hesitated, as if afraid to ask, *What's next?*

Morgan heard a loud hissing sound race toward her. Cold rain pelted down, drumming on the decks, falling so hard that it flattened the sea. For five minutes that seemed like an hour, the rain filled the air and she could barely breathe, much less see the compass. The rain stopped as suddenly as it had started. Wiping her eyes, Morgan saw the wind returning, chiseling jagged seas from the undulating swell. The wind backed her storm jib and forced the bow off course. She let it swing, let the wind get behind her, and let the boat run.

But she felt bold, having survived three knockdowns that might have killed them, and when she saw her chance in a patch of flat water, she jibed back on course. The seas built and the storm settled in—for this was no brief squall, she began to realize, but a storm for sure—and she started working the angles, heading into waves, bearing off down their back sides while holding her southwesterly course to cross the equator, the sooner to put this misery behind her.

Rain slashed down again, chilling her to the bone. But it pounded every bit of salt and perspiration from her body until she felt cleaner than she had in weeks. And when it had raced on, she tied the tiller and jumped below to see how Roscoe was doing.

"Oh, animal." Water bottles had broken loose and flown around the cabin, and the cat was huddled fearfully on her berth, which was soaked from the big wave leaking through the washboards. She hugged him quickly, said, "I can't help you now," grabbed an apple, and raced back on deck.

*A*RCHIMEDES ROUNDED THE GALÁPAGOS, PICKED up the southeast trades sooner than expected, and took off on a broad reach. Now Aiden Page earned his keep, flying the huge spinnaker to capture the following wind. The brightly colored sail looked like a gigantic grapefruit as it strained to get ahead of the bow and it felt sometimes as if it would break the bounds of gravity. The sloop surfed, planing over the regular seas on her flat bottom, trailing a rooster tail like a powerful motorboat.

At last, a smile brightened Tom Slade's grim face. "No stops!"

Which, Aiden knew by now, was Slade's way of ordering, No reefs, no matter how hard it blew. "Even the fucking current's helping out," he howled. *"No stops!"*

They achieved back-to-back three-hundred-mile days that hurtled them across the equator at 100 West Longitude. If they could sustain this rate, they'd hit Fiji in less than three weeks. But that was impossible: even the trades were not 100 percent reliable. Nor could they expect something not to break in the course of sailing flat out for four and a half thousand miles. But even losing the wind on occasion, even stopping to repair a parted halyard or a ripped headsail, *Archimedes* was flying Aiden across the Pacific three times faster than the old girls' *Darling*.

A daunting thought, he had to admit as he watched the water race by. In less than a month he would have to confront Henry Hong. Alone. Unless Charlie was there, alive and well, in which case he had nothing to worry about. But was Charlie likely to be alive if Henry Hong was behind the attack in Panama? Big if, he reminded himself. Add up everything he thought he knew, all the theories in the world proved nothing.

"Tom, I'm going below. Give a yell if you need me." But before he headed down to crank up his laptop for another go at his HHH disk, he loped onto the foredeck to make sure the spinnaker pole was properly seated in its mast track. Ahead of the boat something white lay just beneath the next sea. Big shark? Nurse shark? he wondered in the instant before he saw a square edge.

"Starboard!" he yelled to Tom. "Head down!" and pointed with a full, rigid arm to turn right.

Slade jerked the helm and at sixteen knots the twin rudders skidded the boat swiftly right. Aiden grabbed the shrouds and leaned out to look. "Son of a bitch!"

Slade had already jumped up onto the side deck to get a better angle. "Container." A steel shipping container, twenty feet long, eight feet square, had rolled off a ship. Trapped air or buoyant contents floated it just beneath the surface.

"Hit that at twenty knots we'd know it."

Tom shrugged. "Fucking freighters."

"There's another! Head down! Head down!"

Slade turned to starboard again, off their port tack, and the second container broke surface, bobbing in their wake.

"Maybe we ought to back off a little?"

"Three in midocean? What's the odds of that?"

"What if a whole bunch of them rolled off in a gale?"

"I've seen one or two in an entire passage. Never three."

"I think I'll stand watch on the bow."

"Suit yourself."

Leaning ahead of the jib, gripping the forestay, he watched for more containers until it was his trick at the wheel. In that hour they had moved fifteen nautical miles from the last one they had sighted. The current and wind were active, however, and containers would drift differently depending on weight and how long they thrust freeboard above the surface before they sank. But when Slade surrendered the wheel, he stretched out on the cockpit seat and closed his eyes instead of standing lookout on the bow.

"Aiden?"

Aiden checked the water ahead, sails, and compass, before he answered, "What?"

Slade surprised him with a personal question.

"You married?"

"Divorced."

"How long?"

"Sixteen years, married. Last I checked, the divorce wasn't quite finished. You?"

"Married."

"Where's your wife?"

"I don't know."

"What do you mean?"

"I couldn't stand the sympathy."

"I don't follow you."

"You know, 'I love you right or wrong, especially wrong' . . . I miss her. Good woman. Liked a laugh and always ready to give the ferret a run."

"Excuse me? Ferret a run?"

"Have sex . . . You got kids, Aiden?"

"Daughter."

"Me, too . . . How old?"

"Fifteen."

"I miss the hell out of mine."

"Too much sympathy?" asked Aiden.

"No. Girl kids are different. What does a daughter know? Except, Dad's perfect. She was sure it was all a big mistake."

"How old is she?"

"Ten. Maybe she'll get some perspective by the time she's a grandmother. But not while I'm still alive. How long since you've seen yours?"

"Eight months."

"When are you going to see her?"

"I don't know. I told you, I dropped out after I fucked up.

Disappeared. I thought it might be best for her to make that complete break. Then I missed her so much that I blew it."

"What do you mean?"

"Got drunk one night and telephoned."

"What'd she say?"

"I don't know. I hung up."

"Brilliant."

"Yeah. If I could only, somehow . . ."

"Change the past? Excellent idea. I'd love it. Stop the boat, pick up the 'drowning' sailors, and sail home a hero. Good old Slade, a sporting gent of the old school. Let's make him Rolex Yachtsman of the Year. Fuckers."

"Which fuckers?"

"The sailors. They weren't fucking drowning. If I knew they were drowning, do you think I would have sailed by?"

"No."

"You don't know. You're just saying that. I'd say it, too, if I were going to be shipmates with some poor bastard for a month. I'd say anything he wanted to hear. What I'm telling you—"

He broke off and sat up and stared ahead intently.

"What do you see?"

"Nothing. I'm trying to tell you—"

"What are you telling me?"

"I didn't fucking do it. And if I had to do it over again, I'd do the same thing."

"Sail past a sinking boat?"

"Their boat never sank."

"I heard it did."

"Rumor. It never sank. They abandoned ship for the life rafts, which is the stupidest move anybody could ever make. Never leave the ship. They left the ship. The ship I sailed past and that I knew was not sinking. It never occurred to me they'd be so stupid to leave her for the rafts. Six strong guys could have fished the mast, jury-rigged something, sailed home. Slow, uncomfortably. But home. Instead they panic, and I get the rap."

He stood up and pointed behind them, toward South America, across the Andes, and all the way to the middle of the Atlantic Ocean. "If they only took responsibility for themselves. But you know what they say. You'll never know a man until you've been shipwrecked with him—that's my sad tale, Aiden. What's yours? How'd you do 'em wrong?"

A thunderous crash resounded below. The deck shook as if a refrigerator had fallen three flights of stairs and *Archimedes* stopped dead. Aiden, still sailing at twenty-two knots, slammed against the wheel. Tom Slade tumbled backward down the companionway, his face a mask of astonished horror as the backstay parted with a loud bang.

A multiple-block backstay adjuster whizzed an inch from Aiden's head, tore a hole through the mainsail, and crashed to the deck like a bowling ball. At the same instant, the boat took off again, kicked up to speed by the stiff breeze.

"Head up!" shouted Tom Slade, clawing to his feet. "We hit a container."

"No kidding." Aiden was miles ahead of him, trimming the running backstays to help the mast before muscling the helm. It felt locked up, almost impossible to turn, as if the rudder had taken the brunt of the collison. But he had to head the boat into the wind to take the pressure off the sails before they snapped the unstayed mast and blew the pieces into the sea.

The rudder bearings were grinding ominously and he could feel an awful shuddering transmitted up from the steering quadrant, but he kept heaving on the wheel, knowing that if he didn't turn her around, additional damage to her steering gear would be the least of her problems.

A little helm did a lot for *Archimedes,* and quick off the rudder as always, she swung suddenly up, spilling the wind from the spinnaker, which collapsed in a crazy cloud of nylon. Slade sprinted forward, let fly its halyard, and began hauling the sail out of the water before it wrapped fatally around the keel.

Head-on, what had been following seas rampaged at the bow—lifting it like a cork, threatening to spin the boat sideways—and the powerhouse trade wind blew hard in their faces, luffing the mainsail, which clapped and crackled like skeet guns. Aiden trimmed its flogging sheets. Then he leaped below—afraid they were sinking—to pound plugs in holes and pump if they were. The stripped-out hull was like a long flat tunnel and much of the bottom was visible, as all that covered the ribs and scantlings was a forty-foot catwalk of floorboards laid bow to stern on the centerline.

"Dry up here!" Slade yelled, hanging down through the foredeck hatch. He stuffed the huge spinnaker through the hatch, clearing the decks for whatever came next.

"That's because we struck aft," Aiden yelled over his shoulder.

He was angry enough to throw cowboying "Captain No Stops!" overboard. If Slade's ignoring the container threat slowed them . . . He grabbed a light, a hammer, and conical hull plugs and raced toward the stern, where he saw water gleaming in the bilges.

"Son of a bitch!"

Water was shooting up from the stuffing box where the rudder post passed through the hull. Slade charged up behind him with another flashlight. Both men stared at the geyser that was spraying up with such force that it gushed against the ceiling. Slade said, "For Christ sake."

Aiden whipped off his polo shirt and wrapped it around the shaft. "I'll do this. You run the boat."

Slade turned on the bilge pump and led a hose up the companionway for the hand pump. Aiden started pounding his shirt into the broken gland with a hammer and a flat screwdriver. Easier said than done; the spewing water fought back, pushing the cloth out as fast as Aiden packed it in.

Slade led the spinnaker halyard aft and winched it tight to take the strain off the upper mast, forced the rudder into a fore-and-aft position, and eased the mainsail to give the boat a little headway. Aiden kept on pounding. The water was knee-deep and *Archimedes* was wallowing heavily, before he finally plugged the full circle around the shaft. By then the batteries had shorted out, so they had to pump her dry by hand, a brutal, hours-long job. Finally, the batteries were above water. They got the power sorted out to run the electric bilge pump, which was just able to keep up with the seepage. Night was gathering and both men were stumbling with exhaustion. They shambled up on deck to repair the broken backstay. While they worked, they powwowed their options.

To Aiden's dismay, back was the only way they could go. Back to the Galápagos. The Marquesas Islands, while in the direction they were headed and the trades were blowing, were still more than three thousand miles ahead. Easter Island was slightly closer, two and a half thousand miles but far to the south, and offered no repair facilities they could count on. God, or Neptune, knew what other damage the hull had suffered. Only by hauling her out of the water could they inspect hull and keel and restore her steering.

They eased the boat onto a starboard tack. Close-hauled, playing the sails to take the strain off the rudder, pumping continuously, they took six long days to backtrack their spectacular six-hundred-mile two-day downwind run, half a day more to motor against wind and current into Academy Bay, and a half a day to get permission from the Puerto Aroya port captain for an emergency stop in the strictly protected nature reserve and use of the drying grid. *Archimedes'* damage spoke louder than words that Aiden and Tom Slade were a delivery crew in serious need of repair and they passed easily through the formalities of quarantine and arms inspection—they had none— and a cursory examination of the passports that Tom had had properly stamped when they cleared Panama.

They worked alongside the yard workers repairing the rudder shaft, the broken backstay, and a near-lethal gouge out of the racer's exotic bottom. To Aiden's surprise, Slade actually relaxed. Sailing fast seemed to be more important to him than getting there. Best to get the boat in shape for another assault at the speed records in his private races. In the long run, Aiden reluctantly admitted, it would pay off. With proper repairs and luck—which wasn't running strong, lately—the rudder gland wouldn't open up again halfway to Fiji.

But the lost days were killing him. If Charlie was already on Blind Man Island, and if it was Henry Hong who was stalking Aiden, than Charlie was Henry's prisoner.

MORGAN'S WEATHER FAX HAD NOT lied. Day after day, the vast low pressure system pummeled her with wind, rain, and chaotic seas. Occasionally the wind dropped to a dead calm, as if pausing to rest. But there was no relief for *Molly*. Seas and cross seas continued to attack the boat. With no wind in her sails, she was helpless.

The nights seemed endless. The cloud cover was so thick that it was midmorning before Morgan saw her streaming decks in daylight. When she went below to rest, lumpy seas overwhelmed the self-steering and she had to race back to the cockpit before the boat broached beam onto the dangerous waves. Hour after hour she remained in the cockpit, hunched over the tiller, unable to hold any course, steering only to protect the boat.

She fell asleep. The tiller kicked, slipping out of her numb hand, and smacked her in the face so hard that she wept, first in pain, then exhaustion, then despair. The boat felt heavy, slower to answer the helm. Gradually it dawned on her that something was wrong, that the boat was faltering from more than the impact of the waves. She groped for an explanation, and when she guessed the cause, she accepted with resignation that she had to act. She engaged the self-steering, opened the hatch, quickly stepped inside, and turned on her flashlight. Roscoe was perched on her berth, his wet fur hackled up like a Mohawk, staring at a foot of water sloshing on the cabin floor.

Morgan switched on the electric bilge pump. But she couldn't hear its urgent whine over the hollow, high-pitched banging and crashing of the seas against the hull. Nor could she feel it vibrating underfoot. She plunged her hands into the water to pull up a floorboard, reaching down until her hand touched the pump. It was dead. The water must have shorted out the battery. She felt around for the hand pump, opened the hatch a crack, shoved the hose out, and started pumping, moving the handle up and down, up and down, up and down. When her right arm hurt too much to continue, she switched to her left, which sent shooting pains through her injured shoulder.

Hunched over the bilge, pumping with all her strength, she wanted to cry again. She looked up. Roscoe was on the bunk, at the level of her face, mewing in complete misery. "Poor animal. If I had told you it would be like this, you wouldn't have come, would you?"

He just kept mewing.

Where was all this water coming from? At that moment, the boat staggered as a wave overtook it and spilled into the cockpit. She looked up, expecting to see it pouring through the washboard that protected the main hatch. But very little water came in. Which meant a leak somewhere.

She crawled under the cockpit area and shined a light on the stern, where the electric bilge pump exited. No water. The seal was intact. She backed out, banging her head as the hull leaped and lurched, turned around, and made sure that water wasn't entering through the head. The toilet was dry.

The bow crashed into a trough. She heard a big wave break overhead on the deck. Icy water sprayed around the forepeak. She shone her light on the foredeck hatch. The latches were dogged down tightly. It dripped water on the sailbag under it, but not enough to flood the bilge. She started to crawl backward out of the forepeak, when she felt water pour down the mast.

The seal where the aluminum spar passed through the deck was shot. She touched it, felt the mast move, and jerked her hand back before it crushed her finger. She tied her sweatshirt around the mast and shoved it up into the joint with a screwdriver. It got wet and dripped, but the flood had stopped.

She caught a glimpse of her face in the little mirror above the toilet. Her salt-stung eyes were as red as an albino rabbit's. Her skin was blotched with bruises. And seeing those bruises, she suddenly felt an ache and a pain in every inch of her body.

A heavy sea smashed into the stern. She had no choice but to get back on deck. Crawling through the main cabin, observing the destruction from all the knockdowns, clothing and bedding soaked, gear strewn everywhere, she thought suddenly and unexpectedly about her mother. It was hard to believe she had ever lived on a boat, impossible to picture her living like this. All the years of her early childhood when Morgan was too young to know their life was unusual, her mother—Ms. Perfect Beauty—had lived on a boat. And not a magnificent Hinckley like *Molly P,* but old boats when they were poor. Before Daddy joined up with Uncle Charlie.

"Uncle Charlie rescued us," Mother used to say, punctuating the sentence with a deep sip from her martini—like she didn't want to think about it.

Wearily, she returned to the cockpit. How much longer? In answer, it seemed, lightning plunged from the sky and pierced the water like a flaming arrow. Thunder pealed.

She felt her wet hair start to rise from her scalp. A fierce sizzling noise whipped her head around. A fat, white electric bolt towered behind the boat. By its light she saw a sea that was almost entirely white. As it faded, she sensed something else, something different, but couldn't tell what it was. Thunder boomed. Then a third bolt lit the sky, and by its white flame she saw what she had sensed but not credited. While she was below, one of the big seas that had crashed into the stern had ripped the outboard motor off its lifting bracket.

She gaped in disbelief. Only yesterday she had made sure its clamps were tight. No motor meant she had nothing but the solar panel to charge the battery for the weather fax. But no motor also meant she was entirely dependent upon the wind when she got to Tonga and had to maneuver the boat through the narrow passes.

MORGAN NEVER KNEW when the storm ended. All she knew was rising from a near coma of a sleep, slumped in the cockpit, awakened by a ferocious sun. The sea had settled. The boat was poking along under her storm sails, holding a sort of course to the west and south. Her mouth was dry. She ached all over, and when she eased out of her foul-weather jacket, she found her wrists were red and bloody where the cuffs had ground salt into her skin.

"Cat? Mr. Cat?"

The hatch was closed. She slid it open. "Cat?"

A wet bilge stink rose from below. "Yeccch. Cat? Roscoe?"

He wandered into view, yawned and stretched. He was dry, his fur sleek. He made eye contact and sent a message that he was hungry.

She fed him. Above her raw wrists, her arms were bruised. So were her legs and torso. She stared at the bruise. "I'm getting skinny," she said to Roscoe. "Mom would love it. Skinny at last."

She was deeply thirsty. She drank nearly a quart of water. Then, too befuddled to concentrate on food, she ate several teaspoons of peanut butter. She remembered thinking about her mother, during the storm, which surprised her. So much of the past seemed to have vanished and about all she ever dwelled on was her father, worrying about him being alone and confused. He was never good on his own. The few times that she and Mom went away, they'd find the house a mess, even with the maid. The same man was Captain Clean on the boat, so maybe it was just because he needed his family.

Her boat was a wreck.

She started cleaning up the cabin, pulling her blanket and mattress up on deck in hopes of drying them in the humid air. She picked up the bottles and boxes that had fallen about, drank more water, and pumped the bilge and mopped. She checked on the battery. It was upright, hadn't spilled its acid, thank God. But one of the terminals had pulled loose. She slid it over the lead stud. A spark made her jump and she heard the bilge pump whine. She shut it off to save electricity for the weather fax.

Her GPS had gone missing, washed overboard. She hunted madly for her spare, held it to the sky, and waited, praying it would lock satellites. It worked, thank God, but when she saw her position, she groaned in dismay. 1, 1, 7 North. She hadn't even crossed the equator yet. "Jesus H.," she breathed aloud. "What does it take?"

The weather fax beeped. She ran to it and read the sheet as it rolled out of the machine. Shaking her head, she looked out the hatch to inspect the western sky and discovered yet another truth. All her skills and all her determination—and all her hope—had enabled her to sail to places where the tests kept coming. Nothing could be won for very long. Furious squalls were bearing down on her again. Somehow she had to find the strength to keep *Molly* intact.

S ALOTE GOT ANXIOUS WHEN CHARLIE Page spied on the construction site. What more was there to see?

Gently but firmly, he explained that he had to look down the deep shaft to figure out what they were doing in there. The surf might mask an approach from the sea, but he already knew firsthand that the risk was too high.

Couldn't her brothers watch for him? Wouldn't he be happier

staying home with her? "Home" was a cave high up the hill surrounded by dense jungle and watched over by her brothers. Better still, could they not set sail for Tofua in the Tongatapu group, where her family would take them in? They lived deep in the interior. They were not without influence in the kingdom. They would gladly smuggle in a doctor to examine his eye.

He had no interest in a doctor. The eye had been lost from the moment Jin-shil had stabbed it. If the wound were infected, it would have killed him by now. He was fine with a patch. He didn't need a doctor to tell him what he already knew. And he was adjusting to negotiating with a single eye, moving his head side to side like an owl to gain depth perception.

Every day, he descended the treacherous slope from the caves where they had set up house. He usually took Salote with him. She was strong and agile and alert, and he trusted her to watch his back. Sometimes he went alone.

During these descents he came alive in ways he hadn't felt since he was a kid in the service. It was strangely, even comfortingly, reminiscent of Afghanistan in the late 1980s. Henry's island was a hell of a lot warmer than the mountains of the Hindu Kush. The tropical jungle provided much less territory to hide in, but made up for it with denser cover. Henry Hong's handful of Gurkha officers were as thinly stretched as the collapsing Soviet army had been. Unfortunately, the Gurkhas made up for short-staffing with infrared scopes to see in the dark, and "big-ears" parabolic microphones that could hear men breathing in an ambush. Until he could convince Salote to get her light-fingered brothers to lift some high-tech hardware for him, he was moving down the mountain at a distinct disadvantage.

After eight days spying on Jin-shil's construction site, his patience was rewarded.

A sail appeared on the Pacific. It split in two, as it neared, and Charlie recognized the twin inverted triangles on the noble nephew's two-masted *wa a' kau lua* voyaging canoe. Attention would be focused on the new arrival. Charlie started down the slope.

Salote followed close behind, quick and surefooted as a gymnast despite her tall frame and full body.

He got the closest and lowest down yet—less than two hundred yards from the site, on a level with the slope-side workers' barracks—before the canoe doused sails and the paddlers surfed it between the concrete training walls that protected the channel. Traversing the artificial lagoon, they moored behind the Rivolta 38 that delivered Jin-shil most mornings.

Curiously, Noble Nephew had come without Henry. Charlie wondered whether the Tongan was cutting some sort of separate deal with Jin-shil. But he discounted that possibility. Henry's intelligence was always first-rate. One way or another, Henry would know of the canoe's arrival.

Salote tapped a warning on his back.

His near death at Jin-shil's hands had reawakened instincts and skills nearly two decades old. He released the cumbersome rifle and whirled around, knife appearing magically in one hand, pistol in the other. But Salote was only pointing at the sea. Two dark smudges were perched on the horizon. A single ship was a rare sight. Two in company, unique.

Nor were they passing the island. Their course was headed straight for the harbor. The one in the lead trailed smoke. The smokeless one behind it stood taller and bulkier, square as a car carrier. Why no smoke?

"Barge," said Salote.

Of course. A tug and tow. "Are you sure?"

"They've come before."

As they drew closer, he studied them through the rifle scope. Salote had called it. The lead "ship" was actually a seagoing tugboat with the high bow characteristic of her class. Her barge was far behind her, rising slab-sided twenty or thirty feet above the sea. As it drew close enough to make out details—twin smokestacks, massive towing winch, and an American flag, stiff in the wind—the tug started shortening up, reeling in the tow wire, cutting the distance between the two vessels until the wire itself emerged glistening from the water.

When a short length separated them, the tug belched smoke and started forward again, dragging the barge toward the training walls. In the lagoon, they moved Jin-shil's Rivolta runabout and the noble's twin-hull canoe from the pier and edged both craft against the reef on the opposite side.

"How many times have you seen them?" Charlie asked Salote.

"This will be four."

Miracles must have helped her across the Pacific. She was a sea-beaten old boat, with crapped-out diesels throwing heavy smoke from her stacks. Rust streaked her superstructure; dents and more rust marred her hull. The barge was heavily laden. Its draft numerals showed eighteen feet of hull below the surface. Based upon a similar-size paper-products barge he remembered from Henry Hong's long-ago New York tug takeover scam, Charlie guessed the barge had a capacity of ten thousand tons. Four barges—forty thousand tons. "What's in it?"

"No one knows."

Charlie looked askance at her. Like servants in a mansion, the Tongans tended to know far, far more about the comings and goings on Henry Hong's island than Henry would have liked. Salote shrugged, explaining, "They unload at night. Only Koreans are allowed to help."

He lay back and reached for Salote, who came closer with a smile. "I need a nightscope," he whispered as she pressed against him. "I can't wait any longer. Can you get me one?"

She said she would try. But she looked troubled. Looting the armory under the gaze of the Gurkha officers was difficult. Though not—as his rifle, pistol, and killing knife proved—impossible.

"Do more than try. Go! Go now. Do what you have to do."

She went.

Charlie returned his attention to the tug and barge. Would they off-load tonight under the nose of Noble Nephew, who had just sailed up in his voyaging canoe? Was his arrival concurrent with the barge's coincidence? Or was he part of whatever the hell Jin-shil was launching here?

Noble Nephew might think he was. Certainly he could open the right doors anywhere in Tonga. And close them, too, offering privacy and protection from the government. No patrol boats would come snooping to Blind Man Island if he had put out the word to concentrate their thinly stretched forces elsewhere to protect fish stocks or intercept marijuana smugglers. So he could be led to believe that he was very helpful. But at most, if this operation followed the usual pattern of HHH's South Pacific endeavors, Noble Nephew was merely greasing the skids.

And when whatever Jin-shil was making was finally afloat, helpful Noble Nephew would be left standing on the low beach, holding the bag as the tide rose.

EARLY IN MAY, MORE THAN a month out of Santa Barbara and after seemingly endless days of calm, Morgan Page finally emerged from the doldrums and picked up a fitful wind. Hoping it would blossom into the southeast trades, she headed *Molly* southwest toward her next way point, 10 South 155 West.

It was on-and-off sailing, good for a few hours, then poky, then honking along again. She pored over the weather faxes, to no avail. She saw no course change that would improve matters. While far, far ahead was potential trouble. At 170 West and 5 degrees South, just below the Phoenix Islands, a tropical disturbance had begun circulating. It was spinning winds of twenty-five knots and was moving very slowly west—away from her—but gathering power from warm seas. Near its center the barometer had dropped to 29.2 inches. She made a note in her log to watch it.

Her slow progress, at a point in the voyage where she had assumed she would flying along, started making her crazy, again. She killed time—and staved off moping—by practicing with the sextant. For her, the math was easy. Harder was the physical skill required to align the mirrors to bring the sun or a star down to the horizon. Like playing the piano, she improved with practice. But it still left a lot of the day and night to brood on her slow passage, to worry about the sun giving her skin cancer, and Roscoe falling overboard, and—worst of all—to worry about her father. She was now 100 percent sure that he had telephoned her and was alive, but probably in desperate need. Every second she lost was a second he might die or go crazy and just wander off with amnesia and disappear forever.

The wind died, yet again. She sat under the sun awning, cursing the heat, compulsively patting Roscoe.

"Remember your shot spots?"

She stroked his right back leg, on the hip, repeating the vet's mnemonic: "Right for your rabies shot."

She touched his left hip. "Left for leukemia."

She took his baggy neck scruff in her fingers. "Distemper.

"Ohmigod! Your booster shots. You're supposed to get your booster shots in May. It's May. Ohmigod."

Panic gripped her. What if they had to land at some island, before Blind Man? What if he caught one of those diseases? Or what if they said, *Where's your cat's booster shot? Can't come ashore. Gotta leave him on the boat. Get that cat out of here!*

"I'm nuts." She practiced with the sextant again.

The wind firmed up, then it got weird again. It swung to the south, then all the way over to the southwest. Right in their face. She reached west, which she didn't want to do. The Line Islands speckled the west and the last thing she wanted to do was to start dodging atolls.

She disengaged the self-steering and stayed long hours at the helm, steering much of the night to pinch every advantage out of each shift, stealing distance from the south whenever the wind gave her the chance. It made her less crazy. Something to do, a skill to milk, no time to brood. Nor would the stars let her get too crazy. It was like they sucked bad thoughts right out of her head and threw them behind the boat.

Morning, hot and painfully bright, found her exhausted. But the wind was still veering and backing, east through south to west, east through south to west. "You're supposed to be in the god-dammed southeast, for God's sake. You're the southeast trade wind, remember."

Roscoe scurried below.

"Sorry, cat, I don't meant to sound crazy . . . Come back . . . Please come back."

SHE DREAMED THAT she was sailing a race. It wasn't a total dream. She knew that she was dreaming, but she stayed in the dream, part observer, part actor. She was beating to the windward buoy, struggling to overtake two boats that were pointing higher. Powered up, pointing higher, she had to overtake before everybody got bunched at the buoy. First around the mark, she'd get her spin-naker up and be gone like a rocket on the downwind leg.

Someone started yelling. Like it was her father and Uncle Char-lie, telling her how to race, each in his own way. *Get your head out of the boat. Keep your head in the boat. Feel the wind. Get in their face.*

Bang! The committee boat start cannon. Which made no sense, and reminded her that it was a dream, because the race had already started. Then they started shouting hello, in French.

"Salut! Salut!"

Get in their face.

"Ici!"

Feel the wind, Morgan.

Screw the wind. Get in their face.

"*Arrêtez!*"

Stop? She sat up. The boats she had raced in her dream were sailing alongside. Closer than a city block. They were to windward. She had screwed up. She ought to be overtaking from the windward side. Nonetheless, she was pulling ahead of them, flying by like they were standing still. Winning.

But in fact, the rival boats were standing still, rafted up.

She wasn't dreaming. This was real.

The bigger boat, a forty-foot ketch, was hove to; the smaller, sails furled, tied alongside it. Men and women in skimpy bathing suits were jumping up and down on their decks. And as Morgan watched in bleary-eyed amazement, a guy pointed a gun at the sky. With a loud bang, a flare smoked aloft and exploded red.

"*Arrêtez!*" the guy yelled again, and the woman standing beside him shouted "*Salut, petit yacht. Salut, Molleeee!*"

She couldn't believe her eyes. Or her ears. Two French sailboats were rafted up in the middle of the Pacific, drifting comfortably in the fitful breeze.

"*Salut!*" she called back, and steered toward them.

She was stunned by how bright and pretty everything looked. After a lonely month of water and sky, suddenly the shades of blue and gray were painted over with a green boat and a red boat and a bunch of big white smiles. It felt like a hurricane had hit her. She had not talked to a soul in a month, nor seen a human face, and all of a sudden five people were screaming French at her. More French than even an A student could hope to understand, though it was clear that they were waving for her to come join them.

"*Le chat! Le chat!*" they cried, pointing at Roscoe, who had climbed up on the cabin roof to check out the excitement.

On both boats, people jumped below and popped back up, waving cats.

They had an orange tiger on the little red sloop, a black tabby with a white blaze on the green ketch. At that, Morgan finally gathered her wits to call across the few yards that separated them, "Does anybody speak English?"

"*Anglais*. François. François. English!"

A smiling guy with long blond hair and a tiny bathing suit low on his skinny hips, called, "Catch a rope. Come say *bonjour!*"

"Okay. Wait. Let me drop my sails." Everything was happening so quickly. She still couldn't believe she was with people. They looked wonderful. She quickly lowered and gathered the main, leaving the headsail for control. François stepped forward with a coiled line.

"Wait, let me lock up my cat. *Le chat.*" She could not remember how to say in French, *He will kill your cats.* Nor that he was late on his booster shots and might catch something from them. She grabbed him, hustled him below, and closed him in his carrier, where he howled in indignation. She slipped him a can of tuna, left him licking the oil from the top, and jumped back up on deck. By then the French sailors had rigged fenders on the side of the ketch. François heaved a line. Morgan caught it and let them pull her to them.

François had the bluest eyes she had ever seen. He looked like he was college age, or a little younger.

Morgan extended her hand over the lifelines and said, "My name is Morgan."

"Morgan?" He stared at her. "It is you?" He turned to the others in astonishment and called out in delight, "*C'est Morgan!*"

"*Non!*"

"*Oui. Oui. Morgan. La jeune fille Morgan.*"

"*Incroyable!*"

"Excuse me," said Morgan. "You know my name?"

"*Bien sûr.* Of course we know your name."

"What?"

"You're the Morgan everyone's talking about."

BOOK FOUR

SEA
TRIALS

MAY–JUNE 2002

B EWILDERED AND AFRAID, MORGAN STOOD frozen
against the lifelines, with her hand still sticking out. François
seized it and pumped vigorously. "On the radio."

Radio? She listened to the BBC World Service every night she
could pick up the shortwave broadcast. She wasn't on the news.
"What radio?"

"Ham radio. The cruisers talk. The network."

"I don't know what that is."

"They check in every night. Everybody asks about Morgan. Have
you seen *la jeune fille Morgan* in her little blue boat. But your boat
name is different."

"What do you mean?"

"We didn't think when we saw you coming. We didn't recognize
it was you."

"How would you—" This was wack. How did they—

"Your boat is named *Molly*. They said it was *Roscoe*."

"Roscoe? . . . Roscoe's not a boat, Roscoe's my . . ." She looked
down at her boat, down the open hatch, where, hearing his name,

Roscoe started yowling. What was—ohmigod, Wayne? Was that it? she wondered with a rush of gratitude. Had they somehow caught him and he lied to protect her . . . Smart lie. Very believable. Why wouldn't a girl name a boat after her cat—but who was asking?

"Morgan, may I present my mother, Aileen? And my stepfather, Alain."

Numb with fear, Morgan shook their hands. *Who was asking about her?* Why? What do they know? What do they want? All for a stolen boat?

François introduced the young couple on the little red boat as Jean-Paul and Lilly. Their sloop and François's parents' ketch were sailing in company for Tahiti and had rafted up when the wind stopped, François explained. Everyone shook hands. Lilly kissed her cheeks.

Aileen spoke slowly in French to invite Morgan to have lunch with them and she found herself in a scene she could not have imagined even half an hour ago, crowded around a cockpit table under a gaily striped awning, surrounded by French people—three of whom were smoking cigarettes—eating from a plate of raw fish marinaded in lime juice and drinking very small sips from a glass of white wine, which she soon put aside. The first sip that touched her tongue felt like someone had whacked her with a big, soft pillow.

François's mother sat next to her, put the younger Lilly on the other side, and positioned François across the table to translate.

Morgan listened for some clue how to escape. She was going to have to tell a lot of lies.

"Where are you going?"

"New Zealand."

"Long, long way. You should stop with us in Tahiti."

Yeah, right, thought Morgan. Here comes the ham-radio girl. Papers please. Passport. Port clearance. "What do they say on the radio?"

"Your little blue boat is like a ghost ship. People saw you in the Marquesas."

"That wasn't me. I haven't been there."

"And Moorea."

"No."

"Fiji. Someone even said they saw you in Easter Island."

"I have definitely not been in Easter Island."

"Were you never in all those other places?" François smiled.

"No."

"Like a ghost, like a—what do they call, a 'Flying Dutchman.' Wait till we tell them. We caught the Flying Dutch Girl."

"No!"

"*Pardon?*"

"*S'il vous plaît*—" No way she could explain it in French. "François. Please tell them—ask them—not to radio."

"No?"

"I don't want anyone to know . . . Please?"

He looked. He shrugged. He turned to Aileen. "*Maman. La jeune fille...*" Speaking way too fast for Morgan to follow.

His mother asked, "*Personne?*" No one.

"*Personne,*" said Morgan.

Aileen looked at her husband. Alain was leaning back, with his head thrust out from under the awning to study the sky. "Alain!"

Alain shrugged and asked Morgan, "*Personne?*"

Morgan shook her head.

"*Pourquoi?*"

"My father wonders why?"

She looked from François to his mother to his father. They seemed like a happy family. Although the father seemed kind of withdrawn and was eyeing her in a strange way, like if his wife weren't around he'd put a gross move on her.

Somehow she had to persuade them to forget they had ever met her. She tried to see herself through their eyes, a girl on her own. They couldn't be worried. She was obviously enough of a sailor to have gotten this far. In that way, she was one of them. She decided to take a chance on sailor solidarity.

"Tell them that I am running away from home."

François looked at her closely. "Are you?"

"Yes."

"You are so fortunate," he whispered.

Taken aback, she asked, "What do you mean?"

He glanced at his parents. They were smiling vaguely, unable to follow his excellent English. "*Ma famille*—my parents, they are always running away from home. *Sailing* away from home. Like vagabonds? So I can't."

Maybe he wasn't in college, she thought. He was more like seventeen. She asked, "What if you stayed in one place?"

"Or ran away on *another* boat?" he said with a significant glance at *Molly*.

Great, thought Morgan. Not only will every boat with a ham radio be watching for me, but this guy's mother will be, too.

Who was asking about her? Her mother? With a sudden stab of fear she imagined her mother chasing across the Pacific on a bigger boat. She could do it. Morgan wouldn't put it past her. And sail circles around her, too.

Mom's a sea dog, Daddy used to say. A natural, born with fins. Even though Morgan couldn't mold the sea-dog image to her last sight of her mother's waggle-fingering good-bye at the taxi Morgan was in, she wouldn't put anything past her.

François was staring, looking desperate. Morgan whispered back. "My boyfriend's waiting in New Zealand. He would be really pissed if I sailed in with another boy."

"But we would be only friends."

"I don't think he'd believe us—I'm sorry. It wouldn't work."

What if it wasn't her mother? But who? *I've got to get out of here.*

"What is his name?"

"Who?"

"Your boyfriend."

"Paea."

"A Polynesian name?"

"He's from Tonga."

Aileen asked something and François explained. Morgan sat thinking furiously. Of the boys in her life, the first name that popped into her head was neither Toby, nor Rick in Geology. But sweet Paea, whom she hadn't thought about in ages. Her brain was being logical. No way Toby of Larchmont, or Rick at Stuyvesant, would ever be in New Zealand. While Paea's parents had sent him to school there. So that's why Paea popped in her head. Lies were logical, that way, leading one into another like thread following a needle.

Aileen flashed Morgan a smile and replied slowly in French.

François said, "I told *maman* you have a Tongan boyfriend. She says, 'Very handsome men, the Tongans.' "

"I heard that." She had to get them off this subject. "What is your ham radio? Is it like the SSB?"

"Oh, no. It's low power. For cruisers who don't have big generators to run single sideband."

Alain paused in the midst of lighting a fresh cigarette to interject something about the SSB in French. François translated. "My stepfather says, 'The people's radio, for those who aren't rich.' He's a Socialist."

Alain winked at Morgan and clenched his fist in the air.

"Could you show me?" she asked François.

"*Bien sûr.*" They disentangled themselves from the cramped cockpit and Morgan followed him down the companionway. It was a pilothouse ketch, so it had windows that lit the saloon with views of the blue sea. François's mother had cozied it up with gingham curtains and bright cushions. Green sprouts and herbs grew in pots, which hung balanced in gimbals, and Morgan felt suddenly so lonely she thought she would cry. I'm homesick, she thought. I want to go home.

François invited her to sit at the chart table. Beside a sextant box was an old-fashioned-looking radio with a microphone connected by a curly wire. She stared at it, and felt tears start to burn her eyes.

Could she just call and say, *Hi, Mom? I'm fine. Don't worry. Back soon . . . In a year.*

She picked up the microphone. "Can this radio all the way to Paris or New York?"

"Not directly. People with bigger radios on land would relay your message or an e-mail or maybe connect you to a telephone."

"Show me."

"Later. The net is not up until evening."

"You can't just do it without the network?"

"It's easier. All the boats hear you. One that's in the best position can help relay your signal . . . I could try the higher frequency, but it will take a long time."

"No, don't." What was she thinking? It would be crazy to call her mother. What if a message were traced back to François's boat? What if people started asking questions? She was just homesick. She'd get over it. Then a strange thought struck her. What if her father was holding one of these in his hand right now? Except, how do you radio people who don't exist?

"All the boats hear you on the network? How does that work?"

François said, "Everyone checks into the net in the evening. There's a roll call. When my turn comes I say, 'S/V'—sailing vessel—'*Mais Oui.*' Then I stand by until they are ready to hear the weather where I am. We tell each other about the weather. Relay messages. Report emergencies. And boat watches. That's how they know about you. Someone asked, 'Who has seen S/V *Roscoe*?' "

"They *all* know about me?"

"None as much as we know." François smiled. "Are you really, really positive you wouldn't like a shipmate?"

"I don't have room. There's barely space for my cat." She could hear an occasional angry howl coming from her boat. "Who asked for the sailing vessel *Roscoe*?"

"I don't know. I think it only said to tell the net manager. The person who is the host."

What if it was not her mother? My God, what if it was her father?

But how would he know she was out here? "François, what did you mean *relay* messages?"

"The net passes them on. If someone leaves a message for you and someone else sees your boat, or can hear you on the radio, they relay it. Like, Morgan, if your family wonders where you are for so long? Is your boat okay? So other boats watch for you and report when they find you."

She weighed the clunky old microphone in her hand. If her father was on a boat, still headed for the island, would he want to be "watched"? Not if he'd deliberately run away. But could she somehow warn him about Mr. Hong?

"François, do you listen often?"

"Every night. What's there to do on the boat but read? There's no TV."

But what were the odds that her father might be listening? Infinitesimal. Except, what if he hadn't gotten to Blind Man Island yet and was still on a boat that had a ham radio and he was checking weather? How could she pass up even an infinitesimal chance to warn him he was in danger?

"Could you relay a message for me?"

"Is this message for Paea?" François asked unhappily.

"No. No, it's for my father."

"What is the name of his boat?"

That threw cold water on her fantasy. "I don't know."

"Then how can I relay a message to him?"

It was silly, anyway. One chance in a million, but she felt crushed.

"Wait!" She didn't need a boat to broadcast her warning through the network. She only needed a boat *name*. A name that would catch her father's attention if by a miracle he overheard it on the radio.

She said to François, "He could be on the Sailing Vessel *Molly P.*"

"That is your boat."

"No. Mine is *Molly P 2*. Relay it to *S/V Molly P.*"

"What message?"

Morgan thought hard. This was tricky. How to warn her father in a message anybody could hear, without Mr. Hong finding out? "Let me write this down." The French boy gave her a pencil and she printed slowly.

"Can you read that?"

François read aloud, " '*S/V Molly P.* Island dangerous. Tell François on *S/V Mais Oui* new coordinates minus BC birthday. Love. Kitten.' I don't understand."

"He will."

François liked that and he smiled. "A cipher. A secret code. But if he is in danger, everyone will know where he flees."

"That's the real code. They don't know who BC is. And they don't know BC's birthday, so they won't know what number to subtract to decode his coordinates."

"But he is not really in danger?"

"No, of course not. It's kind of a joke. We kid around a lot. He'll be so happy to hear from me. And he'll probably send you a joke back. Will you send this and listen for an answer?"

"How will I tell you?"

Cold water again. "I will radio you as soon as I'm near a radio."

"You can sometimes telephone a land radio to relay."

"Then I'll try that, too. Soon as I hit land." She wrote down *Mais Oui*'s call sign.

They went back up on deck, Morgan feeling both a little silly and slightly reconnected to her father. How could she not try?

Alain and Jean-Paul were studying the sky and François said, "My father says we've got bad weather coming."

"Could you ask him about the trade wind?"

Alain faced her and made eye contact. When he spoke, it was sea captain to sea captain. For a second she felt like a complete and total adult.

"My stepfather says we'll have good southeast wind tomorrow, but first savage squalls tonight."

She groaned inwardly at the thought of fighting more squalls. "I better get going."

Alain raised a hand. *"Attendes!"* He spoke rapidly, with broad gestures at sea and sky.

"My stepfather says that if you pass to windward of the squalls when you're on a close reach, you will enjoy better wind."

"What if I'm running downwind?"

François translated.

"Ah." Alain smiled. He began his answer with another wink. He spoke, slowly, at length. Morgan heard a good part on her own. She thought she misunderstood, until François translated.

"He says that squalls are like your eyes, Morgan. They present two faces, soft blue, hard green. They overwhelm, then they leave you with nothing."

Morgan glanced at François, who rolled his eyes as if to say, *Parents!* But Aileen smiled a tight smile and eyed her husband closely. Morgan nodded for him to continue. Alain sounded a little New Age-y—if not plain weirdly coming on to her—but the fact was she had several times found herself mysteriously becalmed in the wake of a squall. If the French sailor knew a way out of the problem, she wanted to hear it.

"Knowing these faces, he says, you make the squall your friend when you run ahead of it—if the squall does not appear too strong—on a starboard tack when the wind is strong, jibe to port when it grows weak, back to starboard when it is stiff again.... Wait . . . Ah. I see. He says stay to the equator side to get better wind when the squall has passed. The wind is weaker toward the pole. So on your course to New Zealand, you will let the squall overtake on your left."

Morgan nodded. *"Merci beaucoup!"*

Alain shook his finger, no.

François said, "My stepfather says that only a fast boat can do that safely."

"I have a fast boat," Morgan said. *"Merci,* everybody. Thanks for lunch."

François, Alain, and Jean-Paul pushed *Molly* off. Morgan raised her mainsail. The breeze was still light and bouncing around the compass like a yo-yo, but the French boats fell astern with surprising speed.

She went below to let Roscoe out, but before she opened his carrier, she stole a curious look at herself in the mirror over the toilet. What was François's father looking at her that way for? Was she somehow different? First the California surfer gawking at her and now a cigarette-puffing old Frenchman. What were they seeing? But all she could see was that she was sunburned and had lost weight, which made her eyes look bigger. I'm getting skinny. It can't be that. I wasn't fat. Not *fat* fat.

Roscoe howled. She let him out. "Sorry about that, Mr. Cat. It was for your own good . . . Now, why are *you* staring at me? Oh, the lying. I *know* I don't have a Tongan boyfriend. But I had to lie. That way they won't rat me out. They'll think I'm sailing for love . . . We're on the radio, stupid! Don't you know what that means? I *know* I lied. I lied twice. We're not sailing to New Zealand, either, remember?"

Remember, for sure. Remember a lot. Three years ago it was Paea who taught her how to make a sailing canoe fly like a gull. The son of the man whom Uncle Charlie and Daddy called "Noble Nephew" when they thought no one was listening, Paea was exactly her age and had been as eager as she to escape from the grown-ups. After a few days racing on the lagoon, they had sneaked away one morning and sailed halfway around Blind Man Island to the northeast shore.

Giant waves steamrolling across the Pacific crashed on those shores. But Paea showed her a partly built harbor. Work on it had stopped, as if it were abandoned to the pelicans. But its seawalls— training walls, Paea called them—allowed a safe landing through the surf if you were really good, and Paea was an incredible sailor, like he'd inherited every navigator gene from every Polynesian explorer since time began.

They pulled the canoe onto the sand and played on the beach. He showed her the volcano vent and they dropped rocks down it and counted how long they took to hit bottom. Paea told her a really cool legend about a giant crocodile that climbed out of it to eat Tonga's enemies.

They swam and then dozed in the warm shade of a sloping palm tree. She remembered the underground rumble of the surf crashing on the outer reef and the light flickering as the wind rustled leaves like snare drums. A fat white trade-wind cloud blew in from the ocean and got stuck in the notch between two volcanic hills.

She remembered thinking at the time that it was as if she were making up an incredible fantasy. And if that were not fantastic enough, Paea suddenly climbed the tree and knocked down a coconut, which he bashed out of its husk. Then he lay beside her and drilled holes in it with his knife and dribbled the sweet milk into their mouths. When he propped himself up on one elbow and smiled down at her, she thought she could feel the heat of the sun radiating from his dark skin. For a long time they just looked at each other and she started thinking, If he kisses me, it'll be my second kiss this week and I'll bet it will be better than the first.

The first had been a disaster—only three days earlier—with Angelo, the mailroom boy. First-ever real kiss. Not just cheeks. But real lips, tongue, a total face-sucking kiss. Angelo was only sixteen—he had had to get written permission from his mother to come on the company trip—and somehow he had gotten the idea that she was fourteen when they started hanging out on the plane. Soon they were sprawled in her open-air room that was called a *fale* and the adults were all off drinking and they were fooling around, Angelo calling her "boss's daughter" and tickling, and all of a sudden they started kissing. It felt pretty good. So good that after a while she got a little scared and said, "I really don't want to go too far."

Angelo laughed. "Too far?" He suddenly seemed a lot older and it was like she had accidentally walked into a room full of strangers.

"Yeah, but I'm only twelve and maybe—"

"Twelve?" He rolled off the sleeping mat onto the floor. "You're only *twelve?* Jesus, I could get killed for kissing you."

"You wouldn't know if I hadn't told you."

"Jailbait, oh, man. I'll get fired."

"I won't tell."

To prove it, she reached to tickle him again. He tickled back, but at arm's length, like she was some stupid little sister, and she had pretended to giggle almost as if she'd made a conscious decision to stay twelve for a little while longer.

But only three days longer, it turned out. Three days later on the beach.

She remembered everything. All the stuff she'd heard about your mouth getting dry and your chest locking up like you couldn't breathe, and your heart racing and your legs getting weak, turned out to be all true. So it was the best first kiss anybody had ever had. Paea—mega-cute—turned out to be really nice. In the sailing canoe races, he had blocked the one boat that might have beaten her. So cute and so nice that she sometimes wondered what would have happened if his father hadn't scooped him up and sent him back to his boarding school, leaving them no time for a real good-bye before her parents dragged her back to Larchmont. Who knew? It was long ago. Nearly three years. Three years was a fifth of her life. Twenty percent. And if you counted real life as not starting until you were ten, then 60 percent.

But one thing she did know and would cherish forever: She was most glad that when Paea kissed her, he only had to bend halfway because she was already rising to him, which made it a perfect kiss for both of them, like they owned it together. If a storm drowned her tomorrow, she would never have to regret wasting such a moment.

Not a lot of kisses since.

Good-dork-friend Toby was hopeless in that department. Besides, Toby was really just a guy friend. There were two boys in Geology who were cute, but one was clueless, the other already had a girl-friend at Music and Art. So at a party Dr. Melton had talked her into going to, guess which Geology boy had hit on her—like she was going to be his dish on the side? Like volcanoes would erupt in Central Park?

She would have had face time with the clueless one if she hadn't quit the science project; something might have clicked . . . Then there was that funny moment with Chris, the California surfer football jock, who had surprised her with a hangdog expression, like he liked her but didn't know what to do about it. For a guy with as many girlfriends as he had had last summer, it was still weird how he had treated her, like he was maybe a little awed. Today's creepy look from the Frenchman was too weird to count.

But Paea had really left her stirred up. So stirred that on the long, two-day plane trip back from the Blind Man Island Company Christmas, she had out of the blue asked her father what age he thought a girl should be before she went all the way with a boy. She had shocked herself, even though he had always been easier to talk to than her mother because he didn't try so hard to give his opinion but had a way of seeing where she was. But it was too much for Daddy. He got all red, put down his drink, and stammered that he'd seen a survey that 65 percent of girls said they wished they hadn't busted their virginity too soon.

But at school, she said, it seemed like everybody was doing it.

Uncle Charlie, who she thought was sleeping, suddenly nudged Daddy. "Pass the ball before you drop it, pal."

Morgan had thought, Oh shit. But Uncle Charlie had talked to her like he talked to her about racing, like it was a subject worth plenty of thought. "If 'everybody's doing it' is like anything else in life, you can figure that half who claim they're doing it are exaggerating and a quarter are outright lying. But why don't we assume for a minute that half the girls are actually doing it? What does that mean?"

"That means half aren't."

"You're a genius." A big smile. Except Mom was right. Uncle Charlie's eyes, which mirrored hers and Daddy's, never smiled. Like there was another Uncle Charlie standing behind him with a gun in his back. Still, he always said good stuff. "Just remember, no one girl is a statistic. Which means no one girl has to rush. A girl should take her time. Do it for herself, not to please someone else. And definitely not so she can have a story she can tell her friends."

THE HAM-RADIO VOLUNTEER boat-tracking network—on which an increasingly frustrated Jerry eavesdropped every evening with *Baltic Nights'* powerful receivers—warmed up with a position report from those sailboats currently wandering the South Pacific that chose to join in. Seventeen of them, this evening, scattered east, south, and west, Panama to Easter Island to Fiji.

Jerry listened as the network controller took their weather reports. Other land-based operators in New Zealand, Hawaii, and the U.S. mainland helped relay e-mail and voice traffic. The information garnered was reprocessed on various Internet Web sites dedicated to the health and well-being of the far-flung voyagers and the desire of friends and relatives to keep in touch. One even allowed Jerry to track all the vessels on an electronic chart.

But there was no law that said every sailor had to participate. So far, none of the reporting vessels was *Archimedes,* the Open 50 on which Aiden Page had raced out of Balboa. *Archimedes'* captain was supposedly heading for New Zealand, Jerry had learned at the marina. But who knew where they'd stop along the way? And what was to prevent Aiden Page from jumping off on some island in the middle of nowhere? After seven months on the run, no one could risk computerized immigration checks. Grass skirts and pencils would be Aiden's scene.

Jerry was not big on doubts. Only losers indulged in them. But seventeen sailboats scattered across *seventeen million square miles of ocean?* Even if there were seventeen more boats *not* reporting to the ham net, give me a fucking break.

Zip, too, were the results of Jerry's radio queries about Aiden's little girl, Morgan. A hundred rumors, but none that pinned down the location of the sailboat *Roscoe.*

The only good thing about being stuck on a sailboat was endless time for research, and she burned up the Baltic 70's high-speed Internet satellite connection, scrolling news stories and business-section puff pieces about Aiden Page as a Wall Street guy.

Reading his Portraits of Grief obituary for the fourteenth time, she finally asked herself, What if he's not just running *away?* What if he's running *to?*

That sent her back to Aiden's years at HHH & Company. Which launched a deeper search into Henry Ho Hong. Which took her to Web sites for the South Pacific kingdom of Tonga. One listed the names of every island in the group, inhabited and uninhabited. Suddenly, Jerry's hard work paid off. One of the uninhabited island names popped up in an insipid family Web site run by an out-of-work stock analyst, a former HHH & Company employee, who had posted photos and text from his Christmas vacation three years ago.

Fast-forward to Aiden's kid stealing a boat. Because, maybe, just maybe, Morgan Page wasn't running *away,* either. Maybe she, too, was running *to.*

When "the boss," the pushy bitch with the New York and Asian accent, sat-phoned for a progress report, a supremely-pleased-with-herself Jerry played a very strong hunch.

"I could use some help locating his kid. And something tells me you know where she's going."

"I don't know anything about children."

Good, thought Jerry. She's lying. Which means I'm right.

"About the kid. I'm going to say something. You say yes or no. Blind Man Island."

"Never go there," said the woman, in a voice so cold that Jerry concluded that Morgan Page definitely was headed there. Which presented Jerry with a hell of a shot at snatching Morgan along the way. Precisely where would be determined with the help of young Ahmed, *Baltic Nights'* handsome navigator.

F INALLY, THOUGHT AIDEN, WE GET lucky.

They picked up the southeast trades soon after steering a repaired *Archimedes* southwest of the Galápagos Islands. Up went her huge yellow spinnaker; calms, head winds, squalls, and floating containers departed for other oceans, and the sleigh ride began.

Days blurred past. They crossed 100 West at 3 degrees South, beating their last time by two hours. "Downhill to Fiji!" Tom Slade howled, high on a potent mix of adrenaline, rum, and dexamphetamine. "Full on and no fucking stops!"

The breeze increased until it was blowing near a Force 6— unusually powerful for the trade wind, although May was said to be an excellent month in these waters. It built big seas, with white crests everywhere and spray whipping the decks. But they were long and remarkably orderly seas—exactly the conditions *Archimedes* was built for. She screamed along, surfing waves, and hurtling across troughs like a skipped stone. Under such dependable conditions, they rarely had to touch a sail.

Off watch, between catnaps and monitoring lines, blocks, fittings, and chafing gear, Aiden continued to slot the compact disk of his HHH files into the nav-station computer. Though he kept an ear cocked for a hail from Slade. At the speeds *Archimedes* was making, emergencies tended toward full-blown and abrupt. Hour after hour Aiden pored through the transactions he had recorded. Sometimes he felt like he was banging his head against *Archimedes'* sturdy hull, until, finally, there formed in his mind the murky beginnings of a strange scenario about Henry Hong's secret deals.

Of the four private acquisitions, he ruled out two. A chemical plant that Henry flipped immediately after buying appeared to have been a cut-and-dried transaction. Henry bought it cheap and sold it at a huge profit to an Asian group. Similarly, the shipping line Aiden had helped him snatch from its creditors was soon out of business, Henry having sold most of its ships for scrap; a wry e-mail from a coast-guard inspector noted Henry Hong's contribution to maritime safety that winter by breaking up the "rust buckets" before they sank. Neither company, Aiden was sure, would have held the U.S. attorney's interest for very long.

That left the trans-Pac tug-and-barge outfit, Halborson Towing, and the international construction company, Lewis & Minalgo. Here, too, negotiations seemed straightforward enough. Both contracts had been drawn by outside lawyers, at Henry's insistence. Though he had not shut Charlie out of the construction company deal. In fact, Aiden recalled, it had been Charlie who had defended it, even after Aiden had found a better one for sale.

Suddenly Aiden saw a pattern. Stunned, he spoke out loud, though there was no one to overhear in the clattering, pounding hull. "Jesus H. They're connected."

The tug-and-barge-company acquisition and the purchase of a heavy construction outfit that specialized in site preparation had always seemed to be two unrelated, separate deals. All they had appeared to have in common was that both firms had been cascading into bankruptcy, both had been mismanaged by the founder's heirs (so what was new there?), and both had drawn particular attention from the U.S. attorney.

But the secret buys were connected by stronger similarities. Both companies were 100 percent American owned. Both had been in business for many decades. Both had the security clearances required to do business with the government and the military. Both had customers overseas. Halborson Towing had recently moved into the Pacific trade. Lewis & Minalgo Construction had worked many years in the Far East.

Seen in that light, the two companies made an excellent match. Halborson specialized in delivering heavy equipment and building supplies and offered the scheduling advantage of controlling its own container-transfer operation. Lewis & Minalgo required dependable delivery of bulldozers, drill rigs, steel, stone, and cement to remote sites. Which, Aiden had to admit, actually made Henry Hong look pretty smart. Although he wondered why Henry hadn't joined them into one efficient concern.

He was back at the helm nearing the Marquesas one particularly windy night, driving by the stars and getting ready to piss Slade off by taking a reef in the main, when he saw the lights of a ship. It was the first vessel they'd seen since leaving the Galápagos. He watched carefully, to determine that their similar courses—the ship appeared to be heading farther south of west than he was—would not intersect in a collision.

It showed a puzzling combination of lights. Instead of fore-and-aft white ranging lights—the relationship of which would tell him the direction it was steaming—this one showed what looked like three lights stacked one atop another. A tug towing a barge was something he expected to see in the Long Island Sound, more than in the middle of the South Pacific. Then he spotted a green and white combination far behind it. And that's exactly what it was, he realized—a tow chugging south-southwest at eight knots, probably headed for Tahiti. The tugboat and barge were separated by a half mile. The wire that connected them, deep in the water.

He jumped below for a handheld VHF and radioed the tug, wondering if they would speak English or even take notice. Many wind sailors didn't talk to ships—except to radio a frantic, last-minute *Look out! Don't hit me!* But he had always spoken to ships on the Sound and along the Gulf of Maine and knew they appreciated a sensible courtesy call. In this case, the tow captain would warn him if he was traveling in company with other tugs.

Ordinarily he would announce his vessel's name and particulars, but the habits of running had solidified, even in the middle of an empty ocean, and he radioed only, "Evening, Cap. We're going to pass a couple of miles behind your barge on 260."

The reply was immediate, in a broad Texas drawl. *"We've been watching you, buddy ... We're having a little trouble making out your range light."* A polite suggestion that a ranging light had burned out.

"We're under sail."A polite reply revealing that *Archimedes* was not a powered vessel required to show a range light.

"Very funny. Radar says you're steaming at twenty-two knots."

"We're making twenty-two knots, but we're not steaming."

"Have it your way. Thanks for the heads-up."

The encounter put him in mind of the Halborson Towing deal again, and in the short time it took *Archimedes* to race across the barge's wake, the strange scenario he had been mulling over took shape. Not yet a scenario, more like a fleeting speculation—a spooky *Could it be this that I don't know that I know?* But he recalled that HHH's tug-and-barge investment had literally blown up in Henry Hong's face when a Halborson dynamite barge exploded while stopped by the coast guard in the Sea of Japan.

How big an explosion was that? He didn't know. Even though it resulted in the sinking of the tug, the obliterating of the barge, and the wrecking of the Japanese cutter, the incident had been treated as a run-of-the-mill maritime casualty—not the sort of disaster that CNN noticed for longer than an afternoon.

But how much bigger could it have been? Much, much bigger. Modern, seagoing barges could carry ten or fifteen thousand tons— more than a hundred-car freight train—which was a horrendous amount of dynamite. "Little Boy," the first atomic bomb dropped on a city, had detonated an explosive force comparable to twelve thousand tons of dynamite and had killed a hundred thousand people in

Hiroshima—a horrific fact, Aiden recalled with an ache of conscience, that he knew thanks to Morgan's homework.

A nuclear weapon had always been the terrorists' Holy Grail. But who needed an atomic bomb when a barge load of old-tech dynamite could devastate a port city as big as San Francisco or New York?

Assume for a crazy moment that Henry Hong wants to assemble enormous amounts of dynamite and deliver them undetected? He secretly buys an established American construction company that could legitimately purchase the explosives, and an American-flagged towing company to transport them.

Aiden supposed if he hadn't been in the World Trade Center when the terrorists attacked, he would not be thinking along these lines. But the attack had made everything and anything—every crime—seem possible. Maybe he wouldn't have thought of it if Henry hadn't been so anxious to buy bankrupt disasters even after Aiden found him better deals. Even then, he might not have considered it if he hadn't learned that Henry's surrogates had expanded Halborson into trans-Pacific barge tows.

Gazing ahead of *Archimedes*, beyond the stars that lighted the sea, he pictured in his mind a big twin-diesel, oceangoing tugboat. Flying the American flag, it is towing a ten-thousand-ton barge under San Francisco's Golden Gate Bridge—or New York's Verrazano. Her crew is typical of an offshore boat: the captain and chief engineer, American; deckhands and cook, Filipinos or Poles or Malaysians, whoever is currently cheapest on the international labor market. Her paperwork's in order; she's a regular, here; the coasties might even know the captain by name. Her manifests attest to a bulk cargo of cement or newsprint bound for a well-documented but phantom business in Oakland or Brooklyn.

If you've infiltrated the deckhands, they slit their officers' throats while you light the fuse. Then you cut the towline and steam away. Or if you are martyr-minded, don't even cut the cable. The "fuse" would be very complicated, of course, but you can hire experts. Any mining engineer could wire it. A radio detonator would let you live to kill again.

Simpler yet, wire a GPS to the detonator, set for the coordinates of the harbor. The beauty of a hidden GPS detonator is that it can be set ahead of time and is guaranteed not to explode before it reaches "ground zero." With her deadly cargo disguised, and the GPS installed ahead of time, the crew delivering the dynamite could be total innocents.

Chilling. Fantastic. Paranoid. Henry Hong could be assembling the explosives and delivery system to level a city.

With Aiden Page's help? Could he plead ignorance? After agreeing to being blackmailed into silence? And not daring to ask why?

A question more to the point spiraled paranoia into absurdity: Why would Henry Hong destroy an American city? He wasn't a terrorist, he was a businessman. He wasn't an Al Qaeda fanatic. He wasn't even a Muslim. In fact, it was impossible to imagine Henry Hong fanatical about anything, beyond making a buck.

"Aiden?" The voice startled him. Tom calling from the companionway, as he always did before relieving the watch. "Should I make some coffee?"

"I'll do it," Aiden called back, as always.

He boiled water. The dark, windowless hold was lit by the flickering kerosene burner. He measured out the coffee, losing count as shadows jumped around him. A sea roared over the top of the boat; Tom had shaken out a reef and *Archimedes* had accelerated into the high-speed submarine mode she adopted whenever he drove.

Assume for a moment, against all logic, that Henry Hong really is a terrorist. For whatever reason. Just assume it. Why would he set up such a complicated scheme? There had to be simpler ways to deliver dynamite, even tons of dynamite.

Henry Hong's original "business," as Aiden understood it, had been based on investing funds siphoned out of China by corrupt politicians and army officers. Powerful people with all sorts of access to all sorts of materials. Why cut elaborate deals to buy legitimate construction and shipping companies? Why not simply purchase his ten thousand tons of TNT from one set of shady friends, tugboats from some other crooks, documents from skilled Indian or Chinese forgers, and a flag from Wal-Mart?

Secrecy, in a word. Security of the mission.

Dealing with crooks meant that too many of the wrong kind of people would know too much. The sort of people likely to fall into the hands of the "cops" for unrelated crimes. Too many shady friends who would sell him out to save their own skin. Too many secrets in the hands of others. Too many witnesses.

I'm a witness, he thought. If Henry Hong intended to destroy an American port, wouldn't he safeguard the attack by murdering the clueless employee he had coerced into helping set it up—before the dumb schmuck finally put two and two and two and two together?

Take that what-do-I-know to its logical conclusion: the 9/11 attack had probably saved his life. Total paranoia. Although it would surely account for who had chartered a Baltic 70 to send gorgeous Jerry and "brother Joe" to attack him in Panama.

STARING DOWN THE slope at the construction site on the water's edge, Charlie Page watched the Korean laborers off-load another barge under the lights in the middle of the night. It was the fifth shipment he knew of. Salote had seen the first three. Then there was last week's barge. And now this one, which had arrived after sunset.

They were using forklifts to off-load pallets, whose contents were concealed by shrink-wrap. The shapes pressing the shrink-wrap looked like some contained fifty-pound sacks, and others, five-gallon pails. What was in them was driving him crazy. It could be cement sacks and tar buckets. Or plaster and spackling compound. Or anything at all that was powder and liquid.

He shook his head with a mirthless smile at a bleak private joke: rocket fuel. Henry Hong and Jin-shil were competing with the scamsters down in the Tongatopu group to launch tourists into space.

Fuck this. He was going down there. Salote stirred, suddenly frightened. He stood up, handing her the rifle. "Wait here. Kill anybody who tries to stop me getting back."

He took the "big ears" she had acquired—a mil-spec parabolic mike that was small and light enough to carry in one hand. Her brothers had also liberated an accurate, long-barrel pistol with an infrared nightscope. The scope was so sensitive that it revealed— when he paused three quarters of the way down to pan the final approach—a low-light camera that Jin-shil's security people had hidden in a palm tree. They did a nice job; it was aimed at a narrow point on the slope, a defile where loose scree had funneled his descent.

Pausing repeatedly to look and listen, he worked his way around the camera. Suddenly a trip wire was between his legs. He froze, amazed. Somehow he had stepped over it, and then saw it before he caught it with his left foot. Lucky. Before he lifted either foot, he looked for another wire. Dozens. Strung between him and a chain-link fence topped with razor wire, they registered as pale lines on the infrared scope, radiating less heat than the stone had stored from the day's sunlight.

Still standing frozen with the wire between his legs, he focused the big ears and commenced an aural pattern search of the hillside. It covered a three-foot target area and allowed him to tune out the ambient noise of the crashing surf, if not the amplified groans and creaks of the off-loading operation.

He heard no ambush noise, no nervous rustling of hidden men, no one breathing. He switched back to the infrared scope. Between cameras and trip wires, the final approach was blocked. He'd have to come in from the sea to get a closer look. Frustrated, he played the scope over the pallets the Korean laborers were humping off the barge. Not that they were all laborers. He had been fascinated by what he saw of their work ethic. When something had to be picked up, the nearest man picked it up. Laborer, engineer, it didn't matter.

Could they really be building a missile launch site? Not a joke scam for space tourists, but real missiles, like intercontinental ballistic missiles. Where, he wondered, did he get that weird thought? From the dedicated workers down there. At which point it finally occurred to him to ask, What if Jin-shil is not *South* Korean, but *North* Korean?

Easiest spy scam in the world. Korean was Korean. Her politics wouldn't show on her face. Assume that, though it was a stretch. The North Koreans were big on missiles. Henry claimed that they traded them for technology they were short on. Nukes or whatever else the crazies thought they needed. In fact, he wouldn't be surprised to learn that Henry was in on some of those deals.

Except that the shaft was nowhere near big enough to house a farm of missile silos.

Could the shaft be only the entrance to a vast tunnel complex? An underground complex with each tunnel leading to another and only a thin sheet of the volcanic rock between the launch tubes and the surface? Ridiculous. The construction operation was not that big. Besides, even if Jin-shil had a hundred ballistic missiles on Blind Man Island, the United States would blast them to smithereens after the first shot. No. Until he saw warheads pointing out of the rock, he was not inclined to believe that Blind Man Island was a nuclear launchpad. So what was it? And what was in those damned sacks and pails?

Suddenly one of the forklifts streaming in and out of the barge skidded off a gangplank and tipped on its side. The driver went flying, as did its pallet, which scattered a load of sacks beside the concrete seawall that circled the shaft like a collar. The laborers in its path scattered like ants and another forklift driver, attempting to dodge the sacks, lost control of his machine and dropped a pallet that burst open and sent five-gallon pails rolling in every direction.

Charlie Page focused tighter, hardly believing his eyes as he read the labels on the sacks and pails:

MX DRILLING POLYMER

H. MOSKOWITZ MUD COMPANY

E-Z MUD PLUS

HIGH-PERFORMANCE POLYMER DRILLING MUD

Before he could stop himself, he laughed out loud. No one had heard over the noise of the surf, the machines, and their own frantic shouting.

"*Drilling mud?* Oh, Henry!"

Drilling mud was an integral part of a deep-drilling operation. It floated the cuttings away from the drill bit. It lubricated the drill bit. And it lined the ever-deepening shaft, preventing water from leaking in and collapsing the walls.

Is that what you're doing?

Henry Hong had even conned his wealthy wife's father into paying for it. But the South Korean *chaebol* who thought they were backing Jin-shil's South Pacific island "resort" were actually writing checks for a deep-well drilling operation. Henry, you're a pisser. He felt his pulse start pounding. Someone was going to get unbelievably rich. Jesus H. He should have thought of it earlier, if not first off. But it all added up.

There were several reasons to drill. Drill for water; but Henry Hong had no need for water with his distillation plant turning out oceans' worth, and besides, this operation would be down way too deep for water. Drill to tap underground warmth for a geothermal heating system; hardly a pressing need in the South Pacific. Then there was a third and by far most common reason to drill deep shafts. Petroleum.

Jin-shil was a geologist. And it looked to Charlie as if she had discovered in this far northern outpost of Tonga an astonishing source of wealth, of the sort already found in deep oceans off the coasts of

Australia, Indonesia, Africa, Texas, and Arabia. They were drilling for oil.

Charlie's mouth felt dry as sand and his heart was beating so hard he thought it would blow a hole in his ribs. After all the shots he had taken, all the disappointments, this could be his big win at last. Somehow Henry Hong had discovered oil in the South Pacific. Whoever ruled this island would get very rich. *Own-it-all rich.*

Charlie eased away from the trip wire and climbed up the mountain, silently as drifting smoke, to a vantage point, a rocky outcrop from where he could see far across the Pacific. And when he had collected his spirit and gathered his strength, he shouted a prayer, with his head held high and his blue eye burning like a gas flame.

"Help me with this! Help me with this and I'll do anything You want."

FORCED SOUTH OF HER RHUMB line in order to escape the doldrums, Morgan Page could not sail north of the Marquesas as she had originally planned, but had to negotiate between winds disturbed by the mountains if she strayed too close to the Marquesas Islands, and dangerous, hard-to-see low atolls that studded the waters around the Tuamotu archipelago.

She worried as she squeezed between them, although "squeeze" was greatly overstating the situation. From her position, 142 West, 13 degrees South, Fatu Hiva lay a full hundred and forty miles to starboard and the Îles du Désappointement only slightly nearer to port. But every problem seemed to be a big deal. Knowing why she was overreacting didn't help. Her father filled her thoughts, more with each passing day, and not with hope.

She felt both emotional and emotionless, as if her spirit were fraying—like *Molly*'s worn sheets—to the breaking point. She tried to sleep it away in the sultry heat, hours of dozing under her cockpit awning. Hours more she stared at the swell, zoning out on its cease-less, changeless rhythm. But she couldn't sleep or stare mindlessly forever. It got so bad that if she could somehow bike to the Village, she would spill her guts to Dr. Melton.

Only order, her old friend, might save her.

Crouched in the cabin, she spread her log on her berth and wrote lists of her thoughts, her hurts, and her memories. She had lived two lives since the terrorist attack: the black life when she thought her father was dead, though she hoped for a miracle; and the new life spawned by the telephone call, which she feared more and more that she had imagined.

Then why, she asked herself, am I so afraid Mr. Hong will hurt you? The answer was too easy. When I worry about what *will* happen, when I remember reasons in your files to be afraid, I keep you alive.

She tried to drive her thoughts back to the time when she knew he was alive. But she couldn't reach as far back as the Happy Days. Her mind locked up on terrible days, and for a happy memory she had to settle for the last time she had seen him, the long evening before the attack.

When she got to his office, the setting sun was streaming in his windows. She remembered a beautiful late-summer sky, soft blue, so the river shimmered and the buildings uptown seemed painted in pastels. His eyes were crinkled by the sun. Though he had let his hair grow longer than she liked it, he still looked as handsome as a fashion model. But tired, and beaten down. That he had allowed her to take over his computer showed how worn-out he was by then.

All evening, as they slogged through the files, she had been aware of the effort he was making to smile. Although, when he rode home with her, he had actually relaxed enough to flash his old grin and joke that if it went to trial, she would have to take time off from school to lead his defense team.

"Excellent extracurricular on my Princeton application."

"I'll bet they have diversity scholarships for daughters of felons."

He got out of the car and they stood on the sidewalk outside her mother's building silently staring up at the windows, and she had hoped that he, like she, was wishing that somehow they'd both be asked in to stay. Until he hugged her hard, thanked her again and told her what a good time he had had, and made another joke that they should go into business together. Page & Daughter.

"Files preserved."

"Blame game our specialty."

But, finally: "Okay, you better go in." And what were their last words? *See you soon?*

I need a new obsession, Morgan told herself. Or I will never get to Blind Man Island.

It became her sextant—a wise obsession, she told herself—and for a while it helped.

Every dawn, when first light revealed enough horizon to measure star angles, she practiced with her sextant, afraid of the loss or breakdown of her GPS while passing close to atolls barely visible from *Molly*'s decks, and reefs that showed no lights.

A WEEK OF beautiful sailing, with the breeze rock steady and the air like velvet on her skin, put lonely Vostok and Flint—the southeasternmost outposts of the widely scattered Line Islands—in Morgan's wake. She caught up on her sleep, dozing during the day in the shade of her awning. Between naps she did boat chores. In the cool of early evening she knelt by the stove to cook her one solid meal of the day. Dawn was reserved for star shots.

The celestial light show that wheeled across the sky each night grew more and more familiar. Now constellations, bright stars, and planets were her constant guides and the compass the last thing she checked to confirm that the boat was on course.

Time unraveled. Days became miles. She passed the Society Islands far, far to port. Bora-Bora, Tupai, Motu One, fell behind unseen. Empty ocean stretched ahead. Then at last the magic day that she reached Latitude 17 South.

Morgan altered her course to 270 and rode the parallel, due west.

Now Sirius, the brightest star in the sky, set absolutely dead ahead of the bow.

"Dog Star, Roscoe? Remember, Daddy said it's the only dog you like?" Seen from the coast of Maine, Sirius had set way to the south-southwest. Down here, seventeen degrees below the equator, it set due west—two hours after sunset—like a road sign: BLIND MAN ISLAND. STRAIGHT AHEAD. 1,000 MILES.

She continued her obsession with her sextant. Better than dwelling upon the weather fax, which was starting to spew some really scary possibilities. The tropical disturbances she had noted ages ago had spawned new ones. Several joined forces in a deepening low. That disturbance began lumbering slowly southwest.

Just keep going, she thought. The weather fax depicted winds grown to a full gale. And its movement suddenly accelerated to fifteen knots—360 miles a day—still bearing away, west and south, at double *Molly*'s speed.

The fax wasn't forecasting any recurve in her direction. But the boat was sailing on winds that shifted east and even north on occasion, which meant trimming sails day and night, and she found herself constantly observing the sky and the waves and the barometer and imagining the worst. But wasn't worrying about a hurricane—as yet unformed, five hundred miles ahead—better than obsessing about her father?

See you soon?

Soon was never. She had carried his picture in the streets, which were hung with white ash. Day after day she searched for him. They wouldn't let her into the rubble, but she wandered with his picture, wandered in crowds holding pictures, wandered to hospitals, wandered even to the morgue they had hidden in the Chelsea Piers. Had any of them ever been found? Sudden rumors. Someone pulled out alive. A couple of cops. A fireman. No, not true. Anyone? Was anyone found? None that she knew.

One day, when smoke still poured from the rubble and the sidewalks were still crowded with the searchers, she ran into her mother. And her heart soared because she was searching, too, but it turned out she was not searching for her husband, but for her daughter. Ordered home, Morgan had stayed for a shower and a change of clothes and a fresh photograph.

Hope did not so much fade as lurch to death in stages. The first time the mayor announced no one could have survived. The first time heaps of bodies were uncovered in rubble caves where people might have lived, but hadn't. The first time she considered how fire-hose water and river leaks would drown the living. The first time a girder was pulled still glowing cherry red from the fires that would not go out. The first time they allowed machines to clear huge bites instead of digging by hand. The first time old, retired firemen still digging with their hands admitted that all they hoped for were their sons' bodies. The first time the city offered death certificates for missing relatives. The day her mother accepted that offer.

The phony funeral. Grandpa leaving. Osama. Hope faltered in torment, like a subway train staggering to a last stop on shrieking brakes. Dr. Melton. Endless Dr. Melton. Until, suddenly, when she had no reason left to hope, his telephone call.

No dream, she decided with sudden vehemence. His call was as real as the sea under the keel and the wind in the sails. As real as the deck. As real as the tiller. As real as her cat sprawled precariously on the cabin roof. As real as the weather fax beeping in the cabin below. As real as the ocean itself, which was heaving with a peculiar complexity she had not seen before.

Lost in her father, lost in avoiding despair, lost in hope, she had not looked at the weather fax for more than a day. Several sheets were waiting. She read the top sheet as it spilled out.

"Oh shit!"

The forecasters had upgraded the disturbance to tropical storm. Pressure within the system had fallen below twenty-nine inches. Winds were blowing eighty knots. And it was curving south. Fear based on fact, she realized as her mouth turned suddenly dry, was hugely different from obsession.

The storm was curving south, across her path. She looked at her own barometer, and was pleasantly surprised that it had risen, slightly. Although it had recorded a recent pattern of bouncing up and down five-hundredths of an inch. And the sky was clear, except for a few fair-weather cumulus clouds, ahead. She watched them closely for a while, but they did not grow taller.

Then she noticed the swell, which she should have noticed earlier, rolling like a second sea under the trade-wind waves.

I'LL TELL YOU THE FUCKING truth, mate," said Tom Slade. "That storm has no business being here this time of year. Southeast gales, okay, but a tropical hurricane? No way."

Aiden nodded gloomy agreement at the storm swell that was angling down from the northwest. The easterly trade-wind seas formed by the stiff wind had peaks, some of which dissolved in foam. But the storm waves—rounded by distant events—were bigger, deeper, more widely spaced, and rarely broke the surface.

He said, "Last time I saw swells like these was a hurricane coming at Antigua."

"What did you do?" Tom asked.

"Got on a plane and flew home."

Aiden was driving and *Archimedes* was requiring a lot of attention. The unusually stiff trade wind they had encountered as they passed south of the Marquesas had built beautiful long seas. Until the swell began mucking things up, the boat had been surfing 90 percent of the time, the speedo cracking twenty-five and even thirty knots, the helm light as power steering, the hull resonating a deep, almost continuous growl.

Tom looked at his watch. "The weather net is up now. Let me hear what they say." He went down to his radios. He reappeared a while later with printouts and a puzzled expression.

"What's up?"

"It's still moving. Real slow, six knots. If it heads south, we go behind it. If it recurves, we turn tail and try to beat it to Bora-Bora . . . Did you say your kid's name is Morgan?"

"What?" Aiden shot a quick glance at Slade, then looked back at the rushing water.

"Morgan. Your kid's named Morgan?"

"Yeah. What about her?"

"I broke into the weather net to report these swells. After I signed off, I heard some guys behind us—slow boats making for Bora-Bora—they were talking about her."

"My daughter?"

"They're talking about this little girl who friends of theirs met on a boat called *Molly*."

"*Molly?* Are you sure?"

"He was French. You know how they talk—*Molleee*."

"You speak French?"

"I did the Globe Race with a bunch of them."

"What did he say?"

"I only heard half of the conversation; it sounded like somebody they knew rafted up with her a couple of weeks ago."

"That's impossible—"

"I left the radio on. Weather's playing hell with propagation, though."

Aiden bounded below, clapped the SSB radio headset over his

ears. Static was punctuated by e-mail chirps and bursts of conversation, much rendered unintelligible by the atmospheric noise. With the tropical storm radiating electrical interference over much of the western South Pacific, Aiden had slim hopes of hearing anything. But radio waves played all sorts of tricks. They could bounce, loop the loop, and sometimes seemed to go around corners. The static stopped and all of a sudden he heard part of a conversation so loud and clear that it sounded like a Frenchman yelling in the cockpit.

"S/V Molly P. S/V Molly P. *Island dangerous.*" Static broke it up. *Molly P?* His *Molly P?*

Then he heard gobbledygook. Something that sounded like *"BC birthday."* Then growling white noise. Aiden fiddled the radio, up and down, shifting frequencies in three megahertz increments. Hissing. Silence. Hissing. Suddenly somebody said, *"Relay."*

That meant that whoever the Frenchman was trying to talk to wasn't receiving the signal clearly, but someone else was and offering to help by passing along what he heard. A moment later, Aiden heard the Good Samaritan repeating the Frenchman's message a little more clearly. Though the new voice stumbled as if he was reading it from scribbled notes.

" 'S/V Molly P. S/V Molly P. *Island dangerous. S/V Molly P. Island dangerous. Tell François on* S/V Mais Oui *new coordinates minus BC birthday'—whatever the heck that means. Sorry, we're kind of barely readable here. Probably 'happy birthday' and then he says, 'Kitten sends love.' So I guess it's 'Kitten' wishing somebody on the* Molly P *happy birthday. I'd sing it for you except ham rules don't allow music and they'd lift my license.*"

Aiden waited, listening to static, scratching his head and wondering who the hell François was. But he heard nothing more. Fifteen minutes later the net shut down for the night. When he went back on deck, Slade asked what was going on.

"I don't know."

"I didn't think she was old enough to be sailing out here."

"Well, she's with her mother."

It sounded like Penny had somehow bought the Hinckley back and taken off for the South Seas. He wouldn't put it past her. Penny was a piece of work when she put her mind to something. And a dynamite sailor. He nodded his head. "Sounds like my wife got the Hinckley back. I had heard the new owners took her to St. Thomas for the winter. She probably bought it there— Jeez, they must have transited the Canal right after us."

"Any idea where they're headed?"

"Shelter from that misery," he said, eyeing the long swells. "She's a hell of a sailor, but she doesn't take chances."

"Especially with a kid aboard."

"They saw her two weeks ago? . . . Probably making for Tahiti. Penny was there as a kid. Always talked about sailing back . . . I guess she took Morgan out of school for a semester."

Slade said softly, "You could get a plane from Fiji."

Aiden's heart soared at the thought of seeing Morgan. But he couldn't. Not until he had finished with Henry Hong. Not until he had cleared the past. Even then, how could he go back? How could he suddenly show up? Even if the U.S. attorney had no beef with him. There was no going back. And how could Penny afford to buy the *Molly P*? *His* life insurance, that's how. What would he say to the insurance company if he showed up alive? *I was only kidding? I'll pay you back as soon as I get a great job?*

"I don't think that's in the cards."

"I'd think twice about a woman who followed *me* all the way to the South Pacific. In a Hinckley, no less. Hell, I'd retire."

"Coincidence. She doesn't even know I'm here." He shrugged. "She probably brought her boyfriend along to crew."

"Your poor kid. Probably can't wait to get away from them."

"Well . . ." said Aiden. "It's a comfortable boat. Morgan's got her own cabin. Probably brought her cat. She'll be okay."

"Cat?" Tom Slade snorted. "Only use for a cat on a boat is as an anchor."

"No, Roscoe's a hell of a seaman. One time my radar went down in the fog. Cat walked up to the bow and pointed his nose twenty degrees starboard. Warned me to dodge a tanker. We called him Boat Cat."

His heart clung to the knowledge that Morgan was near and it wouldn't let go of the fantasy of seeing her. Could he somehow sneak into Tahiti? Approach Morgan when she was alone—*Don't scream, it's only Daddy*—explain what had happened, what he had done, that he couldn't come back but he loved her and just wanted her to know he was all right and hoped she was all right.

Then what? Wish her a wonderful life?

JERRY FELT LIKE celebrating.

Morgan Page's name kept floating on the airwaves. And if Jerry had guessed right about Blind Man Island, Ahmed calculated there was a fair chance they might catch up with the kid along the seventeenth parallel. So why not celebrate with the young Malaysian himself—so beautiful to look at, and, as it turned out, so eager to please?

Gazing wide-eyed about the comfortable owner's stateroom in the back of the Baltic, he asked, "Doesn't Joe mind?" And Jerry whispered back, "I'll tell you a secret. Joe's screwing your cousin Mohammed."

The little guy gaped, "No!"

"Yes."

Big smile. "I got a better deal."

She closed her legs around him. "You sweetheart, you sure did."

Out at the nav station, the tracking computer started ringing like a four-alarm fire. Jerry whipped on a robe and ran to it. Joe was hurrying from the crews' quarters in the bow. She got there first.

"What?"

"Archimedes!"

The scanners had picked up a weather relay from the captain of *Archimedes*. He had broken his silence to warn the ham-radio weather network of hurricane swells from the northwest.

"He just told us where he is. Thank you, *Archimedes*!"

Joe punched up a satellite weather picture and laid it over the tracking chart. "He's heading smack into a hurricane is where he is."

"That son of a bitch had better not drown," said Jerry.

MORGAN'S BAROMETER FELL THREE-TENTHS OF an inch in the night—which was the steepest drop she had seen since the doldrums squall. And if the plummeting atmospheric pressure was not storm warning enough, by sunup, strange, yellowish mare's tails streaked the sky.

Her gut—or fear—told her it was coming her way. She pored over the chart and debated which way to run. Bora-Bora, in the leeward Society Islands, was out of the hurricane track. But she had long since passed its longitude. To turn around and go that far back would add weeks to her arrival in Blind Man Island.

Should she slow down? Or even heave to and wait it out? But for how long? The fact was, the sky remained relatively cloudless below those high, thin cirrus. Also, the storm itself looked small. Its winds were powerful, but the area it affected was not as huge as the subtropical hurricanes at home that roared up the Atlantic coast.

By midmorning, however, the swell was enormous. She watched, simultaneously awed and frightened by sights she had studied in the classroom. Waves shed their peaks and deepened into swells as they moved away from the source that generated them. And as they traveled, she recognized the effect called "constructive interference": waves that overtook waves moving in the same direction joined forces. These doubled waves dwarfed the trade-wind waves traveling over them. By noon the overlapping wind and storm waves established little wars between their troughs and in that choppy confusion little *Molly* began to suffer.

High in the sky, the wispy mare's tails thickened into a mesh. Below them, clouds spread across the sun. The trade wind slowed. A gust of wind slammed the sails from the north. The sudden shift backed the main. The big sail bellied and the pressure snapped the preventer line Morgan had tied to stop an accidental jibe.

She ducked, just as the boom whipped across the cabin and slammed hard against the sheets with an impact that she feared could break the gooseneck that hinged it to the mast. The entire boat shook. Morgan put her back on course and trimmed the sails. For the first time in weeks she was not running before the wind, but beating ever so slightly into the north and northwest gusts that hit now with increasing frequency.

The boat got hard to point. She blamed the reduced mainsail—she had never seen a boat that hated a reefed main as much as *Molly*—so she ran up the tiny storm jib and shook the reef out. She was taking a risk. It would be very difficult to reef again if the wind got worse.

Down in a trough, under the wind, during a brief moment of relative silence, she heard the fax beep. She set the self-steering—if the wind and seas increased, she would have to dismantle it to keep it from being destroyed—and went below, apprehensively, closing the hatch and the washboards behind her. Roscoe was watching the paper unfurl, but he made no move to bat it, or chew on it, just sat there solemn as high mass.

"Something's up, isn't it, Mr. Cat?"

He looked at her. Like, *Can't you see the obvious when it's staring you in your face?* Like, *Why don't you read the fax?*

She sat on the cabin floor to read it in the dry. Roscoe leaned down from the berth and balanced his front feet on her, like he was reading over her shoulder. He nuzzled her face as she said, "We've got trouble, Mr. Cat."

Her gut had been right. The storm had resumed turning. Instead of slamming south into Samoa, it was recurving southeast, smack on her course to her father. She nodded, feeling strangely cool. "See here, Mr. Cat? It's got our names on it. See? *Molly*, Morgan, and Roscoe . . . And you see what it says down here. Read the fine print: 'We. Are. Fucked.' "

She thought she was cool. But he knew better. And her fear was his fear. His dark irises were so huge that she could hardly see any yellow in his eyes.

"Hey? We're okay. We'll get through this. Somehow. We've got places to go and things to do. Right?"

She compared the latest weather fax to the chart she had folded to display their current section of the ocean. "We'll just make a course behind it." But she didn't need the cat to tell her that her words rang hollow in her ears. *Molly* was already sailing on the edge of her strength. Making any course would soon be impossible. Whatever the storm's track, they would be sailing smaller, private battles in the chaos, steering for survival moment by moment, heading only where the wind and seas allowed and not according to a grand theory. Tactics, not strategy. If the wind increased even slightly, strategy was out the window. Since she had come below, she thought it had grown stronger.

She reached forward through the oval opening that led to the forepeak and placed her hand on the foot of the mast. It was wet; water had found its way through the boot again. But the drippy leak was not what concerned her. It was the humming noise the wind was sending down the mast, and when she touched it, she could feel it vibrating like a tuning fork.

In an attempt to calm herself, she reviewed her actions to prepare the boat and make a mental list of what else she could try. She knew she was putting off going out to the cockpit, but she told herself that to feel cool she had to be cool. "You know what we're going to do, Mr. Cat? We're going to be dogged. Do you know what 'dogged' is? It means we're going to hang in there. No matter what happens, we'll just keep trying minute by minute, second by second. I'll be dogged. You be catted. Okay?" She hugged him, then placed him in his favorite spot in the leg hole of the starboard bunk. "Relax. I'm relaxed. See, I'm even eating."

She chewed on a Power Bar, forced the whole thing down, swigged water, zipped up her foul-weather jacket, tightened the hood's drawstrings, and climbed up on deck. With the boat rocking all over the place, it took forever to reef the mainsail; but at last she reduced it to its triple-reefed smallest, a little triangle that would barely have shaded a hot-dog stand.

Misty rain began to fall from the dense clouds. Then heavy showers, swooping in on powerful gusts. The gusts came quicker until they were almost continuous. She held her weather station to the wind. It nearly tore it out of her hand. Forty knots.

Powerful rain squalls began sweeping the water, rain falling so thick she could hardly see. The clouds got darker, the horizon impenetrable. Then a gust of wind, the strongest yet, broke up the clouds, which scattered in clumps like crowds running across Grand Central when a train was announced.

Now it was a checkered horizon with slashes of light between slits of dark, and suddenly, in a narrow band of light far off her starboard beam, Morgan saw, for just a second, a bright yellow sail race past. Impossible as it was, she knew it was real because everything else was black and white and the sail was as yellow as a crayon sun.

AIDEN PAGE WATCHED FOR KILLER waves and prayed to God that Penny and Morgan *were* sailing to Tahiti and not farther west for Tonga or Fiji. The storm had turned hellacious, with giant swells crisscrossed by crazy rollers that crashed into one another and stacked up like train wrecks. *Archimedes*, beating triple-reefed to windward, was pounding hard.

The radio message that he overheard relayed to the *Molly P* continued to fuel a fantastic dream of meeting Morgan face-to-face, if only for a moment. The words kept churning in his head, like a song heard the night before. Words that the Good Samaritan relayed precisely, and the "mystery words" lost in transmission that he had attempted to paraphrase.

Island dangerous. What island? A repeat or a paraphrase?

Could "Kitten" signing off be more like a private signal to the one person who called her that name?

Am I missing something? he wondered. Morgan knows I'm alive. I telephoned her, for Christ sake. I called her Kitten.

New coordinates minus BC birthday?

What if the sender was not radioing the *Molly P*? What if someone had used the name *Molly P* to catch his attention? What if he was the recipient?

Happy birthday? New coordinates minus BC birthday? Minus. Subtract.

And then he got it, all in a rush. BC. Boat Cat. They had invented a birthday for Roscoe. Christmas Day. 12/25. To transmit his position to Morgan, he should radio his coordinates minus 12/25. Subtract 12 from his degrees of longitude and 25 from his minutes. Subtract 12 from his degrees of latitude and 25 from his minutes. Morgan would then *add* 12/25 to each. Simple and foolproof secure. The kid could be a spy. But weren't kids among adults always spies, operating in "enemy territory"? Look at the stratagems he and Charlie had devised to dodge their overbearing father.

Trapped on her mother's boat, with her mother's boyfriend lurking about, his daughter had stolen a private moment at the radio to send him a message. *I'm nearby, Daddy. I'm looking for you. Radio back. Tell me I'm not alone. Tell me you wanted to telephone.*

Radio François on the sailing vessel Mais Oui *where you are, Daddy, and he will relay it to me. In code that no one but us can decipher.*

Aiden unclipped his harness to run down to the radio, before the shriek of the wind in the shrouds stopped him cold. Not today, Kitten. No signal is getting through this stuff. Besides, it was still a fantasy. What could he say to her . . . ?

"My turn," he called to Tom. They were spelling each other every half hour to stay strong.

"You want to check the radar, first?" Tom shouted back.

The radar showed the storm still turning.

If any boat could race to the relatively less dangerous or "navigable" semicircle behind the tropical storm, it was *Archimedes.* If her crew could keep up with her. They had rigged a storm jib and had readied a storm trysail—a napkin-size triangle of reinforced Kevlar—to give the boat steerage if they were forced to douse the triple-reefed main. They had eaten—stuffed themselves on canned chicken stew—and filled thermoses with hot soup and coffee. They had rested as much as was possible, before the wind shift drove the boat onto the beat.

Aiden took the helm just ahead of a rain squall that made a Maine-coast autumn nor'easter a pleasant memory. Thunder cracked close enough to hurt his ears. Lightning exploded in the purest white. The last thing he expected was a startled roar from Tom Slade.

"Quick stop! I got the mainsheet."

Aiden spun the helm down, and pivoted the boat on her keel. Tom Slade threw himself at the mainsheets, timing the jibe perfectly. They left the jib sheets untouched, which backed the storm jib in a man-overboard maneuver that would have been impressive seamanship on a millpond.

"What?" yelled Aiden, who saw nothing that would have made them stop.

Slade swiped the water out of his eyes. "I saw a boat."

"In this?"

"Wee bitty sloop. Laboring pretty bad. Caught a glimpse on a crest."

"Where?"

"Port beam. Behind us now."

Both men stared into the rain-slashed gloom waiting for another bolt of lightning.

"What do you mean 'little'? How little?"

"I told you. Wee little thing."

With his heart and his mind newly cleaved to Morgan, Aiden had thought instantly of the *Molly P*. But Tom Slade would not mistake a forty-two-foot Hinckley for a "wee bitty sloop," even in these conditions. Nor would such a powerful boat be laboring, yet.

"Tom, are you sure?"

"No . . . But I thought I . . ."

Lightning flashed on a thousand seas. On every wave foamed a broken crest that gleamed like ice. But they saw no boat.

"What course was it on?"

"Ours. Same course. Two-seventy. We passed it. Some poor bastard sailing on a shoestring . . ."

They sailed back and forth, searching—a search stymied repeatedly by blasts of rain and windblown spray that cut visibility until they couldn't see the bow. All the while black cloud settled closer and closer like oily smoke. Finally, as night began to gather, Aiden said, "They could be miles away by now."

"Or a hundred yards."

"Either way, we'd never see 'em."

Slade shook his head and rubbed his eyes. "I get these flashbacks—Aiden, I've had 'em before. But goddammit, that little boat looked so real I could have touched it."

"I'll take the helm," said Aiden. Slade didn't argue. He just kept scanning the water. Nor did he protest when Aiden suggested that, with an hour to go before the night blotted out the last of the dim daylight, they douse the main and set the storm trysail.

As the seas grew chaotic, Aiden tried to shut his mind to all but the essential forces challenging the boat. But Morgan's message intruded. New coordinates meant a change of location. From where? Island Dangerous. There was only one island in his diminished world and Morgan was smart enough to guess its name. But how had she become wise enough to fear its owner?

AFTER A LONG, BRUTAL DAY, Morgan Page was still counting her blessings. *Molly*'s heavy lead keel and light racing rig made her inherently stable—firm below and airy aloft. And she was as prepared as she could be, fed, hydrated, and protected by good foul-weather gear, warm enough for the Gulf of Maine. She had early on lowered her mainsail and lashed it tightly to the boom and had even stowed the self-steering foil and paddle moments before a heavy sea that would have wrecked them crashed over the stern.

But the wind kept rising. And the squall lines came faster. Squall upon squall fused into incessant bombardment by dark rain and explosive wind. The wind made the seas wild. The water turned white. Broken crests bore down on her from every direction. It became impossible to hold a course and all she could do was steer a path through jagged mountains.

A violent gust blew her hood off her head and she heard, unmuffled, the true strength of the wind. What had moaned through the heavy hood was a shriek pitched so high it hurt her ears.

She clamped the tiller under her arm and flipped open her weather station. She could not believe her eyes. Fifty-six knots. And that was in the lee of a big wave. Scarier was the atmospheric pressure. The barometer read 28.8. If it wasn't a hurricane yet, it would be soon. The wind ripped the weather station out of her hand, banged it over the cabin and into the water.

"Shit."

She had no time to mourn the loss of the precious instrument. Thundering down on her was a wave three times bigger than any she had seen. She tried to race away from it, but it overtook her easily, blotting out what remained of the sky, plunging her into near darkness as it curled above her, taller than her mast. She looked up, frozen by terror.

Molly struggled to climb it. A brutal gust slammed the jib. Over she went onto her side as if baring her neck in surrender. But the watery slope channeled another gust under the sail. The tiller went light. *Molly* soared out of danger onto the crest of the monster wave. Thrust high above the surrounding seas, Morgan Page could see for miles in the dying light.

"Oh. My. God."

It looked as if she had been sailing all day through a different, smaller storm. Concentrating, as she had to, to steer her boat, she had not until this moment seen that all the seas she had struggled through, all the breaking waves, all the wind-shredded crests, had belonged to a small storm inside the real storm. What rampaged before her for a brief moment was the real storm—an infinite reach from horizon to horizon of soaring mountains and steep valleys.

Smoke drifted over the mountains—spindrift, she realized, sea spray churned to mist—draping the slopes that plunged into deep ravines, coiling through dark passes. All she could compare it to, the only thing she had ever seen like it, were video images of the war in Afghanistan—the mountains of the cloud-piercing, snow-covered

Hindu Kush. These mountains looked as fierce, forbidding, and vast. But these water mountains roved close around her, ever in motion, leading random charges from every point of the compass and, like volcanoes, heaving countless tons to the sky, toppling to the depths, and smothering anything that dared invade the sea that bred them.

The pinnacle that had thrust her so high began to collapse. *Molly* teetered on the rim of a steeply raked slope. It melted out from under her, transforming slope to cliff. Morgan looked straight down into blackness. For a long second she saw no way out, then a rugged path materialized, snaking a tortured diagonal among the peaks that studded the face. She wrenched the tiller and the boat skied down it, hull shrieking and banging into the momentary shelter of a deep trough.

"Thank you, *Molly*," she murmured. A family cruiser would have rolled over, blown out its hatches, and sunk. But avoiding a fatal bow plant was not the same as holding a course and Morgan had to concede that the sleek little sloop was nearing her limits. The storm had built seas of such power that soon *Molly* would be unable either to point or to run.

Full night fell, pitch-black under heavy cloud, though lightning kept flashing from the squalls and there was never a full minute when the boiling white sea was not ablaze. Huddled over the tiller, Morgan felt too tired and beat-up to think straight, but she had to make a fateful decision.

How many times had she lain awake listening to Daddy and Uncle Charlie and their friends drunk in the cockpit or at the club bar arguing storm tactics: heave to, run, forereaching, drogues and sea anchors, laying ahull? Everyone had their favorite and ten reasons why the others would drown you. Active or passive? Fight, or pull the blankets over your head? Morgan Page's choice was less a decision than an honest admission of defeat: heave to, retreat to the cabin, take Roscoe in her arms, and pray for their lives.

She rehearsed the move in her mind while she waited for the lightning to show her a break in the roaring seas. A bolt split the sky.

Waves collided in blue light. Thunder cracked, so loud it hurt her ears. Again and again it flashed on madness, until she spotted a tiny patch of smooth water, like a secret garden hidden by jagged walls.

Morgan urged the bow into the wind and through it. The wind backed the jib. She tied the helm to leeward. The boat lost headway. The backed jib pushed the bow away from the wind. The rudder turned the bow toward the wind. It worked. Gripped by opposing forces, the boat bobbed along like a duck, drifting a zigzag course downwind while trailing a slick that quieted the angry water chasing after her.

But even stasis had its limits. Before she could open the hatch, a wave broke over the boat and knocked her flat on the cockpit floor. She pulled herself up by her tether, waited for the lightning to make sure it was safe, and opened the hatch.

"No!"

Roscoe scrambled out. The electrical storm had so terrorized him that his hair was standing on end. He eluded her, leaped from the cabin roof to the boom, and sank his claws into the furled sail.

"Come on, honey, come back inside. See I'm going—"

She sensed a shadow racing swiftly at the boat. She lunged for Roscoe. Her tether fetched up when her fingers were six inches from his face. Thunder pealed. Sheet lightning seemed to freeze the seas, the decks, and the cat clinging to the boom in a coat of gleaming ice.

Then the wave exploded over the boat like surf. It flung Morgan back into the cockpit, and when she could see again, Roscoe was gone.

"NOOOOOOOOOOOO!"

She ripped off the shock cord, yanked the tiller to her. The jib filled. The boat leaped. She would find him. He was there, somewhere. He could swim. Lightning flickered. She saw him paddling frantically on a wall of water, an immense, curling sea that buried him.

Fury roared up out of her gut, an animal howl of helpless rage for every loss in an endless year of loss.

"*I hate you!*" she screamed at the sea, and steered straight into it.

Molly tried to climb, tried to carve a course. But the cliff of water shouldered effortlessly under her bow, lifted her hull, and stood her on her stern.

I left the hatch open, was Morgan's last thought as the sea turned *Molly* upside down and the boat fell on top of her. And I don't care.

B Y THE DULL LIGHT OF a brutal dawn, it was clear to Aiden Page that *Archimedes* had lost her race to the navigable waters behind the storm. Fast as the powerful Open 50 was in the hands of two skilled seamen, the storm had circled faster. The seas had grown gigantic in the night, and even Tom Slade conceded that they could no longer beat to windward, no matter how strong her hull and sturdy her rig. They had to turn around and run before the wind.

Easier said than done, however, as catching a sea broadside would end in tears.

It was Aiden's trick at the helm—methodically heading up to meet the charging crests, then bearing away to angle down their back sides—and he refused to hand off to Slade. By now he knew this beast. While he made no claim to be the racer the captain was, and had never seen such seas, he had as much faith in his own heavy-weather boat-handling skills as he did in Tom's. And greater faith in his judgment. Perhaps it was because he had sailed so much with his family instead of a gang of paid professionals. But with seas running close to forty feet, and the occasional rogue wave roaring among them like a runaway express, he had no intention of pulling a Tom Slade "hard-alee-and-hope."

He waited for the light to get strong enough to see two distant crests ahead. The wind had not dropped a bit, and the seas had built even bigger. Though they appeared more orderly than they had been early in the night. Wishful thinking. He took the first crest nearly head-on, looked back from the top, spotted a hundred-yard smooth patch, and, as the crest passed under the hull, shouted over the wind to Slade, who had spotted the patch, too, and was reaching for the mainsheet, "Ease the main." He bore off and kept bearing off until they were headed downwind on a broad reach.

The change in conditions was as striking as it was immediate. The pounding ceased, and the apparent wind over the deck dropped, even as boat speed tripled. Built to race before the westerlies of the Roaring Forties, the fifty-footer tore up the backs of rollers, flew over their crests, and accelerated down their faces.

"This is more like it," said Slade when it was his trick at the helm, although the slightest miscalculation would end in a fatal broach.

Aiden Page stared at their wake. Tonga, Fiji, and Blind Man Island were falling astern at twenty-six knots. Then he looked at the outcast captain, steering with a grin of pure pleasure, and realized that if there was a man in the world he would trust, it was him. "Hey, Tom."

"What?"

"When we get out of this and turn around again . . . ?"

"Yeah?"

"Would you let me charter you for a slight course change?"

" 'Charter' me? Christ, no, mate. I'm already late for New Zealand."

"It's on the way. Blind Man Island."

"Where's that?"

"Seventeen South, 178, 8 West. Above the northern Tonga group. All by itself, and privately owned, so you don't have to worry about clearance or anything."

"Except if a Tongan patrol boat happens along. No thanks."

"You wouldn't even have to stop. Just put me off on the spare raft. I'll pay for it. You just tell the owner it fell overboard."

Tom Slade gave him a look and Aiden added hastily, "It's no big deal. Just something in my life I have to finish up."

"No big deal? . . . It must be a big deal to you or you wouldn't be asking."

"It is a big deal."

"Shit . . . Well . . . it'll save me time not stopping in Fiji."

"Thank you, Tom. I really appreciate it."

"No problem, mate."

"Thing is, I don't want anybody knowing about this."

Slade give him another look. "You might have noticed by now I don't talk to a lot of people. If you want to go pirating onto an island, that's your business. But first, if you don't fucking mind, could we put some concentration into getting out of this alive?"

OSAMA REACHED TO HELP HER, saying in his deep voice, "You're a brave girl."

"Don't you fucking touch me." She yelled it aloud.

He shook her hard, jerking her shoulders, hurting her back. A big hand squeezed her arm and she cried in pain.

"I won't hurt you."

"You *are* hurting me, you bastard. Leave me alone. Haven't you done enough?"

"I'm only trying to help."

"I don't need your help."

"Then get out of the water." His voice had changed. He sounded like Dr. Melton.

Her eyes opened slowly, one, then the other, a green and a blue peering through a crust of salt. It was light. Her head hurt. Her arm hurt. Her back hurt. He jerked her again. Her arm hurt worst of all. She was in water up to her neck.

She looked around. The water was sloshing in a dark tank. The only light came from overhead.

"Roscoe? ...Oh God...Poor little cat." She started to cry. He jerked her yet again and everything hurt. She was cold. She looked some more. "Oh my God...How did I get here?"

She had no recollection of doing it, but somehow she had climbed into the cabin. Her PDF tether was still clipped to the pad eye outside the hatch, and as the boat lurched, the tether jerked her harness. The harness, not the terrorist in her dreams...But if she was inside, why was she in water up to her neck? She was sitting on the floor. She rose to her knees. The water was higher than the berth. They were sinking.

She stood, painfully, and looked out the hatch. The waves were huge. Big waves riding a long, deep swell. But a thin disk of sun glowed behind the clouds, which the wind was shredding into cirrus streamers. The air smelled of jungle or something rotting, something landlike, as if the hurricane had blown trees into the ocean.

The boat was so low in the water the waves were licking the deck.

A thick cable was draped over the cockpit. The lifelines drooped between stanchions that leaned like drunks. When she grew aware of the absence of the shadow of the boom, she turned around. The mast was gone.

I GUESS I should be afraid, she thought. But she felt no room in her heart for fear. It was overflowing with sadness, pain, and defeat. "We got so close, Mr. Cat. I'll bet Blind Man Island's less than a thousand miles. Six or seven days good sailing. With a mast."

Even with a mast, how would she find it? God knew where the storm had blown her. She was probably lucky they hadn't crashed on a reef. Now she was nowhere. God, I'm out of it, she thought. Like my head's on backward. She fumbled for her GPS. The Velcro pocket flap was ripped, her GPS lost. She stepped down into the water. Who cares? she thought. Besides, she had a sextant, somewhere. Exhausted, she crawled through the water, put her head down on the soaking berth, and fell into a dreamless sleep.

The sun was high overhead when she woke, burning through the last cirrus streamers. The seas were lumpy. The wind had stopped. The air was sultry. In water to her waist, she was hot.

Everything hurt. She could move everything, so she had not broken any bones, except maybe a rib, because her right side felt like somebody was sticking her with a needle. She came up with a plan to distract her mind from the pain: she would review everything she remembered since Roscoe had jumped out. It didn't work. She couldn't get past Roscoe, could not let go of the image of him clinging to the boom, clutching the sail. She could not conjure a picture of what happened next. Though she knew he had been swept away. Scoured off the boat like her mast and boom and sails. She couldn't clear her mind of how frightened his last minutes had been. What a terrible way for an innocent animal to die. Walnut brain, Daddy had teased. Only a big enough brain for the day, no room for yesterday, no tomorrow. But he was a fighter and he would have fought for breath until his heart stopped beating. She lay back and stared up at the sky and cried.

The sun was moving. Time was moving. She was thirsty.

She went below and felt around under the water, under the bunk where she kept water bottles, closed her hand around the smooth, flexible tube, and pulled one up. She fumbled off the screw top and drank it dry. "Oh God." It was the most beautiful thing she had ever tasted.

She found another and brought it up to the cockpit. Sitting, listlessly watching as the sea picked the boat high enough to see total emptiness for miles, then slowly lowered it into a watery canyon, it occurred to her that the boat was no lower in the water than when she had first looked out the hatch. The waves occasionally washed the decks, but did not clear the cabin or break into the cockpit.

Maybe she wasn't sinking. Maybe the water belowdecks had burst in when the boat turned over. Maybe her hull was sound.

Lifted again for another glimpse of desolation, she thought to herself, I don't know where land is, I don't know where I am. All I know is I'm out here alone. She remembered not caring whether she died. It seemed reasonable, all things considered, but for some reason she could not explain, she no longer felt so detached. She even thought of trying to bail the water out of the cabin. It hardly seemed worth the trouble. But, on the other hand, the sun kept moving, which meant night would come, and even if she died, it would be nice to have a dry place to curl up out of the wind.

She had no bucket, thanks to the idiots she had stolen the boat from. But she had a pot and, somewhere, a little hand bilge pump. But when she looked down the hatch, she saw that the cabin was almost entirely full. Tons of water.

A potful of water was amazingly heavy. She made a deal with herself: Two hundred pots of water out the hatch before she could rest. But after fifty she thought she would die of pain. As she scooped water into pot number seventy-five, lifted it over her head, and poured it out the hatch into the cockpit, she thought, I can't do this.

One hundred and fifty pots. One hundred and seventy. One-ninety. She collapsed at the foot of the companionway and rested her cheek on the top step. Two more pots . . . She set a new goal. Twenty-five pots. She cut her finger on a sliver of mirrored glass. Probably the mirror from her sextant. Somewhere in the mess she would find the rest of its pieces.

She bailed and bailed, wondering why she bothered.

But the hull felt lighter. Deep in the water, it had wallowed in slow motion, so it had felt sort of steady. Now it was rocking and pitching on the waves. Like it was bobbing on top again. Like a boat instead of a bathtub. As the motion grew livelier, something banged against the hull. So engrossed in forcing herself to keep filling the pot, lifting it, spilling it out the hatch, she paid it no mind at first. It hit harder and she felt the impact vibrate against her knees. As she dumped the next pot, she rose unsteadily to her feet and looked out. Nothing. Just waves and her. The boat was on a crest. Miles and miles of waves. No land, no ships, nothing and no one but her.

It banged again. Under, she thought. It's under the boat. She crawled into the cockpit and looked around, expecting what, she had no idea. An angry shark. A killer whale. The stern pulpit had washed away—she hadn't noticed that before—the stainless-steel tubing just vanished. But the tiller was right where she had left it when she hove to, still lashed to leeward. Which, as her bailing raised the hull high enough to catch some wind, was keeping the boat hove to, zigzagging ahead of the wind at a safe angle to the waves.

Bang! It hit the hull again. She looked forward. The bow pulpit was still in place. Where the mast had stood was a stump about two feet high. The metal was twisted as if some vandal had chopped it with an ax.

The wire shrouds that had stayed the mast from the port side were hanging straight down in the water, taut as a fishing line with a shark on the hook.

"My mast!"

The mast was hanging by the shrouds and banging against the hull when it rolled. How long before it bashed a hole in the hull? She stared at the stays, wondering what to do about it. She had a bolt cutter to cut the stays. If it was still in the tool box. . . . But—a bunch of crazy buts began lurching inside her brain like the junk sloshing around the cabin. But with a mast, she could sail.

Where, with no GPS and no sextant? Screw instruments. She'd been sailing eight weeks under the stars. She would recognize landmarks at night. Star marks. Sea marks? Suddenly excited, she worked her way forward along the cabin, holding the handrail, leaned over the drooping lifelines, and tugged the shrouds. They came easily, at first. A spreader poked through the waves.

"Unbelievable."

The mast was still attached to the shrouds, hanging underneath the boat at the end of the triple wire, which was still attached to the deck. She pulled harder, but it resisted, like something elastic was holding it down. Or a mirror-image Morgan was pulling back on it. It was caught on something.

Where was the top of the mast? Where was the boom?

Clinging to the wire, which was biting into her palms, she tried to piece together a picture of what might be happening under the boat. All three shrouds—upper, intermediate, lower—were attached to the lowest spreader. Two—upper and intermediate—to the top spreader. The upper—the longest—continued to the top of the mast. She pulled on it again. The spreader that broke surface had only two wires on it, so it was the top spreader.

She tried to pull it aboard, but it wouldn't budge. She let go and slumped to the deck to think. Her head still felt screwed on backward. There had to be a way. If she could haul the mast aboard, she could somehow stand it up and rig a sail and turn poor *Molly* into a boat again. Her eye drifted over the deck. The sun was settling into the west. Low as they sat, the winches were casting shadows.

"Duh!"

She jumped down to the cabin, sloshed through the still ankle-deep water, and found a coiled dock line floating in the forepeak. In the box that served as the bottom step to the companionway was a spare winch handle. She tied the dock line to the shroud with a rolling hitch, astonishing herself. "Hey, Mr. Cat . . ." In the midst of her boast, she remembered he was gone, but finished it anyway: "Look at this; rolling hitch, first try . . ."

Weeping again, she wrapped three turns around the powerful jib winch, hauled in the slack, and started cranking. With a purposeful *click, click, click,* the winch drew the shrouds out of the water, pulling the top spread, and then the top of the mast itself, into sight. But strong as the winch was, she raised the mast only that far. Beyond that it wouldn't budge. Something had tangled, she had an awful feeling, around the keel.

A line, a wire shroud, a scrap of sail . . . Think, she thought. It's getting dark soon . . . Pull from another direction. She led the line back to the stern, through a spinnaker block, and back to the jib winch. Now when she cranked she pulled backward instead of into the boat. The line grew tight.

Suddenly she felt a muffled, underwater *thump*. The line popped free and the entire mast sprang to the surface, as if it were floating. It was a victory that grew even sweeter when she saw the boom was still attached. The gooseneck had not broken. The sail she had struggled so hard to lash down in the storm was still partly furled.

She hauled the tangled spars alongside and lashed it midships, aft, and finally at the bow, like she had caught a long, thin fish, or an aluminum eel. As the boat rolled on the heavy swell, the mast banged the hull. She cushioned it with two fenders and collapsed in the cockpit, so tired she was shaking. Time for more water. When she had the strength, she went below and felt around for another bottle. She came up with a plastic jar of peanut butter and was suddenly so hungry that she scooped half the contents with her fingers before she resumed her search for water.

She dreaded the night. It was closing in fast. The sun was sinking. Yellow clouds absorbed its heat. She was cold and wet, and for some reason after all this time at sea the dark scared her. No cat, she thought. Where are you, Mr. Cat? Of all her friends' cats, he was the only cat she knew that would sleep with a person every night and if it was cold would sometimes sneak under the blankets. He would allow her to hug him, really squeeze him. And he never bit. Her. Though if he got really mad, he would growl. Fair warning, Daddy used to warn her. Mr. Cat has spoken.

Already it was too dark to work on the mast. Even by starlight, if the clouds kept thinning. She could hold a flashlight in her teeth, maybe, if she could find one. But no, she would not be able to see beyond the circle of light, which would actually blind her. She would just have to get through the night, hope the sea grew calmer, rest, eat, and get pumped at daylight. She wondered if there was anything in the entire boat that was dry. Anything warm.

Somewhere, she had a fleece sweatshirt kept dry in a plastic bag.

She searched from bow to stern, sloshing through the water. When she found a flashlight that still worked, she continued her search. There, gleaming red through the plastic. She pulled it to the light. But it felt too heavy. The plastic had ripped, the garment was soaked.

She started shivering. It was pitch-black in the boat. She went up to the cockpit. A few fuzzy stars cast thin light. Better than nothing. She wrung out the fleece, pulled off her foul-weather jacket, which was chafing her neck and wrists, and the soaked sweatshirt under it, and pulled the wet fleece over her skin. Yep, better than nothing. She put the jacket back on to block the wind and closed her eyes.

In Morgan's mind, she saw the boat turn over backward, again. Time had stopped as she teetered on her stern, like clock hands rusted at the hour. She remembered, now, being fully aware that the entire boat was falling on top of her. They would land upside down and the hatch was open. I'm dying, she had thought. I'm going to drown. And I don't care.

What miracle had righted it? Sailboats were supposed to right themselves, the heavy keel did the job, but when she had awakened, *Molly* had been so full of water she was inches from sinking. How had she righted herself with all that weight inside? Over and over she saw the boat rear up on its stern. Over and over she felt it fall backward. Over and over she saw the open hatch. Then nothing. And here she was, wet, cold, and alive. She shivered, but not from cold. She had come so close to killing herself. She *had* killed herself. Except something—God—*Molly*—God as *Molly*—had intervened. Miracles. Or dumb luck. Did she deserve it? She had the sudden, powerful feeling that her mother would say no, while her father would say yes. On the other hand, she was wet and cold on a boat adrift in the middle of the South Pacific without a mast to sail or a radio to call for help, or a GPS or a sextant to tell her where she was. All because she got mad at the sea. Like the sea cared whether Roscoe lived or died? I got what I deserved, she thought. I threw a temper tantrum. I got what I deserved.

She was up before the sun, bailing and pumping, and ready to go to work when she had the light.

MORGAN HAD READ about dismasted sailors jury-rigging short masts out of their boom or their spinnaker pole. But wouldn't it be better to step a real mast so the boat could really sail? She could almost hear her mother saying what she always said—echoing *her* mother: If a job's worth doing it was worth doing right. Except first she had to get it out of the water.

Grandpa, she thought, here's another advantage to small boats. *Molly P 1*'s mast must have weighed hundreds of pounds. No way she could lift it. But she had helped tune enough dinghies and club racers to know that little *Molly*'s hollow aluminum spar couldn't weigh more than seventy or eighty pounds—while the boom was probably only about twenty. But when she tried to pull them on deck, they were beyond the strength of her arms.

She summoned up her heroes. Bow "man" Martha McKechnie said a girl could make things work without the muscle. Think! She found another peanut-butter jar and sat in the cockpit trying to figure out what she was doing wrong. The sun was getting brutal. It softened the peanut butter until she was practically drinking it. Add up the hardware, she thought, the rigging, the storm sail still on the headstay, and the mainsail weighted down with pockets of trapped water, and she was dreaming if she thought she could lift it all in one piece.

She disassembled it, hanging over the side, tying each piece so it wouldn't sink, and gradually got on deck sails, boom, and finally the mast itself, at which point she was amazed to discover that it was dark again and the wind, which had picked up as the trades reestablished themselves in the wake of the storm, was getting cool. She put on the fleece, which the sun had dried, and lay down in the cockpit. When she awoke, to midnight stars, she looked for familiar ones while trying to figure a way to raise the mast.

A girl could make things work without the muscle, said Bow "man" Martha. But Morgan could also hear her saying, *Give it up. Stop being so stubborn. It's a piece of cake to raise the boom. Just do it and get going, already.*

I'm going to sail. I'm not stopping for repairs. I'm not going off course. I'm sailing straight to Blind Man Island.

Martha was not impressed. *Blind Man Island?* She could almost hear the laughter. *No way you're sailing to Blind Man Island. You're just a club racer. You're not a rock star.*

Don't tell me I'm not a rock star. Who do you think sailed all the way here?

You're nothing but a little-rich-kid-club sailor who got lucky. So why don't you jury-rig a stumpy little mast out of your boom and limp where the wind blows you?

I'm not just a club sailor, anymore.

Rock stars don't let their cats fall overboard.

"Bitch!" She screamed it out loud and sat up, startled by the sound of her voice. Tears bubbled up. What am I, crazy? Suddenly she was laughing. Poor Martha was probably twelve thousand miles from here innocently practicing for the America's Cup. Then, all of a sudden, she got a brilliant idea. Thank you, Martha.

She set immediately to work by starlight. Martha was right. It *was* relatively easy to stand the short, light boom and lash it upright to the stump of the mast. And while the boom was not tall enough to make a good mast, it did stand tall enough to serve as a crane to raise the mast itself.

Upright in frantic stages. Twice it got away from her when the boat rolled and crashed to the deck. She came within inches of losing it over the side, before she finally had it standing, wobbling thirty feet in the air with its foot lashed to the stump, the lower shrouds steadying it from the sides, and the main and jib halyards temporarily staying it fore and aft.

She was so tired she didn't dream that night and woke up only when the sun was in her eyes. She replaced the temporary stays with the shortened fore- and backstays, rescued the boom, and tightened everything up. There was just enough juice left in the battery to drill holes in the mast to attach the boom's gooseneck.

With six feet missing from the mast, she had to double-reef the main to shorten it. And until she could resew the genoa, she was forced to fly the little storm jib from the abbreviated head stay. Yet both sails filled with the wind. And as Morgan steered west, she thought that the most beautiful sound she had ever heard in her life was the crisp gurgle of water once more rushing past *Molly*'s hull. She tossed the taffrail log and anxiously watched the meter.

"Four knots, Mr. Cat! . . . And wouldn't you be proud?" No response. Sadly, she turned to her log. It beat talking to herself. Besides, navigating by dead reckoning with only a compass and wristwatch, and what she could guess from the stars, made regular log entries vital.

1400 MAY 27, 2002. COURSE WEST-NORTHWEST (280). SPEED 4 KNOTS. POSITION? NOT EXACTLY RACING,

she wrote, moving the pen carefully on the damp pages.

BUT A LOT FASTER THAN LIMPING.

To celebrate, she unshipped the self-steering Monitor, and when the boat was back in its sure hand, she scrubbed herself under pot after pot of cool seawater, shampooing the grime away and toweling off the salt before it settled on her skin.

Tonight, she would hunt out the stars she had sailed under for so long and steer a course that would line them up as they had been before the storm. Blind Man Island had lain in the direction that bright Sirius set each night. If she could see its zenith, when it was highest in the sky, where it set tonight might show her what compass course to sail to compensate for the storm blowing her south.

She combed out her hair as the wind dried it—it was getting long, big surprise after two months—and decided to use the remaining daylight to bring her log up-to-date. By now the wind and sun had dried the paper and she could write without gouging the page.

1600 MAY 27, 2002. COURSE WEST-NORTHWEST (280). SPEED 4 KNOTS. POSITION? (SOMEWHERE WEST OF 160 WEST AND BETWEEN 12??? AND 16??? SOUTH.)

She started with her memories of being pitchpoled. Writing quickly, unwilling to record more than the facts as she recalled them, she described bailing and finding her mast and rigging it.

RIGHT NOW I'M MAKING 4 KNOTS ON COURSE 280, HOPING I'M ANGLING NORTH ENOUGH FOR BLIND MAN ISLAND. TO-NIGHT I'M HOPING TO SPOT SIRIUS'S ZENITH AND SETTING TO GET BLIND MAN ISLAND'S LATITUDE AND TRY TO CALCULATE MY COURSE TO GET BACK UP THERE . . . I'LL NEVER GET ANOTHER CAT. I'D ALWAYS BE COMPARING IT TO HIM. NO CAT WAS EVER SMARTER. NO CAT WAS EVER MORE BEAUTIFUL. NO CAT COULD BE SO NOBLE. I KNOW I'LL MISS HIM FOREVER. NO CAT COULD BE SUCH A FRIEND. BESIDES, I REALLY DON'T FEEL LIKE I DESERVE ONE.

The page got wet again. When she flung her head back to dry her tears, she caught motion in the corner of her eye. She turned to the wake, and there, just nicking the southeast horizon, was a sail.

She watched it draw rapidly nearer, rising against the sky as tall and narrow as a tusk. No spinnaker—it was not running before the trade, which had backed south—but on a broad reach on a course that paralleled hers.

She felt a strange sensation in her chest, an almost laugh—bitter-sweet, part giggle, part snicker. "Sorry, Mr. Cat. But you have to admit it's kind of funny. *Now* I get help?"

At the speed the boat was traveling, it soon became apparent that it would pass miles to port. Too far off to notice *Molly*'s shortened profile unless someone happened to be aiming binoculars right at her.

Among the items that had survived the submersion in the cabin were her father's binoculars, two distress flares, and an orange smoke flare for daylight. She brought them to the cockpit, where she found her emotions in a tangle. She could certainly use help fixing her position and gathering the latest weather forecasts. And she would love to buy their spare GPS, if they had one—she had some cash drying below, out of the wind—but otherwise she really didn't want to see anybody or answer any questions. She had enough canned food and bottled water. Her bruises were painful, but none needed medical attention. And no one short of a boatyard could make her rig any better than she had already done herself.

She stuffed the flares into her jacket and studied the racing boat through the binoculars with an awed "wow" for the rock-star sailors driving her. They had trimmed her towering mainsail and humongous genoa within millimeters of perfection and she was going so fast that the low-slung hull was barely visible in the fine mist of her passing. If bound for Tonga or Fiji—at four times her speed—they would drop anchor in less than a week. Or down to New Zealand in two. It was like watching a jet from a taxi stuck in airport traffic.

Days instead of weeks. What if they were headed for Tonga? Their course looked right. Or even passing near Tonga on their way to Fiji or Samoa. Sailors were generous. How well could she play the kid lost at sea? Convincing enough to persuade them to tow her little boat? Her planing hull would tow easily . . .

Confused, still afraid of the ham-radio gossip, she turned to her log to order her thoughts.

THERE'S A BOAT OVERTAKING ME ON MY COURSE. PART OF ME WANTS TO FURL MY SAILS SO THEY DON'T SEE ME. THE OTHER PART WANTS TO LIGHT A SMOKE FLARE SO THEY DO.

"What would you do, Mr. Cat? . . . I know what you'd say. You'd say, 'Screw 'em, we don't need anybody. We've got each other . . .'

Easy for you to say, Mr. Cat . . . But maybe you're right. They'll ask a million questions. Then they'll dump me in some harbor where they'll ask a million more. Like where are your papers? That's why I made a real mast. So I wouldn't have to stop. I'm not limping. We're really sailing, so what if we're slow?"

She picked up her pen.

> THE ONLY WAY I CAN COUNT ON GETTING TO BLIND MAN ISLAND IS TO GET MYSELF THERE MYSELF. I'M GOING TO FURL MY SAILS UNTIL THEY'RE GONE.

She reached for the main halyard. "Damn." The boat had altered several degrees and was pointing straight at her. She watched it grow larger, overtaking *Molly* like she was standing still.

"Ohmigod, what a beautiful boat."

> OKAY, THE DECISION'S MADE FOR ME. THEY SPOTTED ME. I'LL PULL A "DADDY" AND TALK MY WAY OUT OF IT. OR I'LL GET A TOW. EITHER WAY, BEFORE THIS DAY IS DONE, I'M GOING TO HAVE A HOT SHOWER ON AN ABSOLUTELY GORGEOUS BALTIC 70.

SMALL, DARK ASIANS SWARMED THE Baltic's decks, readying lines and fenders. A blond couple standing behind the helmsman waved to Morgan. The woman looked a little familiar. Both did, in a funny way. They reminded her of Uncle Charlie and Aunt Mary—or like they would have looked if Uncle Charlie hadn't been killed in the World Trade Center before they finished building his new yacht.

Except, of course, they weren't. Just a nice Greenwich-looking couple like you'd meet at the club, smiling and waving. As the Baltic rounded up and glided to a rest, placing *Molly* in her protective lee, the man held a mike to his mouth and called through the loud hailer, "Hello. Do you need help?"

Which was an embarrassing clue that, proud as Morgan was of her jury rig, it must look pretty awful from the deck of a luxurious racing yacht. She cupped her hands to reply, "I'm fine. But could I buy a GPS or a sextant?"

"No problem," said the man. "We've got plenty of spares."

The woman called, "Bet you'd like a nice, hot shower, too. Would you like to come aboard?"

One step at a time, Morgan had already decided. If she didn't ask for a tow, right off, maybe they'd offer one.

"Thank you. That's very nice of you. But what about my boat?"

"The boys'll rig a bridle. We'll take her in tow."

Smiling deckhands hung fenders to protect the Baltic's pristine hull, jumped down, and held *Molly* alongside. The woman offered a hand to pull her aboard. She had a really strong grip, and as soon as Morgan's feet touched the holystoned teak, the Asians jumped back on the bigger boat and pushed *Molly* away.

"My boat!"

It was slipping astern as the big yacht's auxiliary diesels engaged propellers.

The woman took Morgan's arm. "Be a good little Morgan and you won't get hurt."

"You know—"

The guy came at her from the other side, and before she could move or protest, they were shoving her down the companionway. A blast of cold air-conditioning hit her in the face and then they were hurting her arms and dragging her through a varnished teak-paneled saloon.

"Wait! What are you doing?"

There was a door ahead. They were dragging her toward it and scared her so much she screamed, "No! What are doing? Let me go."

The woman released her arm. Morgan saw the woman's hand rise to the ceiling, then descend toward her in a blur. Her face exploded in pain. The woman seized her arm again and looked her straight in the face and said as coolly and calmly as if she were ordering from a menu, "Bad girls get hurt. Are you a good girl or a bad girl?"

Morgan would not answer. Her cheek blazed. Her mind reeled. The next thing she knew she was being dragged through that door and down a narrow corridor, and shoved into a little teak-paneled cabin, starboard side. As the woman started to close the door, Morgan said, "Could I ask you a question?"

"What?"

"Why are you doing this to me?"

The blond woman cocked her head like a big bird. Her eyes were bright and she actually seemed to consider the question. She even smiled, and Morgan had the creepiest feeling that on some level, this was all a game. And indeed, the woman answered in a game-playing way, teasing with a riddle. "Let's put it this way, honey. You're not the fish, but you'll do for bait."

The door swung shut. In her confusion Morgan had one lucid thought and she yelled through it, "Is that why you put my name on the ham radio?"

The door opened. Morgan backed up. "Nice. You got a head on your shoulders."

"Was it you?"

Another game-playing grin. "Ham-radio nets are maintained by selfless volunteers. They saved my client a fortune."

"Client? Who?"

"Can't tell you that."

"Can't? Or won't?"

She switched the grin off like a light. "Don't press your luck, Morgan."

Morgan waited a long, heart-pounding five minutes to open the door a crack. A scary-looking guard was squatting in the narrow corridor. The port was too small to climb out. Where would she go even if she could fit through it?

She felt the hard lump of the flares hidden in her pocket and tasted hope. She could signal a passing ship. Orange smoke by day, flame by night. Except this was only the third vessel she had seen in two months. What if she lit a flare to start a fire? Then what? Sink with them?

A silent Asian barged in with a bowl of Chinese-looking food. She feared they might poison her, but it smelled so delicious and she was so hungry that she finally picked up the chopsticks that came with it.

The meal made her thirsty. The cabin had its own head and she went in there repeatedly for water. No foot pumps on the Baltic, all electric pressure, hot- and cold-running water, though there was no way she would take a shower with all these people around and no lock on the door.

The air-conditioning was freezing, but she had to close the port to keep out the spray. Scared and cold, she huddled on the bunk in her foul-weather jacket, wondering who in the world she could be "bait" for except her father.

BOOK V

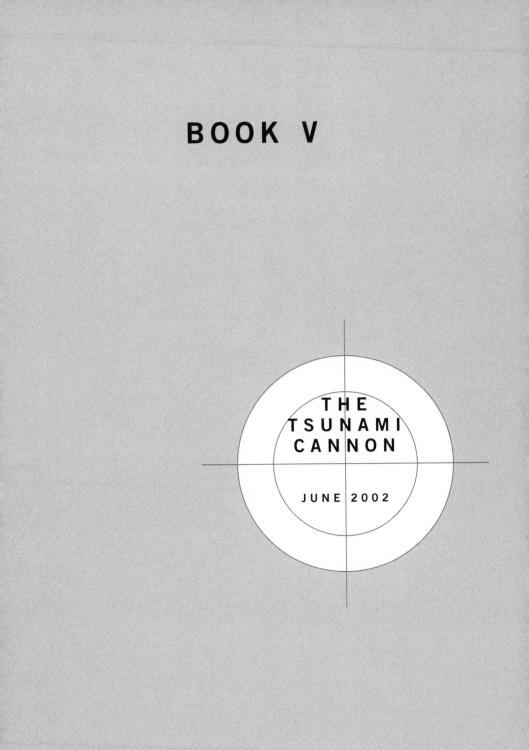

THE
TSUNAMI
CANNON

JUNE 2002

A IDEN PAGE HAD JUST COME off watch and was about to collapse onto a pipe berth when he heard Tom shout a warning from the helm. Before he could grab ahold, *Archimedes* swiveled on her keel and threw him against the nearest ballast tank. He thought they had broached. But as he scrambled up the companionway and the sails crashed across the deck, Tom Slade yelled, "Tell me I'm not seeing things, but—"

Again? Aiden groaned inwardly. Although ahead he did see a minute white notch in the edge of the distance.

Archimedes staggered and, instead of rocketing off on the opposite tack, slipped backward, pounding her rudder. Slade fought the helm. Aiden ran forward. The genoa had hung up on a shroud and was backed. He skirted it around the mast, and when it bellied full, he studied the horizon while Slade steered toward his latest sighting.

"Is that a boat?"

"Could be." More likely, a breaking crest or a bird or a cloud.

Tom Slade had been seeing "sails" ever since they had outmaneuvered the hurricane. Turned around again, and safe on his new course—due west on the seventeenth parallel—to drop Aiden off at Blind Man Island, he was frantic that less fortunate boats somewhere needed help.

"I think it's a sail."

Aiden got the binoculars. Below the white triangle, he glimpsed a dark hull rising on the swell. "Definitely a boat."

Slade laughed, enormously relieved to have finally seen something real. "Must've gotten beat up in the hurricane."

Aiden grabbed a VHF and tried to hail the boat, which looked quite small. No reply.

"Stumpy-looking rig."

When a mile separated the two vessels, Aiden locked on with the binoculars. A wind vane stood off the stern.

"See anybody?"

"Not yet. He's got self-steering."

"What the heck is wrong with that rig?"

"Looks a little short, doesn't it?"

"Crappy-looking jib. You know you see people out here who ought to stay home. Maybe they're hurt."

When a half mile separated them, Aiden said, "That is a tiny boat . . . You know . . . yeah, I can see it now, they've got damage. That's some kind of a jury rig . . . She's lost her stern pulpit . . ."

"How the hell did they get that mast up? . . . Must be a bunch of crew below . . . Well, we'll take the hurt ones to Samoa." He laughed again. And when he complained, he sounded positively cheerful. "Damned if it isn't one thing it's another. Like Neptune's throwing thunderbolts, yelling, 'You'll never get to Fiji.' We should have fucking rowed."

"Tonga's closer," said Aiden.

"Samoa's got a better hospital."

At a quarter mile Aiden said, "Her hull's intact. She's riding high."

"Soon as we're in shouting range, see if we can wake them up.

Tell them to drop her main," said Tom. "We'll come above and try to heave to and drift down on her. Ready—Aiden, you ready?"

"I don't believe it," said Aiden. He rubbed his eyes and refocused the glasses.

"What?"

Aiden passed the binoculars silently to Tom. He shielded his own eyes with shaking hands, and whispered, "Jesus H."

Tom Slade steadied the helm with his knee while he focused. "*Molly P 2*? Isn't that the boat the Frenchies saw? That's no Hinckley."

"*Gimme back the glasses!*" He felt the joy of new life, if only for a second. Because if it were possible, he knew he should run from her and hide. But thank God it wasn't possible.

She must be below. She couldn't be hurt that badly. Not if she was able to raise that mast. Just exhausted, between battling the storm and fighting the pieces back together again.

"That is definitely not a Hinckley," said Slade.

"It's a J/27," said Aiden.

"I *know* that," said Slade. "How the hell'd it get out here? Fall off a freighter? Give 'em a shout! Wake them up."

"Not 'them,' " said Aiden. "Her."

He had completely underestimated her. She hadn't sailed with her mother. And she wasn't bound for Tahiti, either. She was heading for Tonga, for their special island, the one hiding place in the world she might find the selfish fool who got himself drunk enough to place a phone call from the dead.

"Her? How do you know it's a woman?"

"That's no woman," said Aiden Page. "That's my daughter— *Morgan!*" he shouted. "Ahoy, Morgan! . . . *Morgan Page!*"

Silence drifted back as the two vessels closed, rising and falling on the swell.

"Morgan?"

Tom Slade took charge. "We're going to start the engine, sheet up, and work alongside. Put on your PFD and take a line when you board." The diesel alarm whined, the engine cranked over and caught. Aiden felt numb with terror as he stepped outside the lifelines and held on to a shroud. Slade steered for *Molly P 2*'s windward side and, when they were running parallel, edged closer.

"Easy now . . ." Slade called from the helm. "Careful . . . let her come to you . . . Right!"

Aiden jumped down to the smaller boat's deck.

It rolled under his weight. "Morgan?"

He ran the line to the bow cleat and sheeted in her sails. Then he stuck his head down the hatch. "Morgan?"

The little cabin was empty.

A plastic jar of peanut butter rolled in the sink. The port berth had a chart spread on it. "Morgan?" He lowered himself down the companionway, bent double, and duckwalked forward. The forepeak was empty. He whirled around, banging his skull on the low ceiling. Aft of the cabin, the low spaces under the cockpit held only cans and bottles of food and water. Most of them had no labels. The few left were blurred or askew. The mattress was wet.

It was someone else's boat, he told himself. The name a crazy coincidence.

He heard *Archimedes*' diesel grinding alongside and Tom calling, "You okay, mate?"

Aiden stood up in the hatch. "No one here."

Tom was staring down into the little cockpit at what Aiden had missed in his excitement. Beside the tiller sea was a sun-faded PFD, with a tether still clipped to a pad eye.

"No," Aiden said. "That is not possible."

"What's not possible, mate?"

"No way she would take that off. Ever. I taught her never, ever go on deck without it. It was the rule since she was three years old and she never broke it."

"Right," said Tom, with a sad expression that said, *Wrong*. He looked away, unwilling to say what Aiden knew: this was not the first boat found sailing by itself. Everyone breaks the rule one time or another. That's how people fall overboard. *I'll just step up here and reach out for one second—*

Aiden jumped below, knelt by the port berth, and pored over the chart. If he had any doubts it wasn't Morgan's, they died when he saw a triumphant "more than halfway" written beside the Marquesas in her neat, block print. She had drawn a rhumb line straight to Blind Man Island, marked each day's actual passage, meandering above and below it, then so far south in the doldrums to find the trades that she had sailed between the Marquesas and the Tuamotu archipelago. A new rhumb line firmed up at 17 South for a final run west at Blind Man Island. He followed that track of pencil marks straight into the hurricane that had sent him and Tom running for their lives.

At that point—four days ago—her twice-daily GPS fixes and her morning and noon celestial shots ended abruptly. But yesterday her calculations resumed, though she had obviously lost her GPS and smashed the sextant. Question marks sprinkled an area a hundred miles south of her rhumb line—only fifteen miles off, he realized. Though her guess at her longitude was off by more than sixty. From the question marks she had drawn a speculative rhumb line that angled slightly north on 280 and a note to locate Sirius, tonight. He looked for her log, hoping for more details, before the full implication of the time and date of her chart entry struck him. Tonight! "Tom!" he yelled. "She was still aboard this morning. We can backtrack her!"

Turn the boat around and sail straight back on 100 degrees—the reciprocal of her 280 course. Guesstimating the drift effects of wind, waves, and current. A chance in a million—the odds worsening with every mile as they inadvertently angled left or right of her location. But he could see a long way from the top of *Archimedes'* mast. Morgan was a strong swimmer. And the tropical water was warm. He drove sharks from his mind.

Tom jumped aboard. The boat squeaked against the fender he had rigged. He stuck his head in the hatch and handed Aiden a green canvas book that looked like it had gotten soaked. A pen, attached by a string, was folded between pages. "Her log," said Tom. "It was under the cockpit cushion."

Aiden pounced on it. "The closer we get to the time she went overboard, the smaller the search area."

"She didn't go overboard," said Tom.

"Thank God—wait, where is she?"

"Read the last page."

"KNOCK, KNOCK."

Morgan blinked awake. She felt a big boat under her, moving on the swells, but had no idea where she was until she recognized the blond woman standing in the doorway. The way the light fell exaggerated her angular cheekbones, which shaped her face like a preying mantis.

"How you doing, Morgan?"

"Okay."

"Mohammed said you wanted to see me—he's the guy who brought you lunch."

Morgan sat up in a rush. "Yeah, I want to know what you're doing with me."

"Don't worry about it—"

"Could you at least go back for my boat?"

"It's not really your boat, is it, dear?"

All Morgan could think to say was, "What makes you think that?"

"I do my homework—hey, why didn't you take a shower? You look like you've been dipped in salt."

"There's no lock."

Jerry looked at the door. "Oh, jeez. Don't you worry about it. Nobody'll bother you. I'll stand guard."

Still Morgan hesitated.

"My name is Jerry. I'm sorry I hit you before; I get a little pumped when I'm working. Go on, take a shower. You'll feel better. And don't worry, you don't have to get undressed in front of me either." She backed out the door, muttering, "You think you're the only girl who's ever been fifteen?"

The shower—her first in eight weeks—made her forget everything for a little while. It was like floating up to her lips in warm Häagen-Dazs rum raisin, or sleeping in a feather bed, and she dried off with a beautiful clean white towel, thinking, Jerry wants me to feel comfortable so I'll let my guard down. She actually felt a grin cross her face. Jerry had almost succeeded. Might have, if "bait" wasn't such a scary word.

Jerry had left a silky-soft terry robe on the bed and a note. "Your clothes are in the wash. Come back to the main cabin if you feel like a visit."

The guard was gone, the door at the end of the corridor open on the saloon with the white leather upholstery. Jerry was sitting with her feet up on one of the banquettes. "Want a Coke?"

Morgan nodded.

Jerry swung her long legs off the banquette and sauntered into the stainless-steel galley, moving like she had been born to the roll of the boat. "Ice?"

"Yes, please." Ice? Her first in two months.

Jerry was as tall and thin as Morgan's mother and Aunt Mary. She was in great shape, with big strong hands, pink nail polish, and that same knack her mother had of being able to gaze wherever she wanted without letting anyone make eye contact. Her clothes were a little tight, but she'd still fit in for lunch at the club: creamy-white slacks and shirt, daytime jewelry—big rings and small earrings— and a gold watch. She had a couple of small scars on her face. And a smile as cold as Uncle Charlie's.

"So, Morgan, where do you think your dad went?"

Morgan was ready for that. "My dad was killed in the World Trade Center."

"Yeah, yeah, yeah, and you're sailing on a pleasure cruise." Jerry stared. Her pale eyes were sunk deeply in her face, which made her cheekbones even sharper. They mirrored light in the same weird way as Dr. Melton's glasses. "Where were you headed?"

"Tonga."

Jerry crossed over to the nav station and punched up the Tonga archipelago on the plotter's blue screen. "Where in Tonga?"

"Tongatapu," Morgan lied.

After what seemed forever, Jerry said, "I'll level with you, Morgan. Joe and I get paid big bucks to find people who disappear. Do you understand?"

"You're like *bounty* hunters?" Which explained a lot. But was no less frightening. Then Jerry made it more frightening.

" 'Bounty hunter' is a misleading term. Bounty hunters are required by law to adhere to certain rules of conduct. Whereas Joe and I . . . well . . ." She gestured about the cabin, the endless miles of night beyond the windows, and at Morgan anxiously tugging the robe around herself.

"But there's one rule even Joe and I have to obey: If the missing person turns up before we find him, we don't get paid. Okay? . . . So here's the joke: I have the funniest feeling that your daddy is heading for the same place that the people paying us to find him already are."

Could Jerry see her relief at the realization that her father wasn't at Blind Man Island yet? Huge relief that set her heart pounding. It meant that he was still safe from Henry Hong. And from these bounty hunters. "Where is he going?" she asked.

Jerry's eyes squinted up the way they had when she slapped her.

"Don't get between me and work, Morgan. I already warned you, I get pumped. Okay?"

Morgan nodded. There was no way not to.

Jerry said, "All I want is to be the UPS man. Since Daddy's going there anyway, it's no skin off his nose if I hand him over instead of him just walking in."

"I don't understand."

"Yes, you do! I intend to get paid for making the delivery."

"But what makes you think my father is going where they are?"

"I already told you that. I do my research. Just like you do for a school project, I do mine for work. Okay?"

"Okay."

"Here's the real deal. Your dad worked for a very dangerous character named Henry Ho Hong. A name Joe and I have heard once or twice in our own, shall we say, 'checkered' past. A hard man who's made himself a force in the South Pacific. A man whom your average daddy and accountant has no business working for. Unless he's prepared to suffer the consequences."

"My father worked for a private bank called HHH and Company. It happened to be owned by Henry Hong."

Jerry stood up suddenly. "You're not listening to me. I'm telling you that your father has not arrived where you think he went."

"I don't *know* where he went."

"What if I told you he's on a boat heading there?"

"I don't know."

"In fact, I think he's quite nearby."

Morgan felt her face betray her.

Jerry smiled. "That gets interesting, doesn't it? . . . Now, couldn't you and I save everyone a lot of trouble by persuading him to join us here, first, on this boat?"

"Why?"

"You could have a nice reunion. And then we would deliver him where he wants to go. Which happens to be where my client will pay me to deliver him. Where," she said, her voice rising, *"he is going anyway!"*

"You'll kidnap him. Like you've kidnapped me."

Jerry stepped into the galley and came out with a shiny butcher knife. "Now, if we were real kidnappers, would you and I be sitting here drinking Cokes? Wouldn't I call Joe in here to hold you down while I slice off your ear to mail it to your father?" She glanced aft through the galley at the door to the owner's stateroom.

Morgan's stomach suddenly hurt so much it felt like Jerry had plunged the knife into her. When she got control of her breathing, she said, "If you chopped my ear off, you wouldn't know where to mail it."

"Exactly! Bravo! You're so smart. We don't know *where* to mail it. We don't even have his phone number. But we do know the name of the boat he's on."

"You do?" Morgan blurted before she could stop herself.

"Which means we can *radio* him. We've got great radios on this boat, long-range SSB and ham. We can radio for thousands of miles. But how do we get him to answer? Seeing as how he's run away and is pretending to be dead and doesn't want to be caught?"

She waited, staring at Morgan, demanding Morgan answer, "How?"

"We have to radio a message that says very clearly, 'We've got your little girl and we're going to remove her ears if you don't get here . . . real . . . fucking . . . soon.' "

"It's two-way open channels. Everyone will hear you threatening to cut my ear off."

Jerry tilted the knife so it reflected rays of light about the cabin. "The second I saw you, I said to myself, 'That little girl is as smart as a whip.' But *you* don't want the whole world hearing us either, do you, Morgan?"

"What do you mean?"

"Do you want the whole world to hear that your father faked his death? Your mom collected his life insurance—I told you I do my research. She accepted compensation from the funds for victims. *Innocent* victims. She even accepted a trust in your name, in *your name*, Morgan. And why not? It's only right that the terror victims be taken care of in their tragic hour of need. But if Daddy turns up alive, it looks like he's scamming off innocent victims' tragedy . . ."

"He didn't do that! That's not why he ran."

"It's fraud."

"It's not."

"He'll find his ass in front of a judge in a hanging mood."

"He didn't—"

"And good luck to your poor mom convincing the cops she wasn't in on it, too."

"She didn't—"

"So you don't want that heard on the radio either, do you?"

Morgan watched Jerry return the knife to the galley. The pain in her stomach was worse. A deeper fear, a terrible trap.

Jerry popped fresh Cokes and poured them over ice. "See, we have a lot of problems in common, Morgan. Now, I know that this may *sound* self-serving, but you and me, we should be working together."

A IDEN CALCULATED THAT THE BALTIC 70 had a four-hour lead. The trade wind had moderated, but well handled—and Joe had been quite proud of his Malaysian crew—it might be making nine or ten knots. Four hours, forty nautical miles. Slade was coaxing twenty out of *Archimedes*, surfing down the seas, but a lot less climbing them. If he could keep it up, they might catch sight of the Baltic's lights in four or five hours.

Un-fucking-believable, Aiden kept thinking, over and over and over again as night closed in. And yet totally believable. Some-body—most likely Henry Hong—wanted him. He got away. They knew about the phone call to Morgan. Morgan was the way to get him back.

Tom had not pressed Aiden for details yet. He had wondered aloud whether the people on the Baltic had rescued her and for some reason left the boat behind, but did not press him when Aiden assured him it was no rescue. Nor had Aiden had to ask for help. Tom had volunteered to chase the Baltic, saying, "You'd do the same for my kid." Though he had raised the obvious question: "Eight in crew? What are you going to do when we catch them?"

"I'll think of something."

I've got to think like Charlie, Aiden thought. I'm outnumbered, outgunned, and damned near helpless. I've got to be smart. I've got to be clever. I've got to be devious. I've got to get in their faces. Like my father yelled. Counterpunch. *Bam* in the face.

But he felt sick with fear. While a mind-numbing rage boiled deep in his consciousness. Stay with fear, he thought. It would keep him from doing something stupid. Should he get on the horn? Radio-phone Blind Man Island, hoping Henry Hong was behind this? Try to bargain for her freedom? With what? He had nothing to offer but himself, and the minute he surrendered himself, he had no power to enforce the bargain.

"What makes you think they'll be showing lights?" asked Tom.

"They're hiding in plain sight," said Aiden. "If she's showing proper lights, she's just another rich guy's yacht. Plus, she's got no idea you and I exist anywhere near here."

"They know *you* exist," Tom said dryly.

"But they don't know where."

"Do you think they know you signed on with me?"

"I'm sure they tracked me to the Balboa Yacht Club."

"If they did, they'll know I'm heading to New Zealand. If they know their business, they can figure out how fast this boat goes, which'll give them a general idea how far we've come. Especially if they learned we went back to the Galápagos. Point is, if they're reasonably sure we're not in the Atlantic or the Med, they could plot our vicinity."

"I'm sorry. I hope it doesn't come down on you."

Tom shrugged. "Well, it's a big ocean." For the fifth time in an hour, he flipped the radar on for a quick burst. On such a clear night it was unlikely the Baltic had its radar going, but if it did it, its collision-avoidance element would alert the crew to another radar signal.

"Look!"

The monitor showed a single target. It was miles ahead. Making nine knots.

Tom nudged the boat ten degrees to starboard. "Two-eighty? Veering north."

"Turn it off!"

"Only nine knots? Lazy sods doused their spinnaker for the night."

Aiden was afraid to put too much hope in the sighting. The Baltic, while considerably larger than *Archimedes*, was constructed of similar nonmetallic composites that would reflect the same weak echoes as Aiden hoped would conceal their pursuit. But radar was funny stuff. The tug he had encountered near the Marquesas had tracked them on its radar, so there were no guarantees either way.

The distance was about right, though. And the course was similar to the course the Baltic had been sailing when it overtook Morgan, according to her log. But the radar return could also be from an old ship plodding along at nine knots, or even one of the state-run diesel freight boats that plied the vast waters between the island chains.

At 2100, when the sky was thick with stars, Aiden rode a bosun's chair up *Archimedes'* mast, and when he could stand on the upper spreader, he signaled with a tug of the line for Tom to stop cranking the winch. He had a handheld clipped to his harness, but only for the worst emergency, as the VHF transmission could be heard on the

Baltic. While Slade drove and flipped the radar on every few minutes, Aiden probed the dark western horizon with his binoculars.

Seventy feet down, *Archimedes* sliced a track through the dark that glowed phosphorescent green. At the end of a fifty-foot towline, Morgan's little *Molly* skimmed another shiny green path in the bigger boat's wake. Aiden had refused to abandon her. Saving the boat for Morgan made it seem definite that he would find her. Fortunately, she proved as anxious to surf as *Archimedes* and Tom, who had expressed strong doubts, reported little loss of velocity.

Sweeping the dark for a light, he thought, Now what? What if it is them? How do I get her off? Eight in crew, plus Joe and Jerry. Probably armed, while he and Tom carried nothing more lethal than a rigging knife.

Shadow them and radio for help? But they were hundreds of miles from anywhere and who could help? The BBC had reported that relief ships still hadn't even reached the islands devastated by the hurricane.

Suddenly he saw a light. Brilliant white. He fixed his binoculars on it. Only Sirius. A low cloud had moved, revealing the star sinking in the west. He looked back. Little *Molly* was following like a faithful pony. Ahead, moments later, he saw another light, closer than Sirius, and not so bright. When he was sure it was not a star, he looked back once more at Morgan's *Molly*, then closed his gloved hands around a running backstay and plummeted to the cockpit.

"They're dead ahead," he told Tom. "Bear up ten degrees. We'll pass them on the right."

"*Pass* them?"

"Put two miles between us." He switched on a short-range VHF radio. "If they hail us, don't answer."

Slowly they overtook the other craft. The radio in his hand was silent, which was a great relief, but not surprising. *Archimedes* was dark. If Aiden didn't know the Baltic was ahead and hadn't been watching for their light from the top spreader, he, too, would pass unknowing in the dark. Even through the glasses, she showed nothing but an indistinct shadow beneath her light.

Tom said, "After we pass her, then what?"

"How strong is our bow?"

Tom looked over from the wheel for a moment before he answered, "Strong. These boats are built to survive icebergs. If that bloody container hadn't taken out the rudder post, we'd have kept sailing."

"How strong is the Baltic?"

"Fuck," said Tom, seeing where Aiden was going and not liking it. "The Baltic is a custom high-performance cruiser—a rich guy's racing yacht with an impressive win record. But at the end of the day, the Baltic's about money, *Archimedes* is about balls."

"I'm asking you is *Archimedes* stronger than the Baltic?"

"She's a battleship."

"Good."

"But she doesn't have any guns. I have two questions. One, if we ram them, how do we guarantee we don't T-bone the cabin they've locked your daughter in?"

Aiden said, "We're not going to 'T-bone' them in the side. We're going to ram them from behind—square in the stern."

Tom nodded reluctant agreement. The large owner's cabin in such yachts were always in the stern. Morgan would more likely be kept in one of the tiny crew cabins forward of the galley, the nav station, and the main saloon.

"Besides," said Aiden, "they have no reason to *lock* her in. Where could she run?"

"You hope."

And, Aiden hoped, no reason to hurt a fifteen-year-old child. In Panama, he kept telling himself, they had shot at him only *after* he had escaped. "What's your other question?"

"Having rammed them in the stern, how do we deal with eight pissed-off Malaysians?"

"*Vessel overtaking to my starboard,*" the VHF suddenly crackled. "*Do you read me?*"

"Shit! Don't answer that."

"Bloody marvelous," said Tom. "Now the eight pissed-off Malaysians know we're here. Bloody watch changed and the new guy flipped on the radar."

"Vessel to my starboard," came the repeated query. *"Vessel two-point-four miles to my starboard quarter, do you see me?"* And when *Archimedes* still did not answer: *"We are proceeding on 280. Please radio your intentions if you change course."*

"Those lights are funny," said Tom. *Archimedes* was pulling alongside, and the two men were seeing the vessel at a new angle. "Looks like a ranging light. That's not a sailboat."

Aiden stabbed *transmit.* "I read you vessel to my port on 280. What vessel is that, please?"

"This is the motor vessel Empress of Rawalpindi. *Eight-thousand-ton bulker."*

"Oh *shit!"* Aiden whispered. It was a slow freighter, just as he had feared it might be.

Late at night on a dark and empty sea, the watch officer next door was talkative. *"We are bearing copra to our home port Puri, via the Strait of Malacca. Perhaps you have heard of Puri, my friend, across the Bay of Bengal. And what vessel are you, sir?"*

Aiden switched off the VHF. "Jesus fucking Christ, where is that sailboat?"

48

WAKE UP, MORGAN!"

She had pretended to drift off on the white leather banquette as Jerry hammered away at her, alternately teasing and threatening. Anything to gather her strength. Jerry was coldly patient, acting like she had all the time in the world, but terrifying at the same time, as if she had no doubt that Morgan would crack.

"Like I've been saying all night, Morgan. You've got to come up with something that will make him believe it's really *you* calling him and not sneaky old me taking advantage of radio static to pretend I'm a frightened fifteen-year-old. Like a secret code—some little daddy-daughter thing. My father used to call me 'Live Wire.' But only when we were alone. Nobody else knew, not even my mother, the bitch."

She had to warn him. If only she knew whether her father had heard her François message.

"Morgan!"

She had stalled long enough. By now Jerry would believe that she had won. "Okay. Okay, okay, okay. I'll tell him that BC and I both miss him. That will prove it's me."

"Who is BC?"

"He was my cat."

"Your cat's name is Roscoe, sweetheart. Don't fuck with me."

"His nickname was Boat Cat. BC."

"Oh . . . BC. BC. Why does that ring a bell? . . . Hey, where the hell is that cat anyhow?"

"He fell overboard."

"Oh, good—I don't mean that the way it sounds. I was afraid we left the poor thing on the boat. Oh, don't start crying."

"I miss him." It wasn't hard to cry louder—anything to distract Jerry from remembering she had heard François broadcast her "BC code" on the ham radio.

"When this is over, you can get a new cat. Okay, let's do this. Let's radio Dad. Here's our job. Let's review. Two jobs. One, find out where Dad is. Two, tell Dad to meet us where we are."

"*ARCHIMEDES, ARCHIMEDES, ARCHIMEDES.* This is *Baltic Nights, Baltic Nights. Archimedes, Archimedes, Archimedes.* This is *Baltic Nights, Baltic Nights, Baltic Nights.* Here, you try it. It's fun. Like you're in an old movie."

Morgan took the mike. What if he was actually listening? What if he was right now sitting by the radio, a hundred miles away or a thousand miles away? *"Archimedes, Archimedes, Archimedes.* This is *Baltic Nights, Baltic Nights, Baltic Nights."*

"SCREW THIS," AIDEN said to Tom. "I'm going to radio *Baltic Nights* and tell them to come and get me."

"Then they'll have both of you. What the fuck good will that do your daughter?"

"I'll get in the spare raft. I'll tell them they have to put Morgan on a raft so you can pick her up."

"Pray they are honest kidnappers."

"Archimedes can sail circles around that Baltic. We'll spread the rafts out far apart. I'll make them drop her first and sail away from her. Then you drop me and grab her as fast as you can and leave them in the dust."

"And you in the dust."

"I don't see a choice."

Tom said, "Right, mate. They've got you by the balls . . . Well, they're going to be mighty surprised to hear you calling from close by."

"I'm surprised they haven't called me yet."

"Maybe your little girl isn't cooperating."

Aiden went down to the radio. They had to have figured out he was on *Archimedes.* Why hadn't they radioed? Maybe they couldn't get through. He reached for the mike, still hesitating because his entire plan of catching up and ramming them to free Morgan had been based on the fact that Joe and Jerry didn't know that he knew they had taken Morgan.

The instant he radioed *Baltic Nights* to say, "You have something of mine. Let's make a deal," he gave up any hope of surprise.

"Archimedes, Archimedes, Archimedes," crackled in his headset. A woman's voice. "Archimedes. Archimedes. Archimedes. *This is*

Baltic Nights, Baltic Nights, Baltic Nights. Archimedes, Archimedes, Archimedes. *This is* Baltic Nights, Baltic Nights."

"I read you, Jerry," he yelled. "I read you. I read you."

"Let's switch over to a working frequency." They shifted from the frequency reserved for hailing and emergencies to a working frequency in four megahertz. It was a lousy channel, growling and hissing.

Jerry said, *"We have a message for Dad."*

His heart was hammering.

"I'll take it."

"I've got someone here who says that she and BC miss you."

"I want to hear her voice."

"Say hi…"

And then another voice, layered in static. A girl? A woman? He pressed the headset to his ears. It could be her. It could be Morgan. *"We miss you, Daddy."*

But the atmospheric noise muffled her voice too much to be sure.

"I miss you, too, darling. Are you all right?"

The first part of her reply dissolved in static. All he heard was, *"…BC sends love."*

Aiden's breath caught in his chest. It was her.

"Are you all right?"

"…Okay, Daddy. Good-bye. See you soon."

"I'll see you very soon," he shouted into the microphone. "I promise—Jerry! You understand this will be a trade."

"Fair-and-square trade," said Jerry. *"What's your position, Archimedes?"*

Aiden glanced at the GPS. Just as he opened his mouth to reveal his position, it finally sank in that in identifying herself, Morgan had also repeated the "BC code" transmitted by François. His daughter had given him back the advantage of surprise. All he had to do was subtract 12/25 before he radioed his longitude and latitude.

"*Repeat your position,* Archimedes," Jerry demanded. *"Tell us where you are."*

Aiden grabbed the log pencil. He could use the code to tell Morgan he was actually very near. But he was too mind-blown to do the simple numbers in his head. Morgan had put them back in the catbird seat. Jerry had no clue that a sharp-eyed, guilt-ridden delivery captain had spotted Morgan's boat. No clue that they had Morgan's boat in tow. But most important, Jerry did not know how very close he was.

He did the math, then he quickly checked the chart to ensure that the false position didn't place him in the middle of an island . . . Deep water, thank God, far to the east of the Phoenix Islands.

"Five degrees, nineteen minutes South. One hundred and sixty degrees, two minutes West."

Jerry said, *"What are you doing all the way up there?"*

"Dodging hurricanes. Where are you?"

Jerry radioed her position.

Aiden put it on the plotter and his heart leaped. He would never have found *Baltic Nights* in the dark without the radio call. But now he had them in his sights.

"Baltic Nights," he said, working from the false position, "I'm plotting you about seven hundred and twenty miles south and west of me. What do you say we meet halfway?"

There was a delay while Jerry summoned her boat's navigator. They worked out a rendezvous based on the current state of the trade wind and Aiden's false position and their combined boat speed of nearly thirty knots.

Jerry said, "Archimedes, *I expect to see you tomorrow."*

Aiden radioed back, "Take care of my little girl."

"Sooner we hook up, the sooner you see her. Bye-bye, Archimedes."

Aiden whispered, "Sooner than you think, sweetheart," and bounded up to the cockpit.

"Ten miles downwind! No stops!"

• • •

"WHY ARE YOU crying?" asked Jerry. Her angular face was cocked suspiciously, her eyes hard. When Morgan tried to meet her stare, she could tell that the woman sensed that something was off.

"I'm just so happy to hear his voice."

"I told you he was alive."

"I never knew for sure. It's different hearing his voice . . . Can I go back in my cabin, please?"

Jerry patted the banquette. "Stay with me. Don't you want to celebrate?"

"I'm like really wiped. I think I need to be alone."

"How about a drink?"

"No, thank you."

"A little glass of wine?"

"No, thank you." It was like trying to get away from an older kid who wanted to talk you into shoplifting.

Jerry grinned. "I've got some grass that transmutes brain cells into mega-pixels."

Morgan weighed the offer. It would help if Jerry got too high to think straight, but who knew how much that would take and she had to keep her own head clear. Better to put distance between them so that when the time came, Jerry couldn't grab her. "Thanks, Jerry. But I'm way too tired."

"Suit yourself. Big day tomorrow. Daddy's coming."

Alone in her little cabin, Morgan finally allowed herself to smile. *Sooner than you think.*

She checked the corridor. They didn't bother with the guard. Why should they? The weepy little girl had no reason to run even if she could. The guard, she realized now, had just been part of Jerry's plan to terrify her into convincing her father she was actually her prisoner.

Five degrees, 19 minutes South plus the subtracted 12/25 birthday equaled 17 degrees, 44 minutes South.

One hundred and sixty degrees, 2 minutes West plus 12/25 equaled 172 degrees, 27 minutes West.

He was so close. She opened the narrow port and stared into the dark while the spray wet her face. He could be here any minute. But her joy was tempered by fear. Even with the momentary advantage of surprise, what could he possibly do when he got here?

AIDEN COULDN'T RISK alerting *Baltic Nights* with the radar, so he had to plot an intercept that took into account the Baltic 70's new course beating northeast toward tomorrow's phony rendezvous. Tom steered and Aiden went up the mast.

The next thirty minutes were the longest of his life.

He hunted low in the sky for a shadow of a sail against the stars, strained to see a gleam of white hull or a green phosphorescent wake. In the end, it was as simple as a row of lighted cabin ports. He joined Tom on deck.

"A half mile ahead. Let's bear off a little and pull ahead of them."

They passed the lights in silence. Now they saw the immense sails slicing through the stars. When the Baltic was well in their wake, Tom said, "You never answered my question. Having rammed them in the stern, how do we deal with eight angry Malaysians?"

Aiden looked back at the little *Molly P 2* surfing at the end of *Archimedes'* towrope. "That's why we passed them. Any idea if Malaysians are superstitious?"

"Superstitious? Fuck knows. All I know about Malaysians is they're the worst damned pirates on the ocean. No way two of us can fight them."

"We're not going to fight 'em. We're going to scare the devil out of them long enough to get Morgan off."

Aiden jumped into the stern, tied a stopper to *Molly*'s towline, led the stopper to a winch, and cranked in until there was enough slack in the towline to release it. Then he cast off the stopper line and watched his daughter's sea-battered J/27 fall behind them.

"Okay, let's douse the spinnaker."

With Tom at the wheel, Aiden stuffed the huge nylon sail down the main hatch for a quick recovery. In its place he hoisted a small jib, sacrificing speed for nimbleness.

"Head up."

Archimedes carved a ninety-degree port turn and cut across the Baltic's path.

THE MUSIC THUMPING THROUGH THE teak bulkhead stopped abruptly. All of a sudden people started shouting.

Morgan felt the big yacht slow down. It stood straighter as electric furling winches hummed through the deck, reducing sail. She opened the port and pressed her face to the frame. Dark sea. A sprinkling of fuzzy stars. And on the horizon, the first hint of dawn.

The Baltic turned to port, lurching as a wave lifted the starboard quarter, and suddenly Morgan could see what the helmsman and the shouting crew had seen ahead of the bow. It was a truly impossible sight. Twenty hours after they had abandoned *Molly* poking along under jury rig—*twenty full hours,* most of them spent sailing downwind at ten knots, speeding the Baltic 70 nearly two hundred nautical miles—Morgan's little J/27 was poking along under jury-rigged sails, *ahead* of the Baltic.

No wonder they had stopped.

Only one answer made sense. *Molly* hadn't overtaken the Baltic by herself. Someone had helped her. Someone on a fast boat with a towline.

"It's a trick!" she heard Jerry scream. "Heads up, everyone. It's a trick."

"Sheet in!" Joe shouted. "Get her moving. Ahmed. Mohammed. Sheet in! Sheet in! Get this fucking boat moving!"

Morgan stepped into the corridor. All the shouting came from the cockpit. She ran forward, into the forepeak sail locker, climbed a heap of sailbags, undogged the hatch, and climbed onto the bow.

ARCHIMEDES CIRCLED AROUND and came up behind the bigger boat. Main and jib filled. She surged over the back of a trade-wind roller, and surfed down its face. The speedo jumped to twenty-two knots. At two hundred yards, the Baltic was an awkward shadow against the fading stars—circling and yawing, like a drunk trying to see who punched him. At one hundred yards, her decks grew visible in the strengthening light.

"They're sheeting in," Aiden called down to Tom from the mast spreader. "She's getting under way."

The Baltic's crew hadn't seen them yet, having blundered around in a full circle staring at the jury-rigged J/27 last seen in their wake. They were so close, Aiden could see the satellite dome on her sloping afterdeck, the twin steering wheels, the coffee-grinder winch in her cockpit, and a crowd of crew milling around her decks. But now she began to accelerate and his whole plan was falling apart as Baltic's forward motion would lessen the impact even if Tom managed to hit a moving target.

CROUCHING ON THE bow, Morgan Page sensed motion on the sea behind the big yacht. The light was getting stronger, revealing a tall sail bearing down on the Baltic's stern, as yet unseen by its busy crew. On the approaching boat's lower spreader stood a lone figure in a familiar, long-legged stance. High above the deck, he was directing the helmsman with arm signals, guiding him to ram the Baltic.

Morgan's heart filled at a sight so much more real than a hope or a dream or even a voice. He was not dead and he was not a ghost. He was alive. He had understood her message. And he had stopped running away, in order to save her.

But the Baltic's crew was moving into action like a highly trained racing team. One man ran forward; he saw Morgan crouched on the deck but instantly assessed her as unimportant compared to the orders to get the boat moving. She ducked back down into the sail locker and looked for some way to stop the Baltic or slow it down. There was no time to do damage.

But confusion might do.

She yanked her distress flares from her windbreaker and twisted off the flare caps to ignite them. Hissing and popping, they scattered searing-hot sparks on her hands and arms as she ran back down the narrow corridor, and bowled fire and thick orange smoke into the main saloon.

AIDEN SIGNALED FRANTICALLY to Tom. The Baltic was about to evade *Archimedes'* rush. At best they would clip her a light blow, and the advantage of surprise would be lost in a one-sided battle of two against ten.

Suddenly he saw smoke pouring from her companionway. Race-crew discipline evaporated as the Baltic's crew dropped lines, grabbed extinguishers from cockpit lockers, and dove down hatches and companionway to fight the deadly peril of fire at sea.

The sloop lost way, transformed again into a stationary target for the speeding *Archimedes*.

But where in that mess was Morgan?

Twenty-six knots. How soon before someone turned around and saw *Archimedes* surfing down a Pacific roller, straight at their stern? Any second the helmsman would hear *Archimedes'* bow wave. Instead, it was *Archimedes'* wind shadow that betrayed them.

The Baltic's half-filled sails suddenly went slack. Jerry, stationed behind the helmsman, looked up, reckoned the cause, and whirled around in sudden apprehension. Fifty yards separated the two boats, close enough for Aiden to see a blur of faces as the firefighters raced up from below to see what Jerry was screaming about.

The crew exploded into action, grinders sheeting in sails, helmsman spinning the leeward wheel, his watch mate gunning the engines. "They're bearing off," he yelled to Tom. "Turning to port."

Twenty yards of water lay between them as the Baltic answered her helm. Twenty yards shrank to twenty feet. Suddenly she swung broadside.

"Have it your way, mate," Slade muttered, and tweaked the wheel.

Archimedes' bow struck *Baltic Nights* six feet ahead of its stern, sheared off the sloping afterdeck, crushed the sat dome, and parted the backstays. Momentum swept her past the bigger boat and for a second she was free of it. Then the tip of her boom snagged on the Baltic's lazy running backstay, which swung her around and drew her alongside as if a giant squid had grabbed her with a tentacle.

Searching for Morgan from his vantage point on the spreader, Aiden saw six men measure the distance between the two hulls, preparing to spring aboard, when the boats converged. He tightened his grip on the spinnaker halyard, and jumped.

AFTER THROWING THE flares, Morgan Page ran to the forepeak, and climbed out the hatch just as the powerful Open 50 sliced through the Baltic's stern. Now first light gleamed silvery gray on total chaos.

The two boats were tangled up, the Open 50's boom caught in the Baltic's running backstay, and being drawn back to it. Joe was yelling that the rudder was jammed. Jerry was screaming that water was pouring in the stern. A sailor was hustling more fire extinguishers down the companionway. But the rest of the Asians were preparing to swarm aboard the Open 50.

As the boats swung closer, her father swept down from the mast and landed like a giant cat on the end of the boom. Hanging on to the edge of the sail, he jumped with both feet on the boom and freed it. The boats' sterns veered apart.

"Morgan!" he shouted. "Morgan, where are you?"

Morgan jumped for the Open 50's bow. But the distance was too great. She splashed into the water far short of her father's boat, and swam with all her strength, desperate to get away from the Baltic before the crew dove in after her. Behind her, a second loud crack—sharper and louder than the collision—drew every eye. The Baltic's lazy running backstay, stretched taut by *Archimedes*, had been the last thing bracing her enormous mast.

Swaying wildly, the carbon-fiber spar splintered halfway up. The top half plunged to the deck in a welter of stays, shrouds, and spreaders, pierced the cabin roof, and scattered seamen.

"Daddy!"

Aiden looked down from the boom.

"Stop the boat," he roared at Slade, who couldn't see Morgan from the helm, and jumped again, clinging to the halyard. He landed in the water ten feet from her. The boat dragged him another ten even as he tried to swim to her.

"Don't let go," she screamed. "I'm okay. I'll catch up." She ducked her face in the salt and swam harder. Somehow the other man on the Open 50 turned it around, taking the tension off the line her father was holding. A wave picked her up and shoved her toward him and all of a sudden her father was holding her, drawing her tight into one arm and shouting to the other man, "I got her. Go! They're coming after us. Go! Go! Go!"

The line fetched hard. She felt it rip his arm and heard his grunt of pain. It dragged them through the water and he cried, "Honey, pull yourself up to the line." She clawed ahold of his jacket and hauled herself against the flow of the water until she got one, then two hands on the line, which was vibrating with the strain. She held on until she thought she couldn't hold a moment longer. The water was ripping at them and she could feel her father starting to slip away.

The rushing stopped. The line went slack. She thought the Baltic's crew had caught them. But the Open 50 had stopped a short distance from the Baltic to pick them up. Her father looped the line under her arms with a quick bowline and the guy on the boat hauled her over the low transom and into the cockpit. He flipped the bowline off her and dropped it to her father, who stepped into the loop, dragged himself aboard, and collapsed beside her.

"Go, Tom," he gasped. "Before they launch their tender."

INSTEAD OF KICKING *ARCHIMEDES* UP to speed, Tom Slade focused his binoculars on the vessel wallowing two hundred yards astern.

Aiden asked, "What are you doing?"

"I won't leave 'em if they're sinking."

"Tom! Ten to one they've got guns."

Tom Slade turned to Morgan. "You were aboard. Could you tell, were they sinking?"

"I don't know. The whole stern was gone."

"Was she filling up?"

"It didn't feel that way, but I was on the bow. So she could have been. I don't know."

Aiden said, "She had a counterstern. What we took off was above the waterline."

"It wasn't exactly a surgical removal," said Tom. "For all we know, those bloody carbon laminates cracked down to her keel."

"Tom," Aiden pleaded. "It's a well-equipped boat. Big professional crew. They can save her. If they can't, they have life rafts."

"I won't leave them in the rafts."

Aiden said, "They can launch an inflatable and motor over to Morgan's boat. If they have to, they can all fit on it. They can use her radio."

"I don't have a radio," said Morgan

Both men stopped arguing to stare at her.

Morgan asked, "Could we circle around her, get a look at her stern?"

In came the wildly luffing sails and Morgan felt the Open 50 muscle into motion. In seconds, it was laying a white wake. Her father steered a broad circle around the Baltic while Tom inspected it through his binoculars. "She's not at all down at the stern . . . looks like we only took off the overhang, though I don't think I'd want to sail her in following seas."

"Okay?"

Tom took one last long look. "They'll be okay. Not happy, but okay."

Aiden grabbed the VHF handheld and keyed *transmit*. "Joe?" he broadcast. "Jerry? Can you hear me?"

Morgan looked at him in disbelief. "You *know* them?"

"Not well—Joe? Jerry?"

"Aiden, we're sinking," Jerry cried.

"You are not." He glanced anxiously at Tom, who had his binoculars glued to the white hull again. They lost sight of it as both boats descended into troughs.

"Help us."

Slowly they rose to the crest of their next roller. The Baltic rose to its. Tom shook his head. "She's having you on. They're pulling a sail over the hole and they're not even bothering with hand pumps. Fuck 'em."

"Jerry, if you were going to sink, you'd be sunk by now. Who are you working for?"

Jerry dropped the ploy. *"That was a slick move, Aiden. You ought to consider joining up with Joe and me. We could use a guy like you."*

"Who are you working for? Who sicced you on me?"

"I'm not kidding, Aiden. Think about it. It's not like you've got a lot of options in life, being dead already."

"Who's paying you, Jerry?"

"Whereas being dead already could make you a very valuable person to us."

"Who are you working for, Jerry?"

"Neat little kid you have there, Aiden. Cute as a button—like they said about me when I was her age. We could work it so she could see her dead daddy whenever she wanted."

"Who are you working for, Jerry?"

"Come closer. I'll whisper it in your ear."

Aiden snapped off the radio. "Let's go, Tom." Morgan was staring at him, lips parted in an astonished *O*. He said, "I met them in Panama."

Something clanged off the stern pulpit and then something popped against the boom. Gunfire echoed across the water, the sharp crackle of pistols. Aiden pushed Morgan to the deck and lay on top of her.

"Sons of bitches!" yelled Tom. "I was trying to help." Flat on his face, steering from the bottom of the wheel, he headed off onto a broad reach and *Archimedes* scooted out of range.

"Stop!" yelled Morgan.

"What?"

"My boat."

"What?"

"Don't leave my boat."

"Oh shit," said Tom, and now it was Aiden's turn to plead that they not rush off. The J/27 had kept sailing throughout the encounter, but her jib had gotten backwinded at some point, so she was not sailing much faster than the stricken Baltic was drifting. Which left her within extreme range of the pistol fire popping from the Baltic. Bullets were bouncing on the water as they came alongside. Morgan jumped aboard and quickly furled her sails while her father again hooked up onto the towing bridle they had rigged around the strong stump of her mast.

When they climbed back aboard the big boat, Tom Slade told her, "Drive!"

"What course?"

"Try to steer two sixty-five until we're back on seventeen."

"Blind Man Island?"

"Landfall in three days—assuming we're done ramming for a while. Aiden, let's see what's left of the bow."

The Baltic 70 had disappeared astern before Tom and Aiden finished wrapping sailcloth over several significant but patchable holes. A crack in the foredeck looked more ominous. But it stopped short of the chain plate that anchored the forestay to solid structure below. The forestay itself, which was vital, not only to hold the jib, but to support the mast, had survived the collision because it was recessed from the tip of the bow. Although they agreed that the owner would be wise to replace it before his next race.

Aiden told Slade, "I've got some money. The least I can do is pay for it so the owner doesn't take it out of your hide."

"Better than adding 'boat wrecker' to my reputation."

Aiden glanced back to where Morgan was doing an impressive job of steering the Open 50. He said, "Look, Tom. You've gone above and beyond. I can offer you fifteen thousand dollars in cash."

"A stay won't cost fifteen thousand. I've a cousin owns a yard in North Island. I'll do the patching myself, before I deliver."

"The fifteen thousand is to charter you."

"Now where?"

"Still Blind Man Island. But after you drop me, I want you to tow Morgan's boat down to Tongatapu. I know people there who will look out for her."

"Aiden, what the fuck are you mixed up in?"

"I don't know yet. But I do know I can't have her involved."

"I can't take fifteen thousand dollars for that. Ten will cover the damage, the dinghy, and the tow."

"But please don't tell Morgan. I'll tell her when it's time to drop me."

M ORGAN WATCHED THE TWO MEN work their way back to the cockpit. She thought that they had been talking about her. Her father had a big grin on his handsome face, but kept ducking his head. While Tom, a funny-looking wiry little guy who reminded her of a very young Wayne, couldn't meet her eye when she offered him her hand.

"Thank you for saving my boat," she said.

"No big deal," he said. "Your dad would have done the same for my girl."

"I hope your bow's okay."

"Better than that Baltic's stern."

"That's not saying much," said Morgan.

Tom Slade grinned. "We're still floating and still moving, can't ask for more than that."

Tom could not help but notice that Morgan had thanked *him* alone and not her father. She had inherited Aiden's strange eyes, but something remote had crept into hers—a depth to the blue and an edge to the green. He glanced questioningly at her father. Aiden, despite his initial joy at seeing his daughter—and hers at seeing him—looked as uncomfortable as a husband required to explain his failure to come home for the weekend.

Tom figured that if a fifteen-year-old daughter could be half as implacable as his ten-year-old when crossed, the man had a lot of talking to do. But that was Aiden's problem. He himself had been brave enough for one day and it wasn't even ten o'clock in the morning. Definitely time to clear out before the fireworks started.

"Take my watch, Aiden. I'm going to fall on my face. Give you two a chance to talk."

"WANT ME TO take the helm?" Aiden asked Morgan.

"I'm okay."

". . . Quite a boat, isn't she?"

"Amazing."

"She'll turn on a dime . . . Even when you don't want her to . . . Kitten, I . . ."

She looked so alive, and so very beautiful. And suddenly he couldn't see through his tears, or propel words from a throat that filled with joy to be near her. When he could speak again, when he could form the words, he would tell Morgan he loved her and that this was the happiest moment of his life.

She turned from the rushing water to look up into his eyes. "Why did you run away? Did you do it for Uncle Charlie?"

"No," said Aiden.

"Sometimes I told myself that maybe Uncle Charlie had kind of forced you."

"Uncle Charlie helped me, but it was my idea."

Morgan felt a last hope die that he hadn't really meant to do it. "Was it the letter?"

"Only in part."

"Was it that Jerry on the Baltic? Was she—"

"No! I didn't even know about them. They came later."

"Who are they?"

"They're just hired hands . . . like bounty hunters."

"I know they're bounty hunters. Who hired them? Mr. Hong?"

Aiden looked at her sharply. "What gives you that idea?"

Morgan's cheeks blazed redder than her sunburn. "Don't do it again."

"Do what again?"

"You kept so much from me and then suddenly disappeared. I helped you with that letter. I know something was wrong. I think Mr. Hong was in trouble and you got caught somehow in the middle."

"It looks that way," Aiden admitted. "But I didn't know that at the time. It was not part of my thinking."

"Then why?"

"You saw the mess I was in. I was broke. I couldn't pay the mortgages, I couldn't sell anything. I couldn't pay for your school, or credit cards, or anything. You have no idea what it's like to be broke, how it grinds you down."

"But you and Mommy were broke for years before you got rich. You always talked about it—joked about it, like it was fun."

"That was different. This was a lot worse than just being broke. There was no future. I saw no way out. They were coming to get me. By the morning the planes hit, everything had gone to hell. There was nothing left."

"*I* was left."

"I know. But I couldn't do anything for you anymore. If I split, the life insurance would kick in, cover the debts, cover college . . . But if I stayed, I would just drag you down."

"Drag me down? What do you think pretending to be dead did to me?"

"I know I have a lot to answer for. Enormous—"

"But why did you do it?"

"I told you. Everything . . ."

"Daddy, please . . ."

"What?"

"Don't keep saying that. It makes me think I was part of what went to hell and I didn't try to help you."

"I know you tried to help me. I don't mean you. I mean everything else . . . I couldn't face you."

"But couldn't I help? Couldn't I have made that 'everything'
better?"

"Dammit, Morgan. There was nothing anybody could do. I was
in such deep trouble. It would only have gotten worse. I couldn't be
with you. You would be a witness to it. I would have humiliated you
if I ended up in prison. You saw that damned letter. *I* was the one
who was going to get it in the neck."

"But it wasn't your fault. You just got caught in the middle. It
wasn't your fault."

"It was not my fault."

"But?"

Aiden said, "Saying it's not my fault doesn't mean I'm not
responsible." She looked askance. Hastily, clumsily, he tried to
change the subject. "You're different."

"How?"

"Like grown up."

That made her angry. "I'm still fifteen. I don't feel at all grown
up. I don't know what I feel. I thought I'd be so happy to see you—
and I am. I'm so glad to see you—but I feel all ripped up inside."
Suddenly she was blinking tears. She turned, staring to port, and the
boat lurched that way. "Whoa, Nellie. Come back here."

Aiden reached to help.

"I have it," she said quietly.

When *Archimedes* was back on 265, Aiden tried again to change
the subject. "Where did you sail from?"

"California."

"Alone? All the way out here alone?"

"She's a good boat."

"It's a goddamned day sailer."

"No, she's a good little cruiser, Dad. She really is. She'll take
thirty knots without reefing the main—what are you smiling for?"

"I never knew a sailor who didn't love her boat."

"It's not really *my* boat. I was going to take Grandpa's. But he went and sold it. This was the only one I could take—steal— Now what are you smiling for?"

"I'm glad it wasn't any smaller."

"I would have taken a seven-foot Opti if it was the only one. Don't you realize what it meant when you telephoned?"

"Kitten, I'm so sorry about that."

"God, no! It made me so happy. It was so wonderful and so incredible that sometimes I thought I dreamed it or made it up. The shrink thought it was a dream."

"What shrink?"

"Dr. Melton."

"Don't tell me your mother sent *you* to that quack."

"Yeah, well . . . she was worried about me—after the funeral."

"Funeral?"

"*Your* funeral." Again, she felt her face burn red-hot with anger. How could he not have imagined what it would be like for her? "Didn't you think there'd be a funeral?" She thought she would cry. But suddenly she was shouting, "Jesus H. Daddy, they made me sing fucking 'Danny Boy'!"

AIDEN SAID, "I have a lot to make up for."

"Was Jerry right? That you can't go back?"

"I don't see how. I'm sorry."

"Sorry you did it? Or sorry you can't go back?"

"Both."

"Did you *plan* this? Did you know the night before we'd never see each other again?"

"No! No! I had no plan."

But she didn't believe him. "Oh my God, you were going to leave all along?"

"No!" Aiden Page sank to the cockpit bench, planted his elbows on his knees, and held his head in his hands. Like sitting at my desk that morning, he thought. "I was too stupid to make a plan . . ."

"You're not stupid!"

"Not stupid," he admitted. "You're right. But I was blind. Too blind to make a plan. But when the plane smashed into the building, right above me, I knew two things instantly. One, it was a miracle I was still alive. Two, no one would believe I survived. All I had to do was walk away."

"I believed."

"That's because I made that stupid telephone call."

"Stupid? Stupid was leaving, not calling . . ." She felt the tears winning, couldn't stop them anymore. "I understand how you could leave Mom. And you probably didn't even think about Grandpa—I know how hard he was on you. But how could you do it to *me*?"

"I was trying to save you."

"You were trying to save yourself."

Aiden gaped at his daughter, stunned by the realization that he could not deny her accusation.

Her face was shrouded in blighted hope. "Take the wheel!"

Morgan fled below, down the companionway, into the long dark tunnel between *Archimedes'* ballast tanks. By the dull glow of a single skylight in the deck, she saw Tom fast asleep in a pipe berth, blundered past him, and sat on a sailbag beside an elaborate workbench. Her head was ringing, like the ringing noise of the water rushing past the hull. She looked up. Her father had followed her down.

"Aren't you on watch?"

"Autopilot . . . Kitten?"

"Don't call me that. My name is Morgan." She looked around the open hold, so huge compared to *Molly*'s, crammed with sails and gear and tools.

"Morgan. Please."

"What?"

He took her hands in his and rubbed her fingers with his, calluses to calluses. When he reached clumsily to try to hug her, she started crying again. He pulled her to him, held her awkwardly, patting her shoulder. "I'm sorry."

"You don't even know what you're sorry for."

Aiden raised his head. "I'm sorry for disappointing you."

Morgan wept. I can't stand this, she thought. I have to get out of here. I have to get away.

Her father asked in a broken voice, "What can I do to make it up to you?"

"Fix my boat."

I'D SLEEVE IT INTERNALLY," SAID Tom, fingering the twisted metal where *Molly*'s mast had broken. "That's the only way you'll get a weld to hold."

"But where am I going to get marine-grade aluminum plate?"

They were down in the Open 50's hold, having managed the second-hardest part of the job—manhandling the mast and its stump off *Molly* and onto *Archimedes*, with the broken end down her companionway. The hardest part would be putting it back, rocking and rolling on the swell, which the weather report threatened would get worse with a shift in the trade wind.

Tom circled the mast in his hand. "Lop four feet off and use that piece for plate. Cut the track, here. And refit the gooseneck, here."

Morgan's father turned to her with a hopeful rationale. "It'll be a little shorter . . . just a little—like you had a reef in the main."

She shook her head. "She needs her full mainsail. When you reef, she won't point."

Tom said, "How about we cut a length from her spinnaker pole?"

Her father said, "Yeah, peel it open vertically . . . I'd need two pieces. Good idea." He turned to Morgan. "The mast is hollow, right?

We don't want the wall to dimple, because a dimple will bend again, so we're going to shape a sleeve out of a hunk of spinnaker pole, and weld it inside. Then we'll weld the joint. Your mast will be double thick at the point of the break. Doubly strong."

"And we'll pop-rivet above and below the joint, too," Tom chimed in.

"Then what would I use for a spinnaker pole?"

Her father glanced at Tom, and then at a pile of junk in the shadows. "There's some carbon-fiber spars. Thin ones." Tom Slade nodded assent. Her father told her, "I'll transfer your piston and bell ends onto a carbon-fiber pole. Be lighter than aluminum. Stronger, too."

"I'll leave you two to it," said Slade. "I've got a boat to drive."

Aiden chose a fine-tooth hacksaw, cut both broken ends, and smoothed them with a stainless-steel brush.

"Daddy, where'd you learn to do this stuff?"

"I've done all kinds of jobs. If you're going to run a boat, you better know how to fix stuff."

"*Molly P* always went to the yard."

"We were too busy to do our own work."

"Or too rich," Morgan said.

Her father turned his attention to the twisted mast track, hacksawing it below the break, straightening it in the workbench vise. He was smoothing the cut with a file when she asked, "Were you and Mom too rich?"

"Can't be too rich or too skinny."

"How about too greedy?"

He put down the file and looked her in the face for the first time. "Do you think it's that simple?"

When she spoke at last, she stared at her frayed sneakers. "Why was the prosecutor investigating your office?"

"It's very complicated."

"Dad. I'm fifteen. I go to a very good school. I pay attention to what's going on. Particularly since you 'died.' I read the letter. I saw the files. What the hell was going on at HHH?"

Aiden put down his tools and finally looked her in the eye. "What did I think *then* was going on? Or what do I think *now* was going on?"

"What did you think was going on when you worked there?"

"I knew that most of our funds came from Henry Hong. I didn't want to think about the possibility that we might be laundering illegal money—I didn't think it was drugs. I had heard rumors, whispers, that he was helping his contacts in China get money they'd stolen out of the country. But I didn't think too hard on it. It wasn't my side of the business, so I stayed out of it."

"But you suspected the money was somehow not kosher?"

"I suspected maybe."

"What do you think now? Or should I say, what do you know?"

"I still don't think it was drugs. Eliminate government corruption and drugs, the other big source of dirty cash is weapons. So I now have a strong suspicion Henry was selling arms on the black market."

"To terrorists?"

"I don't know. I guess to anybody. There's huge money to be made 'gunrunning' around UN embargoes."

"Which means you helped sell weapons? Illegal weapons. Banned weapons."

"Not deliberately. I was just doing business on Wall Street."

"But the government thought you helped?"

"Maybe at first. But they were only fishing. The problem is . . . they weren't fishing deep enough."

"It's about the 'real deals,' isn't it? What were the folders? 'Tugboats, Bulldozers, Trucks, Drills, and Whatever.' "

"It's just possible that Mr. Hong had a crazy agenda."

"Involving the tugboats and barges or the construction company?"

"Both. I have some weird theories, but no proof. I'm hoping that Mr. Hong can explain everything. I'll find out when I get to Blind Man Island. I would like nothing better than to feel like a paranoid idiot."

"How weird?"

"It is just possible that I might have given him the tools to make a terrorist weapon. A huge bomb. Although even as I say it out loud, it sounds absurd." He told her his theory about the dynamite barge. "I know it sounds crazy."

"Could it possibly be anything else?"

"Some kind of innocent explanation. That's what I'm hoping for."

"Or not innocent."

"Not innocent?"

"Not a bomb. Something else. Something worse."

"I can't think what—I mean, if I'm right, what could be worse than a bomb big enough to destroy a city . . . I can't believe I helped."

"You didn't mean to."

"Want to hear something funny? Sometimes I think that Uncle Charlie and I inside the building had a lot in common with the terrorists flying at it."

"That's wack, Daddy . . . Like what?"

"Attitude. We were all doing exactly what we wanted to do. The hell with rules. The hell with laws. The hell with anybody who got in our way."

She saw his face crumble and she tried to comfort him. She grabbed his hands. "Hey, we all do it. Look at me. I stole my boat."

"So you could find me."

"But it still was a form of 'screw-anybody-in-my-way.' Daddy, I think maybe you're being too harsh on yourself."

He cupped her face in his hands and kissed her forehead and said, "Yeah, I know it all sounds off-the-wall. But there has to be some reason that God let me survive . . ."

That scared her. To Morgan, God was as real as Roscoe's mind had been—a living piece of her life. Whereas, until this moment, her father had always "worshiped" an adult's God, who was only a name. For most people, discovering a real God would be the discovery of hope. But she knew her father too well: a real God was forcing him to see himself as he couldn't bear to.

You're lost, she thought. You're lost in your mind. And you can't help yourself. I know, I've been there.

THE NEXT DAY, as she watched him take chances as they were jumping between the two boats, she worried even more that he would do something dangerous to try to prove that he was actually the good person he had always thought he was.

It was a happy day, talking and kidding around while he finished making her boat almost as good as new. But when he was done hoisting *Molly*'s freshly welded mast back through the collar in the cabin roof and onto its mast step, he confirmed her worst fears.

"Listen, hon. I've asked Tom to tow you down to Tongatapu. I'll catch up with you after I see Henry Hong."

"You're going to see Henry Hong alone? That's crazy."

"I'll tell him what I know. And wait for him to prove I'm nuts."

"But if you're right, he'll hurt you. He'll kill you."

"He can't hurt me. I'll tell him I left a copy of the CD with a lawyer in Panama City."

"Did you?"

"Bluff. It's in my seabag. I'll leave it with you. When you get to Tongatapu, ask Paea's father to stash it in his safe."

"What if he doesn't believe you? What if he hurts you—tortures you—to make you tell him where it is?"

"He won't. It's not his way."

"Oh really? Jerry said that Mr. Hong was a very dangerous man."

"Jerry was trying to frighten you."

"It worked."

For a second, her father grinned back at her. Then he hugged her. "It's so wonderful to see you."

"Can't I go with you?"

"No," he said firmly. "This is something I have to do alone."

"Why, if it's not dangerous?"

"I need you on Tongatapu. You're my second life insurance."

"How?"

"Because you'll be safe with Paea's father on Tongatapu. I will tell Henry Hong that you know I went to Blind Man Island. And that if something happens to me, Paea's father will know."

"But he's Mr. Hong's guy. You and Uncle Charlie mocked him. I heard you call him Noble Nephew."

"He may be naïve. But he's not a criminal. He's just a too-trusting nice guy."

"Daddy, you're taking a terrible chance."

"I have a lot to make up for," Aiden said quietly.

"That's crazy! You're trying to punish yourself for all the bad stuff you did."

"Maybe."

"Jesus H.!" Morgan yelled. "You'll get killed again. Only this time I won't be able to catch up with you."

"I'll be fine."

She looked at him imploringly. "Dad, destroying yourself will destroy me." But his face had hardened.

She said, "When we get to Blind Man, we'll see the situation. Maybe I can stay."

"No. Tom's got an extra inflatable. I'll row in from the reef."

JUST WHEN SHE had lost all hope of stopping him, the trade wind got dicey. It didn't matter at first since they were within a day of Blind Man Island. While it was fitfully backing and veering, it still blew enough from behind to let them keep flying the big yellow spinnaker. But in the afternoon, when they were within thirty miles—and Morgan kept imagining she could see green hills where there was nothing but the endless rim of the sea—the wind suddenly backed halfway around the compass and blew out of the west.

They lowered the spinnaker and began beating on a starboard tack. *Archimedes* demonstrated her hatred of close-hauled sailing—despite a formidable capacity to point—with bone-jarring pounding and enormous douses of salt spray.

"Land!" Morgan cried. "I see it."

A BARREN, DULL-GRAY PEAK PRICKED the horizon like a pencil lead. Beside it crept up a second stony spire, gloomy as the first. But it was over two months since she had seen San Miguel Island sink behind her, and land looked beautiful.

"The two hills! Remember the two hills, Daddy? Over on the windward side?"

They grew slowly taller. Within the hour she saw color below them, a hint of blue green, which got brighter and greener the closer they sailed. And if an emerald set in blue was not pretty enough, now the sinking sun weighed in, lighting the thin cirrus gold. Tom Slade waited until the GPS fixed them fifteen miles off the windward coast, before he finally said what they were all thinking.

"The wind is holding west. It's had plenty of time to build a countersea. If that pass is like any other leeward-side pass I've ever seen, you'll never get a yacht through the reef, much less a dinghy."

Aiden said, "It's a wide, easy pass. Morgan sailed in and out in a canoe when she was only twelve years old." He looked at her. "You remember? What do you think?"

"Tom's right. Even Paea couldn't get the canoe out when the wind shifted. There was an insane riptide and a really mean chop."

Aiden stared at the volcanic peaks spiking up from the green island. "I'll get in, don't you worry. Swim if I have to."

"Daddy, let's get on my boat. We'll sail in together when the wind shifts east again."

"No." He hauled the spare dinghy on deck and began stomping the foot pump.

Morgan watched him pumping like his life depended on it, like as soon as he was in the dinghy, everything would start to work out. Suddenly she saw a way to make the wind work for both of them. She ran below and came up with a chart she had not yet unfolded.

"There's a better way, Dad. Look at this." Kneeling on the cockpit sole, she spread the chart out on the bench and shielded the waxed paper from the spray with her body. "See this little pass and lagoon on the northeast side? I sailed there with Paea. Mr. Hong cut a channel and training walls through the reef. It's not on the chart yet. It's really tricky getting in when the trade is blowing, but with this west wind, you'll be in the lee of the island. You could row in easily."

"Then what?"

"Just walk across."

Aiden measured the island with the calipers. "Eight miles as the pelican flies . . ." He thought on it and flashed her a smile. "Why not? Won't Uncle Henry be surprised seeing me stroll in his back door?"

"It'll be dark soon," said Tom. "If we're going to do it, let's do it . . ."

"Right," said Aiden.

"We'll put her in on a port tack. Ready about?"

Hiding her face to conceal her relief, Morgan jumped to man the running backstays.

THE WESTERLY SWOOPED down the upper hills and roiled seas that made *Archimedes* pound so hard that Morgan feared for *Molly*'s towline. But suddenly, a mile off, they moved into the lee of the island. The land blocked the wind and the surface water lay flat upon the swell.

"Perfect," said Aiden. "I'll row from here."

Tom glanced at the chart in the fading light. "The reef drops off sheer. I've still got six thousand feet of water under the keel. I can motor in closer."

"No, this is fine." He stuck out his hand and asked quietly, "Did you count the dough?"

"Ten grand, all there in cash, as promised, thank you, mate. If I knew how much you were toting in that seabag, I might have knocked you on the head—you sure you don't need to hang on to some of it?"

"No, I'm okay. Funny thing, but I'm actually ahead a couple of bucks working the boats." They shook hands and Aiden said, "You've been a real friend."

"No problem," Tom replied. "Enjoyed the company. Okay, let's launch over the port side. And Aiden? Try to stay out of the towline?"

Aiden tied his bags to the dinghy's seat and they hoisted the little craft over the lifelines. "I will see you real soon," he said to Morgan, hugging her hard and kissing the top of her head. "Thank you for finding me. I love you. I will love you forever."

"I love you, Daddy. Please be careful."

Aiden patted his life vest. "Always." He stepped over the lifelines, lowered himself into the rubber boat, shoved off, and dipped the oars. "Love you! See you soon."

Tom held *Archimedes* hove to, intending to stand by until Aiden was safely inside the cut. But the light was fading fast, and once Aiden had rowed into the shadow of the island, it was too dark to see the training walls. Their last sight of the dinghy was a rhythmic flicker of his oars.

"Okay, little girl. You drive, I'll get some more sail up. Next stop, Tongatapu."

"How long will it take?"

"Three hundred miles on a broad reach? We're towing *Molly* and gotta dodge a heap of reefs, but if we push her, we should be off the harbor before dark tomorrow."

Morgan ran the numbers in her head. Considering how much slower *Molly* was than *Archimedes,* she had less than three hours to make her move.

AIDEN LOOKED OVER his shoulder and pulled harder on his left oar to line up with the low shadows that marked the training walls. On course again, he faced aft, and dug his oars. The first star of the night gave him a reference point, where it hung low in the fading maroon sky. The boats had moved on. It was too dark to see their sails, only *Archimedes'* green sidelight, and the two whites Tom had hung up the mast to indicate a tow. Close behind rode *Molly*'s green and white. When they angled together into a line, he knew that Tom moved beyond the lee and had caught the wind on a fast broad reach.

The water was flat calm and even the swell had turned gentle, gurgling quietly over a reef he could not see in the dark. Again he lined up on the training walls. They were his guide. Stay in line with them and he wouldn't tear the rubber bottom on the coral. But, man, he would not want to be doing this if the trade was blowing. Not without sails down and engine up.

The steep hills reared overhead as he reached the training wall, blotting out what remained of the maroon sky. A missed oar splashed. The sound echoed. He was inside the walls that lined the channel into the lagoon. He didn't want to use his flashlight yet; he wanted to preserve his night vision. As he rowed the last hundred yards, his eyes adjusted sufficiently to see the general outline of the lagoon and where the training wall on his left merged into a pier long enough for a small ship or a barge. Neither was moored there now. Nor did he see any lights showing among the layered lattice of what looked like a loading crane or some kind of drilling rig.

He looked for a place to beach the dinghy. The pier was too high to climb onto safely in the dark. He rowed past it and saw the gleam of a white sand shelf sloping into the water. Just before he got to it, the rubber bow bumped into something and rode partway over it. It looked like a floating log. He pushed off with an oar and, with two strong pulls, ran the dinghy onto the sand. As he stepped out with the painter and dragged it out of the water, he realized it would be foolish to try to cross the island tonight. Even if he could find the trail in the dark, how would he stick to it? Better to set out at first light instead.

He could use the night to adjust to the feel of solid land, which at the moment seemed to be rolling under his feet. Catch some sleep somewhere. There were no mosquitoes, and the air was pleasantly cool and dry.

The stars were thickening into fiery white clumps that cast enough light to see low buildings between the water and the rim of the jungle-clad cliffs. He walked to the crane, which stood straight up at the edge of the lagoon, next to a round wall that felt cool and smooth to his hand like poured cement. When he stepped up on a coral outcropping to see inside, he found it partly covered with a steel lid. Massive as a bank-vault door, it looked about twenty feet across, and what its purpose was, he had no idea.

The low buildings were basically roofs with no walls. The starlight didn't penetrate, so he squinted one eye shut and switched on his flashlight. A machine shop, tools, drill presses, lathes, and workbenches all in perfect order. Another building was a storage shed, stacked with pails of lubricants and sacks of drilling mud. Another looked like a sort of open-air mess hall, with rows of tables and a kitchen range, gas woks, and propane tanks. Wooden stairs led up a slope. On top he found open-air barracks, row upon row of bunk beds sheltered by a tin roof. On each bed was a rolled mattress, a thin pillow, and a folded sheet. Order, order everywhere, he thought, and not one living soul.

The barracks might be the spot to sack out, but it felt a little creepy and for the moment he thought he might prefer to stretch out in the rubber raft with his head on the soft side tube. He followed the beam of his light down the steps past the buildings and the crane and back to the beach. What he had thought was a log that he had bumped into had drifted ashore.

Suddenly he jumped away from it and probed fearfully with the flashlight. It was a dead man dressed in military camouflage. He had an empty holster low on his right thigh, and an empty sheath on his left.

Aiden stared. All he could think of was that the dead man was the spitting image of the Korean greengrocer where he would stop to buy a bunch of flowers before he met Mary at the Gramercy Park Hotel.

What the hell had he stepped into?

He backed away from the body. A rough hand closed over his mouth. A powerful arm circled his throat. He sensed a long blade hovering. But there was no flash of steel in the starlight, no telltale gleam of the naked blade, and the part of his mind that hadn't frozen observed that it was dark with the blood of the dead man at his feet.

THE ATTACKER DRAGGED AIDEN DOWN to the sand. Aiden tried to block the knife.

A harsh voice rasped in his ear, "You picked a hell of a night to come ashore."

"Charlie?" he gasped against the hand covering his mouth.

"Quiet, bro, I only saw one in the night lens, let's just be sure the rest of them split." He held their position for several minutes, stockstill, then helped Aiden to his feet and embraced him powerfully. "You made it. I can't believe you're alive. I hoped . . ." His voice grew thick with emotion. "I just hoped, but I couldn't do a goddamn thing."

Aiden was overwhelmed with joy. Out of nowhere, he had his best friend back. A huge burden of guilt lifted from his heart. And he knew that with Charlie back in charge, everything would be all right. "Let me look at you."

"Don't turn on the light. Wait till we're safe."

At their feet the dark shadow of the body bobbed in the star-speckled water. "Who is that?"

"Security. He got confused when he saw you rowing."

"Who killed him?"

In the dark, Aiden could hear the old big-brother smirk in Charlie's voice. "He was trying to kill *you*, thinking you were me."

"*You* killed him."

"He was about to blow your head off when he exposed his position."

"What is going on?"

"It was an ambush. They figured I'd come down if no one was here. They left one guy."

"Down from where?"

"My cave."

"What cave?"

"Let's go, bro. You'll see when we get there."

"Wait. What are you doing here?"

"You could say I'm in the middle of an unfriendly takeover. You got here just in time. I can use a hand. Shhh! They're coming back."

He pointed toward the training walls. From out at sea Aiden heard the whine of a powerful marine turbine.

"Grab the raft!"

They dragged it deep into the trees. Then Charlie hustled him up the slope. "Hold my belt. Stick close."

"Who are we running from?"

"Uncle Henry and his lady love."

"TOM, DO YOU have a spare GPS?" Morgan asked.

"What for?"

"I have to go back to Blind Man Island."

Tom was at *Archimedes'* helm, eking every ounce of power he could from the wind, which was starting to back. His eyes flickered from the sails, to the stars, to the compass, and for a millisecond at her.

"Sorry, Morgan. That's not on. I promised your father I would deliver you to Tongatapu and that's where we're going."

"There aren't any trails across Blind Man Island."

"What do you mean?"

"I mean my father is stuck there. He can't walk across the island. There are no trails, no paths, no road. And we don't even want to think about him trying to *row* around it in that little raft, do we?"

"What happened to the trails?"

"There never were any trails. There were never any people. Nobody ever lived on the island before Henry Hong built a water plant."

"But Aiden said they have farms."

"The farm plots are connected to the water plant on the leeward side. The windward side is all cliffs and hills, too steep to farm. Besides, the jungle is too thick, and there aren't any pipes."

"You're having me on, dear. He's been there before. He knows there are trails."

"He was there only once. It was a company party. He spent the whole time at the house drinking. I hung out with the kids. They took me everywhere."

Tom Slade laughed, uncertainly. "You *stranded* your dad? Well, aren't you a piece of work."

"So I have to go back and get him."

"Little girl, you don't know what your father's mixed up in."

"But he doesn't either."

"He knew enough to keep you out of it. If it's dangerous, you'll only make it more dangerous."

"No. I'll take him away. I'll take him with me to Tongatapu."

"What if he won't go? Then you're both in trouble."

"He has to go. He'll have to leave the island to protect me . . . Please, Tom. I can save him."

•   •   •

THEY CLIMBED FOR hours, Charlie plunging surely ahead, Aiden scrambling to keep up. He had thought he had gone through many changes since the terrorist attack. But now it was like nothing had changed. Charlie was leading, he was following. Only God and Charlie knew where. They might as well be nine and ten again, sneaking around the hills behind summer camp to spy on the girls' showers.

Charlie stopped in a narrow ravine. "Be very careful. Put your feet exactly where I do . . . Okay. Let's go."

"What was that?"

"Land mines."

"Jesus H." Aiden felt the blood rush from his face, but he had to run to catch up.

Twice more Charlie warned him where to walk.

"Whose land mines?" Aiden whispered.

"The first one was theirs. This is beautiful defensive ground. You could hide here for ten years."

"Charlie, wait!"

"What?"

"I think I heard somebody behind us."

"Salote's brothers. Keeping an eye on the Old Man—that's me."

"Who's Salote?"

"The most beautiful woman in the South Pacific."

"Charlie, what the fuck—"

"Almost home, bro, just hang in there."

They climbed higher in the dark, then paused in a small clearing to catch their breath. "What's that smell?"

Charlie said, "A head."

"A what? The stink—" He looked up and saw stars through the break in the trees. Against the stars, a ragged silhouette.

"Dad told me that when he was in Korea, the Turkish troops secured their perimeter at night by sticking some enemy heads on stakes. Works wonders. They finally leave us alone."

"Who?"

"Henry's goddamned private army. Ran me ragged for weeks. I didn't have a moment to do more than survive. Then I remembered the heads trick—give me your hand."

Suddenly there was light, just enough to see by, and Aiden realized he had been led, unknowingly, inside. The air was cool, the ceiling an arch of stone. Charlie led him ten more steps, into a larger chamber.

A strikingly beautiful Tongan woman threw her arms around him. Tall and full-bodied, she had golden skin, broad cheekbones, and black hair swept back from a high brow. She cupped Charlie's face in her hands, her own face proud. Several Tongan men watched from the shadows, smiling and nodding greetings to Aiden.

"This is Salote," Charlie said, turning to introduce her to Aiden. "Salote, this is my wonderful brother, Aiden, who I never thought I would see alive."

Aiden reached to offer his hand. Then, for the first time, he saw Charlie's face. He recoiled as if he had been stabbed. Charlie grinned. "I should have warned you. But don't worry, I'm in great shape."

"You don't look it."

He'd lost his green eye. He wore a patch over it. His face was drawn. His arms were scarred like he had been raked by claws. Cotton shirt and trousers hung loosely on his frame.

"Save your tears, pal. I'm in my element."

PERHAPS HE WAS, THOUGHT AIDEN, even as he mourned the wreckage of his brother's face. On closer inspection of the whole man, he saw that Charlie was still roped with muscle. His blue eye burned bright with something that could be fever, or a strange sort of happiness.

"Are you hungry, Aiden? Salote? Can we feed our guest? Come, meet Salote's brothers." Aiden took in a cacophony of unfamiliar names and shook hands all around. They were huge men, friendly to him, and clearly in awe of Charlie, who greeted each like family. All wore sidearms.

Charlie led him outside while Salote prepared a meal. Far below, the sea twinkled in the starlight.

"Wait till you taste her cooking. We catch wild pigs up here."

"Charlie."

"Some view, huh? You should see it in the daylight. We're going to build a fantastic hotel, soon as we get this settled."

"What," Aiden asked again, "is going on?"

"I told you, we've got an insurrection going."

"Against Henry?"

"And his wife. You got here just in time. Something's up. Jin-shil finished building down there. They took the workers off on a barge. It's just us and Henry's little army now."

"What is 'up'?"

"I'm still not sure. But it's worth a fortune, and before I'm done—we're done—we're going to own it." He threw his arm around Aiden's shoulders and asked, "What do you think of Salote?"

"It's hard to breathe when I look at her."

"Yeah, well, keep your hands off this one."

"Don't worry, she looks totally in love," Aiden said hastily, wondering whether Charlie knew about him and Mary and was toying with him. I'm going to tell him, he thought. As soon as the rest of this is sorted out. Start over with a clean slate.

Charlie laughed. "I'm not worried. I've discovered the key to controlling women. Be kind. It's a new experience for most of them. Be *very* kind and they'll do anything. You'll remind them of Daddy—or how they'd like to remember Daddy."

Why, Aiden wondered, is he bragging about women? "Bro, we have to talk."

Charlie said what he always said. "So talk. Fill me in. How'd you get here?" he asked, and the brothers stood side by side, gazing down at the starlit sea, while Aiden reported his odyssey since they had become separated in the burning stairwell.

"Panama? How the heck did they find you in Panama?"

"Did you tell Henry I might be alive?"

"I told him it would be a miracle. But when he kept asking, I told him that if you were, you'd come here."

"Morgan says she told Dad I had called. I'm guessing that some pretty good detectives backtracked me to the nuns. The question is *who* hired them."

Charlie looked at him sharply. "Did Dad believe her?"

"No."

"Jesus H., that's all we'd need."

"At the Canal, everybody's stuck in the same bar waiting to transit. I was a sitting duck."

"But how did they pull the snatch?"

Admitting specifics about the kidnapping provoked a dry, "You dumb fuck."

Aiden laughed with him. "Mea culpa. Mea culpa . . . But I kept asking myself, Whose detectives? And whose kidnappers?"

Charlie said, "Same guy who ratted us out to the U.S. attorney. Uncle Henry."

"I figured that out. And I think I know why, which really scares me. And that's what I want to tell you about."

" 'Why' is right down there at the bottom of the cliff," Charlie said bitterly. He pointed at the dark far below. "He's built himself a whole new business, whole new life. And the best way to keep me out of it was to make the prosecutors tie you and me up in knots."

"Out of what?"

"His big win. His home run. Don't you get it?"

"Get what?"

"Henry's moved on again. Gets himself a gorgeous wife, who happens to be a geologist and an amazing fuck—as well as a psychopath and an amateur ophthalmologist—she's the one who slit my eye—and now he's sitting on a fortune. He's quick. Once a refugee, always a refugee. They move quicker than guys like us. The stock market goes south, no problem, split west. But don't forget to burn your bridges. You and me, bro, we were standing on a burning bridge at HHH and didn't even know it. That's why he tipped the prosecutors."

"Maybe. Or maybe he was trying to shut us up . . . What fortune is he sitting on?"

"I was sure, at first, it was oil. Jin-shil's a geologist. And they're drilling deep."

"Oil?"

"Now I'm thinking along the line of diamonds."

"Diamonds? What are you talking about?" Aiden had the funniest thought, unlike any he had ever had about his brother: I know more than he does. He got fooled, too.

"I'm talking about money. Sucking money straight out of the ground."

"Bro—"

"You know what a diamond pipe is?" Charlie didn't wait for an answer, but went on in a rush, "Geological formation, comes shooting up out of the earth. These islands are all volcanic, all recently formed. The 'pipe' is crammed full of diamonds. A diamond mine basically goes down the pipe, plucking diamonds. Still, I'm voting oil."

"I'm missing something here," said Aiden.

"What the fuck do you think they're drilling down there?"

"There could be another way of looking at this," said Aiden. "He's *pretending* to drill while—"

"Oil or diamonds. Trust me, bro, we're talking forever rich."

Aiden said, "Please listen to me. Just hear me out."

"Go ahead."

"Henry bought two companies . . ." He explained the Halborson Towing and Lewis & Minalgo Construction deals.

"I don't recall Halborson."

"You were busy putting out fires."

"What about them?"

"Together the two companies form a weapon."

"Weapon? He's done with weapons."

"Everybody's afraid of terrorists getting their hands on nuclear weapons, right?"

Charlie laughed. "I used to live in fear that Henry would broker a deal for one of them."

"He's got something more dangerous."

"What?"

"Every national security entity from the coast guard to border patrol to the CIA is watching for atomic bombs, right?"

"Right."

"Lewis and Minalgo Construction can purchase industrial dynamite by the barge load. Halborson Towing can tow barges to any port in the world. In other words, Henry Hong can deliver good old-fashioned low-tech dynamite in quantities that equal an atom bomb."

"Deliver? Where?"

"Name your harbor."

Charlie laughed at him. "What the fuck for? Henry's not a terrorist."

"Maybe not," Aiden answered quietly. "But he's got himself a
weapon that terrorists would pay anything for. You just said it yourself. You were afraid he'd broker an atom bomb."

"That was a joke. Henry's through with weapons. He's moving
up, again. Nothing stops him. He keeps improving. He's got his own
country here. He's like the king. He owns everything. But he's about
to lose it."

"How's he going to lose it?"

"I told you. I've put the island in play. I'm running a hostile
takeover."

"What are you talking about?" All these euphemisms made
Charlie sound like a barroom braggart gilding empty dreams with
fancy words. "Business or fighting? You've got land mines—"

"Insurrection. When this started, Henry had a ninety-man light
reaction company. Thirty of them are now on my side. I control the
interior. His guys don't dare step ten feet off the beach."

"Is that why they pulled out down there?"

Charlie hesitated. "I'm guessing they finished up construction
and now the thing will start pumping money."

"Oil?"

"Or diamonds."

"No," said Aiden. "You're wrong."

"Don't tell me I'm wrong. I've been watching for a month. I saw
the barges come in laden. I saw them go out empty."

"Full of what?"

"Drilling mud."

"Yeah, what else?"

"Polymers. Lubricants. Drilling stuff. I watched them unload it."

"How many barges?"

"Five. Big mothers. Five or ten thousand tons each. Barely fit
through the training walls."

Aiden said, "You're wrong, bro. You saw them unload dynamite. TNT, disguised as drilling mud. Maybe they threw some sacks of drilling mud on top, in case the tow got stopped."

"Henry Hong is not a terrorist. He's a capitalist, like the rest of us. Only better at it."

"Is it possible you've been stuck on this island too long to see what's right in front of your eyes?"

"*Eye*," Charlie shot back. "And I will *win* this island."

THEY ARGUED THROUGH the night, fought as the wind turned around and the southeast trade reasserted itself with powerful rain squalls that whipped the jungle, drummed the stone, and raised the distant thunder of breakers pounding the cliffs. "Why would he send those people after me and Morgan?"

Instead of answering, Charlie spoke dreamily to the blackness where earlier the sea had sparkled. "Hell of a squall. Remember Dad growling, 'Ain't fit night out for man nor beast?'"

"Yeah . . . I'm worried about Morgan."

Charlie threw an arm around his shoulders. "Hey, relax. She's safe as houses in an Open 50."

"You haven't seen Tom Slade drive."

"Don't you worry. He can't cowboy towing her boat."

Aiden tried to steer Charlie back on track. "Why did Henry sic Jin-shil on you? He already had you. You couldn't go anywhere."

"Why did he sic Jin-shil on me? Because he was done with HHH and Company. He was done with me. He didn't want to share his new thing."

"You sound a little obsessed with Henry, bro."

"That is ridiculous."

"Is it possible"—Aiden pressed—"that it's bigger than oil? Bigger than diamonds? Bigger? *Deadlier?* If so, we helped set it up. We have to stop it."

"By the time I'm done with him, he'll be stopped. Stopped dead."

His brother *was* obsessed, Aiden thought. Obsessed with a strange private war that had, he realized, now been going on in Charlie's head a lot longer than the past few months on Blind Man Island. He wondered if Charlie had personally cut off the head stuck on the stake. But all he could bring himself to ask was, "Where did you get land mines?"

"Salote and I Rube Goldberged them. Snuck down and lifted dynamite right from under their noses. By the time this war is won, she'll be the deadliest demo man in the South Pacific."

Aiden leaped on the discrepancy. "I thought you said you hadn't seen any dynamite."

Charlie laughed at him again. "They dug a harbor down there. How do you think they blast coral?"

The squalls raced off as swiftly as they had stormed ashore. The fresh trade wind scattered the clouds. Down in the dark, a mile or so at sea, a cluster of red, green, and white lights marked a ship heading for the island.

"Well, well, well, who might this be? Uncle Henry? Salote, dear? Night lens."

She brought him a rifle with a bulky scope.

"Come on, Aiden, let's check 'em out."

They climbed higher in the dark onto an outcropping that allowed them to see almost straight down into the pass and the harbor. Charlie scoped the ship as it entered the training walls. Then he passed the scope to Aiden. "What do you think?"

Aiden took in the extra-high bow, the bridge wings that extended from either side of the wheelhouse, the tall stack to keep seas out of the engine room, and the long, low towing deck aft.

"Big mother of a seagoing tug with a towing winch is what I think." There was just enough starlight to see each other's face and to crow at his brother a triumphant, "Gee, wonder what it's going to tow?"

Charlie had no answer, as though his faith in his oil or diamond scheme was shaken.

"There's an *H* on the stack. As in Halborson?"

"There's another light."

Aiden swung the rifle scope toward it. "Motor launch."

"The Rivolta 38."

The launch raced through the walls and rafted alongside the tug, which had cast lines onto the pier. Within a half hour, smoke stopped jetting from the tug's stacks. Its lights went out. Six men climbed over its rounded side and down a rope ladder. The motor launch whined out of the channel, hurling spray as it turned to the left and disappeared.

"Where the hell are they going?"

"Not towing dynamite." It was Charlie's turn to grin in Aiden's face. "And they didn't even leave an anchor watch, so they're not coming back anytime soon, either. Gee, bro, maybe Henry's stockpiling tugboats. He always had a thing for them."

Just before dawn, when the eastern sky began separating from the sea, Salote came up the slope with plastic water bottles full of a drink that tasted like watermelon and coconut. She sat at a distance, beside a heavily armed Tongan who'd been invisible in the dark, sharing her bottle with the lookout, her eyes rarely leaving Charlie.

"You're supposed to drink this stuff cold," said Charlie. "But the cave didn't come with a fridge."

"Tastes great."

"I don't believe all this about explosives. Why would they bring them all here? Why didn't they tow those barges under the Verrazano and the Golden Gate, like you said? What are they waiting for?"

"Maybe they're storing it here," said Aiden. "Assembling a multibarge tow."

"Or maybe it's drilling mud and not dynamite. I didn't see any dynamite down there. Did you?"

"Maybe they store it underground."

"Maybe it's drilling mud."

"Maybe they store it in that shaft."

"Maybe it's drilling— What the hell is that? Binoculars," he called. Salote came running. "I thought," he said, when he had focused to seaward, "that you sent Morgan to Tongatapu?"

T HE TREE PAEA HAD CLIMBED for coconuts was gone. A huge tugboat was tied to the pier that extended over most of the beach where the palm grove had been. White letters around its stern read *Portland,* and a tattered American flag snapped from its radio mast, indicating that it had voyaged even farther than she had. It looked as rugged as the name on the wheelhouse, *Pacific Trojan.* But it was silent and seemed as abandoned as the rest of the machinery scattered around the lagoon. The trade wind—which had been slapping *Molly* around since midnight—whistled through the crane. The bucket that hung from the crane—it reminded her of a New York skyscraper construction elevator—creaked on its vertical guide rail.

Construction had obliterated most of the pretty cove, except for a short length of beach immediately ahead of the tugboat. She was afraid of running aground there, so she dropped sails and lowered the anchor she had readied earlier over the bow. It hit bottom in ten feet of water and she let the wind drift the boat away from it until she had let out seventy.

"Dad!"

Maybe he was sleeping in one of the huts up the cliff side.

When she was sure no one else was watching, she stuffed her jeans, blouse, underwear, and running shoes into plastic bags, slipped into the clear water, and swam toward the beach. A dark cylinder floating just below the surface scared the hell out of her. She thought it was a shark. But it was only a log.

It wasn't as hot on the beach as last time now that it was late fall below the equator, nor as humid. It fact, the weather was perfect, the air soft. As soon as she was dressed, she yelled, "Dad!"

She walked past the bow of the tug, which loomed over the beach. Its hull had blocked her view of the crane's enormous cable winch—bigger than the one on the back of the tugboat—and a round wall into which the crane's bucket's guide rail descended.

"Dad!"

She took a few steps inland and found his dinghy pulled up in the trees. Deeply relieved, she cupped her hands. "Daaaad!"

She heard a clatter of loose stone. Her father rushed from the steep, treed slope and ran toward her. The last time she had seen him this angry was back in Larchmont when she and Toby came home from the City on the two A.M. train. He had yelled his head off then: Worried sick. At least call. Tell us you're okay. He didn't yell now. He just stared, cold as ice. "What are you doing here?"

She had rehearsed all night on the boat and now she said it in a rush. "I'm taking you with me. I'm taking you to Tongatapu. We'll go to Paea's father's house. And when we're safe there, we can call Henry Hong on the sat phone and tell him what we know. And then if we don't believe him, we'll find somebody we can tell and . . ."

A gaunt figure was watching from the trees. "Who's that?"

Her father's face softened. "Uncle Charlie is alive."

"*Him, too?* . . . You're kidding."

Uncle Charlie waved and started toward them.

"Jesus H."

"You better brace yourself," her father cautioned. "Uncle Charlie looks pretty bad."

"He looks okay from here. Just a little skinny."

"He's been hurt. I'm worried about him."

"What does he have a gun for?" In a holster low on his hip. And farther down his leg, a long sheath knife. "What's—"

"Just brace yourself. He's a little strange. He lost an eye."

She braced. But instead of the stomach-twisting hole in his head that her imagination immediately painted, he wore a patch that made his blue eye even brighter. He was very thin, but he still looked strong and still had his Uncle Charlie swagger. He flashed her a big grin of beautiful white teeth in a sun-darkened face.

"Hello, sailor."

"Hi, Uncle Charlie."

"What's the matter? Don't I get a hug?"

"I sang at your funeral."

"Thank you, dear."

"I sat with your father while he bawled his eyes out."

He had no smart retort to that. But her father said, "Morgan, please. Uncle Charlie's been through a lot. Give him a break?"

"I'm sorry. I'm sorry, Uncle Charlie. But it's really strange seeing you alive."

"Well, it's strange seeing you grown up. You got all skinny. And your hair's longer. Very pretty."

She turned away. His knife and gun were weird. The two of them swinging out of the jungle like a Tarzan movie was weird. His chatting away like nothing had happened was so weird it was almost sick. Then she heard her father say, "Let's get her out of here. It's not safe."

"What's not safe?"

Uncle Charlie said, "Take her into the trees. Let me check out that tug. Make sure they all got off."

"Who?" asked Morgan.

"In the trees!"

He loped to the tug in a funny zigzag that made it hard to tell exactly where he was at any given second, and drew his pistol as he scrambled aboard. Her father watched anxiously.

"Daddy, what is going on?"

"I don't know," Aiden said honestly. "He's got his head full of strange stuff. God, it kills me to see him like this."

Morgan took her father's hand. "I'm sorry I was mean to him, Daddy. I'll be nicer."

He squeezed back. "It's just that—it's very strange to see him not all there . . . You know, hon. He was always more dad to me than Dad."

After a long silence, she asked, "Did you tell him about Mr. Hong?"

"Oh, he knows about Mr. Hong."

"Does he know about the dynamite?"

"He doesn't believe me—here he comes."

They stepped out of the trees when Charlie waved the all clear and joined him on the sand. "Okay," he said, "we've got time for a look." He turned to Morgan with a teasing grin. "Your dad thinks Uncle Henry's stockpiling dynamite to blow up San Francisco."

"He could be right."

Charlie laughed. "You, too?"

Her father whirled on him, but kept his voice low as he struggled to contain anger that flushed his face. "We—you and me—helped him build a humongous bomb."

"I question that." His brother smiled.

"The only question is, Where are they taking it?"

"There's the tug," said Uncle Charlie. "But I see no barge. And no dynamite—other than the explosives that Salote and I copped." He grinned at Morgan, but he wasn't really looking at her. It was just to annoy her father. "Your dad's jealous of my girlfriend. Not only is she beautiful, she helps me make land mines."

"Dad could be right, Uncle Charlie."

"Jesus H.! Okay, you think the dynamite is down in that hole. Come on, Aiden. Let's look."

They hurried to the concrete circle, which was at the end of the pier, beside the tugboat.

"What is this?" Morgan asked. This was new since she had been here with Paea.

"They drilled a shaft. The cable on that winch was completely unreeled when they finished, so it's got to be a mile deep."

Beside the shaft sat a huge metal disk on rails. There were gears and a motor, as if to slide it over the shaft, like a lid. Uncle Charlie climbed onto the structure that held the disk. "Have a look." He still seemed to be kidding around. Morgan climbed up beside him and peered over the edge. Cool air rose from fathomless blackness. "Oh, I know what this is."

"You do?"

"They didn't drill this. It was here already."

"It was?"

"What was here?" Her father had climbed up beside her.

She looked around to be sure. The trees were gone, but she could orient herself by the cliff and the mouth of the lagoon. "This wall around it wasn't here last time."

"The hole was here already? Who drilled it?"

"Nobody drilled it. It's a vent. Left over from an old volcano . . ." They were looking at her, like, *If we did this in school, we don't remember.* "A volcano vent?" she said. "Like a chimney that vented the magma—the lava—the molten rock. This one ended up hollow, when the volcano cooled. The volcano that made this island. It's unbelievably deep. Paea dropped rocks down it. You couldn't hear them hit bottom."

"This hole was here already?" Uncle Charlie asked again, exchanging glances with her father. "But I saw them drilling it."

"No, it was here. Maybe they were drilling the bottom, but this hole was here—it didn't have this thing around it, though, just a ring of rocks and coral. There was no crane. And that track going down wasn't here either— Oh, I see, the track is for that bucket thing."

"It's an elevator," said Uncle Charlie. "The engineers rode down to the bottom in it."

"That would be a scary long way down . . . Anyhow, when I was here, it was just a hole in the beach. Paea said sometimes the waves broke over the edge. Maybe they built this wall to keep the water out."

"They did a lot of pumping," Charlie mused, then he cracked, "Keeping Aiden's dynamite dry."

He jumped down and strode to the tugboat. Her father stormed after him. Morgan caught up.

"You're wrong about that, Dad. Nobody in their right mind would put dynamite down there."

"That's what I said," said Uncle Charlie. "Mouths of babes, Aiden. Mouths of babes."

"Why not?" asked her father.

"What if it exploded? Hydrothermally altered rock—volcano rock—is like really unstable. God . . ." She shivered. "If it exploded, forget it. It would be like tsunami city."

"Tell your father. Hear that, Aiden? No dynamite down this shaft. From the mouths of babes."

"What would happen?" asked her father.

"If it blew up? It could set off landslides . . ."

Her father looked up at the high brow of stone that loomed above the lagoon.

"Not just the cliffs. The land would also collapse for thousands of feet underwater. And that would set off a huge tsunami—"

Aiden trailed his eyes down the cliffs to the ground at his feet. Then he turned and gazed across the man-made lagoon, through the training walls, to the open sea. Was he wrong about the barges? What if Henry didn't have to "deliver" his weapon? Was it right under their feet? He was vaguely aware of hearing Morgan ask, "Dad, don't you get it?"

"Yeah, maybe."

"If Mr. Hong's dynamite is here—down in the vent—then *this* is his weapon."

Charlie grasped Morgan's arm. "What are you talking about?"

Aiden reached over and gently pried his fingers open. "Easy, bro. You're hurting her. Go on, Morgan. Tell him. Tell us both."

Morgan looked into Uncle Charlie's remaining eye and she could tell that it wasn't like he was refusing to believe her. It was more like he really wanted to know. Like he was seeing whole new possibilities. She looked at her father. He nodded. "Tell us what you think."

Morgan picked up a coconut frond and drew in the sand. "Here's the vent."

Her father and uncle leaned close.

"Here's cliffs from up there all the way down to the bottom of the ocean. It's really deep here. The chart said six thousand feet? If an earthquake or a really huge explosion blew down inside the vent and the hydrothermally altered rock was really weak, like ready to collapse, you'd get gigantic landslides."

"Won't hurt anybody out here," said Uncle Charlie. "Maybe break some glass in Henry's palace."

Morgan looked at them. "Are you kidding?" She drew more lines and a circle.

The brothers bent closer. It was like walking Toby through an experiment.

"This is Blind Man Island ... Pacific Ocean ... Over here the West Coast—Washington, Oregon, California. Mexico down here. I sailed almost straight here. There's not much land between the two. So here's what would happen. Landslide here makes a wave. The wave moves northeast—Fiji, Samoa, Tonga are behind it, like a backstop. It's only six inches tall, on the surface, but it's thousands of feet deep. And now it's moving toward America, really, really fast."

Aiden Page asked, "How fast?"

"Six inches?" said Charlie. "Big deal."

"Six inches on *top* of the ocean. Thousands of feet under. So when the tsunami reaches shallow water on the continental shelf, it's forced to climb and it grows taller and taller and taller. Hundreds of feet taller. That's why they're so dangerous. No one sees them coming."

Her father said, "I don't see Henry Hong doing such a thing from his own island. Unless he sells it to somebody."

"Not Henry," said Charlie Page. "Jin-shil. This is her baby. How long would it take the wave to hit the West Coast?"

Morgan said, "I'm not sure. Probably less than a day."

"Fourteen hours," Jin-shil called down from the tugboat.

MORGAN LOOKED UP. SMILING DOWN from the wheel-house wing was a beautiful Korean woman, shielded to the chest by the wing's steel side. Henry Hong stood on her left, stone-faced. On her right stood a soldier, an older Asian man with the steadiest eyes Morgan had ever seen, a snub-nosed assault rifle in his hands, crossed knives on his rank badge, and a British accent.

"Don't even consider it, Charlie," he said. "Even you aren't that quick—remove the pistol . . . the knife . . . the Beretta from your back . . . Excellent . . . Leave them right there on the sand and back away. You, too, sir, back away. And you, young lady . . . Very good. Right you are, Mr. Hong."

Henry Hong murmured, "Thank you."

"Well, I'm embarrassed," said Charlie Page. "The sign says 'Trojan' right on the tug and I missed the connection. Cute trick, Henry. Aren't the old ones the best?"

"It was Jin-shil's idea."

"Where did you hide? I thought I looked everywhere."

Jin-shil spoke in a musical voice. "Not all bunkers contain fuel oil."

Charlie ignored her. He spoke only to Henry. Which made Aiden fear for Morgan. If Charlie was acting on his own advice—change their expectations; make them deal with your game; never play theirs—then the shooting would start any second.

"Just the three of you? Doubly embarrassed. I thought you'd dispatch your entire light reaction force. Or what's left of it."

"They're busy," said Jin-shil. "Taking your caves."

A thin sound snapped high overhead, which could have been gunfire or a boulder rolling through the trees. Henry said, "Minimal bloodshed, Charlie, not that you care. I'm hoping your people will see reason."

"I do care. Upsetting our Tongan hosts with a shooting war is the kind of thing that sends CNN in, and investors out. But I'm curious why you think that a tsunami wouldn't draw some unwanted attention."

"What is this about a tsunami?"

"Jin-shil didn't tell you she's about to blow up an old volcano with fifty thousand tons of TNT to launch a tsunami at the United States?"

"Charlie, you're out of your mind," said Henry Hong. "We're building another water plant for the hotels."

"If you believe that, Henry, you're a bigger sap than I was. You just haven't lost your eye, yet. But you ought to know that rather than bring more tourists to the South Pacific, Jin-shil intends to send the South Pacific to the tourists. Fifty million of 'em who live on the West Coast of North America."

Aiden thought that Henry looked genuinely stumped. Charlie kept at him while the Gurkha captain never took his gun off him.

"Don't you wonder why, Henry? There's no profit in tsunamis. Or is she just the sort of girl who gets her kicks wiping out heavily populated coastal plains? But, Henry, will you give my family a break, for old time's sake? Let my brother and niece go before Jin-shil starts shooting."

"I'll give the shooting orders," Henry Hong said in a low, dangerous voice. "Jin-shil, tell me what Charlie's talking about?"

Jin-shil turned to her husband with a soft smile. "Charlie has guessed that we have built what his niece calls 'tsunami city.' Though I've always called it a 'tsunami cannon.' It helped people get the picture."

"Here? On our island?"

"My first choice was the Canary Islands—there's a fault aimed straight at Boston and New York and Washington, D.C.—but it's too crowded with tourists and bureaucrats to 'load the cannon.' Your island—*our* island—turned out to be much better: isolated, excellent seismic-velocity profile. The entire windward coast is honey-combed with side vents and huge magma chambers. Aimed square at a suitable target and just waiting to be *nudged*."

Morgan could not believe what she was hearing. The phrases "seismic-velocity profile" and "magma chambers" sounded like the Korean woman was a trained geologist instead of a raving wacko. But if she was a scientist, she had to know that her "tsunami cannon" would be the World Trade Center multiplied by millions. People wouldn't have a chance. The tsunami would rush miles inland, smashing everything in its path.

To Morgan's astonishment the woman smiled down at her and confided, as if Morgan's schoolbook explanation to her father and Uncle Charlie made her some kind of local volcano expert, "There was so much room for the dynamite. *Cavernous* magma chambers. Big as Home Depots."

Henry Hong stared, his mouth working. Her father's old boss looked as shocked as Morgan was. But instead of screaming that this was the most horrible thing he'd heard in his life, he said quietly, "That is totally illogical. Even if you could do such a thing, the U.S. would nuke you for revenge."

"It is a totally logical *deterrent*. To deter an enemy attack, we only have to *threaten* to light the fuse. A simple cigarette lighter"—she held up a black-enameled lighter—"will stop an enemy attack before it starts." She glanced down at Charlie. "My people will be able to detonate via satellite. My gift to them will be a phone number. The low-tech fuse is emergency backup, in case the enemy jams the sat-phone signal."

"What enemy?" Henry Hong demanded. "What are you talking about?"

Morgan wanted to scream, *Why do you care what enemy? This shouldn't happen to anybody.*

"We are surrounded by enemies," said Jin-shil. "The United States—"

"Is an ally," Henry cut her off.

Charlie said, "She's trying to tell you that she's from *North* Korea. Not South. And I'd guess that your *chaebol* 'mullets' were actually North Korean Intelligence Service. Aiden, I apologize. You were a lot closer than I was." He glanced at the Gurkha.

Henry said, "Just tell me why, Jin-shil. Why?"

"We are a small nation with many enemies; we have only our spirit and our wits."

"But what do you gain?"

"Time! Time to grow stronger." And suddenly Jin-shil was passionate, gripping his arm, staring into his eyes. "For God's sake, Henry. You know the world. It isn't 1980 anymore. It's 2002! There is no one left to stop the superpower. Why will they make war on Iraq before Korea? Because North Korean artillery is aimed at all the American soldiers occupying Seoul. The artillery was our only shield. Now, until we complete our nuclear shield, we will hold them off with the tsunami cannon."

Henry's head was sinking low on his chest. "I can't believe you would kill so many . . ."

"I *promise* you we will not detonate for any reason other than to protect our nuclear facilities. And our borders. And our integrity."

"How blind—"

Morgan saw tears in Henry Hong's eyes. But Uncle Charlie called up to the tug, like this was some kind of a big joke: "So, Henry, basically, you're sitting on a cannon that Jin-shil promises not to fire unless she—or her 'dear leader' back in P'yŏngyang—decides she has to. At which point, this side of your island falls into the sea, and fourteen hours later, millions of people get killed in a country which has the most powerful military in the history of the world. If I feel stupid, you must feel *really* stupid."

Morgan saw his lightning-quick glance at the soldier. But the soldier had never taken his eyes off him. Nor had Jin-shil responded to his goading and it struck Morgan that her uncle had met his match in both of them. She had to say something because she felt Uncle Charlie was about to explode, and if everybody would just keep talking instead, maybe they would all calm down and stay alive long enough to stop this monstrosity.

She reached for her father's hand. He whispered, hardly moving his lips, "You okay?"

"Can I say something?" she whispered back.

He hesitated, weighing the consequences. "Give it a shot."

Morgan raised her voice. She couldn't quite form a picture in her mind of the tsunami that looked any more real than a computer-generated movie wave. But she had wandered the smoking streets of Lower Manhattan searching for her father and she saw clearly the tsunami's aftermath. The canal behind Grandpa's was filled with splintered houses. Chris and his mom and dad were buried in mud inside their SUV. Their Beneteau lay shattered on a hilltop. L.A. Airport flat as a desert; airplanes stacked against the office towers downtown. Days and days afterward, nothing but flies and terrible smells.

"They're just people," she said to the Korean woman.

"Who are just people?"

"If you can't see that, you're not human."

"I am as human as you are. Would you rather I defend my country with nuclear bombs? The wind blows west across America. Would you prefer radioactive clouds to drift over your land? Radiation sickness? Cancer. Poisoned farms. My way is quick, clean, and simple." She cast Morgan a warm, engaging smile that could not conceal the pleasure she took in describing the effects of radioactive fallout. "You could even call me a humanitarian. But I do it for my country."

Morgan shouted back, "You do it because you want to! Your country is just an excuse!"

Brilliant. Here she was trying to calm things down and now her father had to lay a cautioning hand on her shoulder to calm *her* down. But she had already stopped shouting and was staring at her feet, her gaze fixed on the fragile hydrothermally altered stone that formed the cliffs of the northeast side of Blind Man Island. Had they built that concrete wall around the shaft to keep the water out, or to keep the soft rock from crumbling?

Uncle Charlie threw his hands in the air and yelled, "Don't shoot me! Don't shoot me!"

The Gurkha stared in astonishment and jerked his weapon away from Charlie, as if to prove that he had no intention of triggering it until ordered. A rifle shot boomed off the cliffs. The soldier spun backward, fell against the wheelhouse bulkhead.

Aiden hurled himself on top of Morgan. "Down, down, down!" He covered her with his body, doubled his arms over her head, and prayed for her life.

More shots, and the dull thud of lead hitting steel. But Jin-shil and Henry Hong had ducked down behind the bulwark.

"Salote!"

She ran from the trees. Charlie scooped his guns off the ground. "Get my brother under cover. And the kid."

"But, Charlie—"

"Protect my brother!" he roared.

Salote herded them both behind the round wall just as Jin-shil jumped up with the Gurkha's assault rifle and emptied a clip toward Charlie. Morgan pressed her face to the ground and moaned a prayer. The noise was shattering. Bullets ricocheted like storm spray, grinding and popping against the soft rock. Her ears were ringing when the shooting stopped, her mouth gritty with stone dust. She looked over her shoulder. Jin-shil was coolly loading a fresh clip into the weapon.

"Daddy, are you okay?" she whispered.

"Down!"

"Daddy, we have to stop her."

Charlie ran toward the tug, but the shooting drove him back. Salote pressed her hand on the back of Morgan's head, then laid her own cheek on the stone so they were lying face-to-face, like girlfriends whispering about boys. "Are you afraid?"

"Yes." When the bullets were flying, it had felt about midway between climbing the mast at night and pitchpoling. She reminded herself that she had survived both. But only by staying alert and active. "Salote. Is there more dynamite in the shed?"

"Yes."

"Uncle Charlie said you know how to detonate it?"

"Charlie taught me."

"Can we get it?"

Salote eyed the open ground between where they lay and the dynamite shed. "*I* will. When that crazy woman stops shooting."

Charlie Page ran toward the tugboat again, rolled over the low bulwark onto the towing deck, and raced up the steel ladder on the back of the house. When he got up to the wheelhouse deck, he saw the Gurkha captain, lying very quietly in Henry's arms. Henry had removed his own shirt, revealing a fleshy-white gut, and was pressing it to the man's wound to stop his bleeding. In his other hand was the Gurkha's machine pistol, which Jin-shil had left him to cover her escape.

"Henry!" he called from the back of the wheelhouse. "Of all the times I've wanted to shoot you, this isn't one of them. Time to 'sprit,' Henry. Cut your losses."

He glanced around the corner. Henry hesitated, his face working with grief and sorrow. "She loves me."

"Yes, she does, Henry. But she's also got an agenda. Throw down the gun. If she sets off her tsunami, we'll be the first to die."

Henry extended the weapon toward Charlie butt first. "I'm a capitalist, not a terrorist."

"Where is she?"

Henry Hong shook his head and bit his lips. "Don't hurt her."

"*Henry!*"

"She jumped down to the main deck."

"Shit." Charlie looked over the wing just as Jin-shil ran to the bow and climbed over the high bulwark. As he took aim, she jumped onto the heavy mooring line and ran down it like a circus performer. Ten feet down she slipped and fell, but managed to grab the thick cable with her hands and swing to the pier.

Charlie went down the ladder as fast as he could and rolled over the towing-deck bulwark onto the pier. Jin-shil had climbed up the crane and was just stepping into the elevator bucket.

"We got her now," Charlie told Aiden. "Everything's shut down. The power's off."

Jin-shil reached overhead and jerked the bucket release. The bucket dropped free of the hoist and slid down its vertical track several feet into the shaft before the safety brake slowed its descent.

"Jin-shil, how the hell are you going to climb back out?"

Jin-shil held her lighter up in the sun for all to see. "Keep it simple, Charlie." She cast a beatific smile at Morgan, Aiden, Charlie, and then blew a kiss to Henry Hong, who was watching from the tug.

She jerked another lever and the bucket descended deeper into the shaft, descending out of sight in fits and starts as she struggled with the cumbersome safety brake. "Come on, Jin-shil! You don't want to die!" Charlie pleaded.

"Why not?" her voice echoed up from twenty feet down the shaft. "I'm a Christian."

No one worked the bow who was afraid of heights and Aiden Page finally saw deep in the shaft the means to redeem a wasted life, undo his wrongs, and, with this blessing, live to start anew. He leaped on the wall, pulled off his shirt, and wrapped his hand. Morgan saw instantly what he was doing and screamed, "Don't, Daddy!"

Charlie scrambled after him. "Where you going, bro?"

"I can slide down the rail faster than that bucket. Give me your shirt for my other hand."

Charlie removed his shirt. When his brother reached for it, Charlie knocked him off the wall. Aiden fell hard on the stone, but sprang to his feet, ready to fight. "What are you— Let me do it."

Charlie pulled a small pistol from his ankle and waved it in Aiden's face. "Back off. Give me the shirt. Quick!"

"You won't shoot me."

"If you don't back off, I'll shoot the kid."

"I don't believe you," said Aiden.

"I do," said Morgan.

Uncle Charlie flashed her a smile. "Smart kid. Out of my way, bro."

"Isn't it kind of late in life to save the world, Charlie?"

"I'm not saving the world. I'm saving you."

"I'll save myself!" Aiden yelled.

"Why do you keep forgetting you've got a kid to take care of?"

Aiden threw him the shirt. Charlie slipped his gun in his waistband, gripped the vertical rail, and stepped off the wall. He slid quickly down the rail. The hurrying squeak of the elevator brake suddenly stopped. They heard Jin-shil scream—a cry filled with as much anger as pain—and the sounds of a savage struggle, the thud of fists, rasping breaths, and the clang of metal on metal. Suddenly a gunshot echoed up, and after a long silence, they heard Charlie Page cry out in an animal howl of despair.

His voice trailed away. Morgan closed her eyes and waited, counting as she had when she and Paea timed falling rocks. A muffled thump told her he had finally reached bottom.

Salote leaped up and ran. Aiden jumped for the track.

"No!" Morgan screamed. "Wait for Salote."

"Honey, I have to try."

"Wait. Wait." Morgan threw her arms around him and tried to hold him. "Please wait."

Salote raced back with dynamite sticks stacked in her arms like firewood and a reel of wire.

"No!" yelled Aiden. "If you drop that down there, you'll blow the whole thing up."

"We're not dropping it down there. Volcanic rock crumbles easily. This whole area is unstable. There, Salote. Put it there." Morgan pointed.

"No," said Salote. She carried the dynamite around to the other side closest to the water and stacked it against the round wall, and Morgan saw how the bulk of the tugboat would help focus the force of the explosion against the volcanic stone.

Aiden ran to get Henry off the tug.

From deep down the shaft they heard the creaking of the safety-brake clutch squeezing and releasing the rail as Jin-shil continued her descent.

"Light it," urged Morgan.

"Wait," said Salote. "I have to attach the blasting caps, first. Wait." Tears were pouring down her cheeks. "Charlie said never rush dynamite."

The creaking grew faint. Salote stood up at last and began walking backward, unreeling a long wire. Morgan walked behind her, guiding her with a hand on her back. Henry Hong and Aiden struggled after her, carrying the wounded Gurkha. Salote, deep within the trees, turned a crank, and said, "Get behind me."

Morgan heard Jin-shil's cry of triumph echo up the shaft like an ambulance siren. "Prayers, everybody."

Salote squeezed her detonator.

The dynamite thundered. The concrete collar around the shaft vanished in a cloud of dust. Out of the dust rose an unearthly roar. The ground shook so hard that Morgan feared that Jin-shil had succeeded in exploding her tsunami cannon. She looked up at the cliffs, expecting to see a million tons of stone tumble from the sky.

"Look!" said Aiden.

The land opened around the shaft. Volcanic rock disintegrated and slid into the hole. A crack split open between the shaft and the pier. The thunderous clatter of falling rock was overwhelmed by a cataract of seawater that sluiced out of the lagoon and roared down the shaft. The force of the torrent filling the drill hole, the surrounding vents, and the magma chambers gripped the *Pacific Trojan* and pinned the big tugboat there for hours.

ORGAN WORKED HER BOAT ALONGSIDE the
remains of the pier and tied up behind the Rivolta launch,
which had raced around the island earlier to pick up the wounded
Gurkha, and returned with food and water for the men of the light
reaction company who had trooped down from the cliffs. The trade
wind was strengthening, funneling between the training walls, too
hard to sail out without a motor.

"Daddy?" she called.

He came running from the machine shed, where he had been
trying for hours to negotiate safe passage for Salote's brothers, who
were still holding out in the caves.

"You okay? I'll be done soon, if I can just get Henry to shut up."
He glanced back at the open shed, where Henry Hong was gesticu-
lating at a silent circle of soldiers, and gave Morgan a tired smile.
"He's acting as if punishing Salote's brothers will make up for what
Jin-shil did to him. Anyway, he's coming around. How are you? Are
you sure you're all right?"

Morgan could see that her father had found his own way to put
off grieving. She said, "Dad. I'm so sorry about Uncle Charlie. All I
can say is I know how horrible I would feel if *you* suddenly died—
again. You know, right after I found you alive."

"Yeah." Aiden swallowed hard. "It's . . . I'm just—it's like a hole
in my heart . . ."

She reached out and held him for a long moment. Then she said,
"Dad, would you do me a favor?" She nodded at the Rivolta. "Give
me a tow out of here?"

"Where are you going?"

"California."

"What?"

"I'm going back."

"What are you talking about?"

"I'm going back. I'm going home."

"It's six thousand miles."

"I know."

"Morgan. Now, wait . . ." He glanced back again at Henry and the Tongans and Gurkhas bargaining under the thatched roof. He looked at his daughter. He ran a big hand through his hair. "Wait. Just wait . . . Could we sit down and talk?"

They sat on the pier, legs dangling over her boat. The harbor water was murky with sand riled by the explosion. But beyond the entrance, the Pacific was so blue it glowed.

"What's this about?" Aiden asked.

"I just want to go back."

"That's a long, long sail alone."

"Da-ad. I got here alone."

"Yeah, but your boat needs work, you're low on food."

"I thought I'd sail down to Tongatapu, first. Get supplies. Fix some stuff."

"Is this because you're pissed at me for what I did?"

"I love you, Daddy. Always. But right now I really, really have to go."

"Morgan." He grabbed her and held her so tightly she cried, "Ow!"

"Sorry." He loosened his grip but kept one arm firmly over her shoulders. "Tell me what this is about?"

It took all her effort to speak, and even when she could, her eyes got all warm and she heard her own voice piping like a little girl. "I think I want to see my mother."

"Your *mother?* Well, if you want to see your mother, we'll put you on a plane and you can go see your mother. Though considering how you two get along . . ."

"Dad, I love you. And I'm so happy I found you . . ."

"But . . . ?"

"You haven't always done the right thing."

"I know. I told you, I'm going to do whatever I can to make up for it. Do you believe me? That I'll try?"

"Absolutely."

"But?"

"I used to think that you were a totally good person—like perfect."

Aiden put all his strength into suppressing a flinch. As deeply as it hurt, he realized what a battle it must have been for her to say it. "No one's perfect, hon. It's one of the hardest lessons you learn when you grow up."

"I know that. *Now*. And like now it's obvious. So I'm thinking that if *you* are not as good—as perfect—as I thought you were, then maybe Mommy isn't as bad as I thought."

"Your mother's not *bad*. Bad is like Jin-shil trying to destroy—"

"I don't mean that kind of bad. Just kind of awful—but I think maybe I blamed her for some stuff that wasn't her fault . . ."

"Okay," he said. "I think I understand what you're saying."

"I'm not saying it well."

"You're saying it very well. I understand."

"You really do? Oh, thank God."

"But I *don't* understand why you want to sail this—this—toy. Get on a plane and go home if you want to see your mother, but—"

"I have to sail to California."

"What for?"

"I have to return the boat. I stole it. I want to bring it back."

Her father rubbed his face. "Okay. I can understand that, too, but it's still crazy. You survived the voyage out by a miracle. I can't let you risk your life again . . . I'll sail with you?"

Her heart overflowed at the thought. But she shook her head. "I'd love that. But you can't go back."

"Just as far as the beach." He smiled.

"Yeah, sure. No. It won't work."

"What if we found a way to ship this goddamned boat to its owner?"

"It wouldn't be the same."

"It's crazy. I can't let you do it."

Her strong jaw set. "You can't stop me."

Aiden observed the sturdy knot of muscle, bone, and drive that his daughter had become and concluded it would be easier to persuade a mountain goat not to climb. Jesus, he thought, she looks as tough as my old man. Only by the grace of God had she inherited her grandmother's angelic smile. And a heart to match it.

"I can *beg* you not to do it."

Morgan said, "Please don't."

"I can get down on my knees and beg you not to foolishly risk your life."

"It's not foolish!" she said fiercely. "It's important to me. I got myself here. I'll get myself back."

"Why is that important to you?"

"I came here for you. I want to go back—for myself. On my own. For my own reasons. When I've done that, then I can go back to my life."

"That is totally irrational—" He stopped. What did he know? He cast his gaze toward the open Pacific. "Do you love it out there? Is that it?"

"Not really," she answered. "I was cold, wet, scared, and lonely. But I didn't give it a fair chance because mostly I was worrying about you and not getting caught and everything."

"I've lost Charlie. I could not bear to lose you, too."

"You're not going to lose me. I'm a good seaman, Daddy. I can do it."

"Okay, maybe you can. But the weather's against you. It's too late in the season to go east. Unless you go way the hell up north, around Hawaii, then two thousand miles of heavy seas east, then a brutal slog down the West Coast. You're talking about months and months and months. And if you get held up anywhere, you'll end up hitting the North Pacific in the winter and that will be no picnic."

She looked at him, shaking her head. Then she smiled. "So I'll go the other way."

"What other way?"

"Around the world."

"Oh, Jesus H."

"I'll take it in stages."

"Twenty-five thousand miles, single-handed?"

"Maybe I'll stop in New Zealand. Pick up someone to crew."

"*Crew?*" Aiden exploded. "A fifteen-year-old girl has no business sailing alone with some boat bum who—"

"I'll be sixteen by the time I get to New Zealand."

He caught a nudge in the ribs and another dazzling smile. "Are you enjoying torturing me?"

"Yes."

"Are you kidding me?" he asked hopefully. "Is this whole thing a joke?"

"No." She sobered instantly. "I'm going."

Aiden tried another tack. "Do you have to go right away? Why not hang out awhile? I could use a friend right now." His voice faltered. Every time he thought of Charlie, it was like getting hit in the face. "... And so could poor Salote use a friend. All those big brothers are great, but a little sister ..."

For a fleeting instant Morgan felt thirty years old. Didn't he have a clue that she would be the one to comfort Salote? She looked toward the ocean, a little awed by the depth of her own resolve, and saw, framed by the harbor entrance, a beautiful two-masted Polynesian canoe with tall blue-water bows and sterns and sails of gold.

"Daddy, look! A *wa a' kau lua*. Cool, they're furling their sails. They're coming in."

The upside-down cloth triangles folded against the masts like butterfly wings.

Morgan jumped into her boat for binoculars and scoped the crowded decks. At the steering oar she saw a familiar face. "Daddy! It's

Paea's father." She checked out every face. But Paea wasn't with him.

Henry Hong ran onto the pier. "Is that Noble Nephew?"

"It sure is," said Aiden.

"Of all the bloody times for a bloody visit— Bloody hell!" Henry Hong looked around at the wreckage of the harbor, the tugboat with its wheelhouse windows shattered, and the groups of armed men eating in the shade. "Bloody, bloody hell. Aiden!"

"What is it, Henry?"

"Noble Nephew is on the board of every bank I own. I cannot afford trouble with him."

"He'll be the least of your troubles when he tells the king about this."

"It's your job to make sure he doesn't."

"My job?"

"I need a good man. I want you to take up where your brother left off. Job one, unruffle Noble Nephew's feathers. Explain this mess and keep him away from the king."

"He thinks I'm dead, Henry."

But Henry Ho Hong was issuing orders and for a moment it sounded to Aiden like it was 1999 again, and the chairman of HHH & Company had just hit town like a hurricane. For a moment it even seemed wonderful that Henry Hong could give him his old life back and make him a Wall Street guy again. But only for a moment.

"I'll break the news of your miraculous return. Tell him you had amnesia. He likes you. He always asked about you and Morgan. He'll listen to you. Just get him out of my face. Go on! Hop in the launch. Offer him a tow in— What?"

"I can't go back."

"I'll fix it so you can. You said your wife collected your life insurance? I'll pay off your life insurance."

"I can't go back."

"You'll work for me here. Europe. Asia. Wherever you want. You'll be my CEO, just like Charlie."

"I can't go back."

"You're not listening, Aiden. Take this job and I will buy your life back for you."

"I've already got a job."

Henry Hong made a face. "Sailing *boats*?"

"I've decided to become a consultant."

"Consulting on what?"

Aiden nudged Morgan. "If your mouth drops open any wider, young lady, you'll catch flies."

"Consulting on what?" Henry Hong demanded again, his eyes shooting toward the big sailing canoe. The paddlers were down on the splash rails, lining up with the harbor entrance.

Aiden said, "I'm going to be a projects consultant. I'll vet deals for my client."

"What client?"

"I'll protect him from rip-off artists, hucksters, con men, arms dealers, and offshore bankers."

"Who the hell but me would hire you after what you did?"

"Noble Nephew might."

"Noble Nephew?"

"We liked each other the time we met. Our kids connected— family's no small thing out here. I think I've got a pretty good shot at the job."

"He can't hire a dead man. And he can't make you alive again, which I can."

"I'll serve him privately. Pro bono, if I have to. I can always earn my keep part-time, 'sailing boats.'"

"Your brother always said you were a damned fool."

"Maybe I am. But I'm not a blind fool. Morgan, if you're going, you better get off shore before it's dark."

"Yes, Daddy."

SHE STAYED LONG enough to greet Paea's father and endure another round of "too young, too far, too small." But she could see that he was doing it mostly to be kind to her father and that his voyager eye was satisfied that *Molly* was seaworthy. He gave her his business card to show to the boatyard in Tongatapu.

She asked if Paea would be home soon from New Zealand.

But in the southern hemisphere, Paea's father reminded her, his school's summer vacation didn't start until December. So Paea was stuck in New Zealand for the next five months.

An image of the chart flew into Morgan's mind. Down at the bottom left, in the southwest corner of the South Pacific, New Zealand's North Island and South Island pointed like the first two joints of a finger directly at Tonga. It was only two thousand miles.

THE SHADOWS CAST by Blind Man Island's cliffs were darkening the harbor and their final good-bye was mercifully rushed. Morgan knew she would lose it if she didn't get moving like right now. And while she was excited to get under way, and knew in her heart that she was doing the right thing, she also dreaded the lonely night that lay ahead.

Her father, operating in full Page-brothers charm mode, asked the Tongan noble to help tow Morgan out of the harbor and even invited him to drive the fancy launch while he manned the towline. Just before he paid the line out, when the boats were still touching, she repeated what she had told him earlier. "I am so glad I found you."

Aiden Page jumped down onto *Molly* to hug his daughter one last time. It took him a long while to be able to form an inadequate "I'm glad, too," and a tremendous effort to open his arms and let her go. As he was still struggling to conquer the lump in his throat, his voice grew so rough that he was shocked to hear in it harsh echoes of his own father. But he finally said what had to be said to set her free.

"Maybe, one day, you'll find me again . . . I love you, Morgan."

He pressed a wad of cash in her hand. "Safe voyage."

"What's this for?"

"Do your old man a favor? Buy a radio."